An Ang...

CHRISTM...

Celebrate the holidays with these four stories of Yuletide joy and heaven-sent love.

DEBRA DIER
"The Trouble With Hannah"

"The poignant writing style of Ms. Dier will touch your very soul."
—*Rendezvous*

EUGENIA RILEY
"Tryst With An Angel"

"Both passionate and dramatic, Eugenia Riley's romance are sumptuous reads!"
—*Romantic Times*

AMY ELIZABETH SAUNDERS
"A Time For Joy"

Amy Elizabeth Saunders writes "a beautiful tale...a sweet, simple, and moving story!"
—*Romantic Times*

TRANA MAE SIMMONS
"Chrissy's Wish"

"Readers will remember Trana Mae Simmons's historical romances long after the last page has been read."
—Michalann Perry

Other Holiday Specials from *Leisure Books* and *Love Spell:*

THEIR FIRST NOEL
CHRISTMAS CAROL
AN OLD-FASHIONED SOUTHERN CHRISTMAS
A WILDERNESS CHRISTMAS
A TIME-TRAVEL CHRISTMAS
A FRONTIER CHRISTMAS

Christmas Angels

DEBRA DIER EUGENIA RILEY
AMY ELIZABETH SAUNDERS
TRANA MAE SIMMONS

LOVE SPELL NEW YORK CITY

LOVE SPELL®

November 1995

Published by

Dorchester Publishing Co., Inc.
276 Fifth Avenue
New York, NY 10001

Printed in the United States of America.

Christmas Angels

THE TROUBLE WITH HANNAH

TRYST WITH AN ANGEL

A TIME FOR JOY

CHRISSY'S WISH

DEBRA DIER

THE TROUBLE WITH HANNAH

For my brother, Tom. Any man who takes two teenage girls on their first trip to Disneyland is an angel.

Chapter One

Every visible thing in this world is put in the charge of an angel.

—Saint Augustine

Ethan Fairchild was new to heaven. He still couldn't pass the entrance without pausing to admire the harp-shaped gates of precious pearl. Each time he saw an angel wearing a gold pin in the shape of wings he stopped and stared, filled with awe.

It took a long time to earn your wings. It took even longer to become a guardian angel. Still, he hoped one day to join their ranks. In fact, he had already started his training. Yet he knew he would never win his wings in time to help his daughter, Alyssa. That was why he had come to Raphael, chief of all guardian angels, to ask for a miracle.

"You must understand, Ethan, our mission as guardians is to guide, to give counsel." Raphael folded his hands on his silver desk. "And occasionally, when *He* believes it's appropriate, we are allowed to pull our mortal charges out of danger. But there is only so much intrusion *He* will allow."

"I fear my daughter is in danger, sir. In danger of spending the rest of her life alone." Ethan looked into Raphael's gentle blue eyes and prayed he would understand. "As you know, my wife came to heaven ten years ago."

"Yes, she is one of my most promising students."

Ethan smiled when he thought of his beloved wife. "She was an angel on earth. And so is my daughter."

Raphael nodded. "I have great expectations for Alyssa when she joins us."

"Sir, now that I am here, Alyssa has no one. She has so much love inside her. She needs a family of her own."

"Alyssa has chosen to be alone. We cannot always alter the path a human has chosen. Even if that path is not the same as the one originally ordained. Humans make choices every day. Choices that can alter their destiny." Raphael studied Ethan for a moment, a serious expression on his beautiful face. "Their choices are not always the best ones."

"It is partly my fault. I never coaxed her into the social whirl. Please, sir. Let me try to help her."

"Ethan, you know it's too soon to allow you to return to earth. It takes years to become a guardian." Raphael rested his chin on the steeple of his slender fingers. "And even then, we have had a few problems with overzealous novices. I've just sent a case to Gabriel. One of our guardians actually plucked a soul from his mortal body before his time. I cannot tell you the trouble this one is going to cause."

"But, sir, it isn't only my daughter. I'm also concerned about my granddaughter, Hannah."

"Ah, yes, Hannah." Raphael turned a few pages in the great Book of Life, lying open on his desk, the pearl white parchment sighing softly beneath his fingers. He paused, a frown tugging his smooth wide brow as he studied one of the long pages. "I have quite a few notes about Hannah. And the child is merely ten."

"So you understand why I'm concerned."

"Yes. And I can assure you, *He* is also well aware of the situation." Raphael stood, towering two feet above Ethan. He turned toward the thick white clouds shaping one wall of his office. For a moment he stood there, as though in silent debate, his golden head bowed, his slender hands clasped behind his back. Finally Raphael turned to face him. "Come stand beside me. We shall take a look at the situation."

When Ethan joined him Raphael lifted his hand. The clouds dissolved, mist evaporating in the rays of the sun. A scene unfolded before Ethan's eyes, like the opening act of a play. He stared into the entry hall of a house he knew in Leicestershire, England. It was December 1887, seven months after his own departure from the mortal world.

Alyssa hurried across the entry hall, her footsteps tapping against alternating squares of black and white marble in her effort to keep up with the fleeing governess. "Miss Wentridge, I'm certain if you only give Hannah a chance to explain, you would . . ."

"Explain! That little demon dumped syrup and feathers all over me." Miss Wentridge shook in her outrage, feathers fluttering from her gray hair. "Look at me! Just look at me!"

Alyssa stared down at the woman, and for some unforgivable reason a giggle started low in her chest. Miss Wentridge was short and plump, and with all those white feathers sticking to her face and hair she looked like a partridge during molting season.

Miss Wentridge narrowed her eyes. "Young woman, this is not amusing."

"No." Alyssa coughed, trying to disguise her wayward laughter. "Of course it isn't."

"I can see where your niece gets her lack of discipline, Miss Fairchild."

Alyssa smiled, refusing to take offense when the woman was obviously distraught. "I'm afraid I scarcely know my niece, Miss Wentridge. But in the few days I have spent here I have come to see that Hannah is a child of spirit. She needs a gentle hand."

"Spirit, indeed. That spoiled little heathen needs a good stiff rod taken to her backside."

"Miss Wentridge, it's obvious you and Hannah are not suited. Still, I feel . . ."

"There isn't a decent governess in all of England who would be suitable for that fiendish hoyden."

Alyssa stared down into Miss Wentridge's hard little face, looking past the feathers to the bitter woman beneath. "Hannah is a beautiful little girl who needs . . ."

"Her beauty doesn't hide that black heart of hers." Miss Wentridge curled her lips, as though she had bitten into a lemon. "If I didn't know she was here when her parents were killed in London, I would swear she was the one who had started that fire."

"How can you say something so cruel?"

"You don't know the chit as I do. She has nothing but hate inside her." Miss Wentridge looked past Alyssa, her dark eyes growing round with fear. "I refuse to stay another moment under the same roof with that little devil."

Alyssa glanced over her shoulder. Hannah was standing on the landing of the wide staircase, her hand resting on the balustrade. Bright winter sunlight streamed through the diamond-shaped panes of the window on the landing, sparkling on the gilt ironwork of the balustrade, slipping into the child's pale blond hair, the thick curls tumbling around her small shoulders. She looked like an angel standing on the golden stairs leading to the gates of heaven. Except for the glitter in her huge brown eyes. Hannah was staring at Miss Wentridge as though she wished she could send a thunderbolt through the little governess.

The door slammed. Alyssa turned to find the hall empty. White feathers littered the marble lined floor, the only remains of Miss Wentridge. Dear heaven, why today of all days did the house have to fall into chaos? Alyssa hurried toward the door.

Jared would be returning sometime today. After twelve years of exile, Alyssa had hoped to make his homecoming a happy event.

"Let her go!" Hannah shouted. "She hates me. I don't want her here."

Alyssa paused with her hand on the brass door handle. She glanced back at her niece. "I suspect the woman will not return, but I can't let her walk to town. Not in this weather."

Hannah lifted her little chin. "I hope she freezes to death."

Alyssa stared at the child, seeing the pain behind the ugly words. "I know you don't mean that."

"How do you know what I mean? You don't know me. You don't know anything about me."

The truth of Hannah's words stabbed Alyssa with guilt. She had visited this house a handful of times in the ten years since Hannah had been born. If she had come more often, perhaps she would have seen the way the child had been neglected. "I want to get to know you, Hannah."

"Why?" She stared at Alyssa, her brown eyes far too old, far too filled with pain for her tender years. "You never wanted to know me before."

How could Alyssa explain the circumstances that had torn sisters apart? "We'll talk after I get Miss Wentridge to accept a ride to town."

"I don't want to talk to you. I don't want to talk to anyone." Hannah turned and ran up the stairs, her black skirt flaring over white linen petticoats.

"Hannah!" Alyssa gripped the cold brass handle, resisting the urge to run after the girl. The trouble with Hannah wouldn't disappear in a single day. Right now she had to deal with a plump partridge whose feathers were ruffled.

Alyssa pulled open the door and dashed into the

frigid December morning. "Miss Went . . ."

A man was there. A tall man was standing on the top step, staring up at the house. Alyssa tried to stop. Her foot hit an icy patch on the stone landing. She skidded. "Oh!"

He glanced at her. She caught a glimpse of his face before she plowed into him. He stumbled with the impact. One strong arm came around her protectively as they tumbled backward. The breath whooshed from his lungs when they hit the stairs.

For one brief moment she was flying, riding the hard plane of his body, as though he were a sled rushing down an icy hill. Seven stone steps, then they hit the frozen gravel at the base of the stairs. She bumped her head on his chin.

Alyssa flinched at the sound of his low groan. "Oh, my gracious, I'm so terribly sorry."

She rode the swell of his chest as he drew in a deep breath. The heat of his body wrapped around her with the mingled aroma of leather and sandalwood. She lifted herself up, pressing her forearms against his chest, staring down into a face she hadn't seen for twelve long years. Except in her dreams.

Dear heaven, this wasn't exactly the way she had imagined their first meeting would be. Jared Templeton, the seventh Earl of Greystone, lay flat on his back beneath her. He was blinking, as though trying to clear stars from his eyes.

Oh, my, her memories of him hadn't prepared her for the pure green of those eyes. The green of spring was in his eyes; the green of meadow grass and dew-covered leaves. As his vision cleared those beautiful eyes focused on her face. He frowned, looking at her as though she had fallen from a distant star rather than the top of the stairs. She stared at him, comparing each feature to the memory she kept locked in her heart.

He was more handsome than she remembered. Yet different. Harder. As though the years had turned the charming young man she had fallen in love with to granite. There were lines in his face that had not been there before. Faint lines flared at the corners of his eyes, etched the skin between his black brows, and defined the skin around his full lips. Lines forged with the changing of an eighteen-year-old boy into a man fully grown. A man who had been banished from his home and his family.

She touched his hard cheek, wishing she had been there to witness the events that had carved each subtle line into his handsome face. "Welcome home."

Jared stared up at the woman perched on his chest. Wisps of golden brown curls framed her face. From beneath arched dark brows she gazed at him with eyes that made him feel he was looking into the blue skies of heaven.

She was lovely. Not exactly beautiful. No, she didn't possess the striking beauty of the women he normally chose to share his bed. But there was an innocence in her eyes, a warmth glowing in those celestial depths that lifted her pretty features beyond the exotic. She was without a doubt one of the most attractive women he had seen in a long time.

She brushed her fingertips over his cheek, spreading warmth across his chilled skin. She lay snuggled between his thighs, glowing warmth in the frozen morning, and his body responded to that warmth.

"Are you all right?" She frowned. "You look a bit dazed."

He was shocked to find he had to swallow past a knot in his throat before he could find his voice. "Who are you?"

She looked pleased with the question, her eyes sparkling with a warmth that reminded him of something he hadn't seen in a very long time: honest affection. "You don't remember me?"

"Should I?"

"I suppose not. I was fourteen when you went away. I like to think I've changed a little."

The air turned to stone in his chest as he realized who this enchanting woman was. He should have known. His brother's solicitors had informed him of the current situation at Blackmoor Hall. "You're Vivien's sister."

Her smile faded. "I'm Alyssa Fairchild," she whispered, as though she wanted to distance herself from her sister and the dark memories Vivien stirred inside of him.

Another Fairchild temptress. Was there any wonder he had found her enchanting? Vivien Fairchild could have seduced a saint. The woman had nearly cost him his life. He had lost his family, his home, all he held dear, because of his own foolish infatuation with a woman with the face of an angel and the cunning of the devil. "Perhaps you didn't notice, Miss Fairchild, but I happen to be lying on a bed of frozen gravel."

"Oh, my gracious, I'm sorry." She brought her knee up, bumping him where his body had grown rigid and pulsing beneath her.

Jared sucked air between his teeth.

"I'm sorry."

He looked up at her, intending to tell her what he thought of her clumsiness. He could tear a person to shreds with his sharp words; had done so on numerous occasions. But something stopped him. That innocence. That intriguing warmth that colored her concern for him. "It's all right."

She sat up, pressing down on his chest, shoving the air from his lungs. "Oh, my gracious, I'm . . ."

"Sorry," he said.

"Yes." Her cheeks were red from more than cold. She scrambled to her feet, hit an icy patch, and slipped.

Jared sat up, intending to help.

"Oh!" She sought her balance, windmilling her arms.

"Careful!" He caught a glimpse of her bouncing black bustle before she fell, flat on his chest. He smacked the ground.

She wiggled on top of him. "Are you all right?"

He lay there with frozen gravel biting into the back of his head, wondering if this were some divine punishment for the supreme poor judgment he had displayed at the age of eighteen.

She touched him, cupping his cheek in her warm palm. "Please say something."

He drew in his breath, dragging cold air and a subtle trace of violets into his compressed lungs. He opened his eyes and stared up into the pure blue of heaven.

"Are you hurt?"

She looked so innocent, so incredibly lovely, with her lips parted, her eyes wide, her cheeks full of color. And her skin. Lord, her skin looked as smooth as cream. An erotic image crept into his mind—this woman lying bare upon white silk sheets, her arms reaching for him, her legs brushing his hips as she . . .

She frowned. "You have a strange look on your face."

He released his breath between his teeth. "Miss Fairchild, I want you to slide off of my chest, but I don't want you to try to stand. I'll help you stand. You just slide over to the step. Do you think you can manage that?"

"Of course." She complied, easing from his chest as though he were an egg she was trying to hatch. She plopped down on the bottom step and stared at her clasped hands, an angel at morning prayer.

He stood and stepped away from her, his boots crunching the thin layer of ice that coated the gravel. As the wind whipped at the hem of his black coat, he looked at her gown, her slippers, and knew she must be freezing. "What the devil are you doing out here, dressed like that?"

She flinched at the sharp words, a kitten cornered by a snarling mastiff. He clenched his teeth, appalled at his own anger. What the devil was wrong with him? He never lost control.

Twelve years ago he had vowed never to allow his emotions to betray him again. Discipline was the key. With more discipline he would not have made a mess of things twelve years ago.

He had spent twelve long years burying his emotions, forging his will into iron. Men called him Iron Templeton. Women called him heartless. He liked it that way. And here he stood before this temptress with the heavenly eyes, his emotions swirling like a whirlwind inside him.

She hugged her arms to her waist, glancing down the lane, looking lost and far too tempting. "We should send a carriage after her."

"If you mean Miss Wentridge, I already sent her on her way in my carriage. Feathers and all."

Alyssa looked up at him, a certain wariness in her eyes. "Miss Wentridge was a bit upset when she left."

"Miss Wentridge was furious. And from what I understand she had good reason."

"You have to understand. Hannah is a spirited child. She needs . . ."

"Discipline. Based on what I've heard from her father's solicitors, as well as from Miss Wentridge, the girl has had precious little discipline her entire life."

Alyssa stared up at him, as though she was seeing him for the first time and she wasn't exactly certain she liked what she saw. "Her name is Hannah."

He regretted that look in her eyes. Still, he could never have trusted the warmth he had imagined seeing in those pale blue depths. "The girl will soon learn I will not tolerate the extreme behavior she exhibited today."

"Her name is *Hannah*."

He clenched his teeth, hating the look of disappointment in her eyes. He had seen a similar look in the eyes of women before, but it usually came when one of them realized she had failed to convince him to put a wedding ring on her dainty little finger. The fortune he had accumulated during his exile in New York assured him there would always be women who wanted his company. Beautiful women. Sophisticated women.

But this woman was different. This look of disappointment was different. She was staring up at him as though she desperately hoped he was still something he had ceased to be long ago: compassionate, caring, weak.

"The girl's name is Hannah," she said.

"I know her name."

She smiled at him. "Then why don't you use it?"

"Miss Fairchild, if you had any sense you wouldn't be out here carrying on a conversation." He gripped her arms and tugged her to her feet.

"But it's important you realize . . ." Her words dissolved into a gasp as he swept her up into his arms. She threw her arms around his neck, hugging him as though she were certain he intended to throw her to the ground.

He looked into her wide blue eyes, appalled at his own behavior. He was being harsh. Unreasonably so. Yet it seemed the only protection against her. The woman had the most uncanny way of stirring his emotions. She stared at him, a thousand questions in her eyes. Questions that had no answers. At least none he wanted to acknowledge.

He held her close, so close her breath brushed against his cheek, soft puffs of steam in the cold air. He breathed in her steamy breath, certain he could taste strawberry preserves. He stared at her parted lips, wondering what it might be like to kiss her. Were those lips half as soft as they looked?

"What are you doing?" she whispered.

Excellent question. Was he completely insane? He attributed the momentary loss of reason to the fact that he had been too long without a woman in his bed. "I'm simply making certain I don't end up on the gravel again."

"Oh." She lowered her lashes.

He had the distinct impression he had disappointed her. Again. Why the devil that should bother him remained a mystery. But bother him it did.

Gilbert, the butler, opened the door as Jared reached the landing. No doubt half the servants in the house had witnessed the new Earl of Greystone flat on his back in the dirt. No doubt some of them believed he belonged there. Still, from the smile on Gilbert's thin face, the old man wasn't one of them.

Jared's muscles tensed as he walked across the threshold and entered the house where he had been born. It was like stepping back in time. If only that were possible, he thought.

A scent of lemon oil and beeswax mingled with the fragrance of burning oil. He glanced at the wide sweeping staircase, half expecting his mother to be standing there, as she had been on the day he had left twelve years ago. If he closed his eyes he could still see her, and the glitter of tears in her eyes. It had been the last time he had ever seen her face.

His mother was gone, as was his father. His brother. All of his family. Nothing was left. Except money and property and a title he had never thought to own. Strange, all that was left were things of which he had no need.

Wall sconces cast flickering light against the carved mahogany wainscoting that had graced these walls for a hundred years. Above him a mural stretched across the magnificent plastered ceiling. Angels fought in heaven, and Lucifer fell from grace, banished forever. His chest tightened at the familiar scene that now seemed far too appropriate.

"I imagine it seems strange," Alyssa whispered. "To be home again, after so many years."

He glanced at the woman in his arms. She was smiling at him, a gentle curve of her lips that lit the blue of her eyes like the morning sun touching the eastern sky. He realized in that moment that he was holding her for no other reason than the simple fact that he enjoyed the feel of her in his arms.

She radiated warmth in this place of cold memories. He wanted to cling to her like a lifeline.

He set her on her feet and stepped back, until six feet of cold white-and-black marble separated them. She smiled at him, looking satisfied, as though she could read his mind.

"Welcome home, milord," Gilbert said. "Mrs. Newcombe is gathering the servants for your inspection."

Jared smiled, thinking of the small, gray-haired woman who had always spoiled him. "Maddie is still housekeeper, then."

"Yes, milord." Gilbert nodded, light from the oil lamp behind him reflecting on his bald head. "She had Cook make your favorite cinnamon pastries. Thought it an excellent way to welcome you home again."

Home again. Jared wondered if he could ever truly feel at home in this place again.

Alyssa touched his arm. He graced her with one of his chilliest glares, receiving a smile in return. "After you see to the servants I wonder if I might have a few moments of your time. I would like to discuss Hannah."

Jared stared down into her eyes, seeing that strange warmth flickering there. A warmth that beckoned him, like a frozen traveler seeking the heat of a sheltered fire. "My business associate is due to arrive this morning. We have a great deal of work to do."

"I won't take much of your time."

"I doubt there will be any time this morning."

"Please." She squeezed his arm, smiling up at him, hope shining in her eyes. "Just a few moments. It's important."

For some odd reason he wasn't willing to see disappointment replace that light in her eyes. "Very well. I shall meet with you in the library at precisely half past ten."

Alyssa tilted her head. "*Precisely* half past ten?"

"That's right. I have things to do this morning. I don't expect you to be late."

She nodded. "Half past ten. Precisely."

He turned as she walked away from him, unable to take his eyes from her. She was tall, slender, so light it had been like holding thistledown in his arms. Not at all the fashion. Certainly not the type of woman he preferred. So why the devil did he find her so damn mesmerizing?

She glanced back as she reached the stairs, giving him an impish grin when she caught him staring at her. She started up the stairs, bouncing from one step to another, like a child at play.

Jared clenched his teeth. If the little temptress thought she could wrap him around her dainty finger with just one of her smiles, she had another thought coming. He had learned his lesson twelve years ago, on a cold November morning, when his brother had put a bullet into his shoulder. He would never trust another Fairchild woman as long as he lived.

Raphael waved his hand. Blackmoor Hall dissolved into a thick wall of clouds, leaving Ethan with the memory of Jared Templeton's stern face.

"The man has forgotten what it means to love another human being." Ethan stared up at Raphael. "My daughter is convinced she will never love another man. My granddaughter's future is in Jared Templeton's hands. Something has to be done."

"Yes. Something definitely has to be done. The fates of Alyssa and Hannah are intertwined with Jared's." Raphael rubbed his smooth chin. "Unfortunately, Jared has turned himself into a sculpted figure of a man. He has placed himself on a shelf, high above the touch of human emotion."

"I have to do something to help. Jared will break Alyssa's heart."

"I cannot send you, Ethan."

"But sir . . ."

Raphael lifted his hand, silencing Ethan's plea. "Jared's guardian angel came to see me this morning. She has been concerned about the young man for the last few years. Now that he has returned to Blackmoor, she is worried he will retreat further into his emotional isolation, until no one will be able to reach him. Since I know there is no such thing as mere coincidence, I now realize why she was here."

"Do you think God means for her to help Alyssa and Hannah?"

Raphael rested his hand on Ethan's shoulder. "I suggested she knock Jared Templeton off his shelf. If she can, I believe Alyssa, Hannah, and Jared will find happiness."

Chapter Two

Coincidence is God's way of performing a miracle anonymously.

—Anonymous

Alyssa stood in the hall outside the library, waiting, listening. When the grandfather clock in the hall chimed the half hour, she opened the door and strolled into the room. Jared was standing by the white alabaster fireplace, frowning down at the watch he held open in his hand.

He glanced up when she entered. One corner of his mouth twitched when he looked at her, as though a smile was hidden there, struggling against the frown that tugged his features into a formidable mask. The frown won.

"It's half past ten." She smiled, hoping she

might coax a wayward smile from those tightly pursed lips. "Precisely."

Again she noticed that small twitch of a smile trying to awaken. Again he banished it. He snapped his watch closed and slipped it into the watch pocket of his black silk waistcoat. "I believe you had something you wished to discuss, Miss Fairchild."

Alyssa sighed. Perhaps the man simply couldn't remember how to smile. "It's about Hannah."

"I assume Edward's solicitors have informed you that I have inherited custody of the girl."

"Yes." Alyssa studied this stern-looking man, sensing there was so much more to him than what he allowed the world to see. She perceived an emptiness within him, a loneliness that spoke to her and the longing inside of her. "I thought there were a few things you should know about Hannah."

"My brother's solicitors have already informed me of the child's propensity for terrifying governesses." Jared rested his arm against the mantle. He stared into the fire, his profile as sharp and unyielding as granite. "I understand the girl has gone through seven this year."

Eight, if one was to count Miss Wentridge. Still, Alyssa wasn't compelled to amend the tally. "Hannah is a troubled little girl."

"From what I have gathered, she is an undisciplined little savage."

"No."

"No?" He arched one black brow, his eyes filling with curiosity as he stared at her. Obviously few people dared to contradict Jared Templeton. "Am I to assume you approve of her behavior?"

"Of course not. But you need to understand Hannah. She is a sad little girl. Lonely." Alyssa moved toward him, needing to bridge the chasm she sensed he had carved between them. "And terribly angry."

"Angry? What does that child have to be angry about? She has been spoiled from the day she was born."

"Hannah has been given trinkets all her life. Toys and clothes and various assorted fripperies. But she has never really received what all children desire."

"And what is that, Miss Fairchild?"

"Affection. I believe Hannah was just trying to gain her parents' attention."

"By becoming a demon child?"

"Did you know my sister and your brother spent less than a month each year at Blackmoor Hall? They preferred to entertain themselves in London, or on the continent. While Hannah was left here."

Jared looked down into the fire on the hearth. The light of the flames flickered against his face, illuminating each line etched by time. "It certainly doesn't surprise me to discover your sister had the motherly instincts of an alley cat."

"And your brother took his paternal responsibilities as seriously as a court jester."

He stared into the fire, where golden flames stabbed at three plump logs. The wood crackled beneath the hungry flames, a mournful sound that filled the silence between them. Alyssa watched him, glimpsing the sadness that lingered in this man, wishing she could help him find his smile.

"I'm afraid my parents had the habit of indulging their sons. We were lavished with *affection.*

We had no worries, no responsibilities. The Greystone fortune was enormous. We had solicitors and financiers to tend our inheritance, so Edward and I were allowed to follow our fancies." A muscle in his cheek flickered as he clenched his jaw. "I'm certain you are aware of the disastrous results."

She felt drawn to him, as the sun is drawn each dawn to the darkened sky. She wanted to slip her arms around him, hold him, share her warmth with him. She settled for the simple pleasure of touching his arm. The warmth of his skin radiated through the soft black wool of his coat, a subtle assurance that life still existed beneath the darkness.

He looked at her, his face carved into harsh lines meant to intimidate and repel. Yet there was a longing in his eyes that beckoned her to linger. "You were eighteen when it happened."

"My age hardly excuses my actions." He smiled then, if that taut twisting of his lips could be called a smile. "I was blinded by emotion. Brimming over with misguided passion. In short, I was nothing but a reckless fool."

"You did what you thought was right."

"I challenged my brother to a duel." He lifted his hand from the mantel, bracing his elbow against the cold alabaster as he rubbed his right temple with the tip of his long, slender forefinger. "Hardly a noble act."

"You did it because you thought he had seduced the woman you loved. You had no way of knowing it was Vivien who had invited Edward's attentions. You were young and in love."

"And a man who believes he is under the sway

of this elusive, ethereal, perhaps completely nonexistent emotion, has the right to try to kill his own flesh and blood?" He rolled his eyes, dismissing the argument. "Really, Miss Fairchild, I would think you were at a sufficient age to realize that the concept of love is for children who have yet to clear the stars from their eyes. Love is for fools."

Alyssa stared up at him, unwilling to accept his words. "You don't really believe that."

He frowned. "I see you still believe in the myth. Perhaps that's the reason you are still not married."

Alyssa stepped back from him, reeling as though he had slapped her hard across the cheek. "And you, Lord Greystone? Do you plan to live your entire life alone?"

He sighed, as though growing impatient with the subject. "I plan to marry this coming year."

The blood slowly drained from her limbs as she stood before this man, her dreams dying inside her. He was engaged. Dear heaven, the man she had loved all her life was going to marry another woman. "Does your fiancée share your views on love?"

"I have discovered most women do not consider love a major requirement for marriage. Particularly when a man is rich."

"I see." Alyssa drew air into her constricted lungs. "So you have purchased a woman to be your wife."

Although he didn't move, something flashed in his eyes, something that might have been anger in a man who possessed emotions. In this breathing sculpture of carved ice, Alyssa assumed it was no more than annoyance with a prying female.

"No, Miss Fairchild, I have not purchased a wife. At least not yet."

"I see. Still bargaining over the price?"

One corner of his lips twitched. "I'm still deciding on the merchandise."

Alyssa frowned. "Do you mean to say you're planning a wedding without choosing a bride? Isn't that a bit presumptuous? What if the woman you choose refuses to spend her life with you, no matter how much you're willing to offer?"

Jared rested his chin against his fist. "Everyone has a price."

"I don't believe that is true."

"You wouldn't."

"Because I'm a dried-up old spinster who has never managed to clear the stars from her eyes?"

One corner of his lips tipped upward. It wasn't quite a smile, but it was a start. He narrowed his eyes, like a sleepy lion eyeing his prey. She felt his gaze as he lowered his eyes. It was as though he was touching her, sliding his hands over her, stripping away the black wool of mourning, the prim white linen beneath. Her skin tingled beneath his lazy perusal. Her pulse quickened until she felt the throb of her life's blood in the tips of her breasts. Her own response shocked her; excited her in ways she knew were far from proper.

What would it be like to feel his arms slide around her? The heat of his breath against her cheek. The taste of his lips. The warm brush of his skin against hers. Dear heaven, she had waited so long to experience these things she had only glimpsed in dreams. And now he was here, so close she could reach out and touch him.

He looked straight into her eyes and she realized he knew what she was thinking. "Miss Fairchild, you might still have stars in your pretty blue eyes, but you are hardly a dried-up old spinster."

She moistened her dry lips. "Simply a fool who still believes in love."

"I assume your elusive quest for true love is the reason you are still unwed."

"I can't imagine marrying without love."

He sighed. "Marriages should have a stronger foundation than something as fleeting as emotion."

"And what exactly are you looking for in this wife you intend to purchase?"

He rubbed the tip of his forefinger over his bottom lip as he contemplated her question. "She must be a suitable hostess."

She smiled, realizing the man wasn't entirely as cold as he appeared. "Do you enjoy entertaining friends at your home?"

"A great deal of business is conducted on social occasions."

"I see." Did the man ever do anything simply for the pleasure of it? "So your wife must be able to plan your business meetings—I mean, your social entertainments."

He pursed his lips, obviously annoyed with her. "She must be intelligent, well bred, and reasonably attractive."

"Reasonably attractive?" Alyssa lifted her brows in mock surprise. "Why, Lord Greystone, I would think with your enormous fortune you would be able to purchase a great beauty."

He stared down into her eyes, as though he saw something unexpected there, something that made him uneasy. "You disapprove of me, Miss Fairchild."

Alyssa rubbed her arms, feeling chilled even though she was standing by the fire. "I feel sorry for you, Lord Greystone."

"You feel sorry for me?" he asked, as though he couldn't quite believe her words.

She lifted her chin. "Yes."

He rubbed his fingers across his temple, staring at her as though he was trying to put together the pieces of a puzzle. "Do you mind telling me why?"

"Because you will never know what it's like to feel the warmth of love glow in your heart. You will never be able to look at your wife and know she is there simply because it brings her joy to be near you."

"My approach to marriage is quite practical."

"And cold."

"The world functions on logic, Miss Fairchild. When we court emotion we invite chaos."

"And how do you plan to deal with Hannah? With logic?"

"I intend to find a governess who can handle the child."

"A governess will handle her schooling. What do you intend to do about healing the wounds of neglect?"

He shook his head. "You speak of the girl as though she was some poor, homeless orphan."

"*Hannah.* The girl's name is Hannah."

He released his breath in an impatient sigh. "What is your point, Miss Fairchild?"

"My point is simple: Hannah needs someone to show her she isn't alone in the world. She needs someone to care about her. And I wonder if you can do that, Lord Greystone."

His lips pulled into a tight line, his eyes narrowing in an icy glare. "Hannah is my responsibility, Miss Fairchild. And I take my responsibilities seriously. I will see to it she has a proper upbringing."

Alyssa sighed. "She needs more than clothes and trinkets and things she can learn out of a book. She needs affection."

"She needs discipline."

"Discipline without love will only breed anger."

He lowered his hand to the mantel, his long fingers curling into a fist on the white alabaster, the only outward sign of his growing anger. "You are not exactly an expert on raising children."

"I know what it's like to grow up in a house filled with love and warmth, with parents who freely give their affection."

He huffed. "Vivien was certainly a shining example of what happens when a child is overly indulged."

"Hannah is not Vivien."

"And I intend to give her every opportunity to avoid the temptation of becoming a self-indulgent, spoiled little flirt."

Alyssa hugged her arms to her waist, shivering inside from being near the icy bitterness in this man. "Let Hannah come live with me."

He stared at her, as though she had suddenly sprouted an extra head. "I told you once before, Miss Fairchild, the child is my responsibility."

"That's just my point. Hannah isn't a responsibility. Hannah is an intelligent, spirited, wounded little girl who needs a loving hand."

He studied her for a moment, a cool, assessing

look that stripped away pretense. "If you were so concerned about the child, why didn't you do something before now?"

Alyssa glanced away from his perceptive eyes. She stared at the mahogany bookcases lining the wall behind him, row upon row of leather-bound volumes standing like rigid soldiers before their commander. "I didn't realize what was happening. Vivien and I were never very close. And in the past few years . . . Father was so ill, we didn't travel."

She sensed him watching her, appraising her, but her guilt kept her from meeting his eyes.

"You never came to visit Hannah?"

"A few times." Alyssa released her breath in a ragged sigh. How could she explain how difficult it had been to be around Vivien? Her sister had everything in life—a husband who adored her, a home of her own, a beautiful little girl. And the love of the one man Alyssa had always adored. "I should have realized what was happening. I just thought . . . Vivien always managed to appear the devoted mother when I was here."

"She was always an accomplished liar."

Alyssa refused to allow the barb to stir her to anger. She knew her sister's faults better than anyone. "It wasn't until after I came here a few days ago that I learned how little time Vivien and Edward had spent with Hannah."

"And now you want to save her from her terrible Uncle Jared."

Alyssa looked up at him, seeing anger in his eyes, and more. She had inadvertently hurt him—the last thing she wanted to do. "I didn't mean to imply . . ."

"You didn't *imply,* Miss Fairchild. You made it

very clear you think I'm incapable of raising the child."

She shook her head. "You have other concerns. And now that Father is gone, I have all the time in the world to devote to Hannah."

He narrowed his eyes, a lion about to pounce. "Perhaps you should devote your time to finding a husband and having children of your own. Before you *are* a dried-up old spinster."

His words were shaped into arrows, designed to pierce her heart. And he hit the mark. She felt a twisting inside her, the pain that came from the ragged wound of loneliness. "I would be careful standing so close to the fire, Lord Greystone. After all, ice does melt when it is placed too close to a flame."

He twisted his lips into that sad imitation of a smile. "I assure you, Miss Fairchild, I am in no danger of melting."

She stared up into his eyes, realizing he was safe behind his defenses. She had no way of touching this man. No hope of ever winning the heart she hoped he still possessed. But she knew she would have to try to make him see the need for affection, for the sake of Hannah.

He glanced past her as a knock sounded on the door. At his invitation, Gilbert opened the door and announced the arrival of Mr. Anthony Heyer.

A tall, dark-haired man entered, carrying a brown case in one hand and a plump cinnamon pastry in the other. "Didn't have time for breakfast," he said, dusting crumbs from his chin with the back of his hand. If his easy manner hadn't marked him as an American, his accent would have. "So I raided your kitchen."

"I noticed," Jared said, his dark voice colored with a hint of humor.

"The pastry is . . ." Anthony looked at Alyssa, sweeping his dark brown gaze from the top of her golden brown curls to the tips of her black shoes. "Beautiful."

The blatant perusal shocked her. Still, there was nothing in Anthony Heyer's stare meant to offend. Just a warm look of appreciation. It was enough to make this dried-up old spinster smile.

"You always had an eye for pastry." Jared met Anthony's smile with a frown. "Mr. Heyer and I have a great deal of work to do, Miss Fairchild."

He was dismissing her, without so much as introducing her to this attractive man with the warm brown eyes and the welcoming smile. But Anthony Heyer refused to allow the opportunity to pass. As she drew near, he shifted the case under his arm and offered her his hand.

"Anthony Heyer, at your service." He winked at her. "But my friends call me Tony."

She couldn't help but smile as she looked up into his smiling face. "I'm Alyssa Fairchild, Mr. Heyer."

"Tony. I'm sure we're going to be friends."

Alyssa laughed. "Something tells me being sure of yourself is never a problem with you, Mr. Heyer."

Jared cleared his throat. "If you're through accosting Miss Fairchild, I suggest we get some work done, Tony."

Alyssa glanced over her shoulder at Jared. "I assure you, Mr. Heyer isn't accosting me, Lord Greystone. I find his warmth an unexpected pleasure in this chilly room."

One corner of Jared's lips twitched. "Taking my advice already, Miss Fairchild?"

She could only imagine he meant the advice concerning her own state of spinsterhood. "Perhaps." Without another word she turned and marched from the room, leaving behind a scowling ice sculpture.

Chapter Three

Be not afraid to have strangers in your house, for some thereby have entertained angels unawares.

—Hebrews 13:2

Never in his life had he met a more impertinent young woman. Jared drummed his fingers on a dark green leather desk pad, staring at the papers laid out before him on the wide mahogany desk. How dare Alyssa Fairchild imply he wasn't capable of raising one spoiled little girl?

"I think Hunt is ready to sell." Tony stood beside Jared's chair. He tapped his finger against one of the papers piled on the desk as he continued. "With that tract of land you'll have the entire stretch of Lexington between Twenty-first and Thirty-second."

Did Alyssa Fairchild actually believe she would be better at the task of raising Hannah than he would?

"I wonder what Hunt would say if he knew you were going to set up one of your immigrant orphanages on that parcel. He has a real problem with anyone who has an accent."

Jared shook his head, imagining that starry-eyed little chit trying to raise a child on her own. Why, he could see them now, eating gingerbread for dinner, reading each other stories before going to bed.

"Are you there?" Tony waved his hand in front of Jared's face. "Hello? Can you hear me?"

Jared frowned as he looked up at Tony. "What's wrong?"

"That's what I was trying to figure out." Tony sat on the edge of the desk, a smile curving his lips. "You seem a little distracted this morning. Could it be a pretty brunette has your mind wandering?"

"Brunette?"

"Miss Alyssa Fairchild."

"She isn't a brunette." Jared stared at the spiral staircase leading to the second-story gallery of the library. Sunlight streamed through the French windows behind him, glinting on the scrolled brass ironwork of the balustrade, reminding him of Alyssa's hair. "But she isn't a blonde either. Her hair is . . ." he waved his hand, trying to label that shade of gold and brown, "golden."

"I guess you took a closer look than I did."

Jared slanted a look at Tony. They were both younger sons of wealthy families. Perhaps that was what had drawn them together at Harvard.

Tony had been working for Jared the past seven years as an attorney and business adviser. He was also the only true friend Jared had. "It seemed to me you looked her over fairly well."

Tony laughed. "When have I ever not noticed a beautiful woman?"

Jared's muscles tensed. "Tread lightly around her, Tony. She isn't exactly one of your actresses."

"Relax. I know how to behave around a lady."

Too well. Tony's good looks and easy charm had allowed the man to seduce half the women in New York. Jared stared up into his friend's smiling face and realized he didn't want Tony within ten miles of Alyssa Fairchild. "I want you to leave for London, this afternoon."

"But, I just got here." Tony stared at Jared, understanding dawning in his eyes. "Can it be possible?"

Jared frowned, uncomfortable with the scrutiny. "What?"

"The man who has women literally swooning at his feet for a chance to meet him is afraid of competition." Tony wiggled his eyebrows. "From me."

"I think the bumpy ride from London has addled your brains."

"Really? So tell me, why do you want to send your old pal back to London?"

Jared stared down at the papers, unwilling to examine his motives for sending Tony back to London. "I want you to oversee the repairs to the townhouse. I also want you to interview women for the position of governess."

"Governess!"

"Contact the Fleming Agency. They are aware of the trouble with Hannah. I want an experienced woman, over the age of fifty. Someone who knows the meaning of discipline." He glanced up at his friend. "Someone who might have been able to handle you when you were in the schoolroom."

Tony frowned. "You want me to interview little old ladies who carry a whip?"

Jared smiled. "You have mentioned you have a way with women."

"I didn't exactly have gray-haired tyrants in mind when I said it."

"Narrow the field down to five." Jared leaned back in his chair, the burgundy leather sighing softly beneath him. "Then send them here. I'll make the final decision."

Tony dropped his chin to his chest, a man headed for the gallows.

"There are several theaters in London, Tony." Jared rolled a gold fountain pen between his fingers. "I'm sure you can find a way to enjoy yourself."

Tony grinned. "And you, my friend? Do you plan to enjoy yourself here in the country?"

Jared tapped one end of the pen against the leather desk pad. " "I intend to put this house in order."

"And is that golden-haired beauty going to help?"

"Miss Fairchild is here to visit with her niece, nothing more."

Tony leaned forward, staring Jared straight in the eye. "If I didn't know that you consider one woman as good as the next, I would think you find Miss Fairchild something special."

Jared held Tony's look, the way he would meet the stare of a business rival over a negotiating table—without betraying emotion, thought, or inclination. "Miss Fairchild is nothing more than my late brother's sister-in-law."

"Glad to hear it." Tony leaned back, grinning like a poker player who has just laid four aces on the table. "When I get back from London I intend to get to know the lady better."

Jared molded his lips into a smile he knew revealed none of the turmoil inside him. He managed to mask his emotions as he reviewed the rest of the papers Tony had brought. But they were there, deep inside him, chipping at him like sharp claws on ice.

Three hours later Jared sat alone in the library. He stared out the French windows behind the desk. Sunlight reflected on the snow-covered rose garden, so bright the light hurt his eyes. Yet he stared, emotions churning inside him, some of which had been buried for so long he couldn't even name them.

What madness had taken hold of him? Why couldn't he quell this tempest inside him? Was it coming back to this place where he had lived as a carefree, all too reckless young man? Was it sitting here at his father's desk? Was it all the memories that taunted him?

God, memories lurked in every corner of this house. He kept expecting to see his father walk through the doors of the library, smiling. His father always had an easy smile. Except that day. There had been no smiles the day Jared had been carried home with a bullet in his shoulder. Disappointment and anger had stolen his father's smile.

"You look deep in thought, Lord Greystone."

Jared pivoted in the chair. A woman stood beside the desk. A tall woman, narrow and straight, dressed in a dark gray coat. A black velvet hat sat perched at an angle on her head. A single gray ostrich feather curved from the brim, matching the streaks of gray in her chestnut hair, a touch of frivolity strangely at odds with her austere appearance.

She regarded him with dark blue eyes, smiling as though she knew him, as though she knew every secret he had ever tried to hide. Still, she didn't judge him, only accepted him with that warm smile. Odd, but looking at her, he had the strangest feeling he knew her.

"Who are you?" Jared stood, pushing the chair back against the desk. "How did you get in here?"

"I'm Charlotte Merryweather." She planted the tip of her black umbrella against the Aubusson carpet and folded her hands over the handle, which Jared noticed was shaped like the head of a pink flamingo. "I believe you are looking for a governess."

He frowned. "How did you know of the position?"

"My superior has been aware of the situation here for quite some time."

"I see. Miss Wentridge must have sent a telegram to have reached your superior so quickly."

Miss Merryweather smiled, seemingly amused by this.

"The agency was certainly quick about sending a replacement."

"My superior believes Miss Wentridge was never well suited for this position."

Jared sat on the edge of the desk. "But he believes you are suited to handle my niece?"

"I have had a certain degree of success with children." She turned away from him, tucking her umbrella under her arm as she strolled across the library, the pink flamingo head peeking out from beneath the sleeve of her somber gray coat.

Jared stared at the woman who moved about his library as though she owned the place. "I assume you have references, Miss Merryweather."

"Yes." She paused in front of a painting hanging in an ornate gold frame on one of the carved mahogany panels across from him. "This is excellent work. You can almost feel the rain hitting the dark gray stones. You've captured the true brooding quality that emanates from the Tower of London, almost as if you could see the spirits of tortured souls lingering there."

Jared glanced at the painting. He assumed she had noticed his name in the corner and realized he was the artist. Strange, he hadn't even noticed the painting was still hanging there until this moment.

"Your parents were quite proud of your artistic ability."

The breath stilled in his lungs. "What do you know of my parents?"

She glanced at him over her shoulder, smiling, her blue eyes filled with a gentleness so powerful she glowed with it. "It's obvious your parents were proud of you, Lord Greystone. One of your paintings hangs here in a place of prominence. Another hangs in the entry hall, where every visitor may see it. I suspect there are others hanging in the house as well. Are there more?"

"I don't know." Jared glanced down to the papers piled in neat stacks on his father's desk, certain this woman could read every emotion churning inside him simply by looking into his eyes. "At one time there were others. They may have been removed."

"I doubt it."

Jared drew in his breath. "Miss Merryweather, my paintings are of little significance."

"Do you still paint?"

He hadn't touched a paintbrush in twelve years. He had cast it aside along with all his other frivolous pursuits. "No."

"Pity. It is truly a sin to allow talent to be wasted."

He sighed. "Miss Merryweather, about my niece . . ."

"I should like to meet with her straightaway. The sooner we get started, the better for all concerned. There is much work to be done here."

Jared stared at this tall, majestic woman, seeing the contrast of her military bearing and her gentle blue eyes, wondering how she had managed to control the conversation so completely.

She marched toward the door. "We mustn't waste time, Lord Greystone."

He hesitated a moment, words of dismissal forming in his brain. Yet he didn't speak them. If this strange woman could control him so well, she just might have a chance at controlling his niece.

Jared glared at the ormolu clock that was perched on the carved white marble mantel of the dining room. It was a quarter past eight; Alyssa was late. Slowly, he paced the length of the room, ignoring the footmen who lined the wall like statues, dark blue livery plastered against the pale yellow and white stripes of the silk wall covering. He pivoted as he reached the windows, gold brocade drapes shivering in his wake.

He had told her dinner would be served *precisely* at eight. He paused at the head of the table, staring down the length of polished cherry wood to the empty seat at the opposite end. He wouldn't wait much longer. He would show Miss Fairchild the meaning of discipline. The little vixen could miss dinner as far as he was concerned.

Someone cleared his throat. "Excuse me, milord."

Jared turned, frowning as he saw Gilbert standing a few feet away, alone. "I thought I asked you to escort Miss Fairchild down to dinner, Gilbert."

Gilbert lifted his chin, meeting Jared's glare with a measure of unease in his dark eyes. "I'm afraid Miss Fairchild will not be joining you this evening, milord."

"Is she ill?" Jared asked, careful to keep the sudden concern he felt from his voice.

"No, milord. Miss Fairchild asked me to tell you that . . ." Gilbert cleared his throat. "She said she thought the dining room might be a bit too chilly, and that she prefers to have dinner with Lady Hannah and Miss Merryweather."

"I see." Jared clenched his jaw, resisting the anger that surged inside him. The anger that demanded he find Miss Alyssa Fairchild and shake the woman until all that golden brown hair tumbled from its anchoring pins. Still, he wasn't a man who lost his temper. He didn't intend to start now. "You may begin serving, Gilbert."

Jared took his place at the head of the table. He

stared at the silver candelabra that rose from the center of the long table as Gilbert served the first course. This was hardly the first time he had dined alone. He didn't need Alyssa Fairchild. He didn't need anyone.

But as he ate his solitary meal, his thoughts kept creeping back to dinners long past. The room was quiet, so quiet he could hear the click of the clock on the mantel. This room had never been quiet at dinner. There had always been laughter and conversation. His mother had always believed dinner was a time for sharing the events of the day with one's family.

He stared past the candelabra to the empty chair at the end of the table. A wound throbbed deep inside, a wound he had thought healed long ago. He sipped his wine, forcing the burgundy past the tight knot in his throat.

What was wrong with him? It was useless dwelling on the past. What was done could not be altered. He could only make certain unbridled emotions never betrayed him again.

Alyssa couldn't sleep. She slipped into the library, hoping a book would help divert her thoughts from Jared. The fire had died long ago, and the servants had forgotten to draw the drapes, allowing an icy chill to flow with the moonlight into the room. Winter touched her face, seeped through the thick blue velvet of her robe, the soft white linen of her nightgown. She shivered.

She turned the switch near the door. The flames in the gas lamps overhead rose, flickering brightly against etched crystal globes. Golden light rained upon the burgundy sofas, the tall wing-backed chairs, burnishing the mahogany and brass bookcases lining the walls. From her previous exploration of the library she knew exactly where the novels of popular fiction were kept. After a few moments' deliberation she pulled a mystery from the shelf.

"Having trouble sleeping, Miss Fairchild?"

Alyssa jumped at the sound of that deep male voice. She spun around. The book flew from her fingers as though it had a will of its own. It slammed into Jared's chest. The air whooshed from his lungs as the book fell—plopping end first on his toes. He uttered a half-stifled groan.

Alyssa pressed her hand to her heart, appalled at what she had done. "Oh, my. I'm sorry."

Jared dragged air between his clenched teeth. It took a moment before he spoke, a moment in which he seemed to be counting, slowly, silently. "It's all right."

Alyssa bent to retrieve the book. So did Jared. They bumped, the top of her head ramming the tip of his chin. He fell back, smacking the carpet with his backside.

"Dear heaven." Alyssa stood, staring down at the Earl of Greystone, a nervous giggle tickling her chest. "I'm terribly sorry."

Jared rubbed his chin. "You find this amusing?"

Alyssa coughed, hiding her giggles. "No. Of course not."

He frowned as he studied her. She had the impression he liked to pin labels on each person he met. Yet he was staring at her as though he couldn't quite find a label to suit her. She offered him her hand.

He shook his head. "I think it's safer down here at the moment."

She stared down at him, trying to pull together the tattered shreds of her dignity. How in the world could the man manage to look elegant and sophisticated while sitting on the floor? He was still dressed for dinner, entirely in black, except for his white shirt, which was open all the way down to his black silk waistcoat. "I'm not usually this clumsy."

He folded his arms over his raised knees. "Really?"

"Truly." She stared at his chest, where white linen parted, revealing the shadow of black curls. Those black curls looked silky. Intensely masculine. She couldn't help wondering what it might be like to touch that bare expanse of dark skin and black curls.

Dear heaven, she was staring. She jerked her gaze upward, meeting his eyes. There was no anger in those eyes; just a glimmer of curiosity and something she couldn't identify, something heated that touched her, rippling along her every nerve until she trembled. "As a matter of fact—" she moistened her lips—"I'm not usually clumsy at all."

"I see. Then I must surmise there is something about me that makes you nervous."

"Certainly not." She lifted her chin, hoping to look sophisticated in spite of the fact that her legs were trembling. "There was the ice this morning. And you startled me just now."

He did something unexpected then, something that hit Alyssa like a fist. He smiled. A real smile. A smile that lit the cold depths of his emerald eyes and stole the breath from her lungs. "Remind me never to startle you again, Miss Fairchild. I might not survive the results."

Never startle her again? She nearly laughed. The very sight of the man startled her. She need only look at him and her heart pounded, as though she had been running for miles and finally reached her destination.

He lifted the book from the floor and stood, each fluid movement filled with an easy grace born of power. "You like mysteries," he said, glancing at the title tooled in gold on the brown leather.

"Yes." The heat of his body brushed against her, an unexpected flame in the icy room. Embers burned in this man; scorned, shunned, they survived, hidden deep inside him. She was certain of it. "I understand Doyle has a unique approach."

"Logic." Jared handed her the book, a smile tipping one corner of his lips. "His detective is ruled by logic."

She resisted the urge to step closer to him, seeking the warmth buried deep within him. "You've read it?"

Jared nodded. "It was fairly amusing, although at times I found Holmes a trifle too arrogant, too certain of the world around him."

"Strange." Alyssa hugged the book to her chest. "I would expect you to appreciate a man who is ruled by logic."

He frowned, just a slight tensing of his brow that might have gone undetected if she wasn't so aware of his every expression. "And tell me, Miss Fairchild, by what measure do you judge a man?"

"My father always said you could judge the

character of a man by his deeds. By the people he touched, the lives he helped to make better." Alyssa stared at the window, seeing the reflection of the room in the glass, her throat tightening with the pain of loss. "A good man always leaves a place better than when he found it."

He touched her, a soft brush of his long fingers across her cheek. She glanced up, shocked at the tenderness in his touch, catching a glimpse of that same tenderness in his eyes. He frowned, as though the gesture had shocked him as much as it had her.

He stepped away from her. "How long has he been gone?"

"Seven months. Father had been ill for the past few years. His heart." The chill of the room crept into the space between them. "One morning he just didn't wake up."

"I assume his illness prevented you from entering into the whirl of London society."

"I had a London Season when I was eighteen. Fortunately, my father didn't force me to have another."

"Force you? Don't most women long for balls and parties and all the rest of that nonsense?"

Alyssa laughed. "I suppose. But I'm afraid I found it all terribly stifling. There were so many rules to follow. And I always felt as though I was on display, like a piece of porcelain in a shop window."

"I would imagine there were more than a few gentleman who wanted to take you home."

"A few."

"But not the right gentleman."

Alyssa glanced down at the book she held like a

shield against her chest. "No."

The silence wrapped around her with the chill in the room. She sensed him watching her, as though he wanted to pry away her defenses and peer into the secret places in her soul.

"I'm surprised you didn't enjoy London." There was a restraint in his voice, as though he was testing her responses.

She looked up into his shuttered features. "Now that I live in London I find there are many advantages to living in town."

He lifted one black brow, a cynical glint entering his eyes. "I see you didn't waste time in returning to that stifling town life."

Alyssa's anger flickered at his subtle implication. "Since I didn't have the good sense to be born male I didn't have a choice. Most of my father's property was entailed to my cousin. Father purchased the house in London for me two years ago. He wanted to make sure I had a place to live after he was gone."

He frowned. "I see."

"You really mustn't look at me as though I was a poor unfortunate orphan." Alyssa glanced away from the pity in his eyes. Pity was the last thing she wanted from this man. "I do very well on my own."

"And what of the future? Do you plan to live alone the rest of your life?"

Alyssa squeezed the book to her chest. In her mind she saw the years stretch out before her, each filled with the trivialities of an empty life. "I have found that some dreams have little hope of becoming reality."

"Perhaps you expect too much, Miss Fairchild."

"Perhaps I do." Alyssa lifted her eyes, meeting his steady gaze. "But I won't settle for a marriage based on logic, Lord Greystone."

Jared pursed his lips. "Logic is far more reliable than emotion."

"And far less comforting." She shivered under his icy look. "I'm afraid I've had enough of the chill in this room. Good night."

A muscle in his cheek flickered as he clenched his jaw. "Pleasant dreams."

Alyssa stared out a window of her bedroom, looking up at the sky as she did each evening before going to bed. In her heart she knew her father was still with her, watching over her as he had done all her life. "Greystone is a difficult man, Father. You wouldn't recognize him. Still, I sense a need within him. He's lonely. And so am I."

She hugged her arms to her waist, wishing she could feel the warm embrace of her father's comforting arms. "I wish you were here. I wish you could help me break through the walls of ice surrounding Greystone. I think I'm going to need all the help I can get."

Ethan wiped a tear from his cheek as the image of Alyssa dissolved into clouds. "Is there nothing you will allow me to do? She loves him with all her heart."

"Yes," Raphael said, his deep voice filled with compassion. "Her love for him can light the darkness within him. If he will only turn toward that light."

Ethan looked up into Raphael's gentle eyes.

"Will he marry her? Will she live her life with him?"

Raphael placed his hand on Ethan's shoulder. "I cannot say if she shall live her life with Jared. Much depends on the choices they both make."

Chapter Four

Millions of spiritual creatures walk this earth unseen, both when we wake and when we sleep.

—John Milton

Jared stared down into the fire, nudging a charred log on the hearth with the tip of his black boot, pushing it back into the flames. Behind him morning sunlight slanted across the papers stacked in neat piles on his father's desk. Work demanded his attention, yet he couldn't concentrate. Not on work. His mind kept drifting, as it had since the moment a golden-haired temptress had knocked him off his feet.

He smiled into the flames, imagining Alyssa's face. Last night, as he lay awake in his bed, he had fought to banish her from his mind. Yet she was there, every time he closed his eyes. She was there still, haunting him.

He shook his head, bemused by his own fascination with the woman. Women came into his life, warmed his bed, and left. It was simple. And if occasionally there were tears at parting, something sparkling from Tiffany's worked wonders at drying those tears. Yet Alyssa was different. Diamonds would never dry her tears. He sensed she wanted something more from him than money. Something he no longer had to give.

He shouldn't think of the desire he had glimpsed in her beautiful eyes. He shouldn't remember the softness of her cheek beneath his fingers. He definitely shouldn't dwell on how right she felt in his arms. Even now, memory triggered a response in him, a warmth that heated his blood until it ran hot and thick.

He released his breath in a ragged sigh. The lady wasn't his type. She wanted romance, passion, pledges of undying love. She would get none of those from him. Still he couldn't get her out of his thoughts.

The door to the library flew open, hitting the paneled wall. He glanced up as Hannah stormed across the threshold.

"Look at me!" she shouted, flinging her hands out at her sides.

Jared couldn't help but look at the child. Indeed, she was a most extraordinary sight. Small white feathers dusted her yellow curls, her face, her shoulders. Feathers dripped down the front of her black gown like plump snowflakes.

"She did this!" Hannah pointed to the woman standing behind her.

Jared tore his gaze from the girl to Miss Charlotte Merryweather. Once again he was struck by an odd feeling, as though he had met Charlotte somewhere, a long time ago. She stood with her hands clasped at her waist, her head held high, like a general reviewing her troops. Yet there was nothing military about her eyes. Humor glittered in those dark blue eyes.

"Do something!" Hannah demanded.

Jared coughed, covering the unexpected laughter in his throat. He molded his features into an emotionless mask as he looked at the governess. "Miss Merryweather, I expect you have an explanation for my niece's appearance."

Charlotte smiled, unruffled by his cold glare. "It seems someone secured a bucket of syrup and a bundle of feathers above the door to the schoolroom. When Hannah stepped across the threshold they tipped."

"I fixed them so they would spill on the person who opened the door." Hannah planted her small hands on her hips. "They were supposed to fall on you. You opened the door. You walked into the room before me. You did something to make them fall on me instead."

The feigned look of shock on Charlotte's face was spoiled by the glitter of amusement in her eyes. "Why, Hannah, you don't mean to say *you* put that dreadful trap above the door?"

"I fixed it so . . ." Hannah paused, glancing back at Jared, a thief caught with her hand in the money box.

Jared frowned. "Did you set the trap, Hannah?"

Hannah's lips curved into a plump pout. "She made it fall on me."

Jared studied this angry little girl, uneasy at the certainty that he was out of his element here. "It seems you were snared in your own trap, young lady."

"Oh!" Hannah stamped her feet in her frustrated fury, feathers fluttering from her like snowflakes in a storm. "She did this to me."

Charlotte touched the child's shoulder. "I believe it is time you begin to realize it's important to treat people the way you wish to be treated."

Hannah pulled away from Charlotte's touch. "I don't want you here!"

"That will be quite enough, young lady." Jared kept his voice low, using the same chilling tone he would use with any employee who had gotten out of line. "I shall not tolerate such emotional outbursts."

Hannah stared at him, her brown eyes wide.

He saw disappointment in her eyes, as though she expected more from him than he knew how to give. That made him all the more harsh when he spoke. "You shall go to your room and stay there until you decide to conduct yourself with the decorum of a lady."

Hannah clenched her small hands into fists at her sides. She stared at Jared, her lower lip trembling. "You're a horrible man. I hate you! I wish Father had killed you in that duel!"

Jared flinched inwardly at the hatred in her eyes. "Since he didn't you are now obliged to obey me. Go to your room."

"I hate you!" A sob escaped Hannah's lips as she ran from the room, feathers fluttering in her wake.

Jared stared at the empty doorway. He drew in his breath, trying to ease the tension in his chest, the hurt that one little girl had inflicted with her angry words. How the hell was he going to handle the child?

"You have such a delicate way of dealing with the child."

Jared glanced at Charlotte. "I suppose you think I made a mess of it." His words were clipped as he spoke the truth he didn't really want to admit.

"The thought did cross my mind."

Jared felt like a schoolboy who had taken a test and failed miserably. "I should think it's obvious I haven't spent much time around children."

"Strange, for a man who has established several orphanages in New York."

"How did you know about the orphanages?"

"My superior believes it's important to remain well informed."

Jared stared at this strange woman, wondering how her superior could possibly have known about his work. There were few people in the world who knew he was behind the establishment of homes for children with nowhere else to live.

Charlotte glanced away from him, surveying her surroundings a moment before she spoke. "Do you remember you or your brother ever having tantrums?"

"Never. Why do you ask?"

Charlotte looked at him, her eyes alight with the wisdom of the ages. "You and your brother were raised with a great deal of love and understanding."

Jared tensed. "How do you know about how my brother and I were raised?"

"My superior felt it important for me to know a

little about you and your family before I took this assignment."

"I don't approve of gossip, Miss Merryweather. And I certainly do not care to have the private affairs of my family discussed as though we were performers on the stage. I believe I shall have to confront your superior one day."

"Oh, I believe you shall." Charlotte smiled, as though she was amused with a secret she intended to keep. "I can assure you, my superior does not deal in gossip, Lord Greystone. He meant only for me to be better prepared to help you."

Jared glanced away from her. He stared into the flames, feeling curiously exposed. "If you have a point to make, Miss Merryweather, kindly make it."

"Hannah requires more than a stern hand. She needs to feel as though someone cares about her."

Jared clenched his jaw. "You have obviously been discussing the situation with Miss Fairchild."

"Yes, I have. Quite a remarkable young woman. But I'm certain you must have noticed her exceptional qualities. She has remarkable insight for one so young."

Jared stared into the flames, but it was Alyssa's face he saw, her eyes, her smile, the beauty that came from more than a perfection of features. "You don't work for Alyssa Fairchild," he said, appalled at how his voice had softened with the mention of Alyssa's name. "You work for me."

"I believe you both wish for the same thing, Lord Greystone. I believe you would both like to see Hannah change into a happy, well-mannered child."

"The child needs discipline."

"Yes."

Jared glanced at her, suspicious of her response. "You agree with me?"

"Of course. Every child must be taught discipline. But discipline without gentleness, without understanding, without affection, will bring only anger." Charlotte studied Jared for a moment, as though she was judging his every response. "She really is a dear little girl, beneath all of her anger. Perhaps you should get to know her. After all, you are her guardian."

Jared didn't need reminding. The responsibility of the child sat like a boulder on his shoulders. "As I said before, I don't have much experience with children."

Charlotte nodded, her lips curved into an understanding smile. "I have quite a bit of experience. That's why I'm here, isn't it; to help you."

A strange feeling of well-being poured over him as he held her gentle gaze, like a soft blue light filling him, easing away his tension, assuring him that he could rest his burdens in her capable hands. He clenched his hand into a fist on the mantel. It had been a long time since he had relied on anyone else. "I'm curious. I've seen the result of Hannah's little syrup-and-feather trap before. Just how did you manage to turn the trap on the hunter?"

"We tend to reap what we sow, Lord Greystone."

Jared frowned. "So you didn't have anything to do with it?"

Charlotte shrugged. "By the way, Miss Fairchild is in the tower room, should you wish to see her."

Jared stared at the woman, stunned by her sudden shift in conversation. "Why in the world is Miss Fairchild in the tower room?"

"It seems all the Christmas decorations are stored there. And even though the house is in mourning, we thought decorations for Christmas would be appropriate."

"Christmas." It was little more than a week away. In the past Blackmoor Hall had shimmered at Christmas. It had always been his mother's favorite time of the year.

"Gilbert tells me Blackmoor Hall hasn't been decorated for Christmas since your mother died."

"It doesn't surprise me." Jared stared into the fire, wondering if Vivien and Edward had ever spent Christmas here.

"I thought you might like to help Miss Fairchild find your mother's decorations."

Jared glanced at the woman. "I have a great deal of work to do this afternoon, Miss Merryweather."

"Of course you do." Charlotte folded her hands at her waist, holding Jared in a gentle gaze. "But I hope you remember, Lord Greystone, that we are all given a short time on this earth. It's important to make the most of each moment we are granted."

"I can assure you, I seldom waste time."

"I suppose that is a matter of opinion. Now, you shall have to excuse me. I need to see to Hannah. I believe we shall begin her lessons in painting this afternoon."

Jared stiffened, unaccustomed to anyone counteracting his orders. "I told her she was not to leave her room."

Charlotte smiled. "And I shall tell her you have had a change of heart."

Jared stared, stunned by this woman's impertinence.

"I know you want to do what is best, Lord Greystone. I intend to help you discover just what that is." She turned and left the room, closing the door behind her.

Jared stared at that closed door. He should dismiss the woman. Now. This very moment. Yet something kept him from following her—a sense that she might actually be able to help.

He turned away from the fire and crossed the room, the warmth of the hearth fading as he drew near the desk. He sank into the leather chair and stared at the papers awaiting his attention. The chill of winter creeping through the windows wrapped icy arms around him. He thought of Alyssa, recalling the warmth he always felt when she was near.

The woman and her romantic notions were not for him. It was better for both of them if he stayed clear of her. He lifted a hefty report on the Union Pacific Railroad and proceeded to bury himself in work.

Dust spilled into the air as Alyssa opened one of the many trunks stored within the stone walls of the tower room. Sunlight slanted through the narrow windows, spinning the drifting dust to glittering gold. She felt as though she were on a treasure hunt. Each trunk was stuffed with bounty hidden away long ago, secrets waiting for a curious explorer.

Carefully she eased aside layer upon layer of paper and ornaments, revealing angels with harps and trumpets designed to perch on the branches of a fragrant evergreen, glass balls trimmed in gold, strings of golden beads, white and gold silk bows, small golden candle holders. Everything she needed to decorate a tree. If she had one to decorate.

Alyssa lifted a tall angel designed to sit atop a tree. Golden curls tumbled around a porcelain face sculpted in delicate features. A gown of white silk billowed around her. White feathers sculpted her delicate wings. It was exquisite. She could scarcely wait to see the angel perched high on the treetop. Of course, she would have to convince Lord Greystone that they needed a tree to grace the drawing room.

"That won't be easy, milady," she said, carefully lowering the angel to her bed of white satin. "But it isn't impossible." The man had a generous heart. She knew it. All she had to do was convince him of it.

She lifted a long string of beads from the trunk, turning the golden strand in the sunlight, imagining the little beads glittering in candlelight. The tree would be so very . . .

"Oh, my!" The string broke. Golden beads spilled from her fingers, pinging against the oak planks of the floor like a shower of hail. Hundreds of beads skittered in every direction, streaking across the dusty planks, tapping trunks and walls.

"Wonderful." Greystone already thought she was a clumsy ninny. All she needed was for him to discover she had destroyed his mother's decorations. Well, he wouldn't know of this latest mishap—not if she could help it. All she had to do was recover the beads and re-string them.

She got down on her hands and knees, folded

her skirt to form a pouch and began retrieving tiny golden beads. It was then that she heard the door open. She paused with her hand against the floor. She heard one soft footstep and then . . .

A scuff of a boot on oak.

A startled gasp.

Something heavy crashed against the floor.

Someone groaned, deep and low in his throat. Alyssa cringed. She knew the sound of that groan far too well. She clasped her hand over her lips. She huddled against one of the trunks, hoping Greystone would just get up and go away without ever knowing she was there.

"You can come out now, Miss Fairchild. I know you're here."

Chapter Five

Miracles do not happen in contradiction to nature, but only in contradiction to that which is known to us of nature.

—Saint Augustine

Alyssa peeked over the edge of the trunk. Jared was lying near the door, propped up on his elbows, frowning at her. She wiggled her fingers at him over the edge of the trunk. "Hello."

"Hello." He ran his hand over the back of his head, grimacing as he touched a tender spot.

"Are you all right?"

"I don't think anything is broken."

"Thank heaven."

"I doubt heaven had much to do with this." He picked a golden bead from the floor and held it up between his fingers, one black brow lifting as he looked at her. "However, I assume you did."

She scrambled to her feet, golden beads tumbling from her skirt, clattering against the floor. She smiled sheepishly, aware of how guilty she looked. "The string broke. It wasn't exactly my fault."

"Ah, then I suppose this is a very rare bead." He turned the tiny ball of gold in his hand, reflecting the sunlight so that a tiny spot of light danced upon her face. "I've heard tales of beads such as this."

She frowned, wondering what he was about. "You have?"

He nodded, his brows drawn together in a look of mock seriousness. "Dangerous little buggers. They usually gather on strings, when no one is looking. No doubt this string leapt out of one of these trunks and dashed itself against the floor."

She nodded, trying to match his serious look. "For a moment I feared for my life."

"I assume that is why you were hiding behind that trunk. Protecting yourself against attack."

"Oh, my, yes." She fought the smile tugging at her lips. "I was definitely afraid of retribution."

"Well, I can see it was a good thing I came along. To save you from these little villains."

"And I am so terribly grateful, milord." With a flourish, she pressed her hand to her heart. "Infinitely relieved." *To find you have a sense of humor, milord.*

He studied her a moment, a hint of a smile curving his lips. He was looking at her as though she were some rare creature from a distant realm. Something he couldn't quite understand. Yet there wasn't a trace of anger in his eyes, not a whisper of loathing. She took that as a very positive sign.

He stood and brushed the dust from his black trousers. She watched him, finding even the most commonplace gesture fascinating when performed by this man. Her pulse pounded against the high neck of her gown and she wondered what he would say if he realized just how easily he could set her heart racing. He looked at her and caught her staring. Again.

She glanced away from him, afraid he could see too much in her eyes. She had never truly grasped the intricacies of flirtation. It had always seemed so silly, so artificial. So now, when she wished she could disguise her heart, and flirt and tease as all the women he knew no doubt could do, she discovered all she had to offer was honesty. An honesty that left her far too vulnerable. "I'm on a quest to find decorations for the house. I hope you don't mind."

"I don't mind. Miss Merryweather thought you might need some help." He crossed the distance between them. "Have you found what you're looking for?"

She looked up into the dark male beauty of his face and saw everything she had always wanted. Everything that remained just beyond her reach. "Yes."

He stared into her eyes, like a man staring into a crystal ball, mesmerized by the future he saw unfold before him. Caught in his steady regard, she forgot to breathe. They stood in a column of sunlight slanting through the windows, golden light wrapping around them like a shimmering cocoon. Everything beyond that golden shell faded. There was nothing in her world except this man. And the feelings he conjured inside of her.

He frowned, drawing air into his lungs, as though he only now realized the need to breathe. He turned away from her. He stared into the trunk, as though searching for a lifeline to drag him from a whirlpool threatening to drown him.

"This isn't half of mother's decorations," he said, his deep voice unnaturally husky. He unfastened a brass catch on another trunk and tossed open the lid, waving the dust away with his hand.

The trunk was full, but not with Christmas decorations. Toys crammed the leather-lined interior. Ice skates, sailboats, tennis racquets, balls, and wooden carts lay with wooden soldiers. Alyssa lifted a carved figure from a wooden box. The toy soldier had been well used, his red coat scraped in places, revealing the golden oak beneath, his raised musket chipped from battle.

Jared stared into the trunk, his expression growing thoughtful. "I hadn't realized all of this had been saved."

"Was this yours?"

"The blue army was mine." He took the soldier from her hand, a smile lifting one corner of his lips. "The red army belonged to Edward."

"From the looks of them, you must have had some fine battles."

"A few." He stared down at the old soldier. "Since Edward was older he always managed to be Wellington when we fought the battle of Waterloo."

"Did you ever manage to change history?"

"I'm afraid Napoleon always lost that battle." His shoulder brushed her arm as he bent over the trunk. "But I had my share of victories."

She watched him as he laid the soldier to rest alongside his companions. He brushed his fingertip across the wooden soldiers, a gentle caress saved for old friends. Although he betrayed nothing aside from that single touch, she sensed the sadness that burned beneath the cold facade he allowed the world to see.

She glanced into the trunk, realizing each toy was wrapped with memories. Memories that might well be painful viewed from a distance of years. "I've always believed the ability to forgive is one of the finest virtues anyone can possess. I'm surprised your parents couldn't find it in their hearts to forgive you."

Jared glanced at her, a hard glitter entering his eyes. "Miss Fairchild, I fear you aren't as well informed as you believe you are."

She knew she should remain quiet. It wasn't her place to dredge up the past. Still, she couldn't resist reaching for him. Not when she could feel his pain. Not when she could sense his loneliness as sharply as she felt the blade of her own. She felt connected to him, as she had the very first moment she had seen him years ago. Drawn to him in ways she didn't fully understand. And so she plunged into that dark, dangerous chasm between them, hoping to reach him before it was too late for both of them.

"My father was there the morning you and Edward met on 'the field of honor.' He told me Edward fired first, before the count. He said you fired into the air, when you could have killed him."

Jared gave her a look that warned she was stepping into dangerous territory. "And you think that absolves me of guilt?"

"I think your parents should have realized you were both young. Banishing you to America was a harsh punishment for a youthful error in judgment."

"My parents didn't send me away from Blackmoor, Miss Fairchild. I left. Three months later my mother died. In his letter my father told me she hadn't been eating well since I left. She couldn't sleep. She was torn apart over my decision to leave. She didn't have the strength to fight for her life when she came down with a fever. He had written it all as an explanation. All of it without blaming me for her death."

She touched his arm, braving rejection. He didn't pull away. He didn't acknowledge her in any way. He stood there, stiff and proud and hurting, his muscles steel bands beneath her hand. "It wasn't your fault."

"Wasn't it? Six months later my father died. He had taken to the bottle after Mother passed away. One night he fell in front of a carriage in London. He broke his neck."

She stared up into his eyes, seeing a darkness in those emerald green depths. The darkness of a tormented soul. With all her heart she wanted to heal the wounds she sensed throbbing inside him.

"Now you are well informed, Miss Fairchild." He stared down into her eyes, issuing a challenge, daring her to care for him now that she knew the truth.

"Yes," she said, her voice barely rising above a whisper. She knew her entire heart was there in her eyes as she looked up at him. "And I still think it's time you forgave yourself."

He looked away from her, as though he couldn't accept what he saw in her eyes. "I'm a grown man, hardly in need of your pity, or your concern."

"We all need concern once in a while, Lord Greystone. We all need to know there is at least one person who cares if we live or die."

"I am hardly an orphan in need of your charity." He looked at her then, his eyes as cold as emeralds frozen in ice. "I have all I need in this world—money, power, position."

"Is that truly all you need?"

His lips curved into a cold, sardonic smile. "If I discover anything else that I require, I shall simply buy it."

She stared up into his eyes, reminded suddenly of Midas and the torment he had suffered when he realized any living thing he touched would die. How could a man live believing his touch had brought destruction to the very ones he loved? The answer was in his eyes. He was isolated. Afraid to touch or to be touched. "There are things money can't buy."

"I no longer have a need for any of them." For a moment he stood facing the sunlight that flowed through the windows, like a creature locked in darkness craving the light, not knowing how to reach it. Then he looked at her, his lips drawn into a tight line, his eyes glittering with a pain he couldn't hide. "Remember that, Miss Fairchild."

He was telling her to stay away from him, warning her he would hurt her. She had little doubt he meant it. If she was wise, she would leave this place tomorrow. Still, the idea of returning to her house in London, where the days folded one into the other, each just as empty as the last, left her aching inside. "I thought we might cut one of the pine trees growing near the lake to use as a Christmas tree."

He drew in his breath, a battered fighter relieved the round had ended. "You have my permission to do so, if you would like."

He looked every bit as stiff as one of his wooden soldiers, she thought. Someone needed to grab him and shake him until the guilt he carried cracked and dropped away, like ice chipped from a statue. She smiled, refusing to surrender to despair. The man had forgotten how to enjoy life. And she intended to remind him. "I thought you and I could take Hannah for a sleigh ride tomorrow and allow her to choose the tree."

"Sleigh ride? I have a great deal of work to do, Miss Fairchild. I don't have time to . . ." He paused, as though struck by a sudden disturbing thought. "I suppose we could go right after breakfast."

Alyssa released the breath she hadn't realized she had been holding. "Oh, that would be splendid."

He stared at her a moment, as though he saw something surprising in her face, something that dented his armor. "Tell the child . . . tell Hannah, to be prepared to leave precisely at ten."

Alyssa stiffened like a soldier at review. "Precisely at ten, sir."

One corner of his mouth twitched with a smile he managed to suppress. "I expect this expedition shall take no longer than an hour."

She smiled up at him. The man radiated power; it vibrated in his deep voice, dominated his every gesture. He moved with the confidence of a man who knew people jumped at his command. Well, she was going to change all that.

"You have such pretty hair, Hannah." Alyssa drew a brush through Hananh's hair. The pale strands of silk shimmered in the light spilling from the wall sconce above the vanity. "Like your mother. You're going to grow up to be just as beautiful as she was."

Hannah lifted her eyes, looking at Alyssa in the mirror. "I would rather grow up to look like you."

"Me?"

Hannah nodded, a shy smile curving her lips. "I think you're much prettier than Mother was."

"Oh." Alyssa stared into the mirror, seeing the uncertainty in Hannah's big brown eyes. She was reaching out to Alyssa. Seeking affection. Afraid of rejection. "And I think you will grow up to be much prettier than either of us."

Hannah glanced down at the embroidered lace runner covering the top of the vanity. "I have a maid, you know. I don't understand why you do this every night. Why do you brush my hair?"

"When I was a child my mother would brush my hair every night before I went to bed. I always enjoyed it. I thought you might enjoy it too." Alyssa rested her hand on Hannah's shoulder. "Do you?"

Hannah nodded, keeping her eyes lowered, staring at the top of the vanity. With the tip of her forefinger she rubbed the smooth rosewood through one of the lacy holes in the runner, while Alyssa brushed her hair. "Do you like me, Aunt Alyssa?"

Alyssa paused with the brush in Hannah's curls. "Yes, of course I like you."

"I like you, too. Very much." Hannah looked up, staring into the mirror at Alyssa, her eyes filled with a quiet desperation. "You aren't going to leave, are you? You're going to stay here, with me?"

Alyssa's throat tightened as she looked into Hannah's eyes. "I don't live here, Hannah. One day I shall have to return to my home in London."

Hannah lowered her eyes. "Then you don't want to stay with me."

"Yes, I do." Alyssa slipped her arm around Hannah and pressed her cheek to her lavender-scented hair. "I would like nothing more than to stay here with you."

"Then why will you leave me?"

Alyssa closed her eyes against the tears that threatened. She hugged Hannah, praying the child would one day have the loving home she so desperately needed. "This isn't my home. I'm only a guest here."

"But this could become your home."

Alyssa knelt beside Hannah's chair and took her small hands in her own. "One day your Uncle Jared will marry someone. And she will come to live here."

Hannah curled her fingers around Alyssa's hands. "Why doesn't he marry you? Then you could stay."

Alyssa smiled up into her eyes. "Because he doesn't love me."

"But why not? You're pretty, and nice, and you always smile. He should love you. He should marry you."

Alyssa squeezed Hannah's small hands. "You're a very dear young lady, do you know that?"

Hannah drew in her breath. "Uncle Jared doesn't like me."

"Of course he does."

"No." Hannah stared at their clasped hands. "I told him I wished Father had killed him in that old duel."

"How did you know about that?"

"Mother told me." Hannah looked up, the lamplight shimmering in the tears pooling in her eyes. "She said both Father and Uncle Jared were so very much in love with her that they fought a duel to win her hand."

It was just like Vivien to brag about her conquests even to her little girl. "It wasn't kind to remind Uncle Jared of the past, Hannah. But that doesn't mean you and he can't be friends."

Hannah held tightly to Alyssa. "Do you think we can?"

"Of course I do. You just need to be nice to him. You need to treat him the way you want him to treat you."

Hannah smiled, a light of hope entering her eyes. "Charlotte said the same thing."

"Did she?"

Hannah nodded. "She's different from those other governesses. She doesn't just stand up in front of me and preach at me from a book. And she wasn't really angry at me for trying to dump feathers on her."

"That would definitely make her different."

"We spent the afternoon drawing and painting. It was so much fun." Hannah tilted her head, giving Alyssa a shy smile. "She says I have talent, just like Uncle Jared."

"Well then, you must be quite talented, because your Uncle Jared is a marvelous artist."

"Do you know what I think I shall do?" Hannah chewed her lower lip for a moment, unsure of herself. "I'm going to paint a picture for him. Do you think he would like that?"

"Yes." Alyssa smoothed the yellow curls back from Hannah's face. Tears burned the back of her eyes when she realized how very much she wished she could be here to share Hannah's life. "Now, hop into bed, and I shall read to you, the way my mother always read to me."

Hannah threw her arms around Alyssa's neck. She hugged her hard, as though she was afraid Alyssa would disappear. "Maybe Uncle Jared will fall in love with you, Aunt Alyssa," she whispered against Alyssa's neck. "Maybe you won't ever have to go away."

Alyssa closed her eyes, hugging Hannah close. It would take a miracle to melt the ice surrounding Jared's heart. Still, Alyssa believed in miracles. "Anything is possible, my darling."

Chapter Six

Unless you can love as the angels may
With the breadth of Heaven betwixt you;
Unless you can dream that his faith is fast
Though behoving and unbehoving;
Unless you can die when the dream is past
Oh never call it loving!

—Robert Browning

There was definitely something wrong with him. Jared drew crisp winter air into his lungs, filling his senses with the fragrance of pine. The little excursion to the lake had taken less than an hour. They had the bloody tree strapped to the back of the sleigh. There was nothing preventing him from returning to the stack of papers waiting for him in the library. And still he stood here in a foot of snow, staring at the green branches of the pine, searching for an excuse to spend the rest of the morning with Alyssa.

Her boots crunched against the snow as Alyssa approached him. He didn't have to look at her to know she was smiling. The thought of her smile brought a smile to his own lips. No doubt about it, there was definitely something wrong with him. From habit he scrubbed his features clean of emotion before he turned to face her.

"Look what I found yesterday." Alyssa held up her hand as though she was sharing a special secret with him. An ice skate dangled from her gloved fingers, swinging from a black leather strap. "I found enough skates for all of us. And I was thinking we might teach Hannah how to skate."

"You were, were you?"

She nodded, her smile warm enough to melt a glacier. "Of course, I'm assuming you know how to skate."

Sunlight glittered on the shiny blade of the skate, reflecting light upon her face, but it was the light in her eyes that caught his imagination. Lately, he couldn't look at her without wondering what he would see in those heavenly eyes if he ever made love to her. And he had to admit he had started thinking in terms of *when* he would make love to her.

She tilted her head, giving him a curious look. "Do you?"

He blinked. "Do I what?"

"Know how to skate?"

He frowned at the skate. "It's been years since I skated."

"I'm certain it will come back to you in no time

at all. And Hannah is so looking forward to skating for the first time."

Jared glanced past Alyssa to the girl who stood a few feet away. A small figure dressed in black, Hannah was watching him, expectancy mingling with wariness in her big brown eyes. She wanted him to spend this time with her. And she didn't truly believe he would.

He looked at Alyssa. She was smiling, encouraging him in a way no one had done in a very long time. And he discovered he didn't want to disappoint her. He took the skate, allowing a smile to touch his lips. "I hope you can manage to keep us both on our feet, Miss Fairchild."

She patted his arm. "You can count on me, Greystone."

For the fourth time in three days, Jared lay flat on his back, staring up at Alyssa. He had approached the frozen lake the way he approached everything else in life—as a challenge to be met and won. The ice had a different idea.

Alyssa pressed her hand to her lips, trying to catch her laughter. He stared at her, aware his look lacked its usual glacial edge. The sound of her laughter did something to him, touched him deep inside with the warmth and potency of heated brandy. "I've discovered ice can be very unforgiving of a man who has been away from it for years."

She managed to quell her laughter. Yet she didn't banish her smile. And what a smile it was, filled with an honest affection he had thought never to see in a woman. "Take my hand. I'll help you."

He frowned at her gloved hand. He had been on his own for a long time. He wasn't accustomed to accepting help from anyone. "I can manage."

She gave him a skeptical look, but she didn't press him.

He turned, placing hands and knees on the frozen surface, determined to conquer this icy realm. All the while he was aware of her watching him. He planted one skate on the ice and started to stand. The skate skidded out from beneath him, as though it were connected to a string someone had yanked. He pitched forward, sprawling against the ice, bumping his chin on the frozen surface.

Alyssa's muffled giggle rippled in the cold air. He swore under his breath.

She touched his shoulder. "Let me help, before you damage more than your pride."

He turned his head and looked up at her, expecting to see triumph in her eyes. There wasn't a trace of it. In her eyes he saw only the light of amusement and a gentle concern that might have knocked him off his feet, if he weren't already flat on his belly.

"Let me help."

"All right." He pulled up his legs, pausing for a moment on his hands and knees before he tried to stand. This time, with Alyssa for balance, he managed to plant both feet on the ice.

"Put your arm around my shoulders," she said, slipping her arm around his waist. "I'll steady you until you get the feel of it again."

Heat sluiced through his veins as she snuggled up against him. He looked down into her beautiful face, expecting to see the coy certainty of a woman who knows she has well and truly captured a man's most ardent attention. What he saw instead hit him like a clenched fist in his belly. Innocence. Affection. Pride in him.

He couldn't remember the last time someone had surprised him. Alyssa made a practice of it.

"Just try to remain straight and slide one foot at a time." She patted his chest. "I'm certain you'll have your balance in no time at all."

Looking down into her smiling face, he wondered if he would ever find his balance again. He moved with her as she slid her skates against the ice. He felt like a child taking his first steps, guided by her gentle hand.

"That's it," she said, her pleasure in his accomplishment evident in her tone.

He looked down at her. A curl had escaped the soft roll at her nape, trailing gold down her black coat, tumbling all the way to her waist. He imagined loosening her pins and combs, freeing that glorious hair to tumble around her shoulders—her pale, bare shoulders.

Each stroke of his skates against the ice grew in strength with his developing confidence. Hannah waved to them as they passed her. She stood beneath the bare branches of an oak, near the edge of the lake, skates strapped to her feet, watching them intently, as though her future depended on this skating expedition.

The wind nipped at his cheeks as they glided around the small lake. Alyssa's laughter rang on the cold winter air, like a church bell calling all to worship. He lifted his face, drinking in the winter sunlight, holding the heat of summer close to his side. God, he couldn't remember the last time he had felt this free.

"I knew you would remember how to do this." She smiled up at him as they halted near the edge of the lake. "Now, let's teach Hannah how to skate."

Jared felt her sliding away from him. He wouldn't allow it. Not yet. He tightened his arm around her shoulders, pressing his gloved fingers against her arm, willing her to remain in his embrace.

Alyssa hesitated, looking up at him with a question in her eyes. He didn't want to contemplate the question or the answer he might find should he look too closely at his own motives. He only knew he wanted her near, if only for a few more precious moments. He only knew he wanted to tell her how much he had enjoyed this moment. Yet he had no words.

He kissed her, brushing his lips across the rosy blush winter had painted high on her cheek. Her skin was cold; he sought to warm her. She sighed, startled by his touch. Yet she stayed within his embrace, quivering, like a fawn lifted into the arms of a hunter, unsure of what would follow.

He slid his lips over hers, touching her as he had in his dreams. Heat unfurled like a banner inside him. Her lips fluttered beneath his. He breathed in her sigh, tasting a trace of the strawberry preserves she had eaten at breakfast. He slanted his lips across hers, sensing her innocence, wondering if a man had ever kissed her before. The depth of her innocence shook him. It filled him with a lust that pounded with the sudden rush of blood in his loins.

He wanted her. Here and now. He wanted to take her down on the glittering ice. He wanted to toss her skirts around her waist and plunge into her fire.

He pulled away from her, gripping her arms, shaken by his powerful response to this woman. She swayed in his hold, her eyes drifting open, like a child awakening from a pleasant dream.

Jared swallowed past the knot in his throat. "Hannah," he whispered.

"Oh." She broke away from him so violently, she lost her balance.

He grabbed her arms. Alyssa latched on to his arms, a drowning woman snatching at a lifeline. He set his skates, holding her until she gained her balance.

When she was steady she looked up at him, smiling. "Thank you."

He had the strange urge to thank her. Instead, he released her, watching her as she skated the few yards to where Hannah was waiting. Odd, but the child was smiling as though they had given her the finest gift in the world.

Alyssa stepped back from the Christmas tree, watching as Hannah and Charlotte placed the last ribbons on the dark green boughs. She stood near the gray marble fireplace. Logs crackled on the hearth, radiating a warmth that stroked her back and wrapped around her, as the scent of pine teased her senses.

The tree was everything she might have hoped it would be. It was so tall, the golden head of the angel on top nearly touched the carved plaster-work in the ceiling. The long graceful branches held angels and bows and glass ornaments that reflected the light of the candles attached to each green bough with golden holders.

Alyssa stared at a string of golden beads she had wrapped around the branches, thinking of Jared. She pressed her fingertips to her lips, tracing the curve of her smile, remembering the feel of his lips against hers. Through the last twelve years she had dreamed of his holding her, kissing her, loving her. Always Jared. Only Jared.

Yet her dreams could not compare to the reality of his kiss, of his touch, of being held so close to him, she could feel the warmth of his body through the layers of their clothing. She wanted to believe he might kiss her again one day. Yet she knew better. Instinct told her he regretted that kiss.

Was he still in the library? She had seen him only once since they had returned from the lake, when she had invited him to join in decorating the tree. A shiver rippled along her spine when she thought of the cold look he had given her at the invitation. It was as though he was angry with her. Yet she had no idea what she had done to offend him.

Charlotte touched her arm, giving her a gentle smile. "Lord Greystone is a difficult man to understand."

Alyssa glanced away from Charlotte's perceptive eyes, staring at the wing-back chair beside her. "I didn't realize I was so obvious."

"Love is a powerful force, my child. It radiates from your face like captured sunlight."

"I suppose it's just as obvious to him." With her fingertip, Alyssa traced the curve of a golden rose stitched into the crewelwork back of the chair as she spoke. "Perhaps that's why he is avoiding me."

"He is trying to avoid his own feelings."

"His own feelings." Alyssa looked at Charlotte. "I'm afraid to speculate on what his feelings for me might be."

"So is he, my child. So is he." Charlotte patted Alyssa's arm. "I have a feeling it's only a matter of time before that young man is forced to unwrap all the emotion he has stored away inside him."

"I hope you're right."

Charlotte smiled, her eyes filling with a mischievous light. "You'll see."

Midnight. The grandfather clock in the hall chimed the hour, the deep tones echoing in the quiet house. Jared glanced up from the report he had been trying to decipher for the past two hours. It wasn't unusual for him to work past midnight. The sphere of his business interests was a place he understood, a world he could control, a sanctuary devoid of emotion. Yet he had found no safe haven amid his papers this evening. Alyssa had invaded his sanctum. He had managed to avoid her most of the day, but he couldn't avoid memories of her.

He stood, stretching muscles taut from a tension that had been building inside him since the first moment Alyssa Fairchild had tumbled into his arms. He left the room, abandoning any hope of plowing through the complicated analysis of a mining venture and railroad expansion plans this evening. Something had to be done. Alyssa was far too distracting. He should send her packing. Tomorrow.

His footsteps echoed in the hall, a lonely sound in a house that had once been filled with laughter. As he approached the drawing room, his steps slowed. Alyssa had invited him to help decorate for Christmas. It had been a long time since he had even recognized the holiday.

He paused outside the room, staring inside. The tree stood before the windows, long branches adorned with decorations his mother had cherished since he was a boy. He stepped inside and closed the door, shutting out the world beyond these four walls, as though someone might see him, as though someone might judge him for indulging in the memories he couldn't suppress.

He moved into the room, drawn to the tree and the memories awakening inside of him—his family gathered beneath the tree, his brother racing him to see who would be the first to unwrap all of his presents. Christmas had always been a special time at Blackmoor Hall.

Although the candles on the tree had been extinguished, the fire in the hearth still burned, flickering against pale angels, glowing in the glass balls, glittering against the small golden beads wrapped around each branch. He smiled as he touched one of the glittering beads, thinking of Alyssa.

"Do you like it?"

Jared turned, watching as Alyssa rose from one of the tall wing-back chairs near the fire, an open book in her hands. "It's beautiful," he whispered, unable to look away from her.

The fire from the hearth limned her, stroking golden light across the black wool covering her slender shoulders, slipping light into her golden brown hair. For the first time in twelve years he wanted to paint. He wanted to capture her image on canvas, blend the palette of oils until he discovered the pale cream of her face touched by firelight. "Very beautiful."

A bemused look entered her huge blue eyes as she held his stare. He sensed she was unaccustomed to the affectations of careless flirtations. He had startled her with his blatant appraisal of her beauty. Startled her more by the desire he knew simmered in his eyes. He burned with it. Still, he suspected she had no idea how very much he wanted to hold her, to kiss her, to make love to her until she sang her pleasure to the heavens.

She hugged the book against her chest, as though it were a shield. "I wish you could have joined us. It was marvelous fun decorating the tree."

"I had work to do," he said, aware of how hollow the words sounded in his own ears. "What are you doing up so late?"

"I couldn't sleep." She dropped her book on the seat of the chair and lifted a silver teapot from the cart drawn up beside the hearth. "I thought perhaps a little hot chocolate would help. I made an entire pot."

He drew in his breath, trying to ease the tension within him. "Do you often have trouble sleeping at night?"

"Sometimes." Alyssa glanced down at the silver tea service. "Would you like a cup? The cart was still set from this evening. So we needn't share."

"Please." He moved toward her, watching the play of firelight on her cheek. Propriety dictated a proper distance for a gentleman to keep when addressing a lady, but it was too far to suit him. He paused beside her, close enough to breathe the delicate trace of violets as the fragrance rose with the heat of her skin.

"My father and I would have a cup of chocolate every night before we retired." She glanced up at him, the cup trembling against the saucer she held in her unsteady hand.

He took the cup and saucer she offered, giving her a smile he hoped would reassure her that she need not be afraid of him. Yet, even as the smile shaped his lips, he knew it was a lie. "You must miss him."

"I do." She touched the cameo pinned to the high neck of her black merino gown, staring past him as though she could see her father standing near the Christmas tree. "I miss his conversation, his wit, his wisdom. There are moments when I find myself thinking 'I need to discuss this with Father.' Or I catch myself, after I've read a new novel, thinking how very much Father will enjoy this. Only to realize . . . he is gone."

His chest tightened as he looked down at her. He saw her pain, felt his own shift like shards of broken glass deep in his chest.

She looked up at him, smiling in spite of the tears glittering in her eyes. "I apologize for being so maudlin."

In that moment he felt closer to her than he had ever felt to another human being. He was drawn to her, in a way he didn't want to examine. "There is no need to apologize."

"Father never approved of dwelling on the past. He taught me always to look toward the future." She looked at the tree, her gaze gliding to the angel standing high above them. The porcelain angel stood on the treetop, her arms opened, as though she meant to embrace all she saw. "This is a season to rejoice. We mustn't dwell on all we have lost. There is so much we each have been given in this life."

He lowered his gaze from the angel on the treetop to the angel standing beside him. Alyssa was a creature of light, never delving into the darkness that touched other mortals. And, like a creature banished forever to the underworld, he craved that light. Without thought of logic or consequences or anything but the need within him, he set the cup and saucer on the cart and reached for her.

Alyssa came into his arms as though she were coming home from a long and tangled journey. She slipped her arms around his waist and pressed her cheek against his chest. He held her, needing her warmth, resenting the layers of cloth barring him from touching her as he longed to touch her.

He rested his cheek against her hair, breathing in the innocence and wonder of violets in winter. He needed this, holding her. He needed so much more. He slipped his fingers beneath her chin, lifted her face. He saw innocence in her eyes, and a desire that whispered across the embers burning deep inside him, coaxing flames to flicker and rage.

"Alyssa," he whispered, her name a prayer in the night.

She smiled, as though she liked the sound of his voice shaping her name. "When you kissed me this morning I felt as though I were flying."

The breath stilled in his lungs. "Did you?"

"Yes." She touched his cheek, stroking warmth across his skin. "I've been wondering if you would ever kiss me again."

He looked at her lips, tracing the generous curves, craving her taste. He had spent the day pondering that kiss. Strange; he had kissed a hundred women, yet never had the pleasure of a single kiss haunted him. Until this woman. Had that kiss truly been as potent as his memory suggested? So potent the mere thought of kissing her again had his heart pounding like a locomotive engine at full throttle.

"Would you kiss me, Lord Greystone?" she whispered, her voice barely rising above the crackle of the fire.

Every muscle in his body tightened with the desire to take her. Blood pounded low in his belly, distending hungry flesh, like a lion unsheathing his claws. "I'm not sure that's a good idea."

Her beautiful eyes filled with disappointment. "I'm sorry. For some idiotic reason I thought you might not mind kissing me again."

He swallowed hard. "I want to kiss you, Alyssa. But I'm not certain I can stop at a kiss."

She smiled, a shy curve of her lips that spoke of innocence and romantic notions. "I sometimes feel so terribly lonely. When you kissed me all the loneliness disappeared. Kiss me again. Make the loneliness go away."

She had no idea what he wanted from her. Yet he had no strength to resist what she so innocently offered. He lowered his head, sliding his lips over hers, breathing in her sigh like a drowning man.

She slid her arms around his neck, snuggling

close, her breasts pressing against his chest. Fire spiraled upward from the blaze she had ignited low in his belly, until it flowed through every vein. He slid his lips across hers, fighting his hunger, knowing the battle had been lost the first moment he looked into this woman's heavenly eyes.

He touched the seam of her lips with the tip of his tongue, slipping into her mouth when she opened to him, tasting chocolate on her tongue, letting her taste his desire for her. She moaned deep in her throat, a soft, dark sound, like a contented kitten. But he was not content. Not with kisses.

He pulled the anchoring pins from her hair. He plunged his hands into the mass of curls that tumbled to her waist, sliding his fingers through the golden brown silk, wanting to feel the strands slide against his bare chest. "Alyssa, if you want me to stop, tell me to leave," he whispered against her lips.

"Don't leave me, Jared." She hugged him, her arms tight around his neck. "Never leave me."

With an expertise that seemed sordid in the light of her innocence, he unfastened her clothes. He peeled away the black of mourning, the pure white linen beneath, kissing her, touching her, drugging her with the passion that flowed like fiery brandy through his veins.

"Alyssa," he whispered, lifting her trembling body into his arms. "My beautiful angel."

"I want to be beautiful, for you," she whispered. "Only you."

He trembled at her soft words, needing all the warmth radiating in her voice, needing so much more. He laid her down upon the soft carpet before the hearth, kissing her, stroking her skin, needing all she had to give.

With his lips and his tongue he worshipped her, spreading kisses down her neck, lingering on her breasts, his own pleasure mounting with her every soft moan. He slipped his hand between them and stroked her damp flesh, flaming the embers burning inside her, watching the light dance in her eyes. He saw honesty in her eyes: the honest pleasure of a woman blossoming beneath his touch. And he discovered her honesty a gift more exquisite than any gold could buy.

He moved away from her only long enough to shed his clothes. She stared at him, her curious gaze traveling down the length of him, pausing where his body throbbed and ached for want of her. He held his breath, waiting for some sign from her, appalled at how very much he needed acceptance from this woman.

"Don't be frightened of me, my angel." The heat of the fire brushed his bare skin, but it was her heat he craved.

"I'm not frightened." She lifted her arms to him, an invitation to take all she possessed. "Simply overwhelmed by you, milord."

He covered her, pressing the hard lines of his body against her softness. "I need you."

"I've been waiting for you all my life." She slipped her arms around his shoulders, smiling up at him. Shy, yet unafraid of what would pass between them. "I've dreamed of having your arms around me. And here you are."

He lowered himself between her thighs, nestling his hardened flesh against her softness. He watched her, needing the light in her eyes as much as he needed the feel of her flesh closing around him. He watched her as he altered her body, easing past the delicate veil of maidenhood, plunging into her woman's fire.

She stiffened with the sudden pain. He froze inside her, feeling like a virgin himself. Never before had he touched such innocence. Never before had a woman's body received him so eloquently.

He stroked the curls away from her temple. He kissed her closed eyes, her cheeks, her lips, wanting to give comfort where he had only given pain. "Alyssa, I'm sorry. I never wanted to hurt you."

She smiled up at him. "I'm not as fragile as you might believe. I won't break."

"It will get better, sweetheart. I swear it."

She touched his cheek. "Just having you hold me is more than I have ever hoped for."

She humbled him with her warmth, awed him with her generosity. In that instant he wanted to give her everything he possessed, the very best of himself. He moved inside her, slowly, easing his body within her tight sheath, resisting the urges of his body, the craving for long, hard thrusts.

In time he felt the tension brought by pain ease from her body. In its place he sensed another tension mount, this one born of pleasure. He saw the pleasure in her eyes. He heard the pleasure in her soft cries. He absorbed it all, a man too long without the warm touch of affection. He moved within her, wanting to stay there forever. Yet his body could not resist the siren call of hers.

They moved together, man and woman seeking a glimpse of heaven. And it was granted in the giving, woman to man, man to woman, lifting them beyond earthly bounds where passion seared one into the other.

She shuddered in his arms as he spilled the essence of his life into her. The fire of her passion consumed him, until there was nothing left of him but ashes. And in some distant corner of his mind he realized he would rise again from the ashes, reborn in her fire.

He lay in her arms, joined with this woman, not knowing the beat of his heart from hers, not caring. In time he drifted back with her from the breathless realm, settling into the reality of this time and place.

With his returning breath came the creeping of logic into his mind. He lifted himself above her and looked down into her beautiful face. She was smiling, a soft radiance glowing in her face. He looked into her eyes and saw that part of him he had abandoned twelve years ago. And he wasn't at all certain he wanted it returned to him now.

He felt exposed. The armor that had served him well all these years was pierced in places far too close to his heart. If he opened himself to the emotions he saw in her eyes, he would lay himself bare to every emotion he had buried. And he wasn't certain he could live with the pain.

She touched his cheek, her slender fingers curling beneath his jaw. "What is it? Something is troubling you; I can see it in your eyes."

He drew in his breath, dragging the musky scent of their lovemaking deep into his lungs. "I don't know what came over me. I never planned to seduce you this way."

She smiled. "I think you should know, I enjoyed what happened between us very much."

He was still inside her, where her warmth

bathed him, where the warmth of her woman's flesh nourished him, where the emotion threatened him. And still he wanted to linger. He wanted to stoke the fires within her until she writhed beneath him, until her soft cries sang in his ears. The woman had bewitched him.

"Have I done something to displease you?"

"No. Nothing." He closed his eyes, shutting out the beauty of her face, cringing from the light in her eyes. "I don't believe this is where I would like the servants to find us tomorrow morning. And if we linger, I'm afraid we might fall asleep."

"Oh," she whispered. "I hadn't thought of that."

He hadn't thought of anything, except this woman. He pulled away from her, exposing the flesh that had been warmed by her body to the chill in the room. "We'd better get dressed."

"Yes, of course."

Jared tugged on his clothes, then helped her dress, trying not to touch her smooth skin. When she was once again encased in black wool he escorted her to her bedroom. He stepped back from her as she opened the door.

She stood in the doorway and smiled up at him. He perceived a shifting inside him, a tug on his vitals that drew him toward her like a stallion on a tether. He saw uncertainty in her eyes, the need for reassurance. Yet he had none to offer her.

Emotion flooded him, overwhelmed him. He felt out of his element, in danger of drowning. He clenched his hands at his sides, forcing his feet to stay planted in the hall, when every instinct demanded he take her in his arms. "Sleep well."

He spun on the ball of his foot and marched away from her, feeling as though he were struggling against invisible chains. He needed time to think through what had happened. Calmly. Rationally. He couldn't allow emotion to fog his judgment. Not again. Not ever again.

Chapter Seven

It is in rugged crises, in unweariable endurance, and in aims which put sympathy out of the question, that the angel is shown.
—Ralph Waldo Emerson

Alyssa sat in a Chippendale armchair in front of Jared's desk, staring at the spiral staircase twisting upward to the library gallery. She traced the scrolls in the gilded bronze balustrade, wondering why Jared had summoned her here this morning. She couldn't ask. No, she was much too frightened of the answer.

After last night she had expected to be greeted with at least some small measure of warmth. Instead Jared had scarcely glanced at her since she had entered the room five minutes earlier. She squeezed her hands together in her lap and waited.

"We need to discuss the consequences of last night."

Consequences. Her breath tangled in her chest. She didn't like the sound of this, not one little bit. She looked at him. He had his chair turned at an angle from his desk, staring at some point on the far wall. He looked every bit as distant and cold as he had the first day he had entered this house.

"I've given this a great deal of thought," he said, without glancing at her.

Alyssa swallowed past the anxiety squeezing her throat. "I thought of little else last night except you."

He glanced at her, then looked away, as though he saw in her something that made him uncomfortable. He lifted a gold pen from the desktop, staring down at it as he rolled the shiny cylinder between his fingers. "I believe we should be married as quickly as possible."

Alyssa stared at him, not quite believing his words. "Married?"

He pursed his lips, glancing up from his pen, pinning her with a cold stare. "In case you didn't realize it, Miss Fairchild, there could be complications from what transpired between us last night."

Alyssa stared at this cold stranger. He might have been discussing a business merger instead of the glorious union they had shared.

"You might already be carrying my child."

"Oh." She pressed her hand to her flat belly. In the past she had imagined what it might be like to have a child grow inside her—Jared's child. And now it could be a reality. But the icy glare in his eyes stole the warmth of the moment.

"Necessity dictates a small, quiet ceremony. I shall arrange for a license and schedule a time with the magistrate." He tapped one end of the pen against the emerald leather desk pad, as though he was growing impatient with this interview. "You can be assured I shall handle all of the details."

The way he would handle any business arrangement, she thought.

"Now, I have work that needs attending."

He was dismissing her. Alyssa stared at him, searching for some sign of the man who had touched her so tenderly the night before.

Jared cocked one black brow. "Miss Fairchild?"

"Why do you want to marry me?"

Jared released his breath in an impatient sigh. "I thought I made myself quite clear."

"Yes." She stared past him, unable to hold his icy glare. Snow drifted past the windows behind him, plump flakes glittering like angel tears in the sunlight. "You spoke of consequences."

"Marriage is the logical conclusion to what happened last night."

"Logical." Tears burned her eyes. She stared at the drifting snow without blinking, without allowing her tears to fall. "I thought you might have another reason for wanting this marriage."

"I think it's time you clear the stars from your eyes, Miss Fairchild. If you were still hoping for a fairy-tale romance, you should have considered the consequences before you engaged in last night's activities."

Alyssa flinched at the icy calm of his voice. Did last night mean nothing to him?

He shifted in his chair. "You can be certain I

will always provide for you. As the Countess Greystone, you will never want for anything."

"Except perhaps affection."

He tapped the end of his pen, the only sign of his growing agitation. "Alyssa, I certainly hope you are not the type of woman who will dissolve into a fit of tears each time she is presented with a glimpse of reality."

"In spite of what you might think of me, Lord Greystone, I have faced a fair amount of reality in my life." She squared her shoulders and looked straight into his cold green eyes. "And I find the reality of this situation to be the simple fact that I do not care to marry you."

His lips parted, then closed. He stared at her a long moment before he spoke. "I'm afraid under the circumstances you have little choice."

"And I'm afraid you are mistaken." She stood and marched toward the door, needing to escape before she humiliated herself by dissolving into the tears she could no longer prevent.

"If you walk out that door, you can consider my offer withdrawn."

She hesitated with her hand on the cold brass door handle. "I wish you a happy life, Lord Greystone."

Jared stared into the red and gold flames flickering on the hearth in the library. Heat radiated against him. Yet the warmth of the flames couldn't touch the icy cold inside. It was as though all the life had been drained from him. He heard the soft click of the door handle. He turned, his heart stopping for one brief instant as he stared at the opening door and prayed Alyssa would step across the threshold.

Hannah entered the library, tears sparkling in her eyes as she looked at him. "Aunt Alyssa is going to leave. Today."

Jared rested his arm on the mantel, gripping the edge with his hand. "I'm certain she is anxious to return to her own home."

"You have to stop her," Hannah said, her voice soft and pleading. "Please, you can't let her go."

Jared drew in his breath, dragging the bitter taste of burning wood across his tongue. "Your Aunt Alyssa is a grown woman. She makes her own decisions."

"But she can't leave." Tears spilled down Hannah's cheeks. "Please. You have to make her stay."

Jared looked away from the pain he saw in Hannah's eyes. It was too much like the pain deep inside him. He stared into the flames, fighting to mold his features into an expressionless mask, yet it was no longer an easy task. Not when he felt as though his heart had been ripped from his chest. "I have no way to make her stay, Hannah."

"I thought you might come to love her."

Jared closed his eyes, fighting for control of the emotions that swirled like a tempest inside him.

"I thought you might marry her."

He clenched his fist against the cold alabaster.

"If you married her, she would stay here with us, always."

"Enough!" He glared at the child. "You should be at lessons. Not here, trying to meddle in my life."

Hannah stepped back as though he had struck her. She stood staring at him, a small figure dressed in mourning, a ten-year-old child who had lost everything in the world.

He stared into her stricken face, guilt twisting like a red-hot poker in his chest. "Hannah, I . . ."

"I hate you!" She ran from the room, slamming the door behind her.

He ran his hand over his face, appalled at his actions. Once again he had allowed his emotions to rule him. Once again the results had been nothing short of disaster. He turned away from the fire and marched to his desk. He intended to put his life back into some semblance of order.

Two hours later, Jared sat at his desk, staring out the French windows. A stack of correspondence and reports sat untouched on the desk behind him. The morning had grown gray, as though Alyssa had taken the sunlight with her. Beyond the rose garden, oaks and elms lifted bare arms in supplication, seeking redemption from their frozen fate. The sky had responded with snow. Frozen flakes fell from an expanse of gray sky, swirling in the wind before drifting in dull heaps upon shivering branches, and the graves of roses.

"You look as though you need a friend."

Jared started at the sound of Charlotte's voice. He turned his chair, frowning as he saw the woman standing beside his desk. "How the devil did you manage to get in here without my hearing you?"

"I can assure you the devil had nothing at all to do with it." Charlotte smiled at him. It seemed that all the light missing from the morning was shining in her face. "I suppose you were too wrapped up in your thoughts to hear me."

Jared leaned back in his chair, burgundy leather sighing as it cushioned his weight. "If you have come to preach to me about my behavior toward Hannah, there is no need. I realize I allowed my temper to get out of hand."

"And have you realized your mistake in allowing Miss Fairchild to walk out of your life?"

Jared clenched his jaw. "My relationship with Miss Fairchild is none of your concern."

"I'm afraid it is."

"You are mistaken, Miss Merryweather."

"Am I?"

He watched as she walked away from the desk, wondering again why he didn't dismiss the woman immediately. But something kept him from speaking the words that would send her packing. Something he couldn't quite fathom.

Charlotte meandered along the opposite side of the library, her pearl gray gown rustling in the quiet room. She touched books on the shelves here and there, ran her fingertips over the smooth white alabaster mantel, and paused. She examined a jade figurine of a dragon perched in a niche beside the fireplace as she spoke. "For each person on this earth there is a proper path ordained for him or her from birth. Yet this path can be altered, and not always for the better."

Jared rested his elbows on the arms of his chair and studied Charlotte over the steeple of his fingers. "Is this part of the philosophy you are teaching Hannah?"

She moved to the globe that sat on a mahogany stand near the base of the spiral staircase. "It is part of a philosophy I would like to share with you."

Jared frowned. "I am not your student."

Charlotte smiled, looking at him with such wisdom, he felt as though he were twelve years old again. "The choices you make every day of your life determine the path you will take in this life. For instance, if you choose to allow Miss Fairchild to slip away from you, you will never know the children you might have had with her."

Jared's chest tightened, yet he managed to keep the pain twisting inside him from showing. "There are other women."

"There is only one Alyssa."

Jared squeezed the tips of his fingers together, seeking balance against the emotions threatening to knock him off his feet.

"She loves you, with all her heart."

"Does a woman in love run away from the man who has just asked her to become his wife?"

"If she believes that man has no room for her in his heart."

"She wants a fairy tale. I offered her something more lasting than mere sentiment."

"There is nothing more enduring than love." With her fingertips Charlotte spun the globe. She studied the spinning world as she spoke. "Alyssa will not wait for you forever. She will marry one day. If things are not altered, I believe she will marry your friend, Tony Heyer."

The air turned to ice in his lungs. "Tony?"

Charlotte glanced at him, a smile curving her lips. "You sent him to London to keep him away from Alyssa. And now Alyssa is on her way to London. In time they will meet. An attraction will grow."

Something dangerous twisted inside him,

something dark and ugly, as he thought of Alyssa with another man. "I didn't realize you were a fortune-teller."

Charlotte only smiled. "Each time you see Alyssa, each time you look into the faces of her children, you will think of this day and wonder what might have been."

Jared stared at her, an odd sensation coiling around him, like icy tendrils of fog. For some inexplicable reason he had faith in the certainty of her vision. "Who are you?"

Charlotte glanced away from him, staring at a painting that hung in a gold frame on a panel between the bookcases behind her. "You've always been a talented artist."

It was a simple painting he had fashioned in watercolors when he was eleven years old. He had painted it the day after he had nearly drowned. In the painting a woman carried a small boy from the storm-swollen stream near his home—a woman Jared had never seen before that May morning. A woman who had disappeared before his brother had returned with help.

After the incident Jared had remembered only the light that glowed from her face, the warmth of her embrace as she seemed to fly with him in her arms. He had painted the face of his great-grandmother on that canvas, a fact his father had attributed to the portrait of his grandmother hanging in the gallery. He had painted his rescuer as an angel with wings and a glowing golden halo, a fact his mother had attributed to Jared's youthful imagination.

An angel. Jared's heart crept upward in his chest until each beat pulsed at the base of his throat.

The painting hadn't been there this morning before Charlotte entered the room. He was certain of it. For the first time he realized why Charlotte had always seemed so familiar. "Who are you?"

Charlotte's lips curved into an enigmatic smile. "A friend."

He stared at her, wanting to dismiss the truth he knew in his heart. The truth the logical side of him could not accept. Yet, looking into her eyes, he knew with the same certainty as he knew the sun would rise each morning, that there was far more to life than what could be explained by mere logic.

"You love Alyssa."

Jared didn't try to deny her words. To deny his love for Alyssa would be to deny his own existence. "I never realized I could feel this way about anyone. It's overwhelming."

"You have shunned emotion for a very long time."

"She wants so much from life."

"You can give her everything she needs."

Jared shook his head. "You don't understand. I feel so out of control."

"You are like land that has known nothing but drought for a hundred years. Now that the rains have come it will take time to absorb it all. But you can. You will."

"After this morning I doubt she even wants to see me."

"Go to her, Jared. Alyssa needs you." Charlotte smiled, her face glowing with a gentleness too pure for this tarnished world. "Go to her now, this moment. Before it's too late."

* * *

"You shouldn't have done this, Hannah." Alyssa crossed the length of the drawing room of her London townhouse, a cream-colored cashmere shawl draped across her arm. "You could have frozen to death."

"I took a fur carriage rug with me." Hannah sat in an emerald velvet wing-back chair, holding her hands out to the fire crackling on the hearth. "It wasn't too terribly cold. It truly wasn't."

Alyssa draped the shawl around Hannah's shoulders. "What on earth made you climb into the boot of my carriage?"

"I wanted to come with you."

"Your Uncle Jared will be frantic with worry wondering what has happened to you."

Hannah crinkled her nose. "He won't care. He's probably glad I'm gone."

Alyssa sank to her knees, resting her hand on Hannah's knee. "Hannah, you must give your Uncle Jared a chance to grow accustomed to his new role as your guardian. All he needs is a little time and understanding."

"You didn't give him any time."

Alyssa glanced away from the girl's perceptive gaze, unwilling to allow this child to see the pain she knew she couldn't hide. "That was different."

"Why is it different?"

"We talked about this before. Blackmoor Hall isn't my home."

"It isn't mine either." Hannah gripped Alyssa's hand. "I want to stay with you."

Alyssa cupped Hannah's cheek in her hand. "I would love for you to stay."

Hannah drew her teeth over her lower lip. "Then you won't send me back?"

"Not tonight. But I have to send a message to your uncle. I have to let him know you're safe."

"No. He'll come for me."

"Because he cares about what happens to you."

Hannah shook her head. "Because he wants to teach me discipline. He wants to make sure I don't grow up to be like Mother. I know he does. But I won't be. I swear. I want to grow up to be like you."

"Oh, my darling child." Alyssa looked up into Hannah's tear-filled eyes, a tight band squeezing her heart. "There is no reason why you can't come to visit me. And I shall certainly come to visit you."

Hannah released Alyssa's hand. "You don't want me."

"That isn't true."

"Then let me stay."

Alyssa sat back on her heels, looking up into Hannah's face, seeing the desperation of a lonely little girl. Perhaps she had been selfish. Perhaps she should have married Jared, even though he didn't love her; at least she could be certain Hannah would receive the love she so desperately needed. Still, Jared's parting words echoed in her mind. Was it too late? Would he even consider allowing her to crawl back into his life? "Hannah, when your Uncle Jared comes to take you home I'll discuss the problem with him."

Hannah came to her feet. "I won't go back there!"

"Hannah, please . . ."

"No!" Hannah turned and ran from the room.

"Hannah!" Alyssa struggled with the full skirt of her gown as she came to her feet. By the time she reached the hall, Hannah was already out the front door.

The cold December wind penetrated the wool of her gown as Alyssa ran from her house. In the gathering dusk she saw Hannah in the street, running for the other side, gray slush splashing with her every step.

"Hannah, come back!"

The child didn't pause. She kept running, as though the hounds of hell nipped at her heels. Alyssa lifted her skirts and dashed down the four stone steps leading to the walkway. Without a thought, she dashed into the street. Frigid slush filled her slippers, splashed her legs, chilling her.

A carriage horn blared. Alyssa started at the sound. With the sudden surge of a bolt of lightning her mind registered the reality of a coach and four barreling toward her. The curses of the coachmen peppered the air as he struggled to rein in the leaders. It was too late. They were too close.

"Alyssa!"

Jared's voice reached her a heartbeat before something hard slammed into her. His strong arms closed around her. One moment she was frozen in the slush, the next she was flying. Slush plumed all around them as they hit the opposite side of the street. Jared groaned, taking the brunt of the collision. Slush splashed from the wheels of the coach, hitting them with an icy gray wave.

Alyssa gasped at the sudden chill of the slush soaking through her gown. She struggled against her sodden gown, turning in Jared's arms. She brought her knee up, bumping him somewhere near his thigh. He gasped.

"Oh, my gracious, I'm sorry," she whispered,

looking down into his face.

He lay flat on his back beneath her, an icy cushion of slush beneath his head. His eyes were clenched, and he seemed to be counting, silently, slowly.

She cupped his cold cheek in her hand. "Are you all right?"

He swallowed hard before he opened his eyes. "Fine."

People swarmed around them. Murmurs of shock rippled through the crowd as people recognized the Earl of Greystone lying in the street. A few, including the coachman who had nearly run Alyssa down, voiced their concern. Their collected voices were no more than the drone of a hundred bees. Her entire attention was focused on the man beneath her and the warmth she saw in Jared's eyes.

"Aunt Alyssa!" Hannah pushed her way through the crowd gathering around Alyssa and Jared. She sank to her knees in the slush beside them. "Are you hurt?"

"No." Alyssa tore her gaze from Jared. "I'm fine."

"You risked your life to save her." Hannah stared at Jared as though he were suddenly encased in shiny armor. "I've never seen anything so brave in my entire life."

Jared frowned, seemingly uncomfortable with the praise. "I suggest we continue our discussion inside. I believe we have given London enough of a show for one day."

Alyssa paused on the threshold of her drawing room. Jared was standing near the hearth, one arm braced against the carved white marble mantel as he stared into the fire. He had left Blackmoor without a change of clothes. So there he stood, in trousers and shirt donated by one of her footmen.

The gray trousers ended at the top of his ankles. A belt cinched around his slim waist was the only thing preventing the baggy trousers from tumbling down his slim hips. Jared's broad shoulders tested the stitches of the white cotton shirt. Still, the man managed to look elegant, and powerful, and so very handsome, her heart did a slow tumble in her chest.

He glanced at her, as though he sensed her standing there, watching him. "Is Hannah tucked safely into bed?"

"Yes." Alyssa closed the door behind her, seeking privacy. "I hope you won't be too harsh with her for running away."

He frowned. "Does the child think I'm some sort of monster?"

"No. But she doesn't believe you care for her. She thinks you only want to make certain she doesn't grow up to be like her mother."

He stared into the fire. "It seems I've made a muddle of this."

"It isn't easy dealing with a child who has been neglected her entire life."

"You don't have much trouble." He lifted his face, looking at her in the arched mirror standing above the mantel. "You give of yourself with a generosity that humbles me."

His eyes were filled with a longing that touched her, like the soft brush of his fingers across her cheek. She ached with the pain she sensed filling him.

"For the last twelve years I've dedicated my life to work, where emotion had no place. I didn't trust emotions, you see. Only logic, and discipline. In some distorted way I suppose I thought if I could prove myself responsible and steady, my parents would know. They would be proud of me. Yet, there has always been something missing, a dark empty place inside me. Work couldn't fill it."

"I know what it's like to be lonely, Jared."

"I didn't realize how empty my life was until you came, with your smile and your warmth. I didn't trust my feelings for you. I was a fool." He turned to face her, his need shimmering with the sheen of tears in his eyes. "I know I'm not the man of your dreams, Alyssa. But I love you."

Alyssa closed her eyes, his words piercing her with a joy so intense it hurt. Although he moved as silently as a whisper, she sensed him walking toward her.

"I want you in my life. Now and always." He brushed his hands from her shoulders down to her wrists.

She opened her eyes, staring through her tears at the man who had filled her dreams. She could scarcely believe a moment this precious could be real.

"I want to see your smile first thing in the morning and last thing at night. I want a chance to show you how much I adore you. I'll do anything to win your love."

He was her knight, a warrior wounded in battle, returned to her from the Crusades. And he needed her love to heal him.

"Marry me, give me your joy, your laughter." He sank to one knee before her. He took her hand and pressed his lips against her palm, his warm breath spilling across her wrist. "Marry me, give me your light, your warmth. Marry me, and I'll give you all the love you ever need. Marry me, because without you I'm dead inside."

She sank to her knees before him. Tears spilled down her cheeks, catching at the corners of her smile.

"Alyssa," he whispered, reaching for her.

She threw her arms around his neck. He held her close, cradling her in his arms, holding her as though he drew his very life from her.

She pulled back in his arms, needing to look into his eyes when she confessed her secret. "All my life I have dreamed of only one man. You, my dearest love."

He smiled, his eyes reflecting his relief, his joy. "All my life is yours, my own sweet angel. From this day until the end of time."

Ethan watched as the images of his daughter and her beloved slowly faded into the gathering clouds. He looked up through his tears at Raphael. "And Hannah?"

"With Jared and Alyssa, Hannah shall have all she needs to grow into a happy, beautiful young lady."

Ethan smiled. "Thank you, sir."

"There is someone we both need to thank for a job well done." Raphael turned, lifting his arm to welcome the woman who stood near the entrance of the room. "Charlotte, I believe it is time you met Ethan."

Charlotte glided across the room, golden wings glittering on the shoulder of her flowing white gown. "How very nice to meet you, Ethan."

"Thank you." Ethan held Charlotte's slender hand. "For everything."

"Oh, I had very little to do with it, actually. Without Alyssa, I'm afraid Jared would have faced a frigid future no matter what I had tried." Charlotte smiled, mischief lighting her eyes. "But I must say, I did enjoy helping to knock my great-grandson off his shelf. The young man had become entirely too proud. I particularly enjoyed yanking the skates right out from under him."

Raphael cleared his throat. "I didn't expect you to take my advice quite so literally."

Charlotte shrugged. "Have you told Ethan about his future assignment?"

Raphael frowned. "Not yet."

Ethan looked up at Raphael, excitement thrumming through him like the strings of a harp on Sunday morning. "My assignment?"

Raphael sighed. "It won't come about for some time—not until you are fully ready. But since Charlotte has already revealed too much I might as well tell you the rest. I intend to assign you as guardian for one of Alyssa's grandchildren."

"Grandchildren," Ethan whispered, stunned by the warmth of his blessing.

Raphael rested his hand on Ethan's shoulder. "I'm certain you will make a fine guardian for many generations to come."

"Thank you." Ethan closed his eyes on a silent prayer, content to know he would be allowed to watch over the ones he loved.

Epilogue

It is said, and it is true, that just before we are born a cavern angel puts his finger to our lips and says, "Hush, don't tell what you know." This is why we are born with a cleft on our upper lips and remembering nothing of where we came from.

—Roderick MacLeish

Jared dabbed pale blue paint against the canvas, shaping the gown his wife wore. He had used these same brushes for the past seven years, and never was he more satisfied with the results than when he painted a portrait of his family.

He glanced past the canvas. Alyssa sat on an armchair before the Christmas tree in the drawing room, holding Charlotte, their three-month-old daughter. Their two sons, Michael and Peter, stood on her right, fidgeting, anxious to go on the skating expedition he had promised them.

Hannah stood on the other side of Alyssa. She smiled at Jared when he looked at her, the warm generous smile of a gentle young lady destined to be every bit as irresistible as her Aunt Alyssa. He glanced down at the brush in his hand, silently giving thanks for all he had been allowed to share with his beautiful wife. And with the thought came his gratitude to someone he was certain could hear his silent prayer.

The brushes had been a gift from Charlotte, left beneath the first Christmas tree Jared and Alyssa had shared at Blackmoor Hall, along with a note saying her work was done there. When he had tried to find her he had discovered no one at the Fleming agency had ever heard of Charlotte Merryweather.

It hadn't been a surprise—simply a confirmation of a certainty Jared knew in his heart. A certainty he renewed each day he looked at the portrait of his great-grandmother and saw Charlotte's face. Although he hadn't seen Charlotte again, he sensed she was with them, watching over his family as she had always watched over him.

He blended shades of blue, trying to find the right color for Alyssa's eyes, yet if he lived to be a hundred, he knew he would never capture the light of love shining in the heavenly blue depths. The light that filled their house with love and laughter. The light that had given him back his life.

For a moment he gazed at his family, feeling his

love for them flow like sunlight through him. He glanced up at the angel standing on the treetop, with her arms spread wide to embrace all of them. And he was certain he could see her smile.

EUGENIA RILEY
TRYST WITH AN ANGEL

This novella is dedicated, with love,
to the memory of my Uncle Logan,
who is with the angels now.
He gave so much to this world,
and to his family, with his kindness,
his skills as a doctor, his caring heart,
and his incomparable sense of humor.
He will be dearly missed.

Chapter One

London
1855

Nathan Fletcher returned home to find his bride was missing.

It was the silence, the cold, the darkness, that first alerted Nathan that something was terribly amiss when he returned to the townhouse he and Emily shared in Belgravia. In the wee hours of Christmas Eve Nathan all but blew in the front door, pushed by an icy rain and a battering wind. He deposited his portmanteau on the floor of the vestibule and slammed shut the door only to find himself ensconced in darkness.

As a man accustomed to being pampered, he was annoyed.

"Emily! Gibbons!" he bellowed. "Where are the

cursed lights! It's Christmas Eve, for heaven's sake!"

Only silence answered.

Nathan muttered curses and stumbled about until he located a match safe on the pier table. He lit a kerosene lamp and met his reflection in the gilded mirror hanging above the table—

He saw a scowling Englishman wearing a dripping top hat and soaked greatcoat, his brows a menacing slash across his forehead, his lips a tight line, his jaw set in stone.

Removing his wet outer garments and hanging them on the hall tree, he picked up the lamp and glanced about in consternation. "Where the deuce is everyone?"

He proceeded into the drawing room, lighting the lamps, then starting a fire in the grate to ward off the chill. He felt a lump in his throat as he viewed his wife's daguerreotype on the étagère beyond the hearth. Emily was smiling at him, her face tilted toward him, her dark eyes glowing, her nose upturned, and her pointed chin fixed at an intriguing angle. She was properly dressed in a high-necked silk gown with a cameo brooch at the collar. He wondered at the color of her frock. Could it be the lavender one she had so oft worn? Regret suffused him that he couldn't be sure.

He glanced about at the room so imprinted with his wife's personality, its rococo velvet chairs and silk damask sofa complete with antimacassars Emily had crocheted, its carved pedestal tables cluttered with the knickknacks she had collected—Oriental vases, porcelain cachepots, dried flowers under glass, japanned boxes, and every other imaginable gewgaw. Several recent issues of

La Belle Assemblée peeked out from a large brass urn. The floor was carpeted with a rich pink and blue Savonaire rug, the walls papered in mauve silk brocade accented by framed Landseer oils of cats and dogs and Emily's needlepoint samplers. He paused next to one of her embroideries, a scene of pastoral brilliance entitled "Garden of Heaven."

On a table near the front window reposed the Christmas tree, that novelty made so popular by Queen Victoria's Prince Consort. With candles unlit, toys, angels, paper ornaments, sugar plums, and popcorn strings languishing away in shadow, it appeared a sad rather than a festive touch. The image of the desolate little tree unexpectedly brought a lump to Nathan's throat.

Where the devil *was* she? She couldn't be still abed—no one could have slept through the unholy clamor he'd made while coming through the door.

Nathan lit a taper and left the parlor, heading upstairs to the bedroom. As he moved through the archway, the lingering scent of lavender sachet greeted him; his wife's essence permeated this room. Then, just inside the door, the sight of the huge four-poster mahogany bed—perfectly made, and empty—washed a chill over him.

She had left him. She'd likely gone off to Canterbury again to be with her parents. They would console her for a time, and then, like good British aristocrats, would pack her off back to her husband. Or he would storm after her, bellow at her until she was reduced to tears, and force her to return home. After all, there was his good name, his manly pride, to maintain.

Not that he could blame her for leaving him.

Their marriage had been arranged—indeed, forced—by their families. Nonetheless, when they had wed a year ago on Christmas day Emily had taken it well. Nathan hadn't. From the beginning he'd been intensely resentful and had acted the cad, spending much of his time tending to his import business at the Exchange or gambling at his club on St. James, ignoring his bride—

Except in bed, he thought with self-reproach, gazing at the bed with its sumptuous blue satin counterpane. He'd delighted in exercising his husbandly duties frequently and vigorously, heedless of Emily's response. Even in bed she had surely felt used by him rather than cherished, although she had always performed her wifely duties without complaint.

God, he couldn't blame her if she despised him now! This last stunt he had pulled had likely sent her packing. A week ago they'd had a bitter argument when he'd refused to escort her to take Christmas baskets to the poor in the slums of Westminster. Self-absorbed as always, he had insisted he had a gambling date at his club that he could not break. The next morning, rather than suffer through deserved recriminations from his wife, he had bellowed at his valet to pack his things. He had coolly informed Emily that he was leaving for Paris on business, to buy billiard tables in the Faubourg Saint Antoine. He had told her not to expect his return before Christmas, had steeled himself against her look of angry disappointment and had left—

Then, in Paris, the unexpected had happened. With their first anniversary looming just days away, he had missed her. Guilt had gnawed at him regarding his atrocious behavior. His days had turned sour and empty; his nights had become a torment. Even strolling among the pleasure dens at the Palais Royale, or gambling at Tortoni's, he had no longer felt amused. He had wanted Emily, ached for her. He had missed her occasional smiles, the way her brow puckered when she was thinking, even her little sighs as she lay beneath him in bed. Scoundrel that he was, at least he had not betrayed her sexually during their marriage, but only because, after knowing her, no other woman would suit.

These realizations had left him longing for her, hoping she might forgive him, might give him another chance. . . . He had packed his bag and returned home.

Now she was gone, the house empty.

He was about to leave the bedroom when he spotted the envelope on her writing table, neatly propped up against a row of books. Dread assailed him. He quickly crossed the room to see his name in her elegant script. With trembling fingers he set down his taper and picked up the letter, tearing it open.

As soon as he spotted her signature, obviously blurred by a tear, he knew to expect the worst. With a deepening sense of premonition, he read:

Dear Nathan,

I'm writing to let you know that I'm giving you your long-coveted freedom. By the time you read this I'll be on a steamer bound for the United States. My cousin Rosemary and her husband, Charles, have promised to help me make a new start in America.

I know you never wanted me. I tried to be a good wife to you, tried to give our marriage a fair chance, but you would never meet me halfway. I never felt like more than a possession to you, or a convenience.

Please don't try to come after me. I didn't run to Mother and Father this time because I knew if I did, you would follow me and force me to come home—why, I know not; perhaps to assuage your pride. At any rate, I wanted you to realize that this time it is final.

I shall post you my address later on, so you may institute divorce proceedings if you wish. You can always claim grounds of desertion. I suppose this would be totally in character for you, since you always blamed me for everything that went wrong in our marriage, didn't you, dear?

Despite all, Nathan, I do wish you well and hope you may someday find with someone else the happiness you never found with me.

Regards,

Emily

P.S.: Since you will not be returning home in time for Christmas, I've given all the servants leave until after Boxing Day.

Nathan stared at the letter, stunned and electrified, as lightning illuminated the room and thunder boomed outside. She had left him to go to America in this ghastly weather? Even crossing the Channel tonight had been hair-raising. He shuddered at the thought of her steamer being pitched about on the high seas.

Oh, sweet heaven, what had he done? Had he driven her away forever?

He glanced at the letter again and spotted the date, five days earlier. Too late to stop her now. Oh, heavens! What would he do?

He would go after her, chase her to the ends of the earth if necessary, he decided fiercely. If need be, he would travel to Canterbury to obtain Rosemary's address from Emily's mother; then he would set out.

Why? he asked himself in turmoil. Why, after all this time, all his contempt and neglect, was he at last demonstrating some feeling toward his wife?

Oh, God, did he love her after all? The very question staggered Nathan, leaving him grasping the writing table to keep from falling. He *must* love her, for his throat was burning, his eyes stinging with helpless tears, and never had he felt such aching emptiness.

Setting down the letter, he numbly strode about the room, opening the dresser drawers, the wardrobe, desperately hoping to find some trace of her. Although the lingering scent of her still tortured him, all her things were gone, and he found himself staring only at emptiness. Oh, why had he never realized what she meant to him until he had lost her? He had been such a fool to drive her away like this. . . .

All at once a loud banging downstairs roused Nathan from his turbulent thoughts. Was someone knocking? Could it be Emily?

His heart pounding with reckless hope, he rushed out of the room and down the stairs, flinging open the front door.

A bedraggled lad stood there shivering and holding an envelope in his ragged mitten. "Cable, sir!" he shouted.

Mystified, Nathan handed the lad tuppence, took the telegraph, and went back inside, shutting the door against the cold and rain. With a feeling of impending doom, he ripped open the envelope bearing his name. The words floated past him in unending agony: "Steamer *Invictus* went down in a gale off the Channel . . . .Your wife, Mrs. Nathan Fletcher, on passenger manifest . . . no survivors."

"No!" Nathan shouted. "Oh, God, please no!"

Nathan stood reeling, in shock. The missive slipped through his fingers as he walked, stunned, into the parlor. He paused by the fireplace, resting his elbow on the mantel and shuddering with emotion. His anguish was unbearable.

Emily was gone. She was the best thing that had ever happened to him, and he had driven her away, killed her through his neglect, destroying her sweet young life. She had only been twenty-one years old! He stared at her portrait on the étagère through the blur of his tears, her sweet smile lancing his heart. He touched the glass over the daguerreotype, forlornly hoping he might somehow touch Emily through it.

Her innocent countenance lashed at his conscience. "Oh, Emily," he whispered brokenly, "my sweet darling. I'm so sorry. Now I cannot even beg your forgiveness."

Then, on the shelf above the portrait, he spotted the gold porcelain angel he had recently bought her on a whim, at a shop near Covent Garden. Bittersweet memories threatened to choke off his breath. Emily had loved angels of every kind. They had had a fight that day before he had left for the Exchange, and he had later spotted the statuette in the shop window—a smiling, glittering angel complete with wings and halo. For once he had brought home a peace offering for his bride, and she had accepted the token with a small, reluctant smile.

But she hadn't taken the angel with her. She obviously wanted nothing of his. With trembling fingers, he reached for it—

Nathan wasn't sure just how it happened. Perhaps his hand faltered; the angel slipped off the shelf and fell. He heard a crashing sound, and a split second later Emily's angel lay shattered at his feet.

"No!" he cried, pressing his hands to his temples. "Oh, God, not Emily's angel. Emily, if you can hear me, I'm sorry! I'm so terribly sorry!"

Of course she couldn't hear him. Thanks to his own beastly selfishness she was gone forever. He deserved to have his own life ended as hers had been—cruelly, prematurely.

Yes, he deserved to die—and with her gone now, what else had he left to live for? He had been the worst of idiots, not realizing he loved her until much too late.

Like a man in a trance, Nathan headed for his desk in the corner. He opened a drawer and took out the box containing his grandfather's dueling pistols. Selecting one of the weapons, he quickly loaded the powder, then rammed a ball down the barrel. . . .

Then he heard a funny sound behind him, a tinkling sound, like many small bells softly ringing. He set down the pistol and whirled—

Nathan stared, amazed, across the room. Even as he blinked uncomprehendingly, the shards of the broken angel began to glimmer and shift, melting into a golden mist that began to swirl up from the floor. Mesmerized, Nathan watched the miraculous sight. Then. . . . oh, sweet lord, it could not be! Nathan shook his head, at first certain his eyes were deceiving him—

But no, it was true! Even as he watched in awe, his beloved Emily began to materialize from the mist—softly taking form, spiraling upward like a ghost, slowly becoming more substantial, more real.

"My God! Emily, is it you?" he cried.

"Yes, Nathan, it is I," whispered a sweet, ethereal voice.

"Are you real?"

"Yes, I'm real."

She *was* real! Even as Nathan blinked in disbelief, his bride, now a fully formed, flesh-and-blood woman, glided toward him, smiling at him, her dark eyes glowing luminously. It truly was his Emily, wearing a long white nightgown, her thick blond hair bound in a braid. Nathan gazed at her in stupefaction.

"Emily . . . Heavens, it *is* you!"

"Nathan," she whispered back, "do not worry. I'm here."

Chapter Two

Nathan stared at his wife in awe. Logic told him that Emily couldn't be here, that she couldn't have just materialized from the shards of her own shattered angel. Yet there she stood, seemingly in the flesh, smiling at him. Hungrily, he ran his gaze over her, taking in her delicate silhouette and the way the thin gown clung to her lovely body. He stared at her creamy throat, her beautiful face—the well-remembered heart shape, the smooth brow and bright, dark eyes, the dainty nose, the wide mouth and pointed chin, the slightly flushed cheeks. He gazed at her left hand and saw she still wore her wedding ring.

Whence had she come? he wondered, reeling. Was she real, or a vision? Whatever the source of her manifestation, Nathan felt an incredible welling of joy at having her back with him.

"Emily?" he whispered, his voice trembling with emotion. "Are you truly real?"

"Yes, darling," she murmured, and stepped forward into his arms.

"Oh, Emily," he whispered, crushing his bride close, molding her warm curves against him, burying his lips in her hair and inhaling its well-remembered rose fragrance. "Thank God you are all right! I was so frightened when I received the cable—I thought you had died."

She pulled away slightly, pressing her fingers to his mouth. "Don't speak of that . . . yet."

He stared with concern at her luminous face. "What do you mean, 'yet'?"

She only smiled sadly.

Suddenly Nathan backed away a step. He raked his gaze over her and shook his head in incredulity. "Wait a moment! This cannot be! I received a cable stating that you had drowned. Then I accidentally broke your angel—"

"I know," she murmured sympathetically. "I saw."

"You saw?" he cried.

Her eyes glowed with sorrow and compassion. "I saw you in your despair, Nathan, saw you about to shoot yourself—"

"But you couldn't have!" he exclaimed. "You weren't here! And yet . . . you materialized, like a miracle, from the shards of the broken angel. My God, Emily, how can this be? Am I hallucinating?"

"No, dear," she answered sweetly.

"Dreaming?"

"No."

"Are you a ghost?"

"No, Nathan, I'm a woman. Your wife."

Nathan continued to regard her in mystification. "Then how did this happen? How did you come from being drowned to being alive, and standing right here in front of me?"

"But I didn't drown," she explained.

Heaving a great sigh, Nathan took her arm. "I . . . I think we had best sit down."

They went to sit on the settee together, before the warm fire. In wonder, Nathan studied his bride again, observing her delicate hands, the way wisps of blond hair framed her lovely face. He couldn't believe she was actually here with him, when logic argued this was impossible. He was so terrified she might disappear again at any moment.

He took her hand and spoke slowly, deliberately. "Very well, dear. I've explained what happened to me—how I thought you had died, how I watched you appear. Now tell me what happened to you . . . and how you came to be here with me tonight."

"That is simple," she replied, smiling radiantly. "An angel sent me."

"An angel?" he repeated. "But how?"

"First I must explain about the steamer going down."

"Pray, do."

She eyed him tentatively. "You knew I left you, didn't you, Nathan? You received my letter?"

"I did," he acknowledged tightly. "Just tonight."

"Then you knew I departed for America."

"Aye," he conceded heavily.

She gave a shudder. "The steamer embarked from St. Katherine docks five days ago. The weather turned nasty even as we met up with the

Medway at Sheerness. By the time we reached the Channel the sea was beastly. We were pounded by such huge swells, we were all so terrified." She gazed at him starkly, blinking away a tear. "I felt such regret that I had left you . . . such unexpected sorrow."

He squeezed her hand. "As I did, dear Emily, from the moment I arrived in Paris. God, I behaved like such an ass. I wanted to make amends to you. . . . Then I came home and discovered you had gone."

She breathed convulsively. "I don't know just when I realized the ship was going down. There was only this terrible buffeting and pitching, the groaning and shrieking of the ship's timbers. I remember the hull rolling over, followed by panic and screams, fires breaking out, and everyone scrambling, too late, for the lifeboats. I remember being washed from the decks and landing in the waves—so cold, so powerful and turbulent."

"What happened next?" asked Nathan tensely.

"I struggled for a bit, and everything went black. Later I awakened to see a kindly, wrinkled face hovering over me. At first I thought I had surely died and gone to heaven. But as my vision cleared I recognized a silver-haired woman in humble garb."

"What had happened to you?"

"It seemed I had washed up on a beach on the Isle of Wight, and a kindly fisherman and his wife took me in and nursed me."

"My God, Emily!" Nathan cried. "Then you didn't die, after all?"

She met his triumphant gaze, her own eyes

welling with tears. "No, Nathan," she replied gently. "I think I did die."

For a moment Nathan's heart seemed to cease beating as he gazed at his wife, stunned. How could Emily be dead when her hand was so warm in his, when he could see the glow in her cheeks, the lovely shine in her eyes? Had he gone mad?

"Emily, no," he denied in torment. "You cannot be dead. You're here with me—real, alive, and warm. Don't even say such a thing."

"But I must, my dear," she replied with regret, "because we haven't much time."

A new chill gripped Nathan. "What are you saying?"

She patted his hand. "I shall get to that in a moment, after I finish my story."

Nathan groaned. "If I can bear to hear it. . . ." At her helpless look, he added, "Very well, dear. Please proceed."

A faraway look drifted into her eyes. "Even though I did not drown, I became very ill afterward. I was burning up with fever, in a delirium most of the time—"

"Oh, my poor darling," he whispered. "But you look perfectly fine now. . . ."

She clutched his hand. "I'm not, Nathan. You see . . . I believe I did die tonight."

"You died?"

Her troubled gaze met his. "I became so weak, and my heart felt as if it was barely beating. I felt as if I were sinking through the floor, and the faces of the farmer and his wife grew blurry. I could hear the old woman crying."

"Go on," urged Nathan.

"Then the strangest thing happened," she continued, her eyes suddenly aglow. "I began to feel so light—lighter than a feather, even. And then I floated out of my body."

"My God—you mean your spirit left your flesh?" he asked in amazement.

She nodded solemnly. "I rose up toward the ceiling and turned, staring down at myself. I could see my body dying and hear that poor woman wailing with sorrow. Then an even stranger thing happened."

"What, darling?"

Her face glowed with awe and wonder. "I saw you, Nathan. Saw you accidentally break my angel—saw you in your terrible despair. Watched you go to the desk and begin loading your pistol—"

"But how could that be? You were not here."

She shook her head slowly. "I suppose your anguish drew me somehow. I knew I had to go to you, but I didn't know how." She smiled radiantly. "That's when the miracle occurred."

"What miracle?" He gave a tremulous laugh. "This all sounds pretty miraculous to me."

"I know. 'Twas then an angel appeared before me."

"An angel?" he whispered.

Emily's eyes shone. "Oh, Nathan, she was so beautiful, just as I always thought an angel would look—with a white robe, wings, and a halo. I don't know just how she came to me—perhaps her spirit was released when you broke my angel—but she appeared and she spoke to me."

"What did she say, love?"

"She told me you needed me and I must go to you—"

"She allowed you to live?" he asked with forlorn hope.

"No, Nathan," Emily replied gently. "She told me I could return to earth in human form for just one day. She told me I could have those brief hours to be with you, to help you, to heal the hurt between us . . . and then I must go on to heaven."

All at once Nathan felt crazed with pain. "What? But this cannot be!"

"I'm afraid 'tis true, darling," she replied soberly. "And you must believe me. We have so little time. This is our final chance to resolve things between us—for before Christmas comes I must leave you."

"But—I still don't understand," he cried, looking her over. "You're here, you're human—"

"And I died, darling . . . and came to you from the shards of an angel."

Staring at Emily, so real beside him, Nathan found his mind spinning at what she was telling him. He got up and began to pace, thrusting his fingers through his hair, feeling as if he had indeed lost his mind. "It's just . . . so difficult to believe, that you're here but I can only have you for one day."

"You must believe it." She rose, her expression imploring him. "Nathan, please don't waste our last precious day together with your doubts. Whether you believe me or not, we won't be together for long. Let's not squander what time we have."

"Oh, darling." He pulled her close, inhaling the scent of her, absorbing her warmth. "I just wish I could stand here and hold you forever. I wish I'd seen the truth sooner, before it was too late—"

"It's not too late, Nathan, at least not for you." She stared up at him with emotion-filled eyes. "I still carry a hurt inside me from our marriage. I want that hurt to be healed before I go on to heaven. I want *you* to be healed, Nathan."

Nathan gathered his bride closer with arms that trembled, and spoke past the aching lump in his throat. "I can't lose you again—I can't."

"Nathan, my course has already been set," she murmured. "You *must* believe me—and you must know that we can't change destiny. All we can do now is to make the most of the time we have left."

Observing her face, Nathan realized how utterly sincere she was. What she was saying seemed unreal; but then, so was her presence here. He nodded painfully. "Very well, darling. I won't claim to completely understand this. But if all we have is one day together, I want to spend every minute making love to you."

She shook her head. "No, Nathan. We must first go on a journey together—look at our beginnings, find out where things went wrong, learn where your life will take you from here."

"A journey?" he repeated, bemused.

"Into our marriage," she whispered, "and into the countryside."

"The countryside?"

She continued with fervor. "We shall find a small village where no one knows us and become part of that community for one day. I think we shall find our answers there."

"You are certain?" he asked.

She squeezed his hand. "Yes. And we must be on our way at once. Go prepare the carriage. I shall dress for our sojourn."

"No!" he protested, suddenly desperately afraid of losing her again. "I can't leave you—not even for a moment! What if I come back to find you have disappeared?"

"Nathan, you only have me for this day," she admonished. "The sooner we embark, the sooner we can find our answers together."

He clutched her hands in his own and pinned her with his earnest gaze. "Promise me you'll be here waiting when I return from the carriage house."

"I promise," she assured him. "And I'll be ready."

Giving her one last look of searing anguish, Nathan rushed for the door. . . .

Chapter Three

A light snow was falling as they drove out of London on the Great West Road. Nathan sat next to his bride in the cabriolet, its folding top raised to ward off the chill. He worked the reins and clucked to the gray horse. The animal's hooves thudded loudly in the stillness as they passed snow-blanketed farmsteads, frozen ponds, and wintry stands of trees. The early dawn lingered cold and clear, bright stars still glittering in the dark heavens. Icicles hung from leafless elm, oak, and chestnut trees; an owl sailed over the road and, somewhere in the wooded shadows, a nightingale sang a plaintive song.

Gazing at his wife, Nathan still could not quite believe she was here with him. Yet he could feel her warmth, her body next to his beneath the carriage blanket they shared. She appeared so real and human, her eyes alert, her cheeks bright from the cold. She was appropriately ensconced in a heavy wool traveling cloak, a matching bonnet, and mittens. Before leaving the townhouse, he had grabbed a dry hat, his greatcoat, and a pair of gloves.

His mind continued to reel at all that had happened during the past hour. He had come home to find her gone . . . then he had learned she had died . . . then she had miraculously materialized before him, claiming an angel had sent her to him, and that she could remain for only one day.

Why? What cruel God would send her back to him at the very moment of his despair, only to snatch her away again? Had an angel truly brought her to him? But for what purpose? Why had she insisted they take this journey into the countryside? He stole another glance at her. Heavens, she was so real, so young and innocent. How could her sweet life be over? How could he bear losing her once more?

Perhaps she had been wrong, he mused with desperate hope. Perhaps there was still some way out of this dilemma, and she might be able to stay with him. Yet he could not deny what he had seen with his own eyes—his wife rising from the shards of her own broken angel. His heart sensed that she had spoken the truth, and soon she would be lost to him forever. The prospect was heart wrenching.

Sitting next to Nathan, Emily, too, was lost in thought. She glanced at him, feasting her eyes on the well-remembered lines of his handsome, angular face, his thick, dark brown hair, deep-set brown eyes, straight nose, and strong chin. There was an intensity about Nathan that had always drawn her to him, even when she was a child, and he an older lad who had hardly even taken note of her. She didn't fully understand why she was here now, or why the angel had appeared before her to grant her this reprieve. She did feel intense sadness that she must soon depart this life she had loved so much, leaving behind Nathan, her family and friends. Yet she felt an odd peace and acceptance about going on to the next plane . . . on to heaven.

She sensed her purpose here was not to attend to her own life, her own needs. Her existence on earth was over. She had returned on a mission of mercy, dispatched by an angel. She knew that Nathan needed her—and she must overcome all her doubts and fears and do everything in her power to help him find his way, find happiness and learn to live without her. . . .

Catching him gazing at her, she smiled. "Remember when we met?"

He eyed her in puzzlement. "That is a rather curious thing to ask."

"Do you remember?" she pressed.

Working the reins, he fell quiet for a moment. "Why, of course I do. Wasn't it at Brighton, back when both our families used to summer there at my father's estate?"

"Yes!" Eyes alight, Emily clapped her hands. "Then you do remember! I thought you didn't even notice I was alive at the time."

"Oh, I took note of you, all right. I suppose I must have been around fifteen then, and you . . ." He glanced at her. "You would have been eight."

"You're correct," she acknowledged primly.

A slight smile pulled at his lips. "I remember

when I first saw you, a ridiculously skinny little creature, freckle-faced, with a shock of curly blond hair. You were walking along the beach wearing one of those absurd, voluminous bathing costumes . . . navy blue, as I recall, with white trim."

"Yes! You have it exactly right!"

He chuckled. "When you saw me riding past you grinned, waved wildly, and almost stumbled over your own feet. Then you climbed into one of those silly huts on wheels that the stewards rolled out into the waves, so you could dunk yourself through the hole in the floor with utter privacy."

She giggled. "My, I must have made quite an impression on you! Did you think me silly and childish?"

He gazed at her wistfully. "Actually, I found you rather winsome, like a friendly puppy or a kitten, perhaps."

"My father used to claim I was always into more mischief than a whole basketful of kittens," she confided ruefully.

He regarded her with awe. "Well, for an unbridled child you turned into one fine and responsible adult."

"I suppose even then I had to prepare myself for heaven," she muttered.

They fell into a poignant silence. At last, with unaccustomed tentativeness, he asked, "And what did you think of me, my dear . . . way back then?"

She sighed ecstatically. "I thought you were frightfully handsome, cantering your huge black horse along the beach, wearing that elegant riding suit, appearing so stern, so serious . . . and all grown up."

Nathan grinned. "I was far from it, I assure you."

"You know, I think I fell in love with you that very day."

"Did you?" He appeared delighted.

She nodded. "Oh, it was only a young girl's hero worship then, but I was so drawn to you." She paused. "When did you first come to resent me, Nathan?"

He considered her words with a scowl. "Was it the following summer, when you and your cousins disrupted my cricket practice with old friends from Eaton?"

She threw him a chiding glance. "Please, be serious. I want to know when our problems really started."

He eyed her with keen regret. "But darling, we have so little time together. Please don't make me say things that I may later regret."

"Nathan, we must look at what went wrong," she insisted gently. "That is one of the reasons I am here. We never really talked during our marriage, and we must talk now."

"I suppose," he conceded heavily.

She touched his gloved hand. "Tell me, when did you first start to dislike me?"

"I never disliked you, Emily," he replied with surprising humility. Sighing, he stared straight ahead at the road. "But I suppose I did become most resentful toward both my parents and my grandparents when they began conspiring with your people to arrange our future marriage."

"That would have been when I was twelve."

He nodded. "And I nineteen. It seemed my family always took all of my decisions out of my hands—the choice of my prep school, my going on to the University, my taking over Father's import business at the Exchange. Their demands seemed never to end."

"I guess I never realized quite how much you chafed at it all," she murmured sympathetically.

"I could have stood up to them instead of venting my spleen on you once you became a woman." He laughed cynically. "Actually, I did try to assert my rights once. I told Father I refused to marry you, that an arranged marriage benefitted neither of us, that I wanted to choose my own bride. He even seemed rather sympathetic toward my plight . . ." Nathan's mouth settled into a hard line. "Unfortunately, my grandfather wasn't."

"In what way?"

"He threatened to withdraw the trust he was establishing for me. 'Twas a king's ransom, Emily. And do you know what the hell of it was?"

"Tell me."

Bitterness gleamed in his eyes as he snapped the reins. "I think one reason I caved in to it all was because of Edgar."

"You mean your old friend at Eaton?" she asked.

"Aye. We were always such rivals, and we'd made this silly wager about which one of us would amass a million pounds first. Given my family's wealth, I would have been well-off in any event. But I knew if I lost the trust . . ."

"Edgar would win the wager?"

He nodded grimly. "And that I could not abide."

"So you married me out of pride?"

He regarded her with regret. "My poor dear, I wish I'd just walked away. I might have won the wager, but I lost my soul in the process."

Her face mirrored keen disappointment. "You regret our marriage?"

"No, that's not what I meant!" he cried. "I regret what I did to you. From the moment you came of age and our parents announced our betrothal, I behaved like a cad, never missing an opportunity to make a cutting remark or to embarrass you by showing up late for a social function. I was a self-absorbed, cruel bastard. Perhaps I felt if I insulted you enough, you'd eventually break our engagement. You'd let me off the hook, and I could simply tell my family that the lady had changed her mind. But you didn't. You never had a selfish bone in your body, Emily. You always thought of others before yourself, and that included being a faithful daughter and abiding by your parents' choice of a husband. I don't see how you stood it—but you did, always smiling, forever patient and forgiving about my lapses. God, Emily, why didn't you just show me the door?"

"Because I loved you," she whispered quietly.

He clenched his jaw, as if doing so would hold back the terrible emotion threatening to strangle him. "I never deserved your love. I just want you to remember always that the reason for my abominable behavior was never you. It was bitterness toward my family."

She touched his hand in reassurance. "I think I knew that all along. But it helps to hear you say it."

"It helps?" he repeated with a crazed irony. "Now, when we have no future together?"

She smiled tenderly. "You have a future, Nathan. And we still have this day together. I'm so glad we can communicate now as we never could during our marriage."

"You mean I never communicated," he replied with self-reproach. "You tried so hard. All those nights I languished away at my club. All those beautiful dinners that were ruined when I perversely came home too late. All those evenings you stayed up to the wee hours, monogramming my handkerchiefs or darning my socks by the fire. Then, finally, when I would come home I'd awaken you to sate my own selfish needs." He shook his head. "Why did you continue to tolerate such a scoundrel?"

"I always hoped you would come around in time," she confided. "I knew there was goodness hidden in your heart."

He regarded her starkly. "What made you lose your hope, Emily?"

She stared ahead, blinking away a tear. "I could take the neglect, your coming home in the wee hours, reeking of brandy and smoke. I could bear your anger, even your passion. But when you left me at Christmastime . . ."

"I know," he whispered in torment.

"Mere days before our first anniversary . . ." She paused, shuddering, wiping away a tear. "I sat by the fire and thought of how hard I'd tried to make our marriage work, how you had never met me halfway, not on anything, how you'd never once been kind or tender toward me—"

"How did you bear it?" he exclaimed.

She gazed at him in intense turmoil. "I bore it for a long time because I did love you, despite all. But I couldn't forgive or forget you leaving me at Christmastime. At last your message got through to me, and I realized there was no hope. Months earlier, Rosemary had written, inviting me to come live with her at any time. So I packed my bags and left. And you know what the biggest irony was?"

"What?" he asked, afraid to hear the answer.

Sniffing, she confessed, "As I was packing, it occurred to me that I was finally giving you what you wanted. Like a fool, I'd been trying for a year to make you happy when the only *real* way to make you happy was to tell you good-bye."

"Oh, God, my poor darling," he said, too consumed with self-loathing to beg for her forgiveness, or even to try to comfort her.

Seeing his anguish, she touched his arm. "That was in our past, Nathan. Let's not spoil our day together with too many recriminations. We still have so much to explore, a very long journey to complete together."

He stared at her in misery. If he could endure it. If he could bear losing her for the second time . . .

Chapter Four

The snow had stopped and the sun was peeking over the horizon by the time they reached the outskirts of the little village of Avalon. The clear, cold dawn streaked the western skies with lovely shades of pink, blue, and gold. Nathan guided the horse over a bridge past a frozen, silvery stream, and then the cabriolet clattered onto the snow-dusted main street of the burg.

He glanced down a sweeping row of typical Tudor storefronts, with snowy roofs, icicle-hung eaves, and frosty windowpanes. Not a soul was in sight, save for a scrawny yellow cat seeking refuge inside an orange crate.

He glanced at his wife. "Do you want to stop here?"

She nodded. "Oh, yes. This looks like just the place we're looking for."

"I'll wager you are tired, and hungry."

"Some breakfast would be nice," she agreed.

Nathan halted the horse before an inn whose front windows gleamed with soft light. He glanced at the front door, spotting a large evergreen wreath decorated with pine cones, miniature Christmas presents, china apples, and bright bows. "This place looks respectable enough. Perhaps we should let a room?"

She smiled. "Perhaps . . . but we shan't be spending much time there."

Feeling a twinge of disappointment that Emily was not eager to be alone with him, Nathan hopped down and came around the cabriolet to help her down. He folded back the blanket, caught her beneath the arms and gently assisted her to the ground. Pulling her beneath the eaves of the inn, he gazed at her lovely face, her gleaming cheeks and dark, bright eyes. He brushed aside a wisp of hair on her brow.

"God, I still can't believe this is happening," he murmured. "You look so real, so alive."

"I've never felt more alive, Nathan," she replied feelingly.

"You're not afraid of what is to come?" he asked anxiously.

She shook her head earnestly. "I'll not lose a single precious second to fear."

He caught her close. "But I'm afraid, love. Afraid for you, afraid for myself. How will I bear being without you?"

She drew back slightly, eyeing him sympathetically. "You don't have to be without me now, Nathan."

"But I've wasted so much time," he went on with

intense frustration. "I just wish I'd realized sooner how much you mean to me."

She hugged him tightly. "You've realized it now . . . and that means the world to me."

He clutched her close to his heart, savoring the sweet heaven of her for a long moment. "You're right, love; we mustn't dwell too much on what is to come or we'll go mad." Bucking up his courage, he smiled down at her. "But I don't think I can live for another second if I don't kiss you."

Her smile was all the encouragement Nathan needed. He leaned over and caught her lips tenderly, reverently, trying to communicate through his kiss how precious she was to him. Her lips tasted warm, sweet, so human, and her womanly curves felt so soft and real against him. God, what exquisite torment to hold her this way! He could not believe she was here in his arms, but he would have her for such a short time! Why had he never appreciated her before, or seen what a priceless jewel she truly was? As she had said, he could experience that splendor now, and try not to allow his terrible guilt and fear to cloud their only remaining day together . . .

Emily, too, savored every sensation as Nathan kissed her—the strength of his embrace, his male scent, the heat of his lips on hers. Before, Nathan had always kissed her with arrogance, with passion, even with anger. But now, he wasn't just taking from her . . . she could tell he was truly giving of himself.

Anguish choked her. Why couldn't they have known such glory, such true intimacy, before? Why was she being given the gift of her husband's devotion, only to have it snatched away? Why was it only her death could bring them together?

She quickly cast her doubts aside. Just as she had told Nathan, they must not spoil this day with too many regrets and recriminations. She would lose him tonight, but for now she could love him with all her heart. She felt so cherished, so precious to him . . .

He pulled back and caught a raspy breath, touching the tip of her nose with his gloved finger. "We'd best go inside before we both turn to icicles."

She touched his hand and spoke poignantly. "Nathan, I want you to remember something. . . . "

"Yes?

"Today is not just about looking at our marriage, where we went wrong. It's also an opportunity for us to share all the joys we never got to experience as a couple."

Clenching his fists, Nathan glanced away. "I'm so damned sorry for . . . for the way I neglected you."

"I know, Nathan. But we have today to make up for that. Let's try to cram it with all the happiness we can."

He could barely speak. "Of course, darling."

He opened the door for her, and they entered the inn. A wave of warmth, as well as the sights and smells of Christmas, greeted them. To their right curled a cozy staircase, its gleaming oak banisters encircled with garlands and accented with huge red velvet bows. To their left stood a small Christmas tree laden with candles, sugar plums, miniature clocks, furniture, dolls, trumpets, and tiny baskets filled with candies. The air was redolent with the scent of crisp pine, and the smells of Christmas baking drifting out from the kitchen—gingerbread and plum pudding, ham and turkey, brandied peaches and mincemeat pie, wassail and hot chocolate.

Nathan grinned at his bride. "The place looks—and smells—good enough to eat."

"I agree."

They stepped up to a counter decorated with holly, pine cones, and a large wooden creche. Nathan rang a bell, and a moment later a grinning, potbellied man stepped out through a door at the back of the vestibule. With his white beard and twinkling eyes, his red, suspendered shirt and jaunty striped trousers, he appeared a prime candidate for a role as Father Christmas.

"Well, hello, good folk," he greeted in his booming voice, "and a merry Christmas Eve to you."

"Thank you, sir," replied Nathan. "Our holiday greetings to you."

Pausing behind the counter, the man extended a hand. "Welcome to Benson Inn. George Benson at your service."

Nathan shook the man's hand. "I'm Nathan Fletcher and this is my bride, Emily."

The innkeeper nodded to her. "Welcome, madam." He stared curiously from Emily to Nathan. "You two are out and about early today, I must say."

Nathan and Emily exchanged a conspiratorial glance. "Yes, we decided to drive out from London more or less on a whim," Nathan confessed. "Now we need a respite from the cold, so we were wondering if you might have a room to let—and a space for our horse in your stable."

Gripping his suspenders, the innkeeper rocked on his heels. "You're in luck, sir, for we've one room left—and ample space for your horse in our carriage house." He scratched his bearded jaw. "Although I'm a bit surprised you folks didn't say you're here for the festival."

"What festival?" asked Emily eagerly.

"Every year on Christmas Eve the people of Avalon have an old-fashioned village fair at the town hall, with all proceeds going to the local orphanage, St. Margaret's. 'Tis only a small institution run by the vicar and his wife, but we of the town try to help out where we can."

"How good of you," declared Emily. She turned expectantly to Nathan. "Could we go?"

Regret mingled with tenderness suffused Nathan as he recalled how, only a week earlier, he'd arrogantly refused to escort Emily on a charitable mission. "Of course we'll go, dear, if it will make you happy."

She beamed, and Nathan had his answer.

The innkeeper eyed them wistfully. "That's right, you two young folks should definitely go enjoy yourselves." He sighed. "I remember when I was your age, sir. Had a beautiful young bride like yours. But I was always so busy, not just running the inn but working the fields for our mayor to bring in a few extra shillings. Then, before I knew it, I lost me dear bride to the fever." He forced a smile. "You two should enjoy yourselves while you can."

Gazing intently at Emily, Nathan coughed. "Yes . . . Well, we'd like that room, then, and my wife is hungry."

The man clapped his hands. "I can show you to

our kitchen, and my sister Beatrice will serve you. Or would you prefer that Bea bring you up a tray?"

"Which would you like, dear?" Nathan asked Emily.

She studied his face intently. "I think a tray in our room would be lovely."

Nathan turned to the innkeeper. "Everything smells divine. . . . Please tell your sister to bring up the entire kitchen."

The man chuckled. "Oh, I shall, sir. And I'll see your horse is given a hefty bag of oats."

Nathan registered and paid for the room, and the innkeeper showed them up to the second floor. Emily gasped in delight as they stepped inside the cozy room with its walnut four-poster bed, its Queen Anne armchairs flanking the hearth, its twin dormer windows draped with crewelwork curtains and fronted by window seats hung with homey yellow dimity cushions.

"I believe you have the nicest room in the house," announced the innkeeper proudly.

"Indeed," said Nathan.

"I'll just light the fire for you. . . . "

As the innkeeper lumbered to the grate, knelt with a groan, and ignited the kindling, Emily smiled at Nathan, and he winked back.

The man stood and brushed off his hands. "What else can I do for you, sir?"

Glancing at the flames stirring in the grate, Nathan handed the innkeeper a half-sovereign. "Nothing, thank you."

"Thank *you,* sir," cried the delighted George Benson. "And please let me know if there's anything you need."

The innkeeper left, and Emily fell into Nathan's

arms. They clutched each other close for a long moment as the fire crackled and the room grew warmer.

Appearing enthralled, Emily gazed about her. "Oh, Nathan, look at the lovely quilt on the bed. The fire is so cozy, and it's such a pretty room."

"It's delightful," he agreed.

"You know, we never went on holiday together," she added with regret.

"I know," he said tightly.

She swept over to the window. "Look, it's snowing again!"

He eyed her standing there, her lovely silhouette outlined by the breaking dawn. Emotion choked his voice. "We never watched a snowfall together, did we, love?"

She turned, her expression radiant. "You're learning quickly, dear. Take off your coat, and we'll do so now."

As eager as two children, they threw their coats, gloves, and headgear on the bed and sat down together on the window seat, holding hands and staring out at the lovely fluttering snowflakes, watching the first cloaked citizens brave the streets.

"I never knew this picturesque little town even existed," Nathan murmured in awe.

Emily craned her neck to watch a milk wagon rattle past. "It's amazing what one can see when one opens one's eyes."

Nathan squeezed her hand and smiled at her. "My eyes are wide open now, Mrs. Fletcher. And I very much like what they see."

She was dimpling back at him when a knock came at the door. Nathan called, "Come in!" and a tall, raw-boned, middle-aged woman entered with a huge tray.

The woman, who wore a gray wool gown and a navy shawl, flashed them a kindly smile. "Good morning, loves. I'm Bea Benson. My brother, George, said you two wanted me to fetch up everything in the kitchen."

Chuckling, Nathan stood, walked over, and took the tray, which was heavily laden with a teapot and cups, bowls of preserves, and plates filled with scones and cake. "Thank you, madam. This looks as if it will do nicely."

Beatrice smiled at Emily. "There's hot chocolate in the teapot, ma'am. Thought it would suit well on this chill morn'."

"Oh, yes, it sounds perfect," Emily agreed.

The lady left, and Nathan started toward Emily with the tray. "Where would you like to eat?"

"Here on the window seat?" she suggested.

He glanced about the room, his gaze coming to rest on the cozy bed with its crazy quilt cover. "How about on the bed? I never brought you breakfast in bed, Mrs. Fletcher, did I?"

She eyed him meaningfully. "No, Mr. Fletcher, I don't recall your mind ever being on food there."

As Nathan struggled against a sheepish grin, Emily removed her shoes and then climbed up onto the bed. He paused to eye her, noting she wore the high-necked lavender silk frock that suited her coloring so well. Her hair was fixed in a bun, but charming tendrils fell free about her lovely brow. Nathan found himself longing to pull all the pins from her hair, to undo all those tiny buttons traveling up her high bodice.

It was torment having her here but not being

able to fully express his feelings. He was dying to take her into his arms, to worship and kiss every inch of her.

"Nathan?" she asked uncertainly. "Is something amiss?"

He shook his head and replied hoarsely, "I just wanted to feast my eyes on you."

"You prefer me over breakfast?" she teased.

"Oh, yes." Nathan placed the tray on the bed, then joined her there. He picked up the warm teapot. "Hot chocolate, Mrs. Fletcher?"

"Thank you."

"And would you care for a pastry?"

"Yes, that sounds divine!"

They sipped hot chocolate and nibbled on scones smeared with strawberry preserves and warm plum cake.

"This is wonderful," Emily said, wiggling her stockinged toes.

Nathan nodded, solemnly brushing a crumb from her soft mouth. "It's glorious to share such a happy time, even to laugh together."

"I know," she murmured.

"It's uncanny to think that all the time we were married, we never once indulged in a simple joy like this."

She blushed. "We shared some joys in bed."

He caressed her cheek. "Was it good for you, darling? I always felt I wasn't very considerate of you there."

Her gaze shied away from his. "You didn't want to be . . . I realize that. You were always so filled with anger and resentment. But still there were times—"

"Yes, darling?" he coaxed.

At last she met his eye. "When you were much more tender than you meant to be. It was almost as if you couldn't help yourself. Sometimes when you were sleeping you would reach for me, and just hold me. . . . I felt so cherished then. I felt that for once you were communicating your real feelings."

"Feelings you knew about . . . when I didn't," he said in awe.

"Yes, I knew . . . and that's one reason why I stayed, and didn't give up for so long."

"Bless you for that," he whispered, setting down his cup and staring at her with heartfelt gratitude. "You know, you always were far too good to be true, love. No wonder the angels want you now. No doubt they deserve you far more than I."

They shared an emotional, searching look, and then Nathan leaned over to kiss Emily. He tasted the sweetness of her lips and pulled her closer, the dishes rattling between them. He caressed her spine with his fingertips and nibbled at her earlobe. She sighed with pleasure. Nathan felt as if his emotions would burst inside him if he did not express them.

"Emily, I want to make love to you," he whispered intensely. "I want to show you my true feelings, to cherish you as I never did before."

But she pressed the flats of both hands to his chest. "No, Nathan, not yet," she implored. "We must finish our breakfast, and go on to the fair."

"But why?" he protested in crazed tones. "You're so close to me that I cannot endure not touching you! I'm dying to hold you, to bring us together, to know things are truly right between us. What time we have left is so precious. I don't want to go to the damned fair. I want to spend this time making love to you."

"Nathan, you don't understand," she replied gently but firmly. "This day will be meaningless if you think only of yourself and your own needs. We still have a long journey to take together. I can't leave you until I've shown you the way—how to find happiness in your own life. Otherwise, when I'm gone, you'll be lost again."

Nathan gazed at her for a long moment, struggling between his desire for her and his wish to do whatever would make her most happy. "Very well, darling," he conceded heavily. "I never thought of you first during our marriage, but today I'll try my darndest to remedy that. I won't spoil what time we have left by arguing."

"Thank you, Nathan," she whispered sincerely.

He smiled and squeezed her hand, trying hard to swallow past the knot of sorrow in his throat.

Chapter Five

Soon they left the inn and emerged on the snow-dusted walkway. Holding hands, they headed toward the town hall at the end of the cobbled street.

The snow had stopped falling, leaving in its wake an unseasonably cool, sweet morn. Proprietors were opening doors to cozy shops whose front windows were crammed with Christmas merchandise: a toy shop sported dolls, clowns, cast-iron train sets, and toy soldiers; a butchery displayed hams tied with bright ribbons and a prize goose; a cobbler presented his best button-top shoes and shiny dress boots; an apothecary exhibited men's toiletries and crystal bottles of perfume.

Observing a watchmaker opening the door to his shop, Nathan glanced at Emily. "Should we stop in at some of these places? We never did our

Christmas shopping, you know."

She laughed. "But I did, dear, while you were away in Paris."

Taken aback, he asked, "All of it?"

She nodded. "For both our parents, your brother and cousins, and my sister. I put everything into the post before I left."

He shook his head in wonderment. "I should have known you would have done so. You were always such a good wife, so thoughtful toward others, and I was such a self-centered bastard. Why didn't you give me the boot long ago?"

"You know why, dear," she replied fervently.

His reply came choked. "Aye, because you loved me. Far more than I deserved."

They continued along in silence. A couple of carriages passed by, with families inside. Hearing the childrens' laughter and feeling a tightening of emotion in his chest, Nathan squeezed Emily's hand.

"You know, I never gave much thought to how you spent your days," he remarked. "What did you do for all the time I neglected you?"

She dimpled. "Oh, I cared for our home, shopped, visited with friends, and did charity work with the good ladies of St. Mary's Guild."

"You could have taken a lover," he suggested wryly.

"But I couldn't have!" she protested indignantly. "That is not how proper English girls are brought up to behave."

He chuckled. "But didn't you sometimes want to set me in my place for being such a scoundrel?"

"Not that way," she replied gravely. "I never could have cheated on you, Nathan. Although at times, I must confess, I wondered about you. . . . "

He fell silent, frowning, for a long moment. "I never betrayed you, Emily," he admitted at last.

She glanced at him curiously. "That rather surprises me."

"Don't make me out to be too noble," he went on cynically. "I certainly planned to punish you that way by taking a mistress after we were wed."

"Oh!" Irate, she shoved his arm.

"Only . . ."

"Yes, Nathan?"

He winked at her tenderly. "I found that after knowing you, love, no one else would suit."

Her cheeks hot, Emily glanced away. "I—you never told me that."

"Of course I didn't," he rejoined harshly. "That would have been a kind, loving thing to say, and I had to act the blackguard at all cost, didn't I? My God, Emily, why aren't you furious at me now? You've every right to hate me."

"I don't have time for anger or malice," she replied quietly.

"But weren't you at all resentful of the way I mistreated you?" he persisted. "After all, none of it was your fault. You were pushed into this marriage just as I was."

She nodded. " 'Tis true my parents were adamant that I wed you. But the difference was, I wanted to become your wife, Nathan, even though you never wanted to be my husband. Still, I had high hopes that you might come around in time."

"Hopes I tried my best to dash," he added ruefully. "Heavens, Emily, why did you never do anything to demonstrate your outrage?"

A look of guilty pleasure lit her face. "Oh, but I did, dear."

"No!" he denied. "You never displayed the slightest antipathy toward me."

She smirked. "Didn't I?"

"How, Emily?"

She actually giggled. "Heavy starch, dear," she confided.

He stared at her mischievous face a moment, then snapped his fingers in realization. "So *that's* why all my shirts appeared ready to walk off, and scratched the deuce out of me! And to think of all the times I scolded the charwoman for over-starching them."

"Oh, I insisted on doing your shirts myself," she informed him importantly.

Nathan grinned in awe and admiration. "Why, you minx!"

"I suppose there's still a little of the impish child left in me," she admitted.

He stared at her in awe. "Emily, I never knew you. I missed out on so much. I never realized you are such a joy."

She met his gaze with tender amusement. "A joy to be overstarching your shirts, milord?"

"I'd give my life to have you overstarching my shirts again," he whispered back fervently.

Sharing a bittersweet smile, they approached the steps of the large Tudor hall at the end of the street. Watching a young family—mother, father, and two small daughters—step through the front door, Nathan felt his good cheer dissolving. He stopped in his tracks.

Emily also paused, touching his arm and regarding his wan face. "What is it, darling?"

"This is unbearable," he told her in anguish. "All these families together for Christmas . . ."

She quickly hugged him. "We're a family and we're together, Nathan. At least for today."

Holding her tightly, Nathan gathered his fortitude. "You're right, dear," he said, quickly kissing her brow.

They stepped up to the hall and Nathan opened the door for Emily. Inside, a riot of activity greeted them. In a far corner of the single large room loomed a grand Christmas tree, festooned with garlands, ornaments, and candles. Nearby, a huge fire blazed in an open hearth. All along the walls of the hall were grouped tables piled with various Christmas crafts. Ladies, gentlemen, and entire families were busy tending the wares.

A smiling, ruddy-complected man in vicar's garb stepped up to greet them, extending his hand. "Hello. I'm Reverend Michael Milsap. I don't believe I've had the pleasure of meeting you before."

Nathan shook the vicar's hand. "Pleased to meet you, Reverend. I'm Nathan Fletcher and this is my wife, Emily."

"How do you do?" Emily asked, also shaking Milsap's hand.

The vicar beamed at Emily. "Good to meet you, Mrs. Fletcher. And whence do you folks hail?"

"From London," said Nathan. "We—er—came out for the fair."

"Well, a big welcome to you both," said Milsap. "The wife, Celeste, and I are so thankful the town does this annual homage to the orphanage. You must meet Celeste. She'll be along directly, once she gets the little ones fed and dressed."

"Is the orphanage in your home, sir?" inquired Emily.

The vicar laughed. "Aye, there 'tis, such as it is. The vicarage is large, but drafty as a barn, I'm afraid."

"What can we do to help?" asked Emily.

The vicar gestured about the room. "Well, as you can see, the citizens of Avalon have organized an old-fashioned living Yule fair, and some of the folks will be working at their crafts throughout the day. We've portrait painters, and others making Christmas crackers, pomander balls, quilts, or welcome wreaths. We'd be pleased to have you do your Christmas shopping with us, but you should also feel free to lend a hand if the spirit moves you. A number of the townsfolk pitch in and help the craftsmen each year—it has become part of the fun."

"Why, what a charming custom!" declared Emily.

Nathan winked at his wife. "I rather fancy the idea of helping to make kissing boughs."

The vicar threw back his head and laughed. "I wager we may have a citizen or two working on them."

Nathan and Emily were about to move on when a potbellied, balding man stepped up to join them. The vicar greeted the man with a smile. "Good morning, Tom." Turning to Nathan and Emily, he added, "I'd have you meet our village constable, Tom Stout. Tom, the Fletchers are here from London to join us at our fair."

The man nodded to Nathan and Emily. "Welcome to Avalon. Hope you enjoy the festival."

The vicar addressed the constable in anxious

tones. "Any luck in finding the Kirkland children?"

The man shook his head morosely. "Sorry. I keep spying Kipp about town but haven't been able to nab the little rascal."

At the curious looks from Nathan and Emily, the parson explained. "Three weeks ago the widow Kirkland passed away at her farm just outside town. Left three small children—seven-year-old Kipp, five-year-old Kathy, and two-year-old Lucy. Celeste and I want to take in the foundlings at the orphanage, to try to find them homes as we do for the others, but the orphans have been hiding and we haven't been able to find them."

"Oh, the poor darlings!" cried Emily. "They must be so frightened and cold. And at Christmastime, no less."

The constable spoke up. "I think they're all a'fearing they'll be split up after they go to the orphanage."

"Is this true, Reverend?" Emily asked the vicar.

He shrugged. "I'm afraid 'tis frightfully difficult to find one home willing to take in three orphans." He brightened. "But I didn't mean to burden you with our problems. You two go on and have a good time now."

"We will, Reverend," Nathan assured the vicar as he led Emily away.

Nathan and Emily went past the various tables, watching a group of white-haired ladies put the finishing touches on a patchwork Advent quilt, observing a group of couples assembling Christmas crackers, scrutinizing the work of two young girls constructing a huge gingerbread house, watching an elderly artist transpose the image of a sleeping baby into a cherub on canvas.

Emily spoke up to the young mother who held the sleeping child, a pink-cheeked infant swaddled in a blue blanket. "Your baby is beautiful."

The woman beamed. "Thank you, ma'am."

" 'Tis wee Will's first Christmas," added the child's proudly grinning father, who stood nearby.

"A very special time," agreed Emily, staring at the baby's sweet, rounded face.

Eyeing the finished portrait, Nathan addressed the artist. "I want you to paint my wife next, sir."

The white-haired artist glanced up at Emily and grinned. " 'Twould be my pleasure. She's a rare beauty."

"So she is," agreed Nathan solemnly.

Emily blushed. "Nathan, really—"

He touched her arm. "Darling, I want this," he whispered vehemently. "I want to have something to remember this day by."

At last she nodded happily.

"I work quick, sir," called the artist eagerly.

Nathan glanced poignantly at Emily. "You'll have to. We haven't much time."

As the couple with the baby took their finished portrait and moved on, Emily sat down on the artist's chair. The old man began painting Emily while Nathan watched his wife intently. He committed to memory every lovely line of his wife's face, taking note of the slight pucker of her lips, the dimples in her cheeks, the charming angle of her chin. Perhaps, if he continued to just stand here, loving her, worshipping her from afar, time itself would stand still and there would never be a tomorrow to take her away from him. . . .

She'd said she must leave him before Christmas. A cruel Christmas indeed.

The artist truly was a miracle worker. Within half an hour he held up his brush and grinned at Nathan. " 'Tis done, sir. Come have a look."

Nathan walked around the man and stared at the portrait through suddenly stinging eyes. Heavens, how had the artist known? Nathan gazed at his bride, his Emily. Luminously beautiful. Swathed in white. In an airy portrait bordered with holly and ivy, a halo crowning her glorious countenance.

"You've captured her," he said in gruff tones.

"I have indeed," said the artist, winking at Emily. "She's an angel, all right."

Laughing, Emily came over to join them. "Oh, Nathan!" she cried in wonder. "You were right!"

Over the artist's protests, Nathan paid the man a half-sovereign and asked him to hold the portrait until later. The couple swept on past additional displays until the sounds of a man's curses made them pause before a table where an elderly couple were trying to assemble wreaths, the husband constructing the wire rings and the wife tying on the greenery.

Nathan spoke up to the man. "Well, sir, you had best not allow the vicar to hear that immodest language of yours."

The man, who sported craggy features in a whiskery face, appeared embarrassed, coughing and avoiding Nathan's eye. "Sorry, sir, madam, but I keep snippin' me bloody thumb with the pliers. My rheumatism's such that I ain't nimble like I used to be."

"Rheumatism, my petunias," scoffed the woman. "I keep telling me Harry he's just old and crabby, that's all, and if he don't watch his manners, Reverend Milsap is going to ban him from church and bein' around civilized folk."

"Now, Mildred, I'm just trying to do my part to help the orphans," grumbled the husband. He waved his pliers at Nathan. "Just wait until you two be married fifty years, my boy. You'll see what it's like."

Exchanging an emotional glance with Emily, Nathan murmured, "We can see a lot now."

Emily tugged at Nathan's sleeve. "Could we help them, dear?"

At once he melted at her eager look. "Of course. If it will make you happy."

The couple enthusiastically accepted their offer. Nathan and Emily doffed their outer garments; then Nathan helped Harry cut and twist wires, while Emily helped Mildred assemble the wreaths.

Studying Nathan as he worked, Emily felt great empathy for him, knowing how difficult this day must be for him, to have them spending their time helping others when she knew what he really wanted was to be alone with her. But already she felt she was accomplishing her purpose. Nathan was demonstrating signs of growth, no longer thinking strictly in terms of his own wants and needs. He was doing things he never would have done before: Never before would he have allowed her to choose how to spend their day; never before would he have insisted they pause to have her portrait painted; never before would he have agreed that they should help anyone. Their journey together, however brief and painful, was bearing fruit; these hallmarks of his progress were very important to her. Indeed, she couldn't leave him until he had the skills and the selflessness that he would need to cope with life on his own. . . .

Mildred's voice cut into Emily's musings. "Oh, my dear, you're doing such a splendid job."

Emily stared with pride at the wreath she had just finished assembling. Complete with a huge red bow at the top, it was sprigged with moss, holly, and evergreen, embellished with pine cones and gleaming glass apples.

"Thank you; I do think it is attractive," she replied.

The woman patted Emily's hand. "It'll fetch a pretty price for the orphans. You've an inspired touch, my girl."

Emily smiled.

Suddenly the woman gasped and pointed toward the window. "Well, my land, would you look at that!"

Emily turned to the pane and saw a small, sad face reflected through the frost, the huge dark eyes wistfully taking in the scene. Then, seeing Emily watching him, the child went wide-eyed and dashed away.

"Who was that?" Emily cried.

"Why, young Kipp Kirkland skulking about," replied the woman. "He's been hiding out for weeks now with his sisters. They must all be starved and half-frozen. I must tell the constable."

Emily laid her hand on the woman's arm. "No, please don't."

The woman was aghast. "But, my dear, he and the girls'll be needin' a place out of the cold."

"Don't worry, they'll have one," Emily reassured her.

Leaving the old woman to frown, Emily rose

and swept about the table to Nathan's side. Urgently, she whispered, "We must go now."

"Now?" he repeated in bewilderment. "But I thought you wanted to stay here."

She tugged at his arm. "Please, Nathan, don't argue. There's no time."

He went pale. "But Emily, I thought you said . . . And your portrait . . ."

"Don't worry. We'll be back."

Grabbing their coats, hats, and mittens, they rushed from the building, Nathan's expression still mystified.

Chapter Six

"Emily, where are we going?" Nathan demanded.

He struggled to keep up with his wife, who was all but running by the time they emerged from the hall into the lightly falling snow.

She stopped and pointed ahead. "Look!" she cried, her breath forming white puffs on the air. "It's the little boy—Kipp Kirkland."

Nathan stared ahead, spotting a small, raggedy urchin running through a field between two barren, misshapen trees. "You're referring to the orphan with two younger sisters? But we must go back and inform the vicar and the constable."

She shook her head vehemently. "No. We must help these children." And she rushed off again.

Nathan leaped into step beside her. "Why, Emily? And shouldn't we fetch the carriage?"

"No. He'll hear us pursuing him."

"But why spend our one day together on something like this?" he cried.

Gasping for breath as they marched along, Emily glanced at Nathan in keen disappointment. "Nathan, I must tell you something. I was sent back here to save you. When I came to you, you were suicidal because your life had become meaningless, totally self-absorbed. When your moment of despair came you had nothing to fall back on to redeem yourself. Now, if you don't find more purpose and meaning within your own heart, your own life, you will not benefit at all from the miracle we've been granted, and my mission will have failed."

He grabbed her arm and pulled her close. "Emily, I've already found that meaning and purpose. It's you, love."

But she shook her head and shuddered, wiping away tears with her gloved hand. "Nathan, you aren't going to have me."

She hurried on, and, numb with pain, Nathan followed her. They plodded across the glistening field, still following the child, and finally swept through the gates of a farm. Ahead of them, Nathan spotted a modest stone cottage with a thatched roof piled with snow, and beyond the outbuildings—barn, chicken coop, dairy, corn crib, pig sty—also crested with white. All around the property, corrals, ploughs, wagons, and carts were piled with drifts.

Watching the boy, Nathan felt bemused. Instead of proceeding directly to the farmhouse as he would have expected, the lad hurried past it. "Where the deuce do you suppose he's going?"

"Perhaps to the barn?" she suggested.

But her hunch proved incorrect as the boy continued well past the barn, well, and haystack to a square dovecote on the hillside beyond.

"Why would he be bound there?" Nathan muttered.

Emily shrugged, appearing equally mystified.

As the boy slipped inside the dovecote, Emily and Nathan approached the tall, narrow flagstone building. She glanced at the battered door, which hung by a single rusty hinge. "Why, it looks no better than a pigsty."

Nathan nodded grimly. "Let me go in first, dear."

"Very well."

Nathan slipped through the low, narrow doorway, and Emily followed him. They entered to a cacophony of flapping wings and crying birds. In the dark interior, Nathan sneezed at the odors of dust and feathers. The wretched hut reeked of bird droppings. He glanced overhead. Amid myriad holes in the high thatched roof, at least a dozen doves and pigeons swirled about in vibrant agitation, rippling the spikes of smoky light that filtered in.

Nathan squinted about the shadows, searching for the children. "Kipp? Kipp, are you there?"

In reply, a child coughed and a kitten mewled.

"Kipp?" called Emily. "Please come out. No one will hurt you, child."

At last a filthy, tattered blond lad emerged from the shadows. His pitifully thin face was smeared with dirt; his dark eyes gleamed with mistrust and he wielded an iron spade in one hand.

"Get out a' here, both of ye, or I'll gouge yer eyes out!" he shouted with bravado.

Nathan clutched Emily's arm protectively. "Son, there's no need for threats. We've come here to help, not to harm you."

"Well, we don't need yer help!" declared the child.

In the shadows, another wrenching cough rang out.

Emily smiled at the boy. "No? It sounds to me as if one of your sisters may be ill, Kipp."

The boy blinked at them uncertainly but still gripped his spade.

"Why are you hiding here, boy?" Nathan asked Kipp. "This place is filthy and drafty, no place for your sisters."

" 'Tis the only place the constable don't look!" exclaimed the lad. "I tried hidin' me sisters in the barn, but when our neighbor, Mr. Sturgess, come 'round to feed the stock, he spotted us and ratted on us to Tom Stout."

Emily and Nathan exchanged a helpless look.

Emily edged closer to the child. Leaning toward him, she spoke gently. "Kipp, why are you so afraid to ask for help? My husband and I just visited the Christmas fair in town, and the people of Avalon are wonderful. They truly want to help you and your sisters."

The boy hesitated, his thin jaw tight.

"Reverend Milsap has a place for all of you at the orphanage," encouraged Nathan. "He seems a very nice chap. You can't be afraid you'll be mistreated there."

"Nay, I'm not a'feared of that," Kipp admitted. "It's just . . ." Fighting a shudder, he confided, "If I take the three of us to the orphanage, they'll split up me family. And I promised me mum a'fore she died that I'd keep us all together."

"Oh, Kipp," murmured Emily sympathetically.

"That's a heavy burden for a boy your age," added Nathan.

The boy's sharp features clenched with pride. "I'm man enough fer it!"

A tense silence descended, until the child in the shadows again hacked forlornly.

"Kipp, could we at least see your sisters?" coaxed Emily. "One of them sounds quite ill, and maybe we can help."

The boy mulled this over for a long moment, his young face fraught with vulnerability, his wary gaze darting from Emily to Nathan. At last he called out, "Kathy, bring out the baby!"

Nathan heard sounds of movement; then another frail child—a grimy girl—emerged leading a smaller child. Both girls were hatless, their garments in tatters. The smaller girl was coughing loudly and carried a bedraggled, mewling gray kitten under one arm.

Kipp stepped toward his sisters, protectively placing his arm about the older girl's shoulders. "These be me sisters, Kathy and Lucy."

Emily smiled at the girls. "How do you do?"

Both girls regarded her anxiously and did not reply.

Nathan watched Emily. He saw the anguish in her eyes as she viewed the children, and then she turned to him with a look of pleading.

"Nathan, we must do something," she whispered.

Sighing, Nathan inclined a hand toward the boy. "Kipp, will you excuse us for a moment?"

He nodded curtly.

They stepped outside, into the falling snowflakes. They gazed at each other with heartache and confusion.

"Nathan, we have to help them," Emily beseeched.

"But how?" he asked fatalistically. "The boy is right—if they go to the orphanage, they'll likely be split up eventually."

She waved a hand in frustration. "But if they stay here, they'll surely die! Did you see how filthy and frail they all are? And the baby looks as if she could become quite ill, if she isn't already."

Nathan groaned. "What can we do, Emily? The boy won't let us take them to the orphanage unless they can remain together."

"Then we must promise them that they can."

"How, Emily?" he pressed.

"You must promise it."

He gave an incredulous laugh. "You're saying I should take on responsibility for three orphans? But that is ludicrous! I'd make a wretched father!"

She shook her head sadly. "Nathan, didn't you hear anything I said earlier?"

"Yes!" he cried passionately, moving closer to her. "I heard what you said, love. You said you must teach me how to live without you. But that's impossible because I *can't* live without you!"

For a moment they confronted each other, Nathan breathing hard, Emily facing him with torment and disappointment.

"Nathan, please don't give up," she pleaded, wringing her hands. "And don't forsake those poor children. Don't make me go on to heaven knowing I've failed you."

"Oh, Lord," he whispered, clenching his fists

and gazing distraughtly at the gray heavens. "How can I do this, Emily? I *need* you. And those three children will need a mother."

"I wish they could have two parents, but at least they'll have a father in you."

"Emily, I can't," he whispered miserably.

"You must," she persisted. "I know you can help them. You'll find the strength you'll need. But you must try, for my sake, theirs—and your own."

He was slowly shaking his head. "You're actually saying I should take responsibility for them, even become their guardian?"

"I'm begging you to do so. Nathan, I promise you, you'll benefit from it even more than they will."

Nathan shut his eyes, struggling within himself. What she was asking seemed impossible . . . yet how could he deny her anything, knowing he would lose her forever within mere hours?

"Very well, darling," he conceded at last. "I have a feeling I may fail, but for your sake I shall at least try to help them."

She heaved a great sigh. "That's all I can ask."

Clasping hands and exchanging an empathetic smile, they slipped back inside. Nathan addressed the boy. "Kipp, what if I can promise that you and your sisters will remain together? Will you go with us into town then?"

The boy eyed him dubiously. "I ain't certain, sir."

Emily spoke up. "It's almost Christmas, you know. Wouldn't your sisters like some new clothes, some pretty presents, and a nice hot meal?"

As she spoke, Nathan studied all of the children.

The pitiful yearning on their faces was agonizing to see. "That's right, Kipp," he concurred with a grin. "We'll fetch you into town and get all of you baths, new garments, and all the food you can eat."

Obviously wavering, Kipp glanced from Nathan to Emily. "Will you take us in, sir? Will she be our mum?"

As all three of the children stared wistfully at Emily, Nathan churned in turmoil and spoke hoarsely. "I—I'm afraid I cannot promise that, son. But I do vow that the three of you will stay together. I shall personally guarantee it."

But the boy appeared unconvinced, flashing Nathan an accusatory look. "I ain't sure I believe you. You're sayin' you'll 'elp us, but she won't?"

Emily stepped forward and touched Kipp's frail shoulder. "Kipp, I would love to become your mother, and a mum to your sisters, too. But what my husband is trying to tell you is, as much as I want to care for you, I may not be here much longer."

The boy's throat worked as he swallowed. "Are you ill, ma'am, like me mum was?"

"In a manner of speaking, I suppose I am," she replied gently. She inclined her head toward the baby. "And your baby sister could become very ill, too, Kipp, if we don't get her warm and fed. She could die."

Kipp gazed at the coughing child, then regarded Emily with wrenching anguish in his eyes. Obviously struggling with his pride, he stood with his thin frame trembling and his lower lip quivering. At last, uttering a piteous cry, he dropped his spade and began to sob, throwing his arms about

Emily's waist. She soothed him, patting his frail shoulders and whispering words of comfort.

The emotion too much for him, Nathan turned away. When all was said and done, Kipp Kirkland was only a child, and Nathan felt equally helpless right now.

Chapter Seven

"I think I've been adopted," Nathan said.

"Indeed," Emily replied.

Leading the two older children across the snowy field, Emily watched her husband carry small Lucy and smiled at the endearing sight. Before they had left the dovecote, she had wrapped her muffler about the baby's bare head. The child lay all but limp in her husband's arms, her head tucked beneath Nathan's chin, a tiny thumb stuffed in her mouth. Under one arm was still grasped the mewling kitten. Glancing at the baby's face, Emily could detect cherubic features behind the smeared dirt. Pain clutched at her heart. How she wished she could linger here on earth and be a mother to these children, a wife to Nathan!

She breathed a heavy sigh. What mattered now was that she show her husband the way to his own redemption. What mattered now was that she spend whatever time she had left helping Nathan and the children, ensuring happy futures for them all. . . .

"Lucy does look as if she belongs with you," she remarked to Nathan.

"And it appears we've adopted a cat, as well," he said dryly.

The kitten meowed loudly, and everyone laughed.

From Emily's side young Kipp spoke up to Nathan. "Sir, what will be done with us once we get to the village?"

Nathan grinned. "Well, as we've already noted, you all must first be provided baths, new clothes, and a good hot meal, don't you think?"

"Aye, sir!" piped up young Kathy. "We've had naught to eat but a few moldy crusts of bread."

"Well, we shall fix that!" declared Emily. "And I bet you children haven't done your Christmas shopping either, have you?"

As Kathy chortled in delight, Kipp frowned, obviously uncertain he should be accepting so much charity. Then, after Lucy hacked out another cough, he seemed to relent. "Aye, ma'am, I reckon you're right. 'Twill make the girls happy."

"They should be happy at Christmastime," agreed Nathan. "But to be fair, son, shouldn't we stop by the town hall and let the vicar and the constable know you've all been found? Everyone in Avalon has been frightfully worried about you."

Again, the boy hesitated, his brow furrowed in a tense frown. "I ain't certain, sir."

"Kipp, I promised that you and your sisters

won't be separated," stated Nathan firmly, "and I shall keep my word."

At last, the boy acquiesced. "Aye, sir."

The small group arrived at the town hall. The minute they stepped inside the vicar and the constable rushed up, their expressions astounded. Kipp and Kathy shrank closer to Nathan and Emily, while Lucy clutched Nathan's cravat and hurled a suspicious glance at the men.

"So you've found them, sir!" cried Reverend Milsap.

"Well, would you look what the cat dragged in," added an amazed Tom Stout.

Nathan turned to Emily. "Dear, if you'll show Kipp and Kathy around the exhibits, I'd like to have a word with the gents."

She nodded. "Of course, Nathan. We'll be back shortly."

As soon as she led away the older children, Tom Stout asked, "Where in blazes did you find them, sir?"

"Out at the farm, hiding in the dovecote," Nathan replied heavily.

"Bless their little souls," fretted Reverend Milsap, shaking his head as he gazed at the bedraggled Lucy. "But the wife and I will care for them now."

This pronouncement left Nathan frowning. "Reverend, I have a favor to ask. My wife and I would like to keep the children with us for a few hours, take them back to the inn where we're staying, see that they are given baths, hot food, and new garments. Afterward we promise to deliver them to the orphanage."

Milsap appeared pleasantly surprised, raising a

bushy brow. "You've taken quite an interest in the youngsters, sir."

Nathan smiled wryly. "I'm afraid the only way we could convince them to come into town was to promise Kipp that they won't be separated."

The constable whistled. "But is it fair to give them false hope, sir?"

" 'Tis not false hope," replied Nathan. "If need be, I—that is, my wife and I—will adopt them. I shall be consulting with my barrister first off next week regarding the children's future."

While Tom Stout shook his head in wonder, the Reverend grinned and rubbed his hands together. "Why, bless you, sir! What a wonderful Christmas gift for such needy youngsters. And, considering the responsibility you're assuming for them, of course you may keep them with you for a time."

"We'll have them to the orphanage before nightfall," Nathan assured.

"And you and your wife must join us for Christmas dinner," offered Milsap.

"Thank you, but we really must head back to London," Nathan replied.

"But can't you stay long enough for the children to become accustomed to us?" asked Milsap.

Glancing down at the baby, who was cuddled against his shoulder, staring up at him with huge, trusting eyes, Nathan conceded the point with a nod. "You're right—we'll stay, at least for a time."

Now young Kipp raced up, his eyes aglow, the portrait of Emily clutched in his hands. "Look, sir! We was saved by an angel!"

As the vicar and the constable laughed, Nathan stared intently at Emily as she approached with Kathy. Surrounded by the children, his wife glowed with happiness, her eyes gleaming, her smile bright. Never had she looked more alive, more beautiful to him.

Glancing lovingly at the portrait, Nathan replied hoarsely, "Aye, son. You were indeed rescued by an angel."

With the vicar's blessing the small group headed back for the inn. Upon learning of the children's plight, Beatrice Benson at once volunteered to help the couple tend them. While Nathan embarked on an emergency journey to the village dry goods store to buy new clothing for the children, Beatrice and Emily bathed all of the orphans, even the kitten, in the warm kitchen at the back of the inn.

Half an hour later, walking inside the large room with a huge pile of boxes, Nathan grinned at the endearing scene before him. On one side of the large, square table sat Kipp and Kathy, both with damp hair and wrapped in large towels; the children were gobbling down clam chowder and crackers. Across the table sat Miss Benson and Emily, who held little Lucy. The freshly washed baby was also swaddled in a towel as Emily fed her soup. Across the room, near the open hearth, the well-scrubbed gray kitten lapped at a bowl of milk.

Nathan set down the boxes and grinned. "Well, it looks like you've made great progress here," he remarked to Emily.

"As have you, dear," she answered with a nod toward the boxes. "Did you buy everything in the store?"

"Almost," he replied with a chuckle. He grinned

at the children, noting their finely drawn features, bright eyes, and shiny, fair hair. "My, what a handsome group you are, now that the ladies have scrubbed away all that grime."

Kipp grinned and Kathy giggled.

"They are the prettiest children in the burg, sir," agreed Beatrice Benson.

"They're angels," declared Emily.

Nathan winked at her tenderly. "You should know, dear." He leaned toward Lucy, who appeared pink-cheeked and adorable in his wife's arms. The baby grinned back up at him as she nibbled on a cracker. "And how is our little one doing? I was wondering if we shouldn't try to find her a physician."

"She hasn't been coughing as much since we've been here," said Emily. She touched the baby's soft cheek. "And there's no fever. I'm thinking perhaps she only has a mild cold."

He nodded. "Well, we'll keep her dry and warm. I purchased hats, mittens, and coats for all of the children." He started toward the hearth, where the children's pitiful shoes had been laid out to dry. "However, I forgot to take along their shoes, and the cobbler needs the old ones for comparison." He held up one of Kipp's tattered boots. "I'll wager you could all use a size larger, eh, Kipp?"

The lad grinned back. "Aye, sir."

Nathan grabbed the shoe of each girl, as well, wincing as he noted missing buttons and gaping holes in the soles. "I'll just take these to the cobbler and be back before any of you can wink."

He left, and by the time he returned the ladies had trimmed and dried the children's hair, had dressed the girls in red velvet dresses and white stockings, and Kipp in a black jacket, linen shirt, and dark trousers. Nathan presented Kipp with a new pair of shiny brown boots and the girls with stylish black shoes with gold buckles. Kathy cried out in joy over her pretty gift, and even the baby crowed in delight as Emily buckled on her new shoes.

Once the children were ready, Beatrice clapped her hands. "Oh, don't all of you look like a fine young family."

Nathan glanced at Emily with aching sadness. "That we do."

Kipp tugged at Nathan's coat. "Will you be taking us to the orphanage now, sir?" he asked anxiously.

Nathan knelt beside the boy. "Kipp, you and your sisters may need to stay there for a time," he replied gently. "But remember, I promised that you, Kathy, and Lucy will remain together, and I shall keep my word. I *shall* be back next week to see to your welfare."

The boy beamed. "Aye, sir. We believe you."

Nathan grinned and tousled the boy's hair. "In the meantime, 'tis Christmas Eve, and it has occurred to me that the children at the orphanage could likely use some presents."

"Oh, aye, sir!" cried Kipp.

Little Kathy spoke up fretfully. "We could use some presents, too, sir!"

Laughing, Nathan swept the little girl up into his arms. "But of course, sweetheart. We'll buy out the town if you like. Now, let's all get bundled up!"

Amid cries of joy from the children, they all donned their hats, coats, mittens, and scarves and soon emerged on the front walkway, Emily again leading the two older children and Nathan carrying Lucy. Kipp and Kathy laughed gleefully and raced from shop to shop, eagerly spending the coins Nathan continually proffered. At the toy shop a glowing Kathy purchased a half dozen dolls for the girls at the orphanage, while Kipp lingered over a cast-iron train set before selecting several brightly painted wooden soldiers and cast-iron toys for the boys. The brother and sister stood watching in wonder as the shopkeeper placed the toys in boxes and wrapped them with colorful papers and ribbons. Nathan and Emily, observing the children, exchanged a loving smile.

Next, the group stopped in at the greengrocer's, selecting a huge ham and a fruitcake for the orphans's Christmas dinner. Watching the shopkeeper tie festive ribbons about the gifts, Kathy jumped up and down in glee.

"I never seen a ham so large, sir!" cried a wide-eyed Kipp.

Nathan nodded to the boy. "No one shall go hungry at the orphanage this Christmas, you may rest assured."

The group made its last stop at the village fair, where the children bought dozens of Christmas crackers, popcorn balls, and sugar plums. On the way back to the inn they split up, Emily taking Kipp and Kathy to their room, Nathan stopping back at the toy shop to purchase the cast-iron train set Kipp had eyed so wistfully.

When he entered the room balancing the sleeping Lucy and the wrapped present in his arms, he spotted Emily sitting on the window seat, staring out at the snowfall, a pile of brightly wrapped gifts at her feet. The day was rapidly waning, and the reality that she would soon leave him hit him like a fist in the gut. When she turned to smile at him warmly he bravely winked back.

Nearby, Kipp and Kathy lay asleep on the bed beneath the quilt, looking as innocent and serene as two cherubs. He crossed the room and gently laid Lucy down next to Kathy. The baby at once curled up and placed her thumb in her mouth. Nathan smiled at the touching sight. Drawing the quilt over Lucy, he went to join his wife on the window seat.

He clutched her hands, gazed at her exquisite face, and spoke soulfully. "You look so beautiful with the golden light hitting your face and hair that way. But your eyes are sad, love."

She nodded. "It's getting late, Nathan."

He reached out to smooth down her hair. "I know, darling. I suppose we'd best take the children to the orphanage. By the way, the vicar invited us to stay for dinner."

"Shall we, Nathan?" asked Emily eagerly. "I'd like to. And we'll be bringing along a twenty-pound ham, as well as a huge fruitcake and dozens of popcorn balls and other treats, so I don't think we'll be imposing."

"Emily . . ." He clutched her hands and implored her with his passionate gaze. "Darling, we've so little time left."

"I know." She smiled bravely. "But why do you suppose the children came into our lives today?"

He stared at the bed, a muscle working in his jaw. "So we could experience the joys of having a family—the family we never had together."

"I think you're right."

His anguished countenance met hers. "God, I

never knew it could be this way—holding a small child in my arms, having her trust me, depend on me. Hearing the children's laughter, seeing the joy in all their eyes when we went shopping together. I never realized such happiness could be wrought from making others happy—especially from making *you* happy, love."

"You did, Nathan," she whispered with heartfelt sincerity. "You made me so happy today."

"I wish we could have had more of that together, Emily—a lifetime of bliss."

"You shall find it yet," she said with a wistful smile. "You'll be responsible for the children . . . won't you?"

"I promised, and I shall."

"And I want you to remarry," she added gently.

"Don't even suggest that!" he burst out.

"But Nathan, the children will need a mother," she protested.

He held up a trembling hand. "I cannot bear to think of that just yet."

She touched his arm. "But promise me you will later on?"

He nodded heavily, and glanced again at the sleeping cherubs. "Why do you suppose we never conceived a child together, darling?"

She was silent for a long moment. "Perhaps there was always something coming between us, even as we made love—pride, anger, fear, or mistrust. Perhaps we never gave ourselves to each other fully, in complete love."

"God, how I regret that." He stroked her cheek and gazed at her ardently. "You know, I thought about it—getting you pregnant. I would have had an excuse, then, to be something less than a heartless cad. I would have had to inquire about your health, the welfare of my future heir." He gave a harsh laugh. "I would have had to actually talk to my own wife."

She touched his face. "Nathan, please don't torture yourself."

"How can I help it, when this is all my fault?" he asked in despair. "When we have so little time left and I feel such terrible regret?"

"The children need you now," she soothed. "And I need you to be strong."

He hung his head. "I'll try, Emily."

"Can we take them back with us to London tonight?"

He glanced with terrible uncertainty from the children to her. "Emily, please, come back with me to London alone. Give me a few hours with you before it's too late. I won't abandon my responsibility to the children, you may be sure. But I need to be alone with you."

"What we have here, now, isn't enough?" she asked in a small voice.

He raised her hand and reverently kissed her soft fingers. "It's heaven, darling. And I'm willing to change for you. But I'm also about to lose you forever. Can't I be selfish for just a few hours and have you all to myself?"

"If that's what you truly want," she replied solemnly.

"What I truly want is not to lose you!" His features were fraught with turmoil, his voice breaking. "Emily, I think I lost you before because I didn't love you enough. I won't make that mistake again tonight."

"Oh, Nathan!"

He clutched her close and they kissed tenderly, hungrily, as frost gathered on the windowpane. . . .

Chapter Eight

Nathan asked the innkeeper to bring the carriage around, and soon all six of them—he, Emily, the three children, and Lucy's kitten—were wedged on the narrow front seat of Nathan's cabriolet. All were bundled up, the large-eyed kitten peeking out from the neck of Lucy's coat. The boot of the carriage was crammed with gifts, the ham, and the other goodies.

"The innkeeper said the orphanage is just beyond the bridge, to the south," Nathan told Emily.

"I know the way, sir," announced Kipp proudly.

Nathan grinned at the boy. "Good for you, son. We'll count on you."

Appearing eminently pleased, Kipp twisted about to stare at the boot, where a riot of packages with jaunty ribbons peeked out. "You spent an awful lot of money today, sir. I hope you can spare it."

Over the children's heads, Nathan winked at Emily. "It was my pleasure, son. I've passed too many years thinking only about myself. It's a joy to do something for others for a change."

"Were you always stingy before, sir?" inquired Kipp soberly.

While Nathan uttered a self-deprecating chuckle, Emily answered. "Mr. Fletcher always did possess a pure and generous heart. Sometimes it takes special circumstances to bring out a person's better qualities."

"Are we the special circumstances, sir?" asked Kipp.

"You are indeed," replied Nathan.

Kipp glowed with happiness, evidently completely satisfied.

The carriage clipped over the bridge and, at Kipp's direction, Nathan turned down a narrow lane flanked by drifts of snow and barren trees hung with icicles. They spotted a small country church in the distance and, next to it, a long cottage with a thatched roof.

"Is that the orphanage, Kipp?" Emily asked.

"Yes, ma'am."

Over the children's heads, she leaned toward Nathan and confided, "It appears to be little more than a large hovel."

He nodded grimly. "We'll go in first and say hello. Then we can start unloading the boot."

He pulled the conveyance to a halt before the cottage, whose windows gleamed with candlelight reflected through frost. He hopped down and helped Emily and the children to the ground. The small group plodded through the snow toward the door, with Nathan again carrying Lucy and her kitten.

Nathan's knock was answered by Reverend Milsap, who stood before them dressed in a festive red sweater and dark trousers, a pipe in hand. "Welcome, and a Merry Christmas to you all!"

"Thank you, Reverend," answered Nathan. "And Happy Yule to you."

The vicar motioned urgently. "Come in out of the cold, everyone. We've just put on the Yule log, so you should be plenty warm."

As they stepped inside, Emily glanced around at the interior of the cottage, composed of one large room. At once she was overwhelmed by images of happy humanity. A dozen children of all ages raced about on the flagstone floor, playing and shouting with laughter. Several girls were chasing hoops, a group of boys tossed a ball back and forth, and a toddler marched around, beating a toy drum that was slung about his neck. Emily chuckled at the delightful scene.

The room was dominated by a large, crude table set with more than 20 places, with a boar's head as its centerpiece. The far end of the cottage was filled with a massive open hearth, where the huge Yule log burned. Next to the fireplace a large bake oven was positioned in the stone wall. A woman was tending several iron pots at the hearth, and the smells of turkey and mulled cider filled the air. At the opposite end of the cottage stood a large bed piled with quilts. In a corner, several pine rockers with colorful cushions were grouped about the Christmas tree, and a few presents were stacked around its base. Glancing overhead, Emily spotted a huge loft lined with narrow bunks, obviously the sleeping quarters of the orphans. The overall effect of the bungalow was modest but very homey.

The woman, a smiling, pink-cheeked matron with brown hair worn in a bun, stepped forward to join them, wiping her hands on her apron. "Well, good evening and Merry Christmas."

"Merry Christmas to you," said Nathan and Emily in unison.

The vicar turned to his wife. "Dear, this is Mr. and Mrs. Fletcher, the young couple I mentioned." To Nathan and Emily, he added, "This is my wife, Celeste."

"How do you do?" Emily asked, shaking the woman's hand.

"We're so grateful you folks found Kipp and his sisters," said Celeste feelingly. She smiled down at the children. " 'Tis a pleasure to have all of you here with us on this joyous occasion. Wouldn't you young 'uns like to take off your coats and go play with the other children?"

Kipp and Kathy grew wary, edging closer to Emily and clutching her skirts, while the kitten mewled in Lucy's arms, prompting the adults to laugh.

Emily said to Celeste, "I do hope you don't mind one extra orphan—Lucy refuses to part with her kitten."

Celeste waved her off. "Oh, not at all, dear. We can always use an extra mouser in the barn."

The reverend winked at Lucy. "And with the kitten here tonight, we can all play 'The Vicar's Cat,' can we not?"

The adults laughed again.

A moment later, everyone had to dash out of the

way as several children rushed by playing a spirited game of "Hunt the Slipper." Two freckle-faced lads crawled under the table, while a girl with pigtails scampered behind the curtains trying to find the elusive slipper.

Emily spotted the yearning in Kipp's eyes as he watched the others. "They look like they're having so much fun, Kipp and Kathy. Why won't you join them?"

Still the lad hesitated, and when Kathy threw him a beseeching look, he shook his head.

The vicar grinned at Kipp. "You know, son, we were thinking of playing 'Flip the Kipper' tonight, just for you, we feel so honored having you and your sisters here with us. In the meantime we're counting on a smart lad like you to help the others find that wily slipper."

At the vicar's sincere words the child finally lost the battle with his pride. Grinning, he shucked his outer garments and joined in the fun; Kathy quickly followed suit. Relieved to see the brother and sister cavorting with the others, Emily gathered the children's outer garments, as well as her own coat, hat, and gloves, and handed all to Mrs. Milsap.

Lucy, however, continued to cling to Nathan, and Emily smiled at the touching sight—her husband, so dark, handsome, and serious, holding the small blond child. Her heart ached that she and Nathan had never had a baby together. Yet joy welled in her at Nathan's taking responsibility for the Kirkland orphans. He had made such splendid progress today!

"Well, Reverend," remarked Nathan, "we've a

ham and all sorts of presents and goodies out in the cabriolet."

"You shouldn't have!" protested Celeste.

"It was the least we could do," insisted Emily. She turned to Nathan. "If you'll give me Lucy, perhaps you and the reverend can go unload the boot and stable the horse? I imagine Mrs. Milsap will want to warm up that ham."

"Of course, dear." As Nathan handed Lucy to Emily, the child began to whimper, her little face screwing up in a pout. Emily cuddled the child and spoke to her soothingly as the men stepped out of the house.

"She's taken a real shine to your husband, hasn't she?" asked Celeste, winking at Emily.

Emily patted the fretful child's back. "Indeed, she has."

"Do you two have any children of your own yet?"

Emily shook her head, her eyes lighting with joy as she spotted Kipp across the room, exultantly holding aloft the slipper he'd found behind the pie safe. "No, but I think we shall shortly have *quite* a family."

The woman laughed. "Of course you shall. Michael told me that you and Mr. Fletcher plan to take responsibility for the Kirkland orphans, and I think it's just splendid of you to help them. You're both so young, with so much to give, and all of your lives still ahead of you."

Clucking to the baby, Emily did not reply, her expression solemn. As several happily shrieking children raced by, she shook her head and asked, "How can you manage here, all of you living under one roof?"

The woman shrugged. "Oh, we get by. We have each other, our faith, and our patience, and the Good Lord watching over us. Whenever it seems we haven't a slice of bread left in the larder, or an extra scrap of blanket to ward off the cold, some good soul always comes forward to help us." She brightened visibly. "Michael said the bazaar today earned enough to put on a new roof."

Emily shivered, stepping forward as a draft of cold air hit her back. "It appears to me as if you could use an entirely new orphanage."

"All in good time, dear." She pointed across the room. "Little Lucy seems exhausted. Why don't you go rock her while I check on the meal?"

"Of course."

Emily went to sit in the corner near the tree. As she rocked Lucy, the child at last began to quiet. The baby sucked her thumb, her head resting on Emily's shoulder, her eyelids drooping shut. Exulting in her moments with the child, Emily saw Nathan and the vicar reenter the cottage, their arms heaped with presents. The dozen or so children raced up to watch as the men stacked the presents beneath the tree, and several of the tots smiled shyly at Emily. Nathan and Reverend Milsap made another trip, returning with the ham and other foods.

Removing his coat and hat, Nathan collapsed in a rocker next to Emily. He gazed at little Lucy, who was dozing, then winked at his wife. "She looks about done in for today."

Emily nodded toward the older children, who were howling with laughter as they played blindman's buff," with Kathy the blindfolded one. "The others look as if they're just getting started. But it's so wonderful to see Kipp and Kathy joining in on the fun."

"Indeed." Nathan touched Emily's hand. "The vicar invited us to stay the night. I said no, but I told him I'll be back to see about the children next week."

"But we'll have dinner with them?"

"Certainly, dear. And afterward there'll be an early Christmas Eve candlelight service at the church, just for the orphans. I told him we'd stay for that, as well."

"It sounds lovely," she murmured.

Clutching her hand, he spoke tightly. "Perhaps we can pray for a Christmas miracle, love."

She gazed at him tenderly. "Oh, Nathan. We've already been granted our Christmas miracle."

The two were regarding each other poignantly when the vicar stepped up with a storybook in hand. "Mr. Fletcher, these children are as wild as banshees. At this rate they'll never calm down enough to eat their Christmas dinner. Would you be good enough to read them a story to put them in a more tranquil frame of mind?"

"I'd be delighted," he replied.

The vicar ushered over the children, and they gathered in a circle at Nathan's feet, listening raptly as he read them the legend of "Father Christmas." Emily savored every moment, listening to her husband's deep voice, seeing the awe and magic reflected on the children's faces as they heard the tale.

By the time Nathan finished, the food was on the table and, with expressions of quiet wonder, the children went to take their places. Emily laid the sleeping Lucy on the bed and she and Nathan joined the others, sitting together near the center of the table.

They held hands as the vicar intoned the grace, his voice filled with humble gratitude. "God bless us all this Christmas Eve. Thank you for the bounty you have bestowed on us, and for bringing Kipp, Kathy, and Lucy, as well as Nathan and Emily Fletcher, into our lives this day."

Opening their eyes afterward, Emily and Nathan exchanged a loving glance. They were quickly distracted by a rush of laughter and happy voices as the children popped open their Christmas crackers, happily waving the toys, candy, and paper hats they discovered inside. Soon, with adult assistance, the children were busy heaping their plates with ham, turkey and dressing, sweet potatoes, and hot bread. Toward the end of the meal Lucy stirred, and Emily brought her to the table, feeding her turkey broth and bread.

After all had shared the dessert of fruitcake and mulled cider the group moved toward the tree, and the adults watched in fascination as the children ripped into the many brightly wrapped presents. Emily watched in wonder as Kipp unwrapped his toy train with a shout of glee, and a teary-eyed Kathy hugged her new doll, as the kitten played among the discarded wrappings and bows, her lively antics prompting several orphans to roll about on the floor laughing.

"Oh, Nathan, just look at the children's faces," Emily whispered to him. "They are all so happy."

"Not nearly as happy as you have made me this evening," he whispered back, squeezing her hand.

When all the presents had been opened the group played several rounds of "The Vicar's Cat" and "Flip the Kipper," then everyone bundled up to go to the chapel. Nathan again carried Lucy, and Emily led the two older children. As they tramped across the snow, following the Milsaps and the crew of orphans, he gazed at her wonderingly.

"Why is it I feel as if we've lived our entire marriage in this one day?"

"Perhaps we have," she replied in awe. "Haven't we known more joy today than we knew the entire year we were together?"

"Indeed," he answered with heartfelt sincerity. "Yet it seems so unreal, tramping across the snow with you, knowing that soon . . ." His voice cracked and he couldn't continue.

"I know, dear," she soothed. "Don't think of that now. Just remember all the good times we've shared today."

"Yes, darling." *And tonight we shall share more love than two people have ever known before,* he thought.

The service was beautiful. They all held candles aloft, sang hymns, and heard Reverend Milsap read the story of the nativity. Gazing at his beloved wife reflected in candlelight, Nathan thought of how he'd been given the most wonderful Christmas gift of all—his own angel to love.

But the angels wanted Emily back, and all too soon he must let her go. . . .

The parting with the children at the church door was wrenching, as Kipp and Kathy clung to Emily and Nathan.

"Please, ma'am, can't we come back to London with you tonight?" pleaded Kipp.

"I'm afraid not, dear," she replied, patting his back. "But Mr. Fletcher will be back next week to see about all of you."

"But not you, ma'am?" asked an anxious Kathy.

Shaking her head, Emily smiled at the children through her tears. "You have me in your hearts now. That is what matters most of all."

Nevertheless, the children appeared quite stricken as Celeste stepped up to join them. "Are you certain you folks can't stay the night?"

"No, thank you, madam." Nathan stared down at Lucy, who was blessedly asleep in his arms. "Perhaps you had best take the baby now, Mrs. Milsap, before she stirs."

"Of course."

With more of a feeling of loss than he ever would have anticipated, Nathan handed the darling child to the vicar's wife. He could barely speak during the next gut-wrenching moments, as he and Emily hugged and kissed the tearful Kipp and Kathy, then left.

Clutching Emily's hand as they moved toward the barn, Nathan realized he had lost his heart to her today. Yet part of his heart also lay with the precious family they had discovered together in Avalon. . . .

Chapter Nine

The hour had grown late by the time they arrived at the townhouse in Belgravia. They swept in the front door, ushered in by wind and snow.

Nathan shut and bolted the door, then fumbled about, lighting a taper. Setting it down, he glanced at Emily, who was shivering across from him. "Poor darling, you're all but blue. Come here."

"Gladly." She thrust herself into his arms, and he kissed her cool lips, her frigid cheeks.

"You're so cold, darling, and shaking like a leaf," he fretted, rubbing his hands up and down her spine. "You're not frightened?"

She laughed. "No, just cold."

"I must start a fire upstairs . . . and how does a warm bath sound?"

"Heavenly," she murmured.

"You're heavenly," he replied, kissing her ardently, holding her close until she ceased her shivering.

A moment later he pulled back, eyeing her tenderly. "Before we become carried away I'd best go see to the horse, and bring in your portrait."

She nodded. "I'll start heating up water in the kitchen."

"Don't go off anywhere, now," he scolded. "Promise?"

She wrinkled her nose at him. "I promise."

Kissing her brow, he was off.

Nathan soon returned from the carriage house, bringing in Emily's portrait and setting it on the mantel in the drawing room. He lingered over her angelic likeness for a poignant moment before hastening upstairs to the bedroom to light the fire in the grate. By the time he'd returned to the kitchen Emily had a huge pot of water boiling on the stove. He made several trips fetching buckets of hot water upstairs to fill the porcelain tub.

Soon Emily joined him in the bedroom, staring wistfully at the steaming tub with its charming roses painted around the rim. "Who shall be first?"

Gazing at his wife with profound yearning, Nathan slowly unbuttoned the top button of her collar. "I thought I'd bathe you, darling. It's something else I've never done before."

She blushed deeply. "I've never bathed you, either."

Nathan slowly pulled the pins from Emily's hair, freeing the silken mass and then sliding his fingers into her rich blond tresses and tilting her precious face toward him.

"I'm greedy," he whispered intensely, leaning

over to capture her lips. "I want to minister to you first."

With an ecstatic sigh, Emily kissed him back, absorbing his warmth, his male scent. Delicious shivers coursed over her as his tongue gently pushed inside her mouth. She ran her own tongue over his lips, his teeth, and into his mouth as they clung together for a long moment.

"Oh, darling," he murmured, brushing his lips over her brow, her hair. "My sweet darling . . ."

Slowly, Nathan removed all of Emily's garments—her dress, her chemise; her shoes, stockings, and bloomers. As he worked, he kissed and caressed every inch of her, prompting many an ecstatic sigh.

At last she stepped back and smiled at him, his glorious angel, so eager and unafraid. Nathan's heart pounded in delight as he feasted his eyes on his wife's beautiful body outlined by candlelight—her adorable face, her graceful throat, her high, ripe breasts and her small waist and rounded hips. He lovingly slid his gaze over the golden curls at the joining of her thighs and her long, slender legs. Glancing upward again, he could swear he spotted a halo glowing about her lovely head. His breath caught in his throat.

Then she turned and walked to the dresser, and he followed her, bemused. She took a blue satin ribbon from the bureau tray and began tying up her hair. Staring into the mirror, Nathan watched Emily's lush breasts push upward as she raised her arms. His mouth went dry and he was surprised that his knees still supported him.

He stepped up behind her, wrapping his arms about her, snuggling her against him and cupping her shapely breasts in his hands. Heaven . . . sheer heaven! He heard her sigh of contentment, felt her nestling her bottom sensually against his throbbing arousal. Desire set him reeling. His smoldering gaze met hers in the mirror and they shared a look of profound yearning. She was truly an enchantress, naked and golden in the soft light, with wisps of blond hair pulling free to frame her breathtaking face.

"You've so incredibly lovely," he murmured, leaning over to nibble at her shoulder. "Your skin is so fair and radiant, your smile brighter than dawn. To think that I've never appreciated you."

"You've appreciated me today."

Feeling a shiver rack her body, he turned her in his arms and gazed at her with concern. "You're breaking out in gooseflesh, love."

"But not from the cold," she whispered enticingly, curling her arms about his neck.

With her supple curves pressing against him, passion ran through Nathan with painful intensity. Although he burned to take her to bed then and there, he had already promised himself that tonight he was going to be the soul of patience, the tender, solicitous lover he'd never been before.

"Get into the tub—quickly, now," he beseeched hoarsely.

Smiling, Emily climbed into the tub. Nathan knelt beside her, running the fragrant lavender soap over her body, awed by the beauty of her wet, gleaming skin. He slid the cake seductively over her rounded breasts and puckered nipples, and gloried to her soft, sensual sighs, inhaling her sweet, warm breath as he leaned over to kiss her. He savored her warmth, the taste of her lips, the texture of her sweet mouth, and wished he could go on kissing her forever. After he had cleansed her his fingers lingered between her thighs, probing delicately, and she gasped.

Intently, he observed her face, watching her eyes dilate, her cheeks grow deeply flushed. "I remember how you used to tense up sometimes when I made love to you," he murmured. "Did I ever hurt you?"

Her eyes dark with desire, her lips slightly parted, she regarded him frankly. "I suppose it hurt that there wasn't more feeling between us."

"I won't hurt you tonight, Emily," he whispered with heartfelt emotion. "I promise you."

"I know," she whispered back, leaning forward to kiss him.

"Oh, love." With a groan, Nathan gathered her close, wetting himself with her damp body.

She pressed him away, laughing. "No, Nathan. It's time for me to bathe you—before you ruin that fine suit."

"To hell with my fine suit," he growled.

"Nathan," she reproved.

"Very well," he conceded tightly.

She stepped out of the tub, naked, glowing, totally irresistible. His heart pounding and his breathing shallow, Nathan briskly dried her off, fighting the powerful urge to pull her into his arms and devour her then and there. She was so beautiful, and the dampness, the scent of her, were tantalizing him, driving him mad. Knowing he could have her only fleetingly added poignancy to his already overwhelming need. With trembling hands he helped her into her dressing gown.

Then Emily began undressing *him,* slowly unbuttoning his shirt, roving her lips over his chest, tormenting him with her mouth and hands. With fists clenched and eyes shut, Nathan somehow managed to endure the torture. But when her fingers brushed his manhood as she undid his trousers he could bear no more. Catching her wrist to stay her, he quickly finished the task himself.

Groaning with frustration, he climbed into the tub. As she knelt beside him, he thought of the appealing sight she made, her hair piled in curls on her head, her skin rosy and luminous, her dressing gown gaping open to reveal a shapely breast. He sighed in ecstasy as she ran the soap over his face, neck, shoulders, and chest, slowly lathering the coarse hairs there. As she reached down to cleanse him more intimately, a mighty shudder rippled over him. He slipped a hand inside her dressing gown and caressed her breast, fingering the taut nipple. He heard her helpless moan, then watched her eyes, mindless with yearning, flash to his. Oh, he could not bear it! Moving aside the cloth, he leaned toward her, greedily taking the hard peak into his mouth. Passionately he suckled her, the sounds of her sharp sighs thrilling him beyond reason. He felt her lips press against his hair, while her fingers continued to stroke him intimately.

"Emily, my darling," he rasped, "I don't think I can endure another moment of this. I must hold you, love."

Her face lit by a smile, she rose and grasped the towel. "Shall I dry you, dear?"

"Please."

"If that's what you want," she said primly.

He stood and stepped out of the tub, water sluicing off his painfully aroused body. "What I want, darling," he told her intensely, "is to spend all of eternity with you in my arms."

Her gaze met his, anguished and uncertain. Then a look of utter love settled in as she stepped forward and began drying him off. "We shall have our eternity tonight."

Once again Nathan struggled not to grab his wife as she tenderly ministered to him, rubbing the towel all over his back, his chest, and lower. . . .

But when Emily's fingers again brushed his agonized erection Nathan had reached the breaking point. He caught her wrist and cast the towel aside, his gaze burning into hers. She smiled back in sensual invitation. Groaning his delight, he swept her up into his arms and carried her to the bed. He laid her down and joined her, gently pulling the ribbon from her hair, untying her dressing gown and parting the folds, feasting his eyes once again on her lovely nakedness, the smooth belly, the rose-tipped breasts that seemed made for his kisses—

When she held out her arms to him his bliss was indescribable. He covered her with his nakedness, wrapping his arms around her middle and rooting his mouth to her sweet breast. She was paradise, tasting of lavender and her own special womanly flavor. Her soft belly felt delectable against his chest. He felt her fingers sliding into his wet hair and he moaned in pleasure.

"Yes, Nathan . . . Ah, yes," she encouraged him.

Indeed, Emily felt as if she were already floating in heaven as Nathan kissed her breasts, his slightly bearded face and hair-covered chest deliciously abrading her soft skin. Tears filled her eyes at his sweet wooing, his endearing patience tonight. Almost always before, Nathan had made love to her with passionate urgency. Now he was taking the time to savor and arouse her, to make her feel truly cherished. She loved him so much.

She sighed in delight as he ran his lips and tongue over her breasts, suffusing her with ardent sensation, while his hand slid between her thighs, his fingers tenderly plying her, sending potent strands of desire pushing deep inside her. She cried out at the powerful stimulation. At once he slid upward, until his intense eyes blazed into hers and she could feel his erection probing her intimately.

"I love you, darling Emily," he whispered in a breaking voice. "So much."

"I love you, too, Nathan," she replied exultantly.

"You are a joy and a jewel, the best thing that has ever happened to me," he went on brokenly. "And I've been such a fool. I'm so sorry it has taken me so long to come to my senses—"

She pressed her fingers to his mouth. "No, darling. No more regrets and recriminations. Not tonight."

"But I must know, darling Emily, that I have your forgiveness," he beseeched.

"You have it," she answered soulfully. "And you have my heart. Just love me now. Oh, please, love me."

"I shall, with all my heart." He caressed her cheek and smiled poignantly into her eyes. "Tell me, is it permissible to make love to an angel?"

"Oh, yes, darling. Yes!" she whispered back, tightly clutching him to her.

Nathan kissed her with such aching tenderness that Emily winced with longing. He pulled back, staring into her eyes and burrowing himself into her snug womanhood. She caught a sharp breath and dug her fingernails into his forearms. A moment later she felt swamped with aching pleasure as he pressed home, slowly and steadily sheathing himself, filling her with his vibrant, solid heat. She gasped, stretching upward, frantically seeking his kiss, which he eagerly gave.

"Is it all right for you?" he asked solicitously.

She nodded. "Oh, yes. Never has it felt so wonderful to be with you, Nathan—never so intimate."

"Never has anyone been as perfect for me as you, love," he replied fiercely. "No one can ever take your place. *No one.*"

Half afraid she might try to deny his ardent declaration, Nathan caught her lips in a trembling, tender kiss. He possessed his bride slowly, deeply, exulting in every sweet, shattering sensation as their bodies and souls became one. His mouth on hers, he plied her warm flesh with reverence, with exquisite restraint, until at last she grew impatient, arching her hips and melting into him. Her unrestrained surrender made his passions soar free. He clutched her to his heart and poured himself into her as they both spiraled toward heaven on wings of love. . . .

Chapter Ten

"I must leave you at midnight," Emily whispered.

Nathan and Emily sat downstairs on the parlor settee. Both in dressing gowns, they were wedged together spoon-style, Emily sitting between Nathan's spread legs, his arms possessively crossed over her bosom. A fire blazed in the hearth, filling the room with its warm, cedary scent and the crackling sound of the wood. On the mantel, Emily's angel portrait smiled down at them.

Nathan was in such a euphoric state that at first her softly spoken words did not quite register. When they did he glanced at the clock on the table and saw that only a few moments remained before the hour of twelve; then he stared down at her face in alarm.

"You must leave at midnight? But that is mere

minutes away! You haven't even been with me for a full day as yet!"

She clutched his hand. "It's not how much time we spend together, Nathan. It's the love and happiness we share."

"Oh, God," he muttered. "Why so soon? Why midnight? You aren't Cinderella."

She turned her face up to his and spoke solemnly. "But I'm needed in heaven."

An anguished groan escaped him. "Oh, my darling," he murmured intensely. "No one could ever possibly need you as much as I do." He leaned over and kissed her.

As he drew back, she flashed him a tremulous smile. "You'll be all right, Nathan. I must believe that."

His arms tightened about her. "But—aren't you afraid? I know I am."

She gazed into the snapping flames. "Nathan, do you remember my Irish grandfather?"

He frowned thoughtfully. "You mean old Jack Mullins? Didn't he die while you were still in your teens?"

She nodded. "He told me so many stories and traditions about Ireland, and one was about midnight on Christmas Eve. You see, the Irish believe that at midnight the gates of heaven are opened, and all souls may enter."

Shutting his eyes in torment, Nathan buried his lips in her hair, inhaling its dusky fragrance. "I can't lose you now," he said achingly. "I just can't."

She twisted about to gaze up at him. "Haven't you learned anything from our day together?"

"I learned I love you more than life itself."

"I love you, too," she replied. She stroked the

strong contour of his jaw. "But you learned much else, Nathan. You learned to be joyful."

He swallowed hard. "So I did, love. Because I watched us experience more joy in one day than most people know in a lifetime."

"You learned to think of others more than yourself."

"Yes, I did," he acknowledged, his voice breaking.

Her expression grew radiant. "And perhaps we both learned the true meaning of Christmas—love, happiness, and giving to others."

"Oh, my love." Kissing her brow, her hair, Nathan struggled against the sorrow rising in his throat. "What about hope, Emily? What about hope?"

She tilted her sweet face up to his. "Think of the hope you've given Kipp, Kathy, and Lucy. You won't let them down, will you?"

"Never," he promised fiercely.

"You'll have to be there for them, Nathan," she said quietly. "You can't succumb to despair."

"I'll want to," he confessed.

"I know, darling. But you can't."

"You're right." He pressed his lips to her ear. "You've given me enough love to last a lifetime."

"Oh, Nathan." Her hand tightly grasped his. "You've given me enough love for all eternity."

They cuddled together for a poignant moment, his cheek pressed against hers. Then, all at once, they both tensed as the clock began to chime out the midnight hour. Emily went pale and rose to her feet. Nathan also stood, and they stared at each other in awe and uncertainty.

"Emily, what is it?" Then, hearing the cruel

clock continue to chime, watching her grow more wan, he cried, "No!"

She held out her arms to him, her eyes bright with tears, gleaming with love. "Nathan, hold me. Kiss me good-bye! Now, while there's yet time."

"Oh, God!" Desperately, Nathan crushed his wife close, kissing her cheeks, her lips, her hair. "No, you can't go! I won't let you go!"

"Please, Nathan," she beseeched. "Say it, now."

Gazing at her beloved face through the mist of his tears, Nathan whispered, "Good-bye, my angel," and then he kissed her again, with all his heart. . . .

The clock ceased chiming and Nathan felt Emily slip from his embrace. He saw her gliding away and reached for her, too late. Even as he watched helplessly, the golden mist began to rise up about her and his beloved angel began to fade before his very eyes. He could feel her essence swirling about him, her sweetness enveloping him like a benediction as she drifted away. Disoriented, he tried to find her, to grasp her, but he felt as if his fingers were sifting through sand. . . .

A moment later the mist lifted, and a dazed Nathan stood holding Emily's porcelain angel, miraculously made whole again, in his hand. He blinked at the glittering statuette in disbelief. For a crazed moment he wondered if he had dreamed Emily's being there with him. Had he never broken the angel? Had his bride never appeared?

If so, 'twas a cruel dream indeed!

Then he glanced at the mantel and saw the portrait, saw his beloved angel smiling down at him—

A wrenching cry escaped him. Yes, she had been

here, here to save his soul, here to give him more joy and love than he had deserved. Here to bless him with the miracle of his own salvation. Now she was gone. Gone to heaven.

Clutching the porcelain angel to his heart, Nathan slid to his knees. His shoulders heaved. He wept at having lost his wife, although in his heart he knew he had found her forever. . . .

On Christmas morn, his wedding anniversary, Nathan sat alone in the darkened parlor, drinking brandy and brooding. By rights he and Emily should have spent Christmas day with his family in Mayfair, but like a typical ungrateful son he had neglected even to inform his parents of his plans to go to Paris. He had assumed Emily would tell them. Now there was no Emily; he would have to explain matters to them later on.

Although Nathan's despair was agonizing, it still seemed almost unreal to him that his wife was now dead, especially since they had laughed and loved together mere hours before. He could still smell her in this room, could still almost feel her supple body next to his, could hear the soft echo of her laughter. And her likeness smiled at him vibrantly from the fireplace mantel, as if she had never left him.

But she had left and pain clawed at Nathan's heart. He had decided to allow himself a few hours alone with his morose thoughts before he embarked to bring his wife home. Then there would be funeral arrangements to see to. Afterward he must assume responsibility for the orphans he had promised to care for.

He would go on with his life and become the

person he had promised Emily he would become. He would be strong for her. Even though his beloved wife was gone, she *had* taught him much: that true happiness came from giving, not from receiving; that joy came from selflessness, from placing the welfare of others above his own desires.

But for now, for just a few hours more, he would allow himself to be weak, to miss her, to ache for her with a pain that was soul-shattering. . . .

Nathan had not realized he had dozed until he heard a knock at the front door. Blinking and stumbling to his feet, he moved aside a shade to note the waning day outside. Mercy, he must have slept for hours.

The knock came again. He groaned. When he and Emily had not appeared for Christmas dinner his parents must have sent the coachman to fetch them.

He wended his way to the front door and threw it open. He gaped at the sight before him.

"Merry Christmas, Nathan," Emily whispered. "And happy anniversary."

"Emily! My God!" Staggered by shock and joy, Nathan hauled his bride into his arms, whirled her about, and then pulled back to gaze at her in stupefaction. Emily appeared very much alive—rosy-cheeked, bright-eyed, dressed in a wool cloak and matching bonnet. "Is it truly you?"

"Oh, yes, darling."

"Are you real?"

"As real as the snow on the stoop," she said brightly.

"But . . . did I dream you before?"

She shook her head solemnly. "No, Nathan, you didn't dream me."

"Good heavens . . . but how?" Watching her shiver, he grabbed her hand. "Let's get you inside. I have a kiss for you that should warm your toes."

She laughed. Nathan pulled her inside, shut the door, and gathered her close, kissing her hungrily for an endless moment.

When at last they pulled apart to catch their breath he stared in wonder at her lovely, gleaming face. "I can't believe you're truly here."

"I'm here."

"And you're alive?"

"I'm alive, Nathan."

"You're here to stay this time?"

"Oh, yes."

"Thank God! But how, Emily?"

"I'll try to explain."

Nathan threw his arms around his bride and shuddered with overwhelming relief. "Let's get you in by the fire."

He led her into the parlor and helped her remove her coat and bonnet. They sat down together, staring at each other in awe and joy.

"Can you tell me what happened?" he asked. "I thought you had died and were bound for heaven."

"So did I," she whispered. A faraway, wistful expression gripped her lovely features. "It was so strange, Nathan. After I left you I found myself back in the room where I was dying, floating above my body again. The angel appeared before me once more. Then the oddest thing happened. . . . "

"What, darling?" he asked eagerly.

Radiantly, she smiled at him. "The angel told me my work on earth is not yet finished, that it was time for me to go back to my body—and back to you."

"Oh, Emily!" Nathan exclaimed. "You mean we've been given a second chance?"

She nodded ecstatically. "I think that was the greatest Christmas miracle of all, Nathan."

He pulled her close. "You're the greatest miracle of all, love." Exultantly, he kissed her lips, her hair, her cheek. "Tell me what happened to you then."

"Well, when I arrived back in my body my fever broke. Within moments I felt as if reborn, filled with energy. The fisherman's wife lent me some clothing; then the fisherman took me to Portsmouth in his boat. From there I caught the train back to London."

"Oh, Emily! I can't tell you how delighted I am to have you back!" He clasped her hands tightly in his own. "Merry Christmas, my darling. And happy anniversary. We shall celebrate many, many more, for I'm not going to let heaven have you for a long, long time."

They cuddled together for many moments, basking in the glory of their rediscovered love. Then, between kisses, Emily gazed up at her husband in puzzlement. "Nathan, I can't quite figure something out."

"What, my Christmas angel?" he asked, taking one of her hands and raising it to his lips.

"Why do you suppose I was allowed to live, after all?"

Nathan considered her question carefully; then a heartfelt smile lit his face. "Because, my darling, we had to lose our love to find it. That was the angel's true message, I know. During the day we spent together you helped me save my soul and redeem our love. Now we shall experience the miracle of living our love every day for the rest of our lives. We shall celebrate every day together as if it were our last."

Appearing delighted, she threw her arms about his neck. "Yes, darling, that's just what we must do."

"Starting now . . ." he murmured, nibbling at her throat.

She sighed dreamily. "But . . . when shall we go fetch our new family?"

"Will tomorrow suffice?" he replied. "I don't want to seem selfish, Mrs. Fletcher, but I must have a little more time alone with you before I am willing to share you."

"But you will share me?"

"We'll both share our lives with the children, darling."

She beamed her happiness. "Oh, Nathan, I'm so proud of you."

"Not nearly as proud as I am that you're mine," he said in an emotional voice. "You've given me back my life, Emily. Now come closer, you adorable creature." He pulled her onto his lap. "I'm going to love you until neither of us can breathe."

She dimpled, then snapped her fingers. "Oh, I almost forgot."

He eyed her with alarm. "Don't tell me you're going to spring a new surprise on me?"

"But this is a wonderful surprise," she assured him, her face aglow. "Right as I was returning to

my body the angel whispered something in my ear. A beautiful secret."

"What?"

"Shall I whisper it to you?" she asked earnestly.

He nodded, and she did.

"When?" he asked in elation.

"Before next Christmas. Just think—Kipp, Kathy, and Lucy will be able to share the wonderful gift with us."

A slow smile spread across Nathan's face. "Did the angel know whether the secret will be a boy or a girl?"

Emily laughed. "Angels won't tell everything. That would spoil all the fun."

He touched her nose. "Does this angel know?"

She wrinkled her nose at him.

He leaned over and nuzzled his lips against her chin. "I am going to find out all of this angel's secrets. I am going to unwrap her, savor her, love her, for she's the best Christmas present I've ever had."

With Emily's angel watching over them from the mantel, Nathan and Emily celebrated the miracle of their love. . . .

AMY ELIZABETH SAUNDERS

A TIME FOR JOY

For Shirley

Chapter One

"It's starting again."

Hilary looked up from the cash register and stared at the Christmas tree that stood in the middle of the shop: eight feet of noble fir, decorated with golden trumpets and tassels and angels dressed in Renaissance splendor.

It started slowly, just as it had been doing all morning. A few little white lights began to dim, then glow brighter. A few more went off completely, and then others began to flash steadily, their soft glow growing brighter and brighter. The tree seemed to shimmer, the porcelain angels swaying beneath the fragrant green boughs.

Then, as abruptly as the electrical frenzy had started, it stopped. For a few seconds the tree was dark. Then, without warning, all twenty strings of lights flashed on again.

A few customers, their arms full of last-minute gifts, looked at the performing tree and then went about their business, strolling through the tranquil peach-and-cream showroom of Exclusively Lauren's, sorting through racks of silk peignoir sets and antique tables of sachets and bubble baths and eighteenth-century wardrobes displaying delicately made nightgowns of linen and Venice lace.

For those fortunate enough to be able to afford the merchandise offered at Hilary Lauren's store, the shop was a delight to all the senses. For years, Hilary had searched antique stores, estate sales, and auction houses for the perfect blend of mirrors, light fixtures, and furniture. The peach-and-cream-patterned carpets were reproductions from a Victorian millinery shop in Paris, the wallpaper an exact copy from the boudoir of a Georgian countess. A professional lighting designer had fitted the crystal wall sconces with bulbs that cast the customers in flattering shades of rose and peach. The soft, warm music of baroque composers wafted gently through the air, soothing the happy shoppers. And always, the scent of the delicate sachet filled the shop, a scent that Hilary had blended exclusively for her store at a Paris *parfumerie.*

Yes, it was expensive. But it was that attention to detail that made Hilary's customers feel privileged to pay three hundred dollars for a nightgown.

"Entering Exclusively Lauren's," one magazine article had reported, "feels like being caught in a web of Victorian lace. The modern world recedes, and a fairy-tale beauty captivates the weary shopper."

Flowery, perhaps, but true. At Exclusively Lauren's, everything was perfect.

Until today.

A high-pitched, whirring noise sounded at Hilary's elbow, and she jumped back, staring. The cash register lights flickered, and yards of white adding tape began shooting out like serpentine streamers, piling up on the gleaming cherry counter.

Shirley put a slender hand to her heart, and her eyes met those of her employer.

"It's the ghost of Christmas Eve," she said, treating the mysterious mishap with a levity that Hilary didn't appreciate. That was just like Shirley. Her enthusiasm and good nature prevailed in the face of disaster—and today was turning out to be a disaster.

"When is the electrician supposed to get here?" Hilary demanded. Christmas Eve was one of her most lucrative days. Every year she was descended upon by hordes of businessmen, who seemed to have a genetic flaw that predisposed them to last-minute shopping. Eager to please their wives, they streamed in and out of the store, carrying the mauve-and-pink-striped boxes tied in white ribbon that were Hilary's trademark.

"Owen's said they'd find somebody, but it might take a while," Shirley reassured her. "After all, it's hard on Christmas Eve. Most people are with their families."

Was there a mild reproach in Shirley's voice? She had asked for the day off, but Hilary simply couldn't spare her. Thirty percent of the shop's profits were made in December, and a good percentage of those on the twenty-fourth. And the customers loved Shirley, who was elegant and silver-haired, and remembered their names, greeting each one as if she was a visiting relative.

Hilary, they respected. Shirley, they loved.

The cash register spit out the end of the white tape, gave a high-pitched whine, and died.

"I don't believe this," Hilary said. "I guess we start adding by hand."

Across the store, the light fixtures began a frantic twinkle, and a couple of customers glanced at them, alarmed.

"Where is that electrician?" she asked for the fortieth time since the store had opened. All too clearly she could imagine faulty wires exploding into flame, and thousands of dollars worth of merchandise going up in smoke.

"Don't worry, sweetie, he'll be here," Shirley assured her. "Just relax, and think about your party tonight."

Hilary drew a deep breath. The party. It wasn't just any party, and thinking about it didn't relax her. It was the party of all parties, the invitation she had been coveting for years. It was only after the Seattle *Times* had listed her as one of the city's top ten businesswomen of the year that she had been included on the exclusive guest list.

The invitation to the Vanderheyden Christmas Eve Ball meant that she had made it. The little girl from the suburbs was one of the city's social elite. The thought of the party had occupied Hilary's mind for weeks. She had been to the hairdresser that morning, and her brown pageboy was twisted high into an elegant roll, and her nails were carefully manicured and polished a wintery pink.

All thoughts of her electrical problems faded, and she automatically began straightening a display of silk camisoles beaded with tiny pearls. Tonight was the most important night of her life, the night she would really take her place in the society to which she had always wanted to belong.

In a wild gesture of self-indulgence, she had flown to Los Angeles and ordered a custom-made gown from Petra Bazhenov, whose creations graced the pages of *Vogue* and appeared on at least one Academy Award nominee every year.

Seven thousand dollars; she had spent seven thousand dollars on an evening gown. She should feel guilty, but she didn't. Instead, she felt a warm pleasure whenever she thought of it—shimmering, bias-cut, ice blue silk covered with yards of seed pearls and Austrian crystals.

When she put on the Bazhenov dress the chubby little high school girl who dressed in K-Mart specials disappeared forever. She wasn't Lard-ass Lauren, sitting alone in the cafeteria, pretending she was rich and elegant.

She was Hilary Lauren, rich, successful, and smart, the envy of all the little clear-complexioned blond girls who had snubbed her so many times, in so many cruel, childish ways.

"Hilary?"

Startled, she glanced up to see Shirley, her arms full of pink and mauve boxes.

"Security's on the phone. The silent alarm keeps going off."

"The alarm system isn't even on!" Hilary was reaching the end of her rope.

"I know, hon, I double-checked it. But that's what they say."

"I don't believe this." Hilary took a deep breath and rested her forehead in her hand. "What next?"

"Snow," Shirley suggested.

"Don't be funny. I've lived in Seattle for twenty-nine years and it's snowed for Christmas exactly twice. The last thing in the world I need is snow."

"Then don't look outside," Shirley advised.

Hilary whirled around. Beyond the beveled glass panes of the storefront, Fourth Avenue was a Christmas card scene. Every store, tree, and shrub sparkled with a million white lights. The window displays were at their best, glittering with rich color. Last-minute holiday shoppers were rushing by with their arms full of packages, past doorways hung with rich evergreens. And snow.

It came barreling down from the charcoal skies, a million sparkling white flakes, faster and thicker than any snow in Hilary's memory. Already, the street was white, and the barren branches of the fairy-lit trees were frosted, and the roofs of passing cars were covered as their windshield wipers swung more away.

The shopping crowd seemed delighted with the sudden turn of events, laughing as the white flakes dusted their hair and shoulders. A passing vagrant, wearing layers of tattered clothes and carrying a blanket that seemed more hole than fabric, decided to take refuge in the doorway of Exclusively Lauren's and treat the passing crowd to a spirited and off-key rendition of "Jingle Bells."

"Fabulous," Hilary observed. "That's all we need. Shirley, can you take care of that?"

Incredibly, Shirley was laughing. "What—the snow, or the caroler?"

She stopped laughing at the sight of Hilary's face.

"Sorry, honey. My goodness, don't let it bother you. He's just got a little Christmas spirit."

"Probably a full bottle of it," Hilary agreed.

Shirley hurried to the door. Hilary watched as she smiled at the tattered man, as graciously as if he was a favorite customer, and offered him a few rolled-up bills from her pocket, pointing down the street as she did so.

The vagrant accepted the money with an unsteady bow and smile, gathered his decrepit blanket around his shoulders, and moved on.

Shirley hurried back in, stopping to tidy a rack of satin pajamas. "Mr. Pavarotti's on his way to have lunch," she informed Hilary.

"From which liquor store?" Hilary asked, frowning at the snow, which was getting thicker by the minute.

Shirley's humor wasn't disturbed. "Oh, Hilary, does it matter? We have so much. And it's Christmas, after all. Where's your holiday spirit?"

Hilary stopped, suddenly feeling a chill that had nothing to do with the change in the weather.

Where was her holiday spirit? For the first time in years she felt its absence as clearly as if she were feeling the loss of an arm or a leg.

When had she lost it—that feeling of magic, that indefinable feeling of hope and happiness that touched people in the dead of winter?

She told herself that it was something that simply disappeared with childhood, but she knew that wasn't so. Shirley had it, and she was at least twenty-five years older than Hilary. The passing shoppers had it, laughing at the snow even though it would tangle traffic and disrupt their plans. Even the drunken vagrant on the street, who would probably spend the night shivering in a cardboard box in a dark alley—even he was able to find pleasure in the snow, and sing to the shining flakes that fell from the sky.

And yet she, Hilary Lauren, young, attractive, successful, and well on her way to being rich, with her beautiful home on Mercer Island and one of the most elegant stores in the city—she was bereft of something that they all had.

To the casual observer, no young woman ever had less cause to be unhappy. But there she stood, in the middle of her beautiful store, feeling as if she had been robbed of something precious.

Maybe it was the sudden and surprising sheen of tears that covered her eyes, but she could swear that the dark evergreen in the middle of the room shivered.

It did . . . the porcelain angels and gold silk tassels were swaying slightly; then the light show began again, blinking and twinkling wildly.

As soon as it stopped, she looked across the room at Shirley, who had stopped wrapping packages and was looking at the tree, shaking her head slowly.

Their eyes met, and Shirley lifted her shoulders in a helpless gesture.

Hilary stared out the window at the snow that was rapidly blanketing the city.

"Where *is* that electrician?" she demanded of nobody in particular.

Somebody pinched her arm.

She jumped, looking around.

There was nobody there. Nobody at all. The nearest shopper stood at least ten feet away.

"Nerves," she told herself, and hurried to wait on a handsome businessman who was examining a pink velvet bathrobe with satin lapels and a three-hundred-dollar price tag.

By two o'clock the shopping crowd was peaking, and Hilary and Shirley were doing everything they could to keep up. The cash register was down, and everything had to be added by hand. Each purchase was wrapped in lace-printed tissue, with *Exclusively Lauren's* printed on it in gold script, and then into the striped boxes, and tied with gleaming white ribbon.

The flickering lights had to be explained, over and over again, to curious customers, and the damned electrician was nowhere in sight.

Hilary was restocking a display counter when he finally arrived.

"Does Marie Antoinette shop here?"

Startled, she looked up from her work.

He was tall and had beautiful dark eyes, with thicker lashes than any man had a right to. His dark hair needed cutting, and fell in shining waves over the fraying collar of his denim jacket. He had the chiseled cheekbones and straight nose of a soap opera hero, and long straight legs. His Levi's were ripped at one knee, and his heavy work boots tracked melting snow on the perfect peach and gold patterns of her carpet.

He was looking around at the shop as if he found it slightly ridiculous—the delicate swags of dried roses, the tasseled lengths of rich fabric draped over the tabletops, the nightgowns displayed over gossamer clouds of antique lace.

He held a child by one hand: a little girl, maybe seven years old, with long brown hair that curled down the back of a worn ski jacket. She looked at Hilary with solemn brown eyes. She had purple rubber boots on, and a sticky candy cane in one small hand, the end licked to a pencil-sharp point.

"May I help you?" Hilary asked, suddenly aware that she was staring.

He smiled, as if they were sharing a joke. "I think I'm supposed to help you. Owen's sent me out. I'm the electrician."

Hilary frowned, remembering the last electrician from Owen's, a balding man in pristine coveralls who had installed her alarm system. "I was expecting someone else."

"George Putnam, but he wouldn't come. They sent us, instead."

Hilary looked from the dark-haired man to the grubby little girl, whose candy cane was dangerously close to a display of silk nightgowns. Melted snow dropped from her boots onto the carpet.

"Us? Is this your assistant?" The stress of the day was showing in her voice, she knew.

The little girl looked up and blushed at the annoyed tone of Hilary's voice. She slipped to her father's side, burying her hand more deeply in his. Hilary felt immediately ashamed of her short temper.

The electrician didn't seem fazed at all. "Yup. This is Bashful. Sleepy and Doc and Dopey couldn't make it. Bashful, meet Grumpy."

The child looked up and cast a tender smile at him.

Grumpy! Hilary drew an indignant breath and was about to speak when Mrs. Addington Green the Third passed by with no fewer than eight boxes in her arms. She stopped to smile at Hilary, giving the electrician and his daughter a quick stare. Her eyes were curious, her moonlike face buried deeply in her mink collar. "There you are, Hilary! Will I be seeing you at the Vanderheyden ball tonight?"

"I wouldn't miss it," Hilary assured her.

"Wonderful. We've missed you at the tennis club."

"Maybe after Christmas," Hilary replied. "I've just been so busy."

Mrs. Addington Green gave the handsome electrician a greedy stare. "So I see. Is this a friend of yours, dear?"

"I'm her date for tonight," he said, his eyes sparkling with mischief. "I just came by to see if I should wear the Levi's with the hole in the knee or the hole in the rear."

Mrs. Addington Green blinked and then gave a startled, uncomfortable laugh.

The little girl took her candy cane out of her mouth. "Is your coat made out of real dead animals?" she asked, wide-eyed.

Mrs. Addington Green lost her smile. "Why . . . why, yes, I suppose it is," she said, tight-lipped. "Good night, Hilary."

Hilary glared at the grinning electrician. "Look, Mr. . . . "

"Jake. Jake Burton. And this is Amanda."

"Okay, fine. I called for an electrician, not a comedian. I don't appreciate you making remarks to my customers."

"Sorry." He didn't sound at all sorry. "I guess we'd better get to work. If you'll just drop your underpants, you can show me what's wrong, and I'll take care of it."

Hilary's jaw dropped; she drew in a deep breath and then looked at her hands, which were full of the satin underpants she'd been arranging.

"Sorry. Couldn't pass it up." Again, he seemed not a bit sorry. Hilary was blushing like a teenager.

"Well, make an effort. I'm having a bad day, and I've got a lot to do before tonight."

"Ah, yes. The Voodenweasel ball." He made it sound ridiculous.

"Vanderheyden," Hilary corrected. She turned away from his bright smile and heaved a sigh. "I called you here about the electricity."

"That's usually why one calls an electrician."

"Mr. Burton . . ."

Across the store little Amanda, candy cane, wet boots, and all, was climbing onto a precious Victorian fainting couch and reclining against the antique upholstery. Dreamy eyed, she stared at the Christmas tree.

Immediately, as if on cue, it began its light show.

"There," Hilary said. "Do you see that? It's been like that all day. And not just the tree. The lights, the cash register, the alarm system. And the phone. It cuts in and out, and I'm losing business because of it."

The tree gave a final twinkle and stopped.

"We have a tree," Amanda said helpfully, "but it's naked. We're going shopping when we're done here."

Shirley smiled at the little girl. "Isn't that wonderful?" she asked, apparently seeing nothing wrong with Amanda's wet purple boots on the antique furniture. "What are you buying?"

"Presents," Amanda announced, her cheeks flushing happily. "And Christmas ornaments."

Briefly, Hilary wondered what kind of parents left their Christmas shopping till the afternoon of the twenty-fourth. The irresponsible kind, probably. She turned back to Jake Burton.

"Well, what do you think the problem is?"

Even as she asked, the overhead lights began flickering wildly, and the piped-in music sped up, slowed, and stopped.

"Poltergeists?" he suggested in a very unprofessional, lighthearted way.

"That's what I keep saying," Shirley chimed in, laughing. "The ghost of Christmas present."

"I think it's an angel," little Amanda said, rearranging a sachet display with her sticky fingers.

"Some angel," Hilary remarked.

"Or, it could be power surges. Let me run out to the truck and get my tools, and I'll test a couple of outlets," Jake said.

Hilary noticed that she wasn't the only woman who turned to watch as he left the store.

He probably wasn't as good-looking or charismatic as he seemed, she reasoned. It was probably just the fact that he was so . . . so . . . *male,* in such a feminine environment. He was definitely out of place in the Victorian boudoir atmosphere of the store.

"Do you think my daddy's handsome?" asked a small voice at Hilary's side.

Suddenly aware that she was staring at the seat

of the electrician's jeans, and enjoying it, Hilary blushed.

"Women just love him," Amanda added, as if it was something she had heard often. Her wide brown eyes were watchful, disconcerting.

"Amanda, wouldn't you like to draw pictures, or something?" Hilary asked.

She led the little girl to a cozy chair next to the counter and hastily handed her a pile of her good business stationery and a pen.

There was too much to worry about today. Call and confirm her limousine reservations for tonight. Check with the caterers, who were delivering the food for her Christmas-day brunch tomorrow morning. Call the ad agency, and check that her after-Christmas sale ads were mailed and going to print in the morning paper of the twenty-sixth. Make a phone call to her sister, who was annoyed that Hilary was spending her holiday with "a bunch of pretentious strangers" rather than her own family.

Who wouldn't want to? Hilary wondered, thinking of her sister's tiny, chaotic house, with kids and dogs and football games blaring on the TV.

"Ouch!" For the second time that day she felt the sharp sting of a pinch on her arm.

But no one was there.

"What's wrong?" Shirley asked, frowning, as she looked up over a tidy column of figures.

A nervous shiver raced over Hilary's back.

"Nothing. Nerves, I guess."

Jake Burton bounded back into the shop, laughing and shaking snow from his dark hair. He set a battered toolbox down next to a Victorian armoire displaying a pastel rainbow of silk gowns and smiled at Hilary.

"Okay, boss. Show me the nearest outlets and we'll get down to business."

"Here? In the middle of the store?"

His smile faltered, and his warm brown eyes narrowed.

"This is where you're having problems, isn't it? Unless, of course, you prefer that I stand out on the street with the rest of the commoners, and let you fix your own wiring."

"Sorry," Hilary replied quickly. "I didn't mean that the way it sounded."

"Hey, it's not my problem," he told her, his tone implying that it was hers. "I'm here to fix things and get the hell out. I'm asking twenty-five dollars an hour, and I'd like to be paid in cash."

"I don't pay cash," Hilary retorted, offended at his arrogant tone, "I bill the contractor at the end of the month."

"I don't work for Owen's, I work for myself, and those are the conditions I work under, at least for today."

His words were a challenge—like it or lump it, they said.

Hilary considered telling him to lump it. What was it about good-looking men? They thought that they were superior to everyone, that they had special rights. If only it hadn't taken her so long to find an electrician. . . .

His dark eyes looked as if he was mocking her, and for an awful, long moment she felt like fat little Hilary Lauren again, uncertain of everything but the fact that she was despised.

"Fine," she snapped, "but try not to interfere with business."

She hurried towards the back room, feeling his eyes on her. It made her terribly self-conscious, and she had to remind herself that her winter-white suit was only a size six, and not a sixteen.

She straightened her suit, smoothed her hair, and ducked back into the store, in time to see Jake, a gray gadget with protruding wires in his hand, laughing with a customer.

The woman was pretty, and holding a velvet Dior bustier in each hand.

"Definitely the wine red," Jake was advising her. "The black is nice, but the red is hot."

Hilary dropped her forehead into her hand and took a deep breath.

"Electrician, comedian, intimate apparel consultant," she murmured. "What next?"

"Hilary?" Shirley was hanging up the phone, her face drooping with concern. "That was the limousine service. Their cars are all down because of the snow, and they can't get you to the Vanderheydens' tonight."

Snow. Flashing lights. Burglar alarms. Smart-ass electricians. No ride to the party.

"Merry Christmas to me," Hilary muttered. "What next?"

Chapter Two

He was in her way. Everywhere she turned he was there, stretching out on the floor, with his long legs blocking the flow of traffic, bent over outlets loosening wires, with his rear end on display, talking to customers, and singing along with the music as if he had no idea he couldn't sing.

Ignore him, Hilary told herself, but her eyes were drawn to him, to the slim line of his waist, to the way his shirt stretched over the muscles of his back when he worked, the way his hair shone, thick and dark and unruly.

He had a dimple in one cheek, and his eyes crinkled in an endearing way when he smiled. His hands were strong and masculine, yet strangely graceful as they handled screwdrivers and wires and outlet covers.

But still, the lights flickered and the phone rang,

and the cash register turned on at three and off again at three-thirty.

And Amanda sat behind the counter, making drawing after drawing, a pile of paper building around her and her candy cane growing shorter and shorter.

Hilary tried to stay calm and think of the party tonight. In just three and a half hours she'd be eating boneless pheasant stuffed with wild mushrooms and drinking champagne and dancing in her seven-thousand-dollar gown.

"I can't believe the limo canceled," she said to Shirley.

Shirley straightened her scarf, a rich paisley print fastened with a gold brooch. "It isn't the end of the world," she pointed out with an uncharacteristic lack of sympathy. "After all, you can drive yourself, Hilary."

"Some people don't have cars," Amanda said, looking up from the floor. She was drawing a picture of a man and a little girl, smiling and holding hands in front of a crooked tree.

"That's true," Shirley agreed.

Jake approached the counter and leaned against it as if he owned it. "If you're afraid to drive in the snow, I could drop you off," he offered.

Hilary looked out at the battered van parked in front of the store and imagined it puttering up the stately Vanderheyden drive and herself climbing out in her designer gown.

"Thanks, but I can do it," she said, smiling at the image.

"Then you should go and get changed soon," Shirley suggested, "because traffic's going to be a nightmare. Where did you hang your dress, honey?"

Hilary froze.

Her stomach flipped and she closed her eyes.

"Oh, my Lord."

"What?" Shirley demanded. "What is it?"

Hilary wanted to cry. "I forgot it," she announced, and her voice was small and shaken. "I was so excited, and in such a hurry, I left it hanging over the arm of the couch."

It was ridiculous. It was completely unlike her. She was always organized, always on top of everything. Her evening bag was packed, her diamond earrings waiting in their velvet box, her shoes and stockings waiting in her tote bag in the back room, and *she had forgotten her dress.*

"Wear what you have on," Amanda said helpfully. "That's pretty."

"Not for this party," Hilary said. "It's not good enough. Oh, my God, I forgot it. Can you believe this, Shirley? I forgot a seven-thousand-dollar dress?"

"I can't believe anyone would spend seven thousand dollars on a dress," Jake put in. "What does it do, vacuum the floors and do the dishes when you're not wearing it?"

Hilary was about to answer when a young man appeared at the counter, a bulky ski jacket open over a wine-red chef's apron. He held four large boxes in his arms.

"I'm from Not Just Desserts," he announced. "Where do you want your food?"

Hilary's head snapped to attention. The headache that was starting between her eyes stretched and pulled. "You're joking."

He checked the yellow paper in his hand. "Hilary Lauren? Brunch menu for sixteen?"

"I'm Hilary, and yes, I ordered brunch for sixteen—"

"So, where do you want it?"

Hilary's voice shivered like a winter wind. "At my house. On Mercer Island. Tomorrow morning."

The young man raised his brow and drew his mouth up tightly. "That's impossible. We don't deliver on Christmas, and it says right here—"

"I don't care what it says!" Hilary had never, ever, raised her voice in the store before. But this was different. Her perfect Christmas was falling apart before her eyes, and it was too late to do anything about it. "I know what I ordered, damn it, and I don't forget things!"

Jake Burton raised a dark brow. "What about your dress?"

Hilary ignored him.

"Well, did you or did you not sign this order?" the catering deliverer demanded, offering her the paper.

Hilary seized the order and stared at it in disbelief. "Well, that's my signature, but that's not what it said when I signed it."

The young man shrugged and pointed. "You ordered at four p.m., November the thirtieth?"

"Yes, but—"

"This is your order."

The store was deathly silent. A couple of customers watched nervously.

"It's not the end of the world," Shirley said for the second time that day. "Just put it in your car and heat it up tomorrow. I'm sure everything will be fine."

Hilary reached behind the counter and withdrew her keys. "Shirley, show him my car," she said stiffly. "Put everything in the trunk."

"Got it," the delivery man agreed, relieved.

"And tell your manager that I will never, *ever,* do business with him again."

"Gee, we'll really miss you," the young man said, his insincere tone implying that Hilary had not been the easiest of customers. Shirley hurried out behind him.

The Christmas tree gave a little shiver and sparkle.

Hilary dropped her face into her hands and took a deep, quivering breath.

"Hey, cheer up." Jake pulled her hands away and patted them, as if he had a right to. "Like Shirley said, you can heat the stuff up tomorrow. And as for your dress, you can swing by and change on your way to the Voopenweenie party. If you're a little late, so what?"

His hands were warm and strangely comforting. For a moment Hilary was distracted by the unfamiliar sight of a man's hands holding her own.

She shivered and pulled away. "You don't understand. It *is* important. I've been planning this for months—"

"Plans change. We change with them. On the grand scale of things, so what? So, you miss dinner and get there in time for dancing and general foo-fooing about. There are people out there going without food tonight, and people who don't have enough money to pay their rent, much less throw away seven thousand dollars on a dress. Put it in perspective."

"It may seem silly to you," Hilary retorted, "but it's important to me. And I don't want to be late, and if this day keeps going the way it has been, I'm going to scream. I swear, somebody cursed me!"

As if on cue, the fire alarms began beeping. Hilary rushed through the store, looking for smoke, but found none. She ran back into the office and threw the switch that disabled the alarm.

When she came back into the showroom Jake was packing up his tools, his dark hair falling over his forehead.

"Did you find the problem?" she asked.

"There is no problem."

She *was* losing her mind.

"Excuse me. I thought I heard you say there wasn't a problem."

"There isn't. At least, none that I can find. The current is moving through all the outlets and switches at the normal rate, we're not showing any power surges, the wires are all in order, and nothing is overloaded. The only thing I can suggest is an exorcist."

"What?"

He was grinning again, his brown eyes sparkling as if everything was just swell.

"Or the ghostbusters. Anything else been strange around here? Things going bump in the night? Cold spots, unexplained noises? Has your head been rotating repeatedly?"

How dare he make light of this? How dare he come into her beautiful store and annoy and aggravate her, and lecture her, and then tell her everything was just fine?

"Well, that's all I can suggest. Two-and-a-half hours, at twenty-five per, is about sixty-five dollars."

Hilary took a deep, angry breath. "You've got to be kidding," she said, and her words fell out like rocks hitting the sidewalk, slow and hard.

He had the nerve to look surprised. "The hell I am. I gave you two and a half hours of honest work, and I expect to be paid for it."

"Honest work, my foot! You look at these lights and you tell me we don't have an electrical problem! Sorry, Charlie, I wasn't born yesterday. You're no more an electrician than I am."

The good-natured look vanished from his face. He drew a deep breath and shook his dark hair back from his forehead. "Think again. I know my job, I'm licensed and bonded, and I've just given you two and a half hours of my time."

"You've given me two and a half hours of grief, with nothing to show for it."

From her position behind the counter Amanda looked from her father to Hilary, her brown eyes wide with worry.

Shirley stepped in and laid a slender hand on Hilary's arm. "Don't be hasty, honey. I'm sure that Owen's wouldn't have sent him out if he didn't know his job, and it's Christmas Eve—"

"Stay out of this, Shirley." Hilary never, *ever*, snapped at Shirley, but the last thing she needed right now was a lecture on Christmas spirit. "I'm not about to pay good money for nothing."

Jake Burton was angry. She could see it in the tense line of his jaw and the tightening of his mouth. For a moment he stood, saying nothing.

"You're a real piece of work, aren't you?" he asked after a minute. "You know, I've never understood people like you. Seven thousand dollars on a damned dress, and yet you'll cheat a man out of sixty-five dollars because you're in a cranky mood. Well, I'll tell you what: You call any electrician in the city out here and see if he can find a problem. And he won't. I'd say I hope you feel guilty, but I don't think you would. As far as I'm concerned, you can take your sixty-five dollars and shove it right up—"

"Daddy!"

Little Amanda was on her feet, her dark eyes filling.

"Come on, pumpkin. Let's go." He turned, and bent to pick up his battered toolbox.

"But Daddy—"

"Let's go." There was no arguing with his quiet order.

The little girl hesitated and then turned to Hilary and pressed a paper into her hand. "Here," she whispered.

There was something about the sticky face, the downcast dark eyes, that stopped Hilary in her tracks. Guilt washed over her as the child hurried after her father, her purple rubber boots clumping.

"Merry Christmas," Jake added, and shoved his way out the door. The bells on the door rang furiously as it slammed behind them.

Hilary watched as the two stood in the snow for a minute, and then Jake helped his daughter into the battered green van parked outside the shop. He didn't look back. The sound of the engine sputtered, whined, and then roared.

"Oh, Hilary."

Shirley's quiet voice made her feel even worse. It was that I'm-disappointed-in-you tone, the kind that makes you feel worse than being shouted at.

Hilary looked down at the paper in her hand. It was a drawing of herself with impossibly long arms holding ruffled dresses, surrounded by evergreen boughs and flowers.

"MERRY CHRISTMAS," was written over the top, in childish block letters. "I THINK YOU'RE PRETTY."

Hilary stood in the silent store, surrounded by her beautiful antiques and elegant displays and exquisite racks of silks and satins and crepe de chincs. The music was playing softly, a haunting flute caressing the notes of *Ave Maria.* The Christmas tree stood, a silent witness, the renaissance angels that hung from its boughs floating gracefully in their evergreen bowers.

She felt awful. Cheap and shallow. Shame, dark and ugly, washed over her.

"Hilary—"

She could hardly bear to meet Shirley's eyes.

"Shame on you." Shirley rarely, if ever, was angry, but she was angry now. If she was the type of person that swore, she would be swearing, Hilary knew. "That was terrible. I love you, Hilary, but I am very, *very* ashamed of you. That man was right. What's sixty-five dollars to you? And on Christmas, as well. I don't like to criticize, but you were wrong."

Harsh words, for Shirley. Hilary felt as if she was an eight-year-old who had disappointed her favorite teacher.

"I'm so sorry, Shirley."

"Well, don't tell me. My feelings aren't hurt. I'm just ashamed of you."

Shirley's words stung.

"Shirley . . ." Hilary's words sounded a little quivery. "I'm sorry. I really am. And first thing on Tuesday I'll get hold of Owen's and make sure that Jake gets his money. I really didn't mean to blow up. It's just the lights, and the limo canceling, and the cash register, and forgetting my dress, and everything else." She sighed, her headache pounding against her temples. "Why don't you leave early, Shirl? There hasn't been a customer in since the fire alarms went off, and I know you want to be with your family. I'll close up."

Shirley's face softened, and brightened a little. "Are you sure, honey?"

"Of course," Hilary answered, anxious to relieve the guilt nagging at her.

Shirley gave her a quick hug. "That's wonderful, Hilary. Thank you." She disappeared into the back room and came back buttoning her coat. "You should leave early, too. The roads don't look too good, and you still have to get home and change. And you enjoy yourself tonight."

"I will, Shirley." But would she? Her enthusiasm for the party wasn't as keen as it had been, for some reason. All too clearly she could picture Jake Burton, his handsome face dark with anger.

"You're a real piece of work, aren't you? You spend seven thousand dollars on a dress, but you'll cheat a man out of sixty-five dollars."

The doorbells jangled as Shirley lifted the handle. "Merry Christmas, Hilary."

The words sounded hollow in the empty store, and Hilary suddenly found herself unable to reply.

There was a lump in her throat, tight and aching.

She stood at the counter for a moment, looking at the silent room and feeling very alone.

It wasn't a feeling that usually bothered her. She'd read all the magazine articles—Enjoy your SELF, and Alone doesn't mean Lonely! and all the other self-help columns that reassured her that it was healthy to be independent and single. You didn't need other people, just a good dose of self-esteem.

"What the heck is wrong with me?" she muttered. Hilary wasn't given to self-pity. There were lots of people who'd give anything to be in her Italian leather shoes. It was Christmas Eve, she had the most wonderful job, most fabulous business, and most beautiful dress in the world, and she was . . .

Lonely. She felt completely, utterly alone. It was an empty, hollow feeling.

She took the cash from the cash register back to the office, grabbed her keys, and came out to lock the doors, only to find that she wasn't alone.

There was one customer left in the store.

One woman, who could have been anywhere from sixty to eighty, dressed in the most ridiculous outfit Hilary had ever seen in the tasteful rooms of Exclusively Lauren's.

She wore a scarf made of a million chiffonlike flower petals, the kind old women used to wear over their curlers when Hilary was little. Kind of a cross between a swimming cap and a headpiece from *Swan Lake*. And a giant white sweatshirt over her round figure, decorated with so many sequin snowflakes that it rivaled the Christmas tree for brilliance. She wore Christmas ornaments for earrings, actual round glass *Christmas ornaments,* for goodness sake, one red and one green, as big as baseballs.

And, in a final tribute to bad taste, she was wearing bedroom slippers in public. Giant, fuzzy bedroom slippers in a bilious turquoise color that hurt Hilary's eyes.

She blinked, wishing that Shirley was still here, to gently direct this old loony-tune out of the door.

But she wasn't.

"I'm sorry; we're closed for the day," Hilary said, as politely as she could.

The woman looked at her. She had a very round face, like a moon, with deep, soft wrinkles around her eyes. The sequined chiffon petals of her scarf sparkled around it like white stars.

She had very blue eyes, surprisingly bright for her age, and they were staring at Hilary as if she was the ridiculous one.

"So, you finally noticed me." Not an unpleasant voice. Clear, and almost pretty. It didn't match the owner at all.

"I . . . I was in back," Hilary explained quickly. "Closing up. So if you'll leave, I can lock up."

"Hilary Lauren," exclaimed the woman, "I couldn't leave if I wanted to. I've been waiting for your attention all day, and now that I've got it, I'm not going anywhere."

Astounded, Hilary stared. She didn't know this woman; she was sure of that. She reached for the phone to dial security.

"Don't bother. The phone's out," the woman said cheerfully, just as Hilary put the phone to her ear.

The woman was right; there was no sound on the line.

Hilary slowly dropped the phone back into its cradle.

"May I help you?" she asked hesitantly, trying not to let her fear show. She was alone in the store with a certified nut, one who knew her name, and knew that the phone lines were out.

The woman put her hands on her ample hips and sighed.

"Help me? I wish you would. But I'm afraid I'm here to help you. It's the twenty-fourth, you know."

Speechless, Hilary nodded.

"Good. I was afraid you hadn't noticed that the world outside of Hilary Lauren still existed. I was about at the end of my rope, missy, trying to get your attention. I've flashed lights and pulled plugs and rung bells till I'm half crazy with it. I was just about to set off the sprinkler system."

"You *what?*" Hilary almost shrieked at the woman, this insane person who was standing there looking like a cross between the Sugarplum Fairy and the Pillsbury Dough Boy, and taking credit for the whole day of insanity.

"You heard me," the woman said, and she laughed, a delighted, sparkling laugh. "Wouldn't that have been something? Snowing outside, and the sprinklers going in the store?" The old woman's cheeks glowed pink with pleasure. "That would have taken the starch right out of your underpants!"

"Okay, that's it!" Hilary grabbed her keys and marched out from behind the counter. "I don't know who you are or what you're doing here, but you're leaving, right now. If this is some kind of joke, it's not funny. Not one damned bit."

She stormed to the front door and flung it open. A blast of winter wind rushed through the shop.

"Out. Now. Or I'll start screaming for help."

The woman smiled. "I wouldn't do that. You'll end up looking very silly. And anyway, it's almost five, isn't it? Security should be making their rounds just about now."

"How do you know that?" Hilary demanded, trying not to panic. "And how do you know my name? And what do you know about—"

"Everything all right, Miss Lauren?"

Hilary sagged with relief. It was Dave, from security, his nose glowing red from the cold, snowflakes covering the shoulders of his blue uniform as he made his way up the snowy sidewalk.

"Oh, thank goodness. No, I'm afraid I'm having problems getting this customer to leave."

The old woman crossed the floor toward them, blue fuzzy slippers flapping. She stopped directly in front of Dave and smiled up at him. "What a nice young man," she commented.

"What customer?" Dave asked, peering into the store.

What customer? Hilary repeated silently. *Gee, maybe the crazy old woman practically standing on your feet.*

"That one," she said with a quick nod.

David looked down.

He looked to the right and then to the left, and then, with a carefully blank face, at Hilary.

"Where?" he whispered.

The old woman smiled. "Cut your losses, Hilary.

Tell him I must have left, before he thinks you're losing it."

"I'm losing it?" Hilary repeated. "You're walking around the city with feet like Cookie Monster and you think I'm losing it?"

Dave the security man peered down at his shoes. "Cookie Monster? Miss Lauren, have you been drinking?"

"No, Dave. I meant the woman I'm trying to get rid of, not you. The one with the fuzzy blue slippers and the spangled head scarf."

"Oh. Well, where is she?"

Something was very, very, wrong. The old woman stepped out onto the street, looking like an advertisement for the local nut house, but nobody noticed her. The passing shoppers kept hurrying by, and people on their way home from work, and Dave the security man stood there looking at Hilary as if she'd lost her mind, *but nobody was looking at the woman wearing blue fuzzy slippers in the snow.*

"Do you want me to check the store?" Dave asked very carefully.

Hilary shook her head, frustrated. "No, Dave, she's standing outside, now. Right behind you."

He turned in a circle and then looked at Hilary. He looked behind him again, and the old woman waved a plump hand and smiled. He turned back to Hilary and hesitated.

"Umm . . . Is she still there, Miss Lauren, or did she go away again? Do you want me to check the store?"

"He can't see me," the woman explained gently, beaming at Hilary. "Watch. I'll go back in the store, and he won't be able to find me."

"Don't you even think about it," Hilary ordered. "You're out, and you'd better stay out."

Dave scratched his head, looking worried. "Well, geez, Miss Lauren, that's what I get paid for."

"What?" Hilary demanded.

"Checking the store," he reminded her. "Hey, are you all right?"

"Test him. I'll prove it."

"Okay," Hilary said softly. She kept her hand firmly on the cold brass of the door handle, the only normal thing she could touch.

The old woman walked up to Dave, thrust her face directly into his, pulled her mouth back with her fingers, barred her teeth in a frightful grimace, and crossed her eyes.

"Are you sure you're feeling all right, Miss Lauren? I can call you a cab, if you don't."

Incredibly, he was looking right past the old woman, who was now hopping from one blue fuzzy foot to another, shaking her white spangled head and making noises that sounded like "yada-yada-yada," like a cartoon spring vibrating.

"Oh, my God," Hilary said. Nobody looked, nobody turned to stare, nobody saw. "You're right."

"So, should I call a cab?"

"No. Oh, no thanks, Dave. Everything's . . . fine."

She ducked back into her store, banged the door closed, and turned the key in the lock.

Outside, Dave gave her an uncertain smile and wave and walked off into the snow, on his way to check the next store in the building.

The crazy woman stood outside, her hands on her hips, and shook her finger sternly at Hilary, frowning through the glass.

"Too damned bad," Hilary murmured, hurrying toward the back room. She grabbed her tote bag, checking it briefly, turned out the shop lights, switched on the alarm, and hurried out of her office.

"It won't work, you know."

Hilary gave a strangled shriek and dropped her coat and bag in her panic.

That woman was back, sitting in Hilary's favorite Queen Anne chair, with Hilary's favorite cup in her hands, watching the Christmas tree, which should have been off, and wasn't.

"Great balls of fire, Hilary, you scared me! Don't scream like that."

Hilary tried to speak, choked, gasped for air, and tried again.

"Deep breaths, please."

Hilary gulped one in. "Okay! Okay!" She bent over and picked up her things, never taking her eyes off the crazy woman, who sat smiling, as if everything in the world was all right. "Okay," she whispered, and struggled for words. When they came out they came in a great, hurried rush. "All right. I don't know how you got in, or what you want, or why you're doing this, but I'm listening. Just tell me what's going on and what you want, and I'll do whatever I can, but please, please, don't hurt me."

The woman looked a little hurt. She gave a tired sigh and raised her mournful blue eyes.

"Hurt you? Oh, Hilary. How could you even think such a thing? For twenty-nine years I've done everything I can to keep you from being hurt. I've done a fine job, for the most part. The only pain you've had is what you've caused yourself. Please, sit down, dear, and I'll explain everything."

Hilary hesitated, her hands quivering.

"You see, dear, I know you quite well, and I care for you very much. My name, by the way, is Joy."

"Joy," Hilary repeated, clutching her keys. "How can I help you, Joy?"

Again that sparkling laugh, clear and high and oddly youthful. "But that's *my* line, Hilary. You see, I'm your guardian angel."

"I'm out of here," Hilary replied.

Chapter Three

She rushed down the sidewalk, her tote bag banging against her knees, slipping in the snow. The parking meter had expired, and there was a ticket on her car.

She seized it without looking, cramming it into her pocket as she fumbled for her keys.

She dropped her keys twice, fished for them in the slush with shaking fingers, and put them into the lock.

It was a hallucination, plain and simple, she told herself, though there was nothing really plain or simple about hallucinating. She clambered into her car, slamming the door behind her and locking it.

She laid her head on the steering wheel of the Volvo, breathing hard, deep breaths.

After a moment she raised her head. Everything

was normal. Traffic went by, moving slowly because of the snow, still falling from the darkening sky. White Christmas lights sparkled up and down the sidewalks, outlining the winter-bare tree branches. A Metro bus rumbled by, its windows bright in the darkness. The normal sights and sounds of the city at rush hour.

The car felt safe and familiar. She turned over the ignition, switched on the heater, and turned on the radio. For a minute she sat shivering, listening to Julie Andrews singing *Silent Night*. She checked her watch. Two hours to get home, change, and get to the Vanderheyden party.

She indicated, waited, and pulled out onto the busy street.

"Look out for that Dodge. He's about to slide!"

Hilary screamed and slammed on the brakes.

A gray car to her left slid harmlessly past her, regained control, and straightened itself.

Joy was sitting in the passenger seat next to Hilary, her hands neatly folded in her lap, beaming.

"Get out!" Hilary screamed.

"Oh, goodness gracious."

"Get out! Now! Out!"

"And if I hadn't been here, you'd have been sideswiped—"

"Out of my car!" Hilary shrieked, slapping the steering wheel and bouncing on the seat, enraged.

"You're holding up traffic," Joy pointed out reasonably. "And all they can see is you, sitting alone in the car, having a tantrum."

Car horns were sounding behind Hilary. She glanced in the rearview mirror, and then pulled forward.

"You aren't here. I'm losing my mind."

"No you're not," Joy responded. "And I can't go anywhere. At least, not 'til Christmas morning. Special assignment."

Hilary set her jaw tightly, focusing on her driving. The windshield wipers slopped back and forth, pushing the heavy snow out of the way.

"Now," Joy said brightly, "if you've quite finished your tantrum and are ready to listen, I can explain. It's Christmas Eve, and that's the day that guardian angels—"

"You're not my guardian angel."

Joy straightened indignantly, her round chin thrust out. "Oh, yes I am, missy, and you'd best get used to it. I've done a lot of work for you, and I'd appreciate a sight more gratitude and a lot less attitude, thank you."

Hilary braked slowly for a red light, shifted, and turned to glower at Joy. The traffic lights reflected red off the sequined sweatshirt.

"Gratitude! I have a party to be at in less than two hours, you've ruined my day, and you want gratitude! Look at me—I'm a wreck! I'm sitting here arguing with a hallucination and you expect gratitude."

Joy crossed her pudgy legs comfortably. "What about the time you tried to take your tricycle down that hill, and I pushed you off before you could be killed?"

Hilary stared. She remembered the incident distinctly, though she had been only four. She remembered the glorious speed, the wind rushing through her hair, and then the hard scrape of asphalt beneath her leg as she tumbled off onto the side of the road into the grass. The trike sped on and was crushed beneath the tires of an oncoming car.

"And remember the night, when you were thirteen, you planned to sneak out to that party with Tammy and Diane?"

Hilary remembered. She had met them at the Seven Eleven store up the street, but her conscience got the better of her, and she had gone home, instead.

Tammy and Diane had never made it home. They had gotten in a car with some older boys, who had been drinking. The police had fished the car out of the Green River the next day. Nobody had survived the wreck.

"And there were a million other times that I did little things for you. Some you don't even know about."

Hilary maneuvered the car silently onto the freeway, thanking God for front-wheel drive. The roads were solid white with snow. Abandoned cars sat in the median, lit by the rosy glow of the streetlights. Traffic was crawling.

"Like what?" she asked at last.

"Do you remember when your mother decided you were too old to sleep with your teddy bear anymore?"

She had been nine, and the bear had gone with her everywhere since she was two. One eye had been missing, his fur patchy. She had come home from school one day, and Freddy was gone from her pillow. Her mother told her they had sent him to the dump. She had cried as if a friend had been murdered.

"I remember." Funny, how it still brought tears to her eyes. She glanced over at Joy, and saw an answering sheen in her blue eyes.

"Nobody has the right to take a Christmas present back," Joy said softly. "Here, Hilary."

And incredibly, there was Freddy, sitting in Joy's ample lap. He was smaller and more shabby than she remembered, but it was Fred, his poor bear nose pushed and flattened to one side where he had been slept on, one eye still missing, and his stuffed arms worn thin.

Hilary blinked rapidly as she turned the car onto the Mercer Island exit, trying to see past the tears.

The snow fell thicker, blowing in white ghosts around the halos of streetlights.

"And now that you believe me," Joy said softly, "we have a few things to talk about. Including the way you treated your future husband, earlier."

The Volvo swerved and slid, and Hilary turned into the skid, her heart pounding as she brought the hood of the car back into a straight line.

"Tell me you're joking." She knew, *knew,* that Joy was talking about Jake.

"I am not, and of course I'm talking about Jake," Joy said, seeming to read Hilary's thoughts. "And I'd worked everything out so beautifully. But you and your bad attitude, you just had to mess things up."

Hilary thought of the handsome electrician and his cocky attitude and battered Levi's and decrepit van and sticky daughter. No. Definitely not. She would marry a stockbroker, or a newscaster, or . . . an astronaut, or *someone.*

"You," she said between gritted teeth, "are *not* my guardian angel."

"Oh, yes I am, young lady."

"Oh, no you're not!"

Joy leaned over the gear shift and thrust her chubby face into Hilary's. She was quivering with indignation, setting the sequin disks on her stupid head scarf into sparkling motion.

"You listen to me, Miss Smarty-pants. I have certain obligations to meet, and one of them is a thorough character accounting every Christmas day. And let me tell you a thing or two: No matter what kind of shape your Visa card is in, where it really matters your account is pushed to its limit! Now there are certain things you have a choice about, and certain things you'd better choose wisely, and *this is one of them.*"

Hilary glowered back and glanced at her watch. One and a half hours to get to the Vanderheyden party and here she was, driving home in the snow, arguing with some figment of her imagination who was wearing a jogging suit and fuzzy slippers.

"You," she said between clenched teeth, "are not my guardian angel. My guardian angel does *not* shop at K-mart."

"There's nothing wrong with K-mart," Joy returned indignantly. "What a nasty little snob you've become, Hilary. As to my attire, how good I look on the outside is in direct proportion to how good you look inside. If you think I don't want a nice gown and iridescent wings, think again. Or maybe something in a nice Renaissance look; all those Michelangelo colors with nice drapery. But until you shape up I'm stuck with polyester fleece."

Joy settled back into her seat with a sniff. The windshield wipers slurped back and forth, and on the radio Perry Como sang the praises of letting it snow.

"And by the way," Joy added, "you're not going to that party, Miss Know-it-all."

"Be quiet," Hilary said. "You're not here, and I don't hear you."

When she glanced over again the passenger seat was empty, except for the small, battered teddy bear, which sat looking up at her with one button eye.

Unable to resist, Hilary reached over and patted him gently, smiling at the familiar feel of soft stuffing and threadbare coat.

"Hi, Fred," she whispered, as if he could hear her. For a moment she felt a quiet thrill of magic, as if she was a little girl at Christmas again.

Her condominium was silent and spotless, the white carpets and furniture as clean and pure as the snow outside the picture window.

The Bazhenov gown lay draped over the arm of one couch, sparkling ice blue and white in the dim light. The pearls and crystal beads glistened like a promise.

She changed quickly, sliding the bias-cut silk over her slim figure, and twirled in front of her full-length mirror. Perfect.

She glanced over her shoulder in the mirror as she touched up her makeup—smoky gray shadows under her blue eyes, a soft wine color on her lips. She glanced back again, but there was no sign of Joy.

She went into her silent bedroom and sat on the rose-strewn Laura Ashley comforter as she pulled on her stockings. Her dyed-to-match high heels with their delicate ankle straps were still in her tote bag, in the car. She'd change there, she decided, after she had waded through the snow.

The dress made her feel like a princess. Nothing in the world had ever fit her so well, had ever moved like the silk against her body. She knew, without vanity, that it changed her looks from pretty to stunning.

One last quick look in the mirror, and she hurried through the quiet rooms. She stopped by the tree, a stunning noble fir covered with hundreds of shimmering, jewel-toned ornaments. Trumpets and apples, drums and bells, porcelain cherubs and fur-robed Father Christmases, and delicate angels with fragile wings.

"Don't think about angels," she said aloud, glancing nervously about the room.

Luckily, there was no sign of Joy.

Good, Hilary thought. It was too much to have to worry about, tonight. Imagine, trying to tell her that she was destined to marry Jake Burton. She could imagine what it would be like. She could just picture him now, sitting on the spotless white couch, his work boots on the perfect white marble coffee table, putting his coffee cup on the antique tea table next to the Tiffany lamp.

There'd be no Vanderheyden party for her then. What would they do on Christmas Eve?

Stay home, like other married couples. Amanda would be putting cookies and milk by the hearth, pretending she still believed in Santa Claus. Hilary would put a French braid in the child's long dark hair, and she would have a velvet dress with a falling lace collar waiting for her for Christmas morning.

She and Jake would stay up long after Amanda was sleeping, drinking hot buttered rums and putting together things like bicycles and doll beds, and he would swear at the directions and eat Santa Claus's cookies, and she would sit by the fire and laugh at his stupid jokes, and then they would fall asleep under the thick down comforter on Hilary's antique sleigh bed, warm and happy in each other's arms until Amanda woke them, laughing with the joy of Christmas morning, and the magic that it brings. . . .

"Ha-ha!"

Hilary whirled, knocking a glass bird from the tree. It landed harmlessly on the carpet.

Joy stood there, beaming. Her impossible white cap was gone, and her own pale hair showed gossamer white, swirled into a casual knot on the back of her head.

"Caught you!" Joy announced triumphantly, crossing her arms. "Not bad, was it? And just think, if you'd accepted his offer of a ride home, you'd be there with them right now."

"Fabulous," Hilary said. "Just swell. Joy, I don't want the man."

"Could have fooled me. Do you mind telling me what's wrong with him?" Joy bent over and looked at a perfect white poinsettia, floating in a cut-crystal bowl.

"He's not my type. First, I'm a woman that likes a little security, and he's very obviously irresponsible."

"And why is that?" Joy demanded, raising her pale brows toward her cloud of white hair.

"Well, look at him. He can't even afford to dress his daughter decently, and he's driving around in that piece-of-crap old van that looks like it's about to fall apart, dragging that poor little girl off to work with him on Christmas Eve—"

"And do you know why?" Joy asked. "No, you don't have the faintest idea, Hilary. And why was he working on Christmas Eve? You don't know that, either."

"It's not my problem," Hilary retorted, grabbing her coat from the closet and throwing it over her shoulders. "It's got nothing to do with me."

She wasn't surprised when Joy followed her out of the front door and down to the car. She knew it was useless to argue.

She checked her tote bag. Her beaded evening bag was ready, her pale blue satin heels, the velvet box with her diamond earrings. She snapped it open and adjusted the rearview mirror, ready to put them on.

"I'll tell you what is your responsibility," Joy told her, tapping a blue fuzzy slipper on the floor of the car. "That poor little girl is getting cheated out of a proper Christmas. He was taking that money you kept from him and stopping at Woolworth's on their way home. He was buying her ornaments for their tree, and a present to open in the morning. You ruined it, Hilary."

Hilary sat, her hand frozen on the ignition key. "Oh, no," she whispered.

"You and your bad temper," Joy said softly. "My, my, I hate to report to accounting tomorrow."

Hilary couldn't look up. The crystal beads on the cuff of the Bazhenov gown sparkled up at her like diamonds.

"What can I do?" she asked at last, softly.

"Not a darn thing, about the money," Joy said.

"But I can tell you this much: They're on their way home, out by Woodinville, and that 'piece of crap' van is about to break down. They'll have a long, cold walk home tonight."

Hilary started the car and it gave a warm purr.

"Which way do I go?" she asked.

"Good girl," Joy said softly.

When Hilary glanced over the blue fuzzy slippers were gone, and satin slippers with ribbons glowed on Joy's feet.

"Don't expect too much," Hilary said. "I'm still going to the Vanderheydens's as soon as I drop those two off."

"We'll see," Joy said, and she settled back with a complacent smile as they drove off into the snowy night.

Chapter Four

"You're trying to kill me," Hilary said. "I know it. What kind of guardian angel would let me drive in these conditions?"

The farther they went from the city, the thicker the snow. If it hadn't been for the concrete barriers on the freeway, Hilary would have had trouble finding the road. The weather wasn't letting up, either. Snow came down in billowing clouds, was caught by the wind, and swirled into ghostly patterns beneath the streetlights.

Few cars dared to venture out in these conditions. Abandoned vehicles were scattered along the sides of the road, like children's toys that had been left outside.

"Next exit," Joy said. "Take it easy."

Hilary took the curve slowly, sliding a little as she approached the intersection.

"Right on this road," Joy ordered, "and straight, about four miles."

"What road?" Hilary asked, staring at the dense snow. Funny, she must have driven that freeway a hundred times, but everything was unfamiliar, blanketed in white and with all landmarks obscured. It was a rural area, and the only sign of a road was a white flat space stretching through the snowy pines, off into the darkness.

"The radio would be nice," Joy remarked, and it turned on, the dial traveling freely up and down as it searched for an appropriate station.

"—opens tomorrow at a theater—"

"—chains are required on all mountain passes—"

"—record snowfall of twenty inches, with reports exceeding twenty-nine inches in outlying areas. Seattle-Tacoma International Airport is closed—"

"Have yourself a merry little Christmas—"

"That's nice," Joy exclaimed. "I love Andy Williams, don't you?"

"I love spring," Hilary answered. "Look, Joy, are you sure you know where we're going? This is dangerous. They don't even have streetlights out here, and if we break down or get stuck, it could be hours before anyone finds us."

The roads were unmarked by tire tracks. If anyone had come this way, the falling snow had covered their trail.

"Dangerous, indeed!" Joy laughed her sparkling bell-like laugh. "Hilary, you have your guardian angel sitting next to you. How could you be any safer?"

"I could be at a nice warm party, eating pheasant and dancing," Hilary retorted, but she kept on driving down the endless road of white. They passed a small mom-and-pop-type country store with a CLOSED sign displayed in the window.

"Do people really live out here?"

"Don't grumble. Oh, look!"

Hilary stared. There was the decrepit van, sitting on the side of the road, its front wheels in a ditch. She drove very slowly, staring into swirling flakes illuminated by her headlights. All thoughts of the Vanderheyden party vanished from her mind, to be replaced by images of Amanda and Jake, wandering through the biting cold somewhere on these dark, lonely roads.

"Where are they?" she whispered, staring into the darkness.

"There should be a right turn up here," Joy said. "Cutter Creek Road."

Sure enough, the sign appeared. The road was so small, Hilary might have driven right past if she had not been watching for it. The snow was even deeper here, untouched by any sign of cars, and the tires spun a little as she started to climb the hill.

"I don't know if the Volvo can do it," she said.

"We can do it," Joy said firmly.

With a skid and a slide, the car began to climb steadily. Evergreen trees crowded closely along the rural road, their branches heavy with winter frosting. They passed a lonely-looking mobile home on a lot, its windows alight, and then, a mile down the road, a small 1930s-style farmhouse.

"See?" Joy said. "Even if we get stuck, it's nice to know there are people nearby."

On the radio the Mormon Tabernacle Choir was singing *Hark the Herald.*

Joy hummed along. "I like this one," she said.

Hilary squinted into the darkness, the steering wheel clutched tightly in her cool fingers. She had no idea what time it might be. She was lost in an arctic landscape where wristwatches held no authority.

Then she saw them—two dark figures, hunched over, making their way through the white wilderness.

"There they are!" she exclaimed, and relief rushed through her. She turned to Joy, smiling with triumph.

To her surprise, Joy looked a little younger. Her face had smoothed and slimmed, and her white hair looked more luxuriant. The white jogging suit seemed to hang a little looser.

"Good girl," Joy said, and then she was gone.

Hilary touched the horn gently, and Jake turned with a grateful wave as she drove slowly toward them and braked.

He and Amanda stood in the glare of the headlights, shivering, relief obvious on their faces.

Jake's dark hair was white with snow, his sharp cheekbones and aquiline nose brilliant with cold.

Amanda was zipped into her ski jacket, her hood drawn so tightly that only a pale circle of face showed, and two enormous dark eyes.

Hilary leaned over and opened the passenger door, and he picked up Amanda and came hurrying through the snow.

"I take back everything I ever said about foreign cars," he said as he reached the open door. "Am I ever—" He stopped abruptly at the sight of Hilary, sitting in her sparkling evening gown. "Am I hallucinating?"

The wind blew in through the open door with an arctic bite, tossing his dark hair around his face.

"Hello again," Hilary said. "Nice night for a walk, isn't it?"

Amanda's face was white and red, except for her brown eyes, which blinked in astonishment.

"Get in, before you freeze," Hilary urged, turning the heat up.

Jake didn't need to be asked twice. He lifted Amanda into the back seat, brushing the wet snow off her purple boots, and then climbed in himself, slamming the door quickly.

"I never thought I'd say it, but am I glad to see you," he said, leaning back into the comfort of the leather upholstery.

"Are you all right?" Hilary asked, looking over her shoulder at Amanda. Shivering, the little girl nodded.

Hilary shrugged her wool coat off her shoulders. "Here, use this as a blanket. You'll get warmer faster."

"Thanks," Jake said, and leaned into the back seat to tuck the heavy coat around his daughter.

"Okay," Hilary said. "Exclusively Lauren's tundra taxi. Where are we going?"

Jake stared at her again, as if he couldn't quite believe it. "What are you doing out here? Don't tell me the Whippenpoodles are holding their soiree at the Cutter Creek grange hall."

Hilary searched for a plausible explanation and found none. "Would you believe I got lost?"

"I'll say you did. About fifty miles off, I'd guess.

Not that I'm sorry, you know, but you must have the worst sense of direction in the history of mankind."

"Would you believe I felt guilty and wanted to apologize, so I followed your tracks through the snow?"

"No." His blunt answer was spoken pleasantly enough, but it still made Hilary blush.

She looked at his hands, red and white with cold. They were agile-looking, strong hands. He was holding a wet plastic shopping bag.

"Where to?" she asked.

"Straight ahead, about three more miles."

She put the car into gear and proceeded cautiously.

"Thanks," he added. "I was starting to worry about Amanda. Our guardian angels must have been working overtime."

"Not if you're lucky," Hilary muttered, driving into the white flurries, the beads of her Bazhenov gown clicking together.

The house was small, a craftsman-style house that had seen better days, sitting off the road and surrounded by giant pines.

"Wow," Hilary said, "this is really out here."

"Yeah. It belongs to a friend of mine, but he's letting us use it 'til we find a place of our own."

"We have a tree," Amanda said eagerly. "Want to see it?"

Hilary hesitated. She felt as if she'd been driving for hours. Maybe she had. It would be good to get out and stretch.

"Sure, if it's okay with your dad."

"Hey, it's not the Hootenweenie mansion," he

warned her, raising a dark brow at her evening gown.

"Is it warm? Is there room enough to stretch my legs?"

"Maybe and probably not," he replied, smiling, "but come in anyway."

Hilary stopped the engine and followed Jake and Amanda through the snow and up to the small porch. Amanda, her good spirits restored, jumped up and down.

"Look at our Christmas house!" she cried, scooping a handful of snow off the porch.

"Hey!" her father exclaimed indignantly, "I thought you never wanted to see snow again. I thought you were ready to move back to California."

"I like it again, now that I'm warm," the child explained. "Snow's nice, when you're home."

She followed Hilary and her father into the house. Hilary stood shivering while Jake flipped on the lights.

"It isn't much," he apologized with a quick glance at Hilary.

It wasn't. The living room was small—smaller than the guest room at Hilary's condo. The carpets were an indifferent beige; the old sofa slumped. But the windows were good-sized, and there was a charming stone fireplace, and it was clean.

"This is our tree," Amanda said, taking Hilary's hand in her small cool one.

It stood on a little table in front of the window, unadorned except for a string of colored lights.

Hilary felt a flush of guilt.

"He was going to buy Christmas ornaments," Joy had said, *"and presents for Amanda."*

"But we don't have decorations," Amanda added wistfully. "Not like your tree."

Jake was bent over, stacking logs into the fireplace. He looked over his shoulder with a quick, brilliant grin.

"I've got an idea," he said. "To hell with the tree. Let's plug Miss Lauren in, and light her up. She's sparkly enough."

Amanda laughed with delight at the idea of using Hilary for a tree. She reached up and touched Hilary's sleeve with small, gentle fingers. "I like sparkly things," she said softly. "That's the prettiest dress I've ever seen."

Hilary felt a little ludicrous, standing in the shabby room in her seven-thousand-dollar original. The hem was wet and dark from her short walk through the yard. She wondered if the silk would ever recover.

"Have a seat before you go," Jake called out. He was in the kitchen, putting the plastic shopping bag into a cupboard. "Amanda, plug in the tree."

The child tossed her wet jacket to the floor and scrambled to plug in the tree.

Hilary sat in a rocking chair, feeling like an intruder.

Amanda sat back on her heels, staring at the Christmas lights. "It looks like Charlie Brown's tree," she said mournfully.

"Wrap a blanket around it, Linus," her father suggested from the kitchen.

Amanda rolled her eyes.

Music came flooding out of the kitchen, an explosion of glorious trumpets, golden and clear.

"How's that?" Jake asked, appearing with a load of newspaper. He began to crumple it, stuffing it beneath the logs in the fireplace.

"Very Christmasy," Hilary approved. "I love Bach."

"So do I. Amanda and I are going to St. James Cathedral on New Year's for the Bach concert."

"Really?" Hilary said.

"Are you surprised that a lowly, not to mention incompetent, electrician would like Bach?" He put a match to the paper, and the fireplace glowed with light.

"Actually," Hilary replied defensively, "I was surprised that someone as young as Amanda would like Bach."

The little girl turned and smiled. "I don't really," she said. "He's hyper. I like Mozart better."

"Me, too," Hilary agreed.

"I'm starving," Amanda said. "What's for dinner?"

Jake hesitated, and Hilary saw the muscle in his cheek tighten briefly before he answered. "I'll go look around and see what I come up with."

Hilary didn't look as he walked back out to the kitchen and began banging through the cupboards. She couldn't look at Amanda, either.

She stared out the window, at the dark night and the postcard-perfect trees blanketed and draped in sparkling white, and felt sick to her stomach.

There she was, sitting in a seven-thousand-dollar dress, while Jake searched for something to feed his daughter for Christmas Eve dinner, and she felt lower than the slimiest slug that had ever oozed across the earth.

"Sixty-five dollars."

Startled, Hilary looked up.

Joy stood in the doorway between the kitchen and living room, her arms crossed over the bosom of her sparkling track suit, frowning.

"All you had to do was pay him the money you owed him, and you wouldn't have to feel like this."

Hilary glanced at Amanda, but the little girl was stripping off her mismatched socks and apparently didn't notice the woman standing in her doorway.

"Bacon and eggs?" Jake called, his voice studiously cheerful.

Amanda made a throwing-up noise.

"The question is," Joy continued, "what are you going to do about it?"

"Chile and crackers?"

"Okay," Amanda agreed.

Hilary thought about her kitchen on Mercer Island, the refrigerator full of cheeses and dips and cold ham and the boxes of rum truffles and perfect cookies from La Pannier, all ready for unexpected guests. And everything she had ordered for her brunch tomorrow—a brunch that nobody would probably come to, because of the snow.

"Will you stay?" Amanda asked, turning to Hilary with a tremulous smile. "It'll seem more like a party with someone else here."

"Hey," Jake said, standing in the doorway where Joy had been a minute ago, "Hilary has a big party to go to, Amanda Panda. A great, big, fancy party in a house as big as a city, with crystal chandeliers and waiters in fancy tuxedos and violin players. She didn't buy that dress to sit out here in Bumdoodle, Washington, with us. She's afraid we'll plug her in and use her as a Christmas tree."

Amanda giggled at her father, and he beamed

at her, leaning against the wall, a can of chile in his hands.

Hilary looked at them, and the scruffy little tree, and the crackling fire in the stone fireplace. The mantel was decorated with Amanda's drawings—pictures of stars and trees and angels with trumpets, their wings frosted with glitter. The majestic sounds of Bach gave over to a softer, sweeter piece by Handel.

"Actually," she said quietly, "I'd rather not drive until the snow lets up."

Jake looked astounded. "You'll miss your party," he said softly.

"We can have one here!" Amanda cried, leaping up.

"With a bacon and egg and chile buffet?" Jake asked.

"Well, if you don't mind, there's a full catered buffet in the trunk of my car," Hilary said. "It might need to thaw out . . ."

He stood, looking at her with puzzled dark eyes. "Hey, are you sure you're Hilary Lauren? Or did I have a run-in with your evil twin earlier?"

"Daddy!" Amanda cried, appalled.

"It was my evil twin," Hilary agreed. "Do you mind an uninvited guest?"

"I invited you," Amanda reminded her anxiously.

Jake raked a hand through his dark hair. "In that case, I'm not going to be the grinch. If you ladies would like to adjourn to the dining room, I'll head out into the blizzard and bring in the food."

Amanda laughed with pleasure and bounced

from one bare foot to another as Hilary handed Jake her keys.

"We can play games," Amanda suggested, "and play in the snow, and have candles on the table."

"You bet," her father told her. "We'll show those Vippenwheedles how to throw a party."

He slipped his arms into his jeans jacket and smiled at Hilary.

"I'll find the candles," Amanda shouted, running from the room.

He stopped by Hilary's chair and rested his hand on her shoulder for a moment.

"Thanks," he said awkwardly. "It means a lot to her."

His hand felt warm on her bare shoulder, and a surprising tremor ran through Hilary at the touch.

She looked down at her dress, and the lights of the Christmas tree reflected red and green and blue prisms in the crystal beads.

Embarrassed, she shrugged. "She's a beautiful little girl," she said. "I'm glad to be invited."

He accepted her unspoken apology with a quick squeeze of her shoulder and went out the front door, muttering a profanity as the cold hit him.

"Hilary," called Amanda, "come light the candles. I'm not allowed to."

Hilary stood, kicking off her water-stained heels, and padded into the kitchen. When she glanced back into the living room Joy stood by the tree. Her white jogging suit was gone, replaced by a simple, shapeless gown of white. She smiled at Hilary.

"Go for it," she said, wiggling her brows in a very unangelic fashion.

* * *

The preparations for the party took on an intoxicating excitement. Jake carried in sturdy box after box, all bearing the caterer's trademark, until the kitchen counters were cluttered with them. Amanda covered the table with snowflakes she had cut from tissue paper while Hilary warmed the oven.

The mysterious boxes were opened, and Hilary found herself sharing Amanda's delighted surprise as each perfect white box revealed exotic treasures—perfect puff pastries filled with exotic fruits and cheeses, apricot roses on beds of white whipped mascarpone, tiny red potatoes filled with créme fraîche and caviar, cakes of lemon with raspberry sauce, towering plates of ham and roast beef, and miniature loaves of bread with herbed butters. There were orange currant muffins, and peach and ginger ones, and cinnamon pecan ones.

Amanda exclaimed with delight as each exotic tray appeared. She and Hilary let out "Oh's" of delight at the individual glass dessert dishes of fruit, the melons carved into bouqets of peach and rose and yellow roses, with sparkling sugar-frosted mint leaves.

Jake laughed at their simultaneous exclamation. "If that don't beat all," he said in his best "Beverly Hillbilly" voice. "That ain't manly food, there."

"It's pretty," Amanda cried, her eyes sparkling with delight.

"Pretty food is more fun to eat; so there," Hilary agreed, checking on the pastries warming in the oven.

"You-all women folk are mighty silly," Jake deadpanned, but his eyes sparkled at Amanda's happiness, at the way she cried out with surprise at each new sight.

Her excitement was infectious. The tiny kitchen was transformed by the heaped and sparkling platters, the tissue paper snowflakes, the candles that shone among them.

The rich smell of baking food mingled with the clean scent of pine, and the cedar smell of the burning fire. Beyond the lace kitchen curtains, the landscape of white frosted forest sparkled off into eternity, like a fairy tale.

Jake stood back and surveyed the scene, and began laughing. "This is nuts," he said, shaking his dark head. "There must be enough food for thirty people."

"Sixteen," Hilary corrected.

"You're going to have sixteen disappointed guests tomorrow," he remarked.

Hilary shook her head, leaning back against the counter. "I doubt anyone will bother showing up, with the roads as bad as they are." She began stacking empty boxes.

"Here's a big one we haven't even touched," Jake observed.

"Amanda, that's your job," Hilary said.

Amanda left the table in a shot and pounced on the sturdy carton. "It's like opening presents," she bubbled, and gave out a noisy whoop as she revealed the floral arrangements—twenty cut-glass bowls filled with white roses and evergreens and opal frosted baby's breath, with three white candles in each.

"Can we light them?" she asked, breathless with pleasure.

"That's what they're for," Hilary replied, smiling. "You're the decorator; put them around the house."

Amanda hurried from kitchen to living room, thrilled with her new task. "This is the most exciting Christmas we've ever had," she called.

Hilary took a plate of steaming ham from the oven and stopped still with surprise. "It is for me, too," she admitted, laughing softly. "This is really fun. Maybe because it's so full of surprises."

She turned to find Jake smiling at her. "It certainly is," he agreed, and there was a warmth in his eyes that caused her heart to do a sudden unexpected flutter.

The table was so crowded that they ate in the living room, sitting on the floor at the coffee table in front of the fire. Amanda opened the curtains so that they could see the snow and put Christmas carols on the stereo.

The little room was transformed by the bunches of roses and evergreens, and the glow of the white taper candles. Outside, the storm stopped and the moon appeared from behind the cloud cover, sparkling on the enchanted forest of white frosted evergreens and the snowy hill leading down to the empty white road.

"What's that?" Amanda suddenly asked, pointing at the rocking chair.

Hilary turned to look, half expecting to see Joy there with her feet up.

Instead, she saw Fred the bear, sitting in genteel shabbiness, appearing to watch the festivities out of his one good eye.

"Oh, him?" Jake asked. "He was sitting out in the car with the boxes, so I brought him in. He looked like he needed a good party."

"Is it yours?" Amanda asked Hilary, disbelief showing on her little face.

Hilary nodded, and swallowed a mouthful of brie with almonds before answering with mock dignity. "That's not an *it,* it's a *he.* That's Fred the bear, and this is the first Christmas we've spent together since I was nine."

"Poor Fred," Amanda said, easily stepping into the make-believe world where teddy bears had feelings. "He must have been lonely."

And suddenly, without warning, there it was—the Christmas feeling that Hilary had missed so keenly. It rushed over her without warning, in a flow of sparkling lights and evergreens and carols and snow. The magic was back.

It was here, in this tiny, rural house, in the way Amanda saw everything through new eyes, and the way Jake's smile shone on Hilary when she made his daughter smile. The Christmas spirit was wrapped up in the room the way the house was tucked into the snow, but it was as mysterious and beautiful as the moonlit sky.

"Hey, are you crying?" Amanda asked, her dark eyes wide with concern. "Is it because you're missing your party?"

Hilary lay her hand on the child's shining brown hair. "No, I'm very glad I did. This is much more fun."

Jake pushed his plate away with a satisfied look. "It certainly is more fun for me," he agreed. "The Poopendoodles's loss is our gain."

"Vanderheydens," Hilary corrected, "And it's my gain, too."

She hadn't meant the words to sound flirtatious, but somehow they did.

Across the crowded coffee table Jake's eyes met hers and locked in a warm gaze. For a few seconds the air was electric, and Hilary looked away, her cheeks warm with a self-conscious blush. She suddenly felt as if her feelings were on display for Jake to read. She shouldn't be having feelings like this for a man she barely knew.

"I guess I should leave soon," she said, looking down. "Now that the snow has stopped."

"It's a long drive," Jake reminded her, a worried line appearing between his dark brows.

"Don't go," Amanda pleaded. "Spend the night!"

"Look at it out there," Jake said. "I'd feel a lot better if you waited until morning."

Why, he's genuinely worried about me, Hilary realized.

"Look at it," Amanda echoed, pointing out the window. "See that wind?"

Hilary looked out at the snowbound yard and an extraordinary sight met her eyes.

The wind was gusting through the yard, catching the snow and blowing it in misty sheets. The ancient pines were swaying as if they had come alive.

And directly above her car, on a long, overhanging branch of pine, was Joy.

She was hanging from the tree limb like a little girl playing on monkey bars. She wore a determined expression on her face, and her white skirts flew up around her chubby legs as she kicked rhythmically, swaying back and forth.

The swaying limb sagged lower and lower.

"Oh, for heaven's sake!" Hilary exclaimed, rising anxiously to her feet.

"That's quite a wind," Jake observed. "I know

this probably isn't your ideal way to spend Christmas Eve, but maybe you should consider staying."

There was nothing in his voice to suggest he might have seen Joy, swinging from the sagging branch with the grim concentration of an Olympic contender on the uneven bars.

But apparently Joy heard him. She began to shout, and her voice rose above the whistle of the wind as she punctuated each word with a mighty kick.

"She's . . . not . . . going . . . *anywhere!*" And with her last mighty, thigh-baring kick, the heavy branch snapped.

Amanda leapt to her feet, and Hilary froze with disbelief as Joy disappeared in a shower of sparkling lights.

The branch, in a cloud of flying snow, descended with frightening speed toward the Volvo. It hit the windshield with a thump and crash that Hilary felt to the bottom of her snow-stained satin shoes.

The wind died suddenly, and the yard lay silent and white.

"I hope you have insurance," Jake said after a long pause.

Hilary let her breath out with a tired sigh, and her shoulders slumped as she looked at the jagged hole where her windshield had been, the bough sticking out of it. "I guess we're having a slumber party," she said.

"Did you see how it sparkled?" Amanda asked. "Right before it fell, it sparkled."

"It sparkled, all right," Hilary agreed. "You wouldn't believe how it sparkled."

Chapter Five

"Well, since Amanda wanted to play games," Jake announced, "the first one is called 'Save the leather upholstery.' What do you think?"

Hilary thought Joy was very lucky that she could disappear at will, or she might hear some very uncelestial thoughts.

"Sounds like a plan," she agreed.

Amanda was already running for her rubber boots.

"I'll take care of it," Jake said as Hilary reached for her coat. "You can't go out like that."

Amanda looked up at Hilary. "You can't play in the snow," she observed mournfully. "Not in that dress."

Jake laughed. "Amanda Panda, I'm sure the last thing Hilary wants to do is play in the snow."

Amanda looked crestfallen.

"Sure I do," Hilary announced suddenly. "If you have anything here I could change into, I'd love to play in the snow."

Jake looked at her, puzzled. "You're kidding."

"I'm not."

"You don't strike me as the play-in-the-snow kind of girl."

Hilary wondered why she felt mildly insulted. "Well, you're wrong. Do you have something I can wear?"

"Well, yeah, but I can't guarantee the fit."

"We'll improvise," Hilary declared.

"Okay," Jake agreed. "This way, please, madam."

He lead Hilary into a small bedroom, Amanda following behind.

The room was small and simple, obviously lacking a woman's touch. Laundry was simply thrown into a mountain on the floor and the bed was unmade. School pictures of Amanda were displayed on the dresser—Amanda showing a toothless smile, Amanda wearing crooked pigtails and looking out with wide, solemn eyes.

But no pictures of her mother, and Hilary wondered where she was, why she was so conspicuously absent from her daughter's life.

"Welcome to Boutique Burton," Jake announced in an exaggerated French accent. "Today, we show the new winter line. We call it, the stuck-in-the-snow look."

Amanda giggled and climbed onto the bed to watch as her father produced clothing from the dresser drawers.

"Ze plaid flannel shirt," he announced, waving an oversized plaid shirt in dark blues and greens.

"It says, 'I'm rugged, I'm manly, I'm freezing my *derriere* off.' Just the thing for your Christmas soiree."

Hilary couldn't help joining Amanda's laughter. Jake was so masculine that the elaborate flourishes and supercilious pose were ridiculous.

He produced worn Levi's, a bulky sweater, and, with great aplomb, "The very latest in fashion accessories—le great big socks. Two pair, this season—one for ze feet, one for ze hands. We call this the 'I have no mittens' look."

"Thank you, Monsieur Andre," Hilary said, accepting the pile of clothing. "If you'll just direct me to the fitting room—"

"Right there," he said, dropping the silly accent and pointing Hilary toward a tiny bathroom. "Come on, Amanda, let's find you something warm."

Hilary closed the door quietly behind her, shivering as she slipped out of the Bazhenov gown. It slid to the cold tile floor with a silken whisper, pearls and crystals clicking softly.

Hilary looked at the shimmering mass of silk with a small, regretful smile, thinking of all the trouble she had gone to, and the party she had longed to be invited to.

"Well, that was a nice waste of money, wasn't it?" a voice asked in her ear, and Hilary jumped, her hands crossing over her chest.

Joy sat on the edge of the claw-footed bathtub, beaming.

Hilary heard Jake and Amanda talking somewhere in the house and turned on Joy.

"Was that necessary?" she demanded in a furious whisper. "That bit with the car?"

"I think so," Joy replied, with a smile that gave new meaning to the word *angelic*.

"Do you have any idea what that will cost me?"

"Less than that useless dress," Joy answered. "My goodness, Hilary, what a waste of money."

"Thanks to you," Hilary muttered, slipping on Jake's faded jeans. The waist was baggy, and the legs needed to be rolled up.

"You should be thanking me," Joy replied. "After all, aren't you having fun?"

"I'm handling it," Hilary admitted.

"I would think so. I told you he was perfect for you."

"He is *not*. He's nothing like the man of my dreams—"

"I beg your pardon," Joy interrupted, "but don't presume to tell *me* what you dream. I know what you dream about, and I pay attention. You wanted somebody kind, but not a pushover. You wanted somebody capable, who handles crises well. Somebody you can count on when the going gets rough. You wanted somebody good-looking, and somebody who could make you laugh. You wanted somebody who loves children, somebody who loves life. And I found him and put him right in front of your nose."

Hilary buttoned the flannel shirt over her ice blue silk brassiere. "I also wanted somebody with a good social position and bank account. Or did you forget about that?"

Joy gave an airy wave of her hand. "Oh, that. That's not important."

"Like fun it isn't."

"Hilary, you are so exasperating. Now you get your butt out there and have a good time. See if you can do something about that Christmas tree. Amanda's terribly unhappy with it, and it's just not one of those things that men do well."

"By the way, Joy," Hilary asked, lowering her whisper, "just where is Amanda's mother, anyway?"

"Why don't you ask?" Joy suggested, and disappeared.

The landscape lay silent and perfect, blanketed in sparkling white. The cloud cover had broken up, and stars sparkled between silver and blue shadowed clouds.

Jake trudged across the yard, holding a blue plastic tarp, his boots crunching in the snow, and Hilary and Amanda followed behind in his deep footprints.

"Like good King Wenceslaus," Amanda said, stepping from one deep footprint to another.

Jake pulled the heavy pine bough from Hilary's broken windshield and tossed it to the ground.

"What a mess," he observed, opening the door. He began tossing out pieces of broken glass and broken branches.

"Here, I'll help," Hilary said.

"No, don't. You might cut your hands. My gloves are thick."

Finally he and Hilary unfolded the blue plastic tarp and spread it over the car, weighting it down with pine boughs and rocks.

"At least if it snows again, it won't do any more damage," Jake observed.

"Thanks." Hilary straightened, wiping the snow from the socks she wore over her hands.

Jake began laughing.

"What?"

"Look at you. You don't even look like the same woman I met today."

Hilary looked down at her outfit—a pair of giant rubber boots, an oversized down jacket, sock-covered hands, and a striped muffler tied around her head like a scarf.

Her light brown hair had slipped loose from its elegant twist and was falling in breezy strands around her face.

"I look ridiculous," she admitted.

"You look great," he corrected.

Her heart gave a funny flop. What kind of man could think she was attractive dressed in odds and ends of oversized clothing?

A good one.

"Look!" came Amanda's cry, and they turned to see her bounding across the snow, dragging a saucer-shaped disc of battered metal. "One of those sled things!"

"Oh, boy," Jake said. "We're not going to get out of this. Amanda found that thing in the garage, and she's been waiting for snow ever since. Are you up for it?"

Hilary didn't hesitate. "Hey, are you kidding? It's been years since I've been sledding. Point me to the nearest hill."

They plowed down the snowbound road together, their boots leaving deep furrows behind them. They could have been anywhere—in an enchanted Bavarian wood or lost in the dark, mysterious forests of Russia.

There were only the three of them in an enchanted world of sparkling white, wandering into the moonlit night.

"We're like the three kings," Amanda said, staring up at the sky. "Which one is 'the yonder star,' do you think?"

"Take your pick," Jake said. "There's enough of them up there."

He began singing, *"We three kings of Orient are, bearing gifts we traverse afar . . ."*

Amanda joined in, her soft, clear voice high over her father's off-key baritone. After a moment Hilary joined in.

Their voices sounded small in the dense night, muffled by the snow. The only other sound was the crunch of their booted feet.

"There's the hill!" Amanda shrieked, her glowing face bright with excitement. "Let's run!"

"You run," her father told her, "and we'll catch up. I may go out to play in the snow in the dark of night, I may sing to the stars, but I'm an old man, and I don't run up hills."

Amanda took off, the snow slowing her. She lost her knit hat once, stopped to retrieve it, and continued on.

Jake and Hilary continued on at a more sedate pace.

"This is her first sledding trip," he explained. "You just don't get a lot of snow in L.A."

"How long have you been here?" Hilary asked, glancing at him. In profile, his movie-star face was even more handsome.

"Two weeks. That's why we're living out here. We didn't have time to find a place; that's why we're borrowing this house. It belongs to a friend of mine whom I went to college with. He usually rents it, but it just happened to be empty. It's not the Ritz, but it beats sleeping in the van."

Hilary wondered what kind of man would pack up his daughter and drag her hundreds of miles away without even having a place to live.

"Wasn't it hard on Amanda? Packing her up and leaving her family and school right before the holidays?" She tried not to sound judgmental, but it took an effort.

It reminded her too much of her own childhood—her mother, who cared more about sitting in bars than taking care of her own children, the eviction notices tacked to the doors of their shabby apartments, the sudden moves made in the middle of the night to avoid paying rent.

Amanda was halfway up the hill, dragging the sled by a fraying rope. She turned and gave them a happy wave.

Hilary looked at Jake. He was watching her with a grim expression, his mouth a tight frown.

"We didn't have a choice," he said. "It was time for a fresh start."

A fresh start. How many times had Hilary heard that, growing up? They were empty words. A fresh start in another crowded apartment, or a ramshackle house, or with her mother's newest boyfriend, who was just like the other one. A fresh start to the same old hand-to-mouth life.

"It's not fair to children," she said softly, without meaning to speak out loud. "Amanda deserves better."

Jake's dark eyes narrowed. "Well, thank you for that pearl of wisdom, Miss Exclusively Lauren. How nice of you to enlighten me. Unfortunately, the rest of us don't live in your caviar-on-artichoke-leaves kind of world, and sometimes things don't happen the way we'd like. I guess it's easy to sit in judgment on the masses when you're born with a silver spoon in your mouth."

Hilary flinched at his stinging words. "I didn't mean—"

"Like hell you didn't."

He stalked ahead in the snow, and Hilary hurried after him, the cold air stinging her cheeks.

"And I wasn't born with a silver spoon in my mouth," she informed him. "I've lived in a lot worse places than you can imagine."

He didn't answer.

Hilary walked behind him, the snow bunching under her feet.

The magic was gone from the night; the adventure was over. She was simply trapped in a ramshackle house somewhere outside Woodinville, with a hole in her windshield and in the company of a man who didn't much like her.

Funny, how that hurt.

"I'm sorry," she said, and something in her voice caught his attention. "I'm really sorry. I didn't mean to imply that you're a bad father. As a matter of fact, from what I've seen you're a very good one. I guess I was thinking of myself."

He stopped and looked at her, curious.

"I didn't have a very nice childhood," she confessed. It was not something she shared with people, and the words felt awkward as she spoke them. "We . . . we moved around a lot. My mother . . . well, she was an alcoholic first and a mother second. It was hard on us. We were never as good as the other kids, never had the same things they did. It was rough on me."

He stood quietly for a minute. "Not a caviar-on-artichoke-leaves kind of life, huh?"

Hilary shook her head with a rueful laugh. "More like surplus processed cheese and stale food bank bread."

He shook his head in thoughtful disbelief. "You could never guess, to look at you now."

"I hope not," Hilary said. "That's the point."

"The point of what?" he asked. "The ritzy store, the country clubs, the big parties?"

"I guess," Hilary answered softly.

From far up the hill Amanda gave an impatient shout. "Hurry," she called, dancing from one foot to the other.

"Come on," Jake said, "the rest of the Swiss toboggan team is getting impatient."

He took Hilary's hand in his as they hurried up the hill, and it felt secure there, warm and right.

First Jake went down the hill with Amanda, and Hilary waited at the top as they made their laborious way back up, dragging the disk. Then it was Amanda and Hilary's turn. They settled together on the cold metal, clutching the handles in cold fingers.

Jake gave them a push and they were off, sailing through the crystal-clear, snow-washed night, the earth singing past them, the wind rushing over their faces.

Hilary let loose a delighted shout at the sensation of speed and cold, and Amanda, held firmly on her lap, shrieked with laughter.

They slid and bumped and spun their way to a breathless stop, and the night seemed oddly quiet again.

"I like coming down," Amanda said, "but walking back up isn't much fun."

"That's the price you pay," Hilary told her.

Amanda slipped her small mittened hand into Hilary's as they started up the hill. "Is there snow every Christmas here?" she asked.

"No; enjoy it. Mostly it rains."

"Too bad. We never had snow in California. This is the best Christmas we've ever had."

They were quiet for a few minutes, and Hilary thought how good it felt, to hold a child by the hand.

"Do you like your mother?" Amanda asked suddenly.

Hilary looked down, startled by the question. Amanda looked very small and fragile, her wide brown eyes anxious.

"No," Hilary said honestly. "No, I don't. She's not a very nice person."

Amanda seemed as startled by Hilary's answer as she had been by Amanda's question. "You're supposed to like your mother," she said, her eyes troubled. "Everybody else does. The kids at school all do. They have nice mothers."

And I don't. The words were as clear as if the child had spoken them.

Hilary knew. She remembered too clearly the sense of isolation, watching the other girls getting picked up after school in nice cars, wearing new dresses, their moms who brought cupcakes for the class on their birthdays.

But not for Hilary the Hippo, in her thrift store dresses and fraying sneakers. There were no ballet lessons or Girl Scout meetings or slumber parties with the friends she never had. She ate, and ate, and ate, trying to fill the hole where her heart should have been.

Amanda was looking up at her, waiting.

"Do you like your mother?" Hilary asked, because she knew that Amanda wanted her to.

"No." Hilary knew, all too well, the guilt the child felt over the simple admission. She waited.

"She ruined everything," Amanda went on. "She took our money and made us lose our house. She went away all the time and never called."

Hilary felt a rush of anger for the woman who had so callously mistreated this gentle, lovely child.

"That stinks," she said.

Amanda nodded. "She's a cocaine addict," the little girl added, and the careful words spoke volumes.

"My mother," Hilary said, "is an alcohol addict."

"That stinks, too," Amanda said, and smiled tenderly up at Hilary, who understood.

They continued up the hill, their fingers clasped together like the fragile friendship that had grown between them.

The last trip down the hill the three of them took together, laughing as they tried to fit onto the tiny round toboggan. Jake climbed on first, sitting cross-legged, and then Hilary climbed onto his lap.

She couldn't help blushing at the unfamiliar sensation of his body fitted next to hers, and the way his arms circled around her. His breath was warm on her cheek.

Then Amanda climbed on top, and Jake groaned and carried on about the weight, and demanded that he be allowed to sit on top.

Amanda and Hilary refused to budge, Jake finally admitted defeat, and, with a combined effort, they set the disc off down the hill.

Hilary laughed all the way down, feeling the cold wind singing over her cheeks and Jake's solid grip around her waist, and the way Amanda clung to her shoulders. They sailed down the white silk ribbon of hill, the three of them, stars and trees and ground shooting past, their delighted shouts rising into the sky.

"Now I know why they say, 'laughing all the way,' in *Jingle Bells,*" Amanda said when they came to a stop. "This is the best Christmas ever."

"Christmas Eve," her father corrected. "Christmas is tomorrow. And we'd better get you to bed if Santa Claus is going to come."

Amanda was too tired to offer any more than a token argument, and the three of them started back toward the house.

Hilary felt very small in the ice-white enchanted forest that went on into eternity. Above them, the sky was like midnight blue velvet dusted with diamonds, silent and watchful.

Chapter Six

The tiny house seemed to glow with light, welcoming them back into its pine-scented warmth.

They shed boots and mittens and scarves as they entered, clumps of snow melting on the worn carpets.

Jake built up the fire while Hilary and Amanda collected the wet clothes and hung them in the bathroom to dry.

"Bedtime, Amanda Panda," Jake called.

Amanda gave a cry of dismay. "But I'm having *fun*."

"The snow will still be here in the morning," Hilary soothed her.

Amanda brushed her long dark hair back from her face with a troubled look. "Will you be here?"

Hilary ran a hand over Amanda's silky hair. "Sure."

"Promise?" The experience of a million broken promises hung in the tremulous word, and Hilary felt a flash of anger for Amanda's mother, wherever she was.

"I always keep my promises."

"Because you're a hard-ass?"

Hilary choked back a laugh. "Did your dad call me that?"

"When we were leaving your store today he said, 'You can always count on a hard-ass.' Can you?"

"You bet," Hilary said.

"Nightgown time," Jake announced, appearing in the bathroom doorway. "The fat guy in the red suit is on his way."

Amanda rolled her eyes, making clear that she was far too mature to believe, but couldn't suppress the excited flush that washed over her face. She scampered from the bathroom to her bedroom, clad only in a bulky sweatshirt and Minnie Mouse underpants. Hilary heard her pulling open dresser drawers.

"So, I'm a hard-ass, am I?" she asked Jake, picking up Amanda's jeans and hanging them over the towel rack.

He had the good grace to color a little, but his dark eyes sparkled and he showed a crooked grin.

"Out of the mouths of babes," was his noncommittal reply. "How about a glass of wine?"

"Are you changing the subject?" Hilary asked, laughing.

"What subject?" he returned, assuming an innocent air.

She followed him to the living room, where he had cleared away the remnants of their feast, and relit the candles in the rose and evergreen arrangements.

A bottle of chardonnay stood on the coffee table, a decent brand from a local Washington winery. Two mismatched glasses stood beside it.

The fire crackled in the stone hearth, shedding its rosy glow over the room, and the windows shone like paintings of winter landscapes.

"Nice," Hilary said, accepting a glass from him.

"To Christmas," he said, lifting his glass to her.

"To Christmas," she echoed, raising her own. Their eyes met, and a warm electricity crackled between them.

I want you, his eyes said.

I want you, too, hers answered.

They both looked away and drank. Somehow the simultaneous act of putting lips to glass seemed terribly intimate. Awkwardly, Hilary looked away, at the tiny fir tree in its red and green metal stand. Its lights seemed to glow brighter above its fragrant branches.

"Those jeans are soaked," he commented, looking at her borrowed Levi's. "Let me find you something else to put on."

His practical words broke the spell.

"Great," Hilary agreed, grateful. "Then I can help you with the kitchen."

Amanda appeared in a too-short nightgown, her legs looking long and thin beneath the flannel hem. "Okay, cookies and milk for Santa," she announced.

"That fat old geezer," Jake remarked. "Let's give him some of that goose liver stuff, and leave the cookies for us."

Amanda shrieked with mock dismay at this sacrilege, and Hilary laughed.

"You're a candidate for a lump of coal if I've ever seen one," she told Jake. "Come on, Amanda, let's make Santa a proper plate."

Together, they chose an assortment of appropriate delicacies, and Amanda placed it by the fire. "I didn't hang my stocking," she reminded her father.

"Well, Santa might not do stockings this year." His voice was studiously cheerful. "He's probably fallen behind, what with the snow and everything."

"But he'll still bring presents?" Amanda's eyes were troubled.

"You can bet on it. Unless you've been very, very bad. Like, staying up three hours past bedtime."

Reassured, the little girl flew to her father and hugged him tightly around the waist. "Okay, I'll go to bed."

Hilary stood back, her wineglass cool in her hands, watching as the two embraced, and the way Jake's hand stroked his daughter's hair and the way Amanda's face shone. If she'd had a father like that, she thought, how different her life might have been. How lucky they were, wrapped in the circle of their love. She knew that even if they had dined on canned chile and saltine crackers, if Santa Claus hadn't come at all, they would have been just as happy at the end of the day.

She felt awkward, alone, an intruder.

"Hilary?" Amanda was smiling at her, with her small, innocent face glowing. "Can I sleep with Fred the Bear?"

Hilary looked at the old rocking chair, where Fred sat, battered and wise-looking.

"Of course," she answered, surprised, and handed him to Amanda.

The little girl beamed. "Good. He looked lonely."

She gathered Fred tightly to her chest, and the sight reminded Hilary of her own childhood.

"How long do you plan to carry that ratty old bear around?"

"Forever. And when I have a little girl, she'll want to take care of him."

How her mother had laughed at the idea that anyone would want the threadbare toy. But there stood Amanda, beaming with happiness as she held Fred to her heart.

"Good night, Hilary," she said, and Hilary received her first full-fledged hug from the little girl. She returned it gratefully, burying her face in the soft brown hair.

Oh, if you were mine, she couldn't help thinking, *what I wouldn't do for you.*

"Sleep tight," she told Amanda, and watched as Jake led her from the room.

She busied herself tidying up the remnants of their Christmas feast, humming along with the radio as she heard their low voices murmuring back and forth in Amanda's room.

She felt very domestic, and found herself pretending that she did this every night. They would have dinner together and play Scrabble, or watch a video. She would help Amanda with her homework, and she and Jake would talk about their days at work. Then, while he was tucking Amanda in, she would do the dinner dishes, looking out the window at the dark pine trees. . . .

"Very different from your usual daydream."

Joy was sitting at the kitchen table, leaning her

head on one graceful arm.

Hilary did a double take. Joy looked very different. In fact, she was hardly recognizable as the same pudgy, track-suit clad intruder she had met earlier.

Her pale hair had half fallen from its knot and hung in gossamer waves down her back. She appeared to have lost at least thirty pounds over the course of the evening, and her face was unlined, her complexion glowing with a translucent brilliance. The simple robe she had changed to earlier had become a satin gown of gleaming white that caught the light in shimmering folds.

And most amazing of all, she had wings—almost transparent, iridescent wings like some fantastic, opalescent butterfly.

She smiled at Hilary's astonishment and gave her new wings an experimental flutter. "Stylish, aren't they?"

"Fantastic," Hilary whispered.

"Oh, I've seen better. So, you're in here wallowing in some Betty Crocker fantasy. Wife, mother, doer of dishes and scrubber of toilets."

"That's intrusive," Hilary whispered, slapping the dishcloth indignantly to the counter.

"That's my job," Joy answered, with such a clear, radiant smile that it was impossible to be angry. "And it was a nice fantasy, Hilary. Much better than the one about the senator."

Hilary blushed.

"Seven hours 'til sunrise," Joy observed. "That's when I report to accounting."

Hilary glanced at the kitchen doorway. Jake and Amanda were still speaking quietly behind Amanda's partially open door.

"How am I doing?" she asked.

Joy beamed and smoothed her satin skirts. "I think my appearance speaks for that. Of course, I would like some kind of commitment."

"Like what?"

"I'd like to know that this isn't some kind of spiritual one-night stand. I want you to keep on this track, to keep your heart open and stay focused on what's important. Mind you, there's nothing wrong with a good business, but it shouldn't come first in your heart."

"What else have I got?"

"What else do you want?" Joy asked. "Honestly, Hilary."

I want Jake, Hilary thought. *Not just Jake, but Amanda with him. I want to be part of their family, I want them to love me the way they love each other.*

"Good girl," Joy said. "Take care of it. But keep in mind, he's not a pretentious man. He won't be impressed by who you know or what restaurants you go to or the fact that you wear Chanel suits. You need to open up, let him know who you really are."

"I need to change," Hilary said softly.

"I found you some long johns."

She jumped, and found herself staring at Jake, who was offering her a pair of thermal knit long underwear.

"Not glamorous, but clean and warm," he said.

"Thanks." Hilary accepted them gratefully. "I think I'll change."

"High time," remarked Joy.

When Hilary emerged from the bathroom Jake was sitting at the kitchen table, wrapping a present for Amanda, while Joy watched with interest.

Actually, he was trying to wrap a present. He was folding and unfolding the paper, staring at it with a bemused expression.

"Want help?" Hilary asked.

"How did you guess?"

"Normally," Hilary said, "I don't like to perpetuate sexual stereotypes. However, there are some things men just shouldn't do, and one of them is gift wrapping."

She pulled a chair up to the table and sat next to him, swiftly reorganizing his purchases. There was a pad of drawing paper, a box of colored pencils and a package of felt-tip pens, and a scented doll in a cologne bottle–shaped package.

Swiftly and expertly, she wrapped them in the holly-printed paper. "There."

He leaned back, tilting his chair on its back legs.

"Pretty sparse," he observed, looking at the small packages.

"Sometimes it happens," Hilary said. "Amanda doesn't strike me as a particularly greedy little girl. She'll be happy with whatever she gets."

"That makes it worse," Jake said. "If she was a spoiled little monster, I wouldn't feel so guilty."

Hilary studied him for a moment. "Hey, do you mind if I contribute?"

He raised a quizzical brow. "It's a little late for last-minute shopping, isn't it?"

Hilary went to the living room and returned with her tote bag. "Here," she said. "She likes sparkly things."

She took out her miniature evening bag, brand-new and ordered to match her dress, and emptied it. "Very glamorous," she assured Jake, waving the beaded bag. "Little girls love glamorous things."

"Spoken like an expert," he said. "Do you have nieces?"

"No. Two nephews, who are interested only in noise and destruction. But I was a little girl once."

She added her silver hand mirror and hesitated. "Are her ears pierced?"

He nodded, and Hilary added the blue velvet jewelry box that held her quarter-carat diamond studs.

He flipped open the box and gave her a sharp look.

"Tell me these are fake."

"They're fake," Hilary lied, "but very sparkly."

"You wouldn't bullshit me, would you?"

"Do I strike you as the kind of woman who would?"

He took his time about answering. "Honestly, Hilary," he said at last, "I don't know what kind of woman you are. Earlier today I would have said you were a coldhearted, materialistic phony of the worst kind. Tonight, I don't know. You seem different."

Hilary carefully Scotch-taped the end of the wrapping paper over the velvet box. "It's the clothes," she said, nodding at the oversized plaid shirt and the long johns. "My new image from Chez Jake."

"I like it," he said.

They sat in comfortable silence while she wrapped the hand mirror and evening bag, listening to Christmas carols on the radio.

"I'll make sure Amanda takes care of those earrings," he said. "You know as well as I do that they're real."

She looked up, blushing. "Do you mind?"

"Where my daughter's concerned I have no pride," he admitted. "And this has been a wonderful night for her. I'd like her to have something to remember you by."

A sickening, hollow feeling rolled through Hilary's stomach. Tomorrow she'd return to the city and her well-ordered life, and this magical Christmas Eve would become a memory.

She looked at the little pile of packages in front of her and hesitated.

"Would you like to go out sometime?" Her words were quick and awkward.

"What? Like on a date? You're asking me out?"

"Why not?" she asked defensively, not looking up.

"I didn't think I'd be your type."

She looked at him and saw the surprise in his face. Surprise, and something else. He was happy. His mouth was curved into a pleased smile, a dimple showing at the corner.

Joy sat across the table, her chin resting on her hands, beaming with approval.

Hilary gave her a get-lost look and turned back to Jake.

"I think," she said carefully, "that meeting you and Amanda may be the nicest thing that's happened to me in a long time. I think you're exactly my type."

"I can't take you anywhere you could wear that seven-thousand-dollar dress," he said quietly.

"Well, I'll save it just in case Chuck and Di drop by," she answered, laughing. "What do you think?"

He reached across the table and took her hand. "I think," he said, "that you're very beautiful. And

I think there's a very gentle heart under Miss Lauren's hard-ass exterior. And I think . . ." His voice trailed off and he looked down at their hands—his large and callused from work, the nails bitten off, and hers smaller and paler, with perfectly manicured pink nails.

Their eyes met and they leaned toward each other, drawn by the welcoming light that showed in each other's faces.

A whisper of breath escaped Hilary, a dove-soft sigh, right before their lips met.

It was right. It was bliss. It was a kiss like nothing she had ever felt. His mouth was sweet on hers, sending satin-soft fire through her veins. His fingers trailed over her cheeks, in her hair, onto her neck, touching her as if she was something precious.

And when he leaned back and looked at her, Hilary felt beautiful, truly beautiful, for the first time in her life.

She was stunned, shaken. She smiled unsteadily and reached up to touch his hair. It was as soft as it looked. She let the thick dark silk of it fall between her fingers.

"Alleluia," Joy said, and Hilary jumped. "Just as the clock strikes twelve. You timed that perfectly, Hilary. And now I think I'd better leave. I have a feeling this is one of those places where angels shouldn't tread."

There was a soft rustle of wings, and Joy's chair crashed to the floor.

Jake jumped. "How did that happen?"

"I guess I did it," Hilary answered vaguely.

He glanced at the fallen chair, sitting at least four feet out of Hilary's reach.

"Come on," she said hastily, "Let's get these presents under the tree."

They were quiet as they placed the packages under the little tree.

"I wish I could have done more for her," Jake said softly.

"Hey, you love her," Hilary said. "That's worth a lot."

He put his arm around her waist and pulled her next to him, kissing the top of her head softly. "Thanks."

They stood there for a long time, and then she raised her face to him, and he kissed her again.

His shoulders felt strong and warm beneath her hands, and the line of his back was straight and smooth. Her body curved against him as if it had been made to do so as their lips met again and again. Sensations of heat and darkness rolled through her, leaving her body simultaneously shaken and melting.

"I should stop," he murmured, his voice husky against her ear.

Hilary stared up at him with eyes full of wonder.

"No," she whispered. "Please don't."

"Are you sure?" he asked, and his dimple showed. "I'm not some cheap little tart, you know. If you don't call me in the morning, I'll die of shame."

Hilary's laugh was shaky. "Better than call you, I'll cook you breakfast. What do you think?"

He lifted her face toward his, and his dark eyes were full of heat and light. "I think I'm starting to believe in miracles again. How about you?"

"I think I believe in a lot of things I never considered before," Hilary said, and then his mouth covered hers again.

She woke in the early hours of the morning and for a minute didn't remember where she was.

Jake slept next to her, his long body curled around hers, his hand on her shoulder. His heartbeat was solid and strong against her back, his breath warm against her ear.

She sighed with delight, burying herself deeper under the warm blankets, looking around the dark room.

He had been perfect. His fingers had touched her like fire, awakening and electrifying her senses. Her body had fit perfectly beneath his; his skin had felt like warm velvet to her. Their lovemaking had been stunningly perfect, as easy as if they had always been lovers, but as new and wonderful as if it had been their first time.

She touched his hand, and he sighed in his sleep, a happy, deep sound low in his throat.

After a minute Hilary slid out of bed. He slept on, the symmetrical lines of his face shadowed in the faint moonlight that came through the window.

Hilary slipped his flannel shirt on and padded silently into the living room.

Outside, the snow lay white and perfect. The world seemed new and beautiful to her, sleeping peacefully beneath the moonlight as it waited for Christmas morning.

She stood for a few minutes, hugging herself, listening to the silence.

In front of her the little noble fir stood, proud and straight, barren save for its single string of lights. A Charlie Brown tree, Amanda had called it.

Hilary walked into the silent kitchen and picked up the scissors from the table, where they lay in the scraps of wrapping paper.

She hesitated only a second, and then returned to the living room and picked up her Petra Bazhenov gown from the arm of the couch.

She turned it inside out and saw where the strings of pearls and crystals had been fastened on with careful stitches.

She cut one thread, and then another. She sat cross-legged in the soft glow of the Christmas tree lights, snipping until a string of Austrian crystals came loose from the satin and slid to her lap. Then a string of pearls. Then another.

"And you said this dress was useless," she murmured to Joy, but there was no reply.

Dawn was coming, pink and cold over the snow-covered hills, before she went back to bed. She crawled in next to Jake, and he pulled her against him without waking.

She closed her eyes, wondering at the incredible sensation of his body next to hers. She had never imagined that it could feel like this to simply fall asleep next to someone, she thought, and then slipped off to sleep.

Amanda's cries of happiness startled her into the real world.

Next to her, Jake gave a reluctant groan.

"Look!" screamed Amanda. "Look at my tree! Look!"

"Is it on fire?" Jake called, sitting up in bed.

Hilary opened her eyes. He was more beautiful

in the morning light than he had been in the night. His skin was golden, and the hair that covered his chest was dark and soft looking.

She couldn't resist touching it, and he caught her hand in his and brought it to his mouth, kissing her fingers.

"Come look," Amanda cried from the other room.

"Welcome to the world of children," he said to Hilary. "Either we go look at her or she'll come in and look at us."

Hilary grabbed the flannel shirt from the floor next to the bed. "I think we'd better go look."

She grabbed the discarded long johns and hastily pulled them over her long legs.

"Hey."

She turned to look at Jake.

"You're beautiful," he said simply, and she felt her cheeks heat with pleasure.

"So are you," she answered, and they exchanged a smile full of memories and promises.

"Okay," he called, pulling on his jeans and leaving the bedroom, "what's the tree doing that's so . . ."

His voice trailed off, and Hilary smiled as she stood up and followed, raking her fingers through her tangled hair.

The little tree was alight with yards and yards of shimmering beads. Strings of tiny round ones, cascades of square-cut ones, teardrop pendants and strands of pearls. They caught the light and reflected it, like a million rainbows. It was an angel tree, a snow queen's tree, a confection of glitter and light.

Amanda stood, quivering with delight, her eyes

huge and glowing, clutching Hilary's worn-out bear to her heart.

Jake stared too, confused, and then realization dawned.

"How about that Santa Claus," he said softly.

"It wasn't!" Amanda cried, and she rushed to her father and caught him around the waist. "It wasn't, Daddy. It was an angel, a genuine truly one. I *saw* her. She had on a dress that was all sparkles, and wings as tall as she was, and stars in her hair. I swear it! An angel did it!"

Jake stood, shirtless and shoeless, shaking his head with a bemused smile.

"An angel," he repeated. "Did you ask her to make coffee before she left?"

"It was!" Amanda repeated, a little desperately.

"You bet it was," Jake said. "I don't know about the wings, but it was an angel, all right."

"I saw her, too," Hilary said, and Amanda's face glowed with delight.

"Did you? With stars in her hair, and in a sparkly gown?"

Hilary nodded. "That's her."

"Does she make coffee?" Jake asked.

"No!" Amanda burst out. "That's your job, Daddy." She shook her head in disbelief. "Have you ever heard of anything so dumb?"

"No," Hilary agreed. "Everyone knows that angels don't make coffee. Its the most ridiculous thing I've ever heard of."

"As ridiculous as a seven-thousand-dollar tree?" Jake murmured to her, silent laughter in his eyes.

Amanda was dancing around the shimmering tree, her long, tangled hair flying.

"At a price like that, I expect to be invited back

next year," Hilary told him.

"Invited back? You're assuming that we'll let you leave."

They exchanged a secret, silent smile.

Amanda whirled past, her nightgown and hair flying.

"Look at her," Jake said, "She's lost it. She's out of her mind with joy."

"That's understandable," Hilary replied. "I've gone out of my mind with Joy a time or two." She laughed at her own joke, and Amanda joined in, seizing her by the hands and spinning her around.

Jake shook his head and went to make coffee. Hilary and Amanda spun in circles until the room shimmered like a rainbow, and outside the little house the sun climbed and dazzled across the snow-covered hills, as pure and brilliant as a promise of love.

TRANA MAE SIMMONS

CHRISSY'S WISH

To the little angels in my family: Brandon and Ransom Simmons, my grandsons; Rebecca and Emily Haavik, and Diana Cantner, my nieces.

Chapter One

Chrissy stretched to her tiptoes and looked out the cabin window, searching for her Aunt Polly until she saw her drawing a bucket of water from the well shaft. Aunt Polly balanced the bucket on the rim of the well while she untied it, then set it on the ground. Straightening, she placed both hands in the small of her back, arching and staring at the sky while she worked her fingers back and forth.

All at once, Aunt Polly bent forward and covered her face with her hands. Though she couldn't hear her, Chrissy knew her aunt was crying again. She could see Aunt Polly's shoulders shaking, and her own throat tightened as tears filled her eyes.

Aunt Polly had cried last night too. She probably had thought Chrissy sound asleep, but she'd heard her through the bedroom wall. She'd been puzzling once again over what to give her beloved aunt for Christmas, which was only two and a half weeks away, and she'd tossed and turned instead of slipping straight into sleep as she usually did.

Chrissy rubbed at her eyes and stepped back from the window. Recalling her aunt's reddened eyes at breakfast, she quickly dropped her hands. She didn't want Aunt Polly to realize she'd been crying too. Though her aunt had spoken in her usual, it's-going-to-be-a-wonderful-day voice this morning, Chrissy had caught the worry behind the cheerfulness. After all, she was five years old now—a big girl. Even that mean old rooster didn't bother her anymore when she gathered the eggs all by herself.

She lifted her chin in imitation of the tilt she saw so often on her aunt's face and crossed the small cabin floor to her bedroom. Closing the door behind her, she stood with her hands on her hips and stared at the ceiling.

"I guess You're not hearing me real good," she said out loud. "Or maybe You think I'm se . . . selfish. I heard Tommy's mama telling him after church last week that he was being selfish 'cause he put so many things on his Christmas list. All's I asked for was a dolly, You know."

She stood for another second, then crossed to her bed. Kneeling, she pressed her palms into prayer and bent her head, closing her eyes.

"Preacher Jim always says I can be heard anytime I want to talk," she said. "Daytime or nighttime. I just got to be sin . . ." She frowned and pursed her lips in thought, then nodded her head. "Oh, yeah. Sincere. I think that means I shouldn't take up time for silly things. Me wanting Aunt

Polly not to cry all the time's not silly, is it? And I think I know why she's crying, even if she keeps telling me things are fine and dandy."

She glanced at the ceiling once more, her head cocked as though expecting a reply. When none came she bent her head.

"At church Sunday, all my friends had their papas with them," she continued. "And the papas were awfully nice to the mamas when it got time to leave. They helped them into the buggies, and I even saw Mr. Pyle kiss Mrs. Pyle when he thought nobody was looking. They aren't a mama and papa yet—Mr. and Mrs. Pyle, I mean. But Aunt Polly says they're gonna have a baby of their own real soon."

She shifted a little to ease the discomfort in her knees, then clenched her fingers tighter as she went on. "I know You probably seen all this, too, since Preacher Jim says You see everything. Didn't You see Aunt Polly's face when everyone started going home? She looked so lonesome. She helped me into the wagon, but she had to climb in by herself. She's got to do 'most everything by herself, now that Mr. José's got so old, and she don't have much time to laugh and play with me anymore. Can't you please send somebody, so Aunt Polly will be happy again? Amen."

For a full minute Chrissy kept her head bent over her intertwined fingers as she thought over her words. She'd done it right, hadn't she? She wasn't asking for herself. She only wanted Aunt Polly to smile again.

"Uh-oh," she said. She heaved a small sigh and spoke again. "I really, really want this mostly for Aunt Polly. But it's not right to not tell the whole truth. It's almost like a lie, Aunt Polly says. So I've got to tell You that it would be nice for me to have a papa, too. I guess he'd be my uncle, but that'd be all right. And Aunt Polly being happy would make me feel happier, too, so maybe that's kind of selfish."

She took a deep breath and said with extreme effort, "If You want, You can keep the dolly. Amen, again."

"Have you got everything?" Josephine asked Matthew.

"You've asked me that ten times, Jo," Matt replied. "What more do I need than the letter? The donkey's right over there, and you've made me change my clothes three times. If I don't look like an old prospector by now, I might as well forget it."

"They call them burros these days," Jo said in exasperation. "Prospectors carry their tools and supplies on burros."

"Burros, donkeys, whatever. Mary rode into Bethlehem on an ass, but for some reason that's considered a derogatory term now."

Jo cupped her chin in her palm and stepped back to study Matt one last time. The corporeal body he'd chosen looked adequate, and there was no trace of angelic demeanor in his stance. He stood hunched over a little, and his face was covered with a scraggly beard. She wrinkled her nose a tad, but they'd both agreed a man traveling around with his burro for months on end would probably not bathe too frequently.

As angels, she and Matt never had to worry about body odors, but when one of them took on a corporeal form they had to keep in mind the physical attributes of humans. They didn't want any slip-ups when talking to a man like Sam Butler. For a human, he was darned intelligent, and he wouldn't be easy to manipulate.

"Oh, dear." Jo glanced skyward. "Chrissy's praying again, Matt. She's only five, and she doesn't realize that answering her wish can take a little time."

"She's really worried about Polly," Matt replied. "Polly and the ranch are Chrissy's whole world."

"Well, it's time Sam Butler accepted his responsibility." Jo crossed her arms, and her wings fluttered on her back. "After all, he's Chrissy's uncle, the only other blood relative she has left. I can't see why that man's been so stubborn about not checking on his brother for over six years."

"You know why," Matt told her. "He didn't want to see Christine, Chrissy's mother. He didn't think he could stand to see her married to his brother, Ron. That's what started their quarrel to begin with."

"I suppose," Jo said in resignation. "But I'd like to think that if he'd ever gotten Christine's letter, he'd have gone to see how she was doing."

"He's going to have the letter in a few minutes, if you'll let me get out of here. And I'll deliver the rest of the mail from the pouch that got overlooked after the train wreck after I give Sam the one from Christine. If things go right, Sam will be on his way to the north of Dallas by morning."

"And when he gets there he's going to find out that Christine's dead, too—that she died in childbirth," Jo said. "But he'll just have to face it. I hope he doesn't turn away from Chrissy and Polly. They need him badly."

Jo watched Matt stare at the dusty little town down the road, where Sam Butler ran his saloon. The instructions they'd received with their assignment of fulfilling Chrissy's Christmas wish had been completely clear. They were to retrieve the letter Christine had written over five years ago, informing Sam of his brother's death, and deliver it to Sam.

She and Matt had done some hurried background checking, and she had to admit it didn't look very promising. They'd had tough assignments before, but never one with this much potential for failure. They both hoped Heaven knew what it was doing—pairing up a hard-bitten, embittered man like Sam with the sister of the woman Sam had once loved.

"He's Chrissy's uncle," Jo reminded both herself and Matt when she read Matt's thoughts, which were mirroring her own. "As bitter as Sam is, I'm sure he'll want his niece to have a better life than she will if Polly can't hold on to the ranch."

"Chrissy's Polly's niece, too," Matt said. "And Polly's always been proud of her independence. She's not going to be real happy about someone moving into her life and trying to take over. She's always had pretty much of a free rein, what with her father being sickly all those years and her being in charge of running the household. She even raised Christine after their mother died."

"Too, it's going to be hard for her to admit she's failing for once in her life and needs some help. We've discussed all this already, Matt, and we both agree Sam Butler seems like a truly unlikely candidate to help Polly. She didn't much care for Sam when he first came courting Christine, and she made no bones about the fact that she was glad Christine chose Ron instead."

Jo fluttered a few feet above the ground and nodded toward the burro. "Well, we have our assignment to start off with. We have to deliver the letter. Then we can stay around and see what happens, but we can't interfere."

Matt deliberately replied to her in a crackling voice. "Wal then, I guess I better get crackin'." He plopped the battered and stained felt hat he'd been holding in his hands on his wiry gray hair and spat a wad of tobacco juice on the ground.

"Matt!" Jo said in a horrified voice. "You're chewing tobacco!"

"T'baccy," Matt said with a grin. "Why, don't 'cha know? T'baccy's 'most as important to an old feller like me as my burro."

He winked at her and turned away to walk to the burro, affecting a limping gait. The small animal lifted its head at his approach and let out a loud hee-haw.

With a chuckle, Matt said, "Yeah, I think I look pretty funny, too, but that's nothing compared to how I smell. You and me will just have to tolerate it, though." Picking up the lead rope, he led the burro toward town.

Sam Butler pulled his dun stallion to a halt atop a rise. The horse immediately blew out an exhausted breath, scattering flecks of foam from its muzzle, and Sam patted its damp neck. He'd pushed Dusty damned hard, but not beyond the bounds of the stallion's endurance. After a few hours' rest he could count on Dusty to be ready to go again. And he might have to do just that, depending on what the next few minutes brought.

To the west, the first flames of a brilliant magenta sunset lit the sky. Sam ignored the panorama in favor of studying the layout of the ranch yard below him. There was a small log cabin, a fairly large barn set off to the back, corrals, and another tiny shed. Smoke curled from the chimneys of both the cabin and the shed, so the shed probably housed a ranch hand or two; he didn't see a bunkhouse.

Huh. After six years he'd have thought his brother's spread would be something a little more substantial than this. Still, he had to remind himself that he didn't know how long Ron had been dead. The envelope on the letter the old prospector had delivered two days ago was too ragged and water-stained for him to make out more than the address, and Christine hadn't dated the letter. Damn it to hell, why hadn't she written him again when she didn't hear from him? He probably could have checked with the post office and tried to find out exactly how long ago the train wreck had happened, but from the minute he touched that letter all he could think of was getting to Christine.

The door of the little shed opened and a woman emerged. Oh, God. Was that Christine? About all he could tell from here was that she had the same golden hair and lithe figure. Her walk, though, when she started toward the cabin, didn't have the bounce he remembered. The hard years she'd spent on a Texas ranch could account for the change. He'd seen plenty of women go from young to old in too few years in this harsh land.

Damn it, why hadn't she tried harder to get hold of him? Sam's fist thudded on his saddlehorn, and Dusty half reared and snorted his displeasure. When Sam had the horse under control again he glanced down at the ranch yard to see that the woman had noticed him. She stood with one hand shading her eyes, gazing in his direction. A second later she almost ran into the cabin.

"Well, hell," Sam muttered to himself. "No sense settin' up here wasting time when I've pushed myself like a madman for two days to get here."

He nudged Dusty forward and rode on down the rise. When he was about a hundred yards from the cabin the door flew open and a shot rang out. The bullet plowed into the dirt and kicked up a plume of dry sand near Dusty's front hooves—too near. The stallion rose in a full rear this time, and Sam cursed both it and the shooter under his breath as he reined the horse back to earth.

Sam had sense enough not to urge Dusty onward. Gritting his teeth, he jerked his hat from his head, hoping he was close enough to be recognized.

"Hello!" he shouted, anger making his voice sharp. "It's Sam! Can't you tell?"

The feminine figure slipped out the door, still holding her rifle at her shoulder. "Sam who?" she called back. "Sam Butler?"

"Yes, damn it!" he yelled. "Can I ride on in now?"

The woman lowered the rifle, but Sam noticed as he rode closer that she kept her right hand positioned near the trigger guard. She stood in the shadows thrown from the cabin by the dying sun, and it wasn't until he was ready to dismount that he could tell she definitely wasn't Christine. In fact, he immediately identified her as Christine's older sister, Polly.

Polly, the old-maid harridan, he'd derisively called her in his mind, although she was only two years older than Christine. He felt the chip settle on his shoulder instantly.

"I want to see Christine," he said instead of greeting Polly. "I got a letter from her."

He almost missed Polly's smothered gasp, but he saw her shoulders sag and the rifle tremble in her hands. For a few long seconds, she only stood shaking her head, her mouth working as though she was trying to speak. Finally she managed a few words in a choked voice.

"You . . . you couldn't have. No, oh, no."

"Damn it," Sam growled, "I know you've always thought I was a son of a bitch, but I'm not leaving here until I see her. She's got a right to tell me herself if she doesn't want to talk to me."

He took a step closer and watched Polly's face crumple. She made no attempt to ward him off and even set the rifle down against the cabin. He stopped a foot from her, and she closed her eyes briefly, then looked up at him.

God, she was almost the perfect image of how he had imagined Christine in his mind after six years. The golden hair was a little less wavy, but Polly had always worn her hair tied back. Wisps of what he'd once told Christine were honey-blond sweetness curled around her face, and she hadn't gained an ounce. In fact, she looked like she'd lost some weight.

He'd been avoiding her gaze, partially because

he knew his own confrontational attitude was showing on his face and partially because both sisters shared the same brilliant emerald eyes, which could bring a man to his knees. But she cleared her throat, and he instinctively met her eyes.

A hammer thudded into his stomach. Instead of the haughty sternness he'd expected, held-back tears sparkled in her eyes. He saw pain swimming there, tinged with despair. Spontaneously, he reached out and cupped her upper arms with his hands.

"What is it?" he asked in a softer voice. She shook her head mutely, and a stab of compassion tore through him. He had to make an effort—a huge effort—not to pull her into his arms and soothe away her misery. Only quickly reminding himself that this sister would not welcome any sympathetic gesture on his part kept him from following through on his impulse.

"Polly," he said, "what's happened? Where's Christine?"

Polly gulped back a sob, then stepped away from him. Turning, she raised a hand and pointed to a small fenced plot west of the cabin. Beneath a cottonwood tree growing on the bank of a creek were two wooden crosses, not one, as he had expected after learning about his brother's death.

The hammer thudded into his stomach again, this time followed by a splintering in his heart. He bowed his head, striving fruitlessly to keep back his own tears. He thought he'd been ready for the sight of Ron's grave—he'd had two days to prepare for it. But the twin cross beside it had the effect of shattering his resolve.

He felt a faint brush on his sleeve and saw Polly's hand. Without one thought of all the past dissention between himself and Polly, he turned and swept her into his embrace. Burying his face in her neck, he choked on his grief, his shoulders heaving.

Polly held Sam to her, just as she held Chrissy whenever she suffered either a physical or emotional hurt. He was much more of an armful than Chrissy, though, this huge man she'd always thought of as much too unemotional and egotistical for her bubbly sister. Now, though, all she could think about was how much she was feeling his hurt—as deep as her own had been when she held Christine in her arms and watched the life flow out of her—as deep as it had been when she helped José lower Christine's body into the ground.

"Ah, God. Ron. Christine," she heard Sam mumble.

She hugged him in return, then brushed her hand across the back of his ebony hair. Tears streaming from his eyes soaked her neck and the shoulder of her dress. His iron-clad grip left her little room to breathe, but she couldn't bring herself to struggle against him.

Something inside her shattered in response to their shared grief. The ranch's hired hand, José, had grieved for Ron and Christine, but he hadn't loved them both as deeply as she and Sam had. Even after five years she still missed her sister desperately.

Overcoming her own misery, Polly stroked Sam's back comfortingly and whispered, "It's all right, Sam. Go ahead. You won't start healing until you let it all out. And even after that it takes time."

Sam shuddered deeply, then lifted his head and wiped at his eyes. "I'm sorry," he mumbled.

Unthinkingly, Polly reached up and touched his face. "It's all right," she repeated. "Truly, it is."

"Thanks," he said. He glanced again at the gravesites and took a step away from her. "I want to go over to the graves and have a minute to myself there."

"Go ahead. I . . . Sam, I just want to ask you something first. It'll only take a second."

Sam nodded, and Polly continued. "You mentioned receiving a letter from Christine. Sam, she's been dead five years."

"God," Sam groaned. "It . . . well, the letter has lain somewhere in a mail pouch after a train wrecked. I just got it."

"Did . . ." Polly hesitated a moment, then plunged on. "Did Christine tell you she was with child?"

Sam's gaze swung back to her, wonder on his face. "No," he almost breathed. "The child . . . ?"

"Her name's Chrissy," Polly responded with total love in her voice. "I named her after her mother."

"Chrissy," Sam repeated. "Will you let me meet her?"

"Of course," Polly told him with a smile. "After all, you're her uncle. If you'd like to stay for a while, I can move in with her for a day or two. There's a cot I can use."

"Please. I'd appreciate that a lot." He turned to walk toward the tiny graveyard, shoulders bent and hands thrust into his pockets.

Polly watched him go with a surprising ache in her heart. Funny how she'd always disliked him. Still, she wasn't one to do a total about-face in her feelings regarding someone without a valid reason. Right now she felt empathy toward Sam because of their shared grief, yet too many times she'd listened to Christine complain about Sam's high-handed, standoffish attitude. Only after Christine had met Ron, Sam's more easygoing, openly affectionate brother, had Polly seen true love blossom in her sister's eyes.

Sam had a right to get to know his niece, but Polly would be darned if she didn't kick his butt right off the ranch if he so much as once gave Chrissy even one of those condescending looks Christine had so often had to tolerate.

Chapter Two

Polly heard clumping footsteps cross the back porch as she moved the perking coffeepot to the side of the stove. Sam must have stabled his horse and decided to come in the rear of the cabin. He gave a short rap, then entered the kitchen and hung his hat on the rack beside the door.

Shrugging out of his coat, he said, " 'Preciate the invite to stay overnight. Barn's pretty snug, though, and I could pitch my bedroll out there if you'd rather."

"That won't be necessary," Polly assured him. "I've already set up the cot in Chrissy's room."

"Is she asleep this early?"

"She's getting into her nightgown and will be out in a minute. She's excited about meeting you."

Though she and Chrissy had already eaten, Polly assumed from the look of Sam's horse when he rode in that he hadn't stopped recently for a meal. She stirred the pot of stew rewarming over the fire, then reached for a loaf of bread to slice. After a moment she realized she hadn't heard Sam cross to the table and turned to invite him to sit.

"I'm not a rancher," Sam said without preamble before she could speak. He still stood by the rack, his coat in his hands and a forbidding look on his face. "Never had no desire to punch cows or clean horse dung off my boots."

"Pardon me?" Polly asked, confused as to the meaning of his comments, which seemed totally unrelated to their discussion of Chrissy. But a sense of premonition prickled into a tightening band around her chest.

"I don't plan on having to work up a sweat to make a living," Sam replied.

Polly gritted her teeth and bristled. "No, you might end up with a callused finger and not be able to deal the cards so easily when you gamble!"

"The world needs businessmen just as much as it needs beef to eat," Sam said with a shrug.

"I'd hardly call a saloon a business," Polly fairly snarled. "At least not a respectable one. But then, it fits in with your past style of living."

"Just a damn minute. . . ."

"I'll thank you to remember that I have a small child in this house," Polly broke in. "You *will* watch your language while you're in my house."

"Yours? My brother started this place."

"And just who do you think's been keeping it going for the past five and a half years? Giving Chrissy a home? Feeding her? Caring for her, while you sat around a card table and let your body start running to fat?"

Polly bit back a satisfied grin when Sam sucked in his stomach. He hadn't really put on that much weight, and she fought a flush when she remembered that the reason she even knew he had gained a few pounds was because she'd held him so close a while ago. Maybe she should try to hang on to the sympathy she'd felt for him then, instead of letting this discussion deteriorate so rapidly into an argument. A tiny warning bell kept ringing in the back of her mind. She just couldn't figure out whether it had something to do with the meaning she sensed hidden behind Sam's words about ranching or the tingling in her hands when she recalled the feel of his silky hair and bunched muscles.

Chrissy barreled into the kitchen and slid to a stop. Craning her neck back until Polly felt sure the little girl would end up with a knotted muscle, she gazed up at Sam. Her golden hair spilled riotously down her back and her piquant face held a mixture of awe and something Polly couldn't determine. Wistfulness, perhaps?

When she glanced at Sam she saw his face mirroring Chrissy's. Definitely wistfulness, then uncertainty. Sam's fingers clenched on his coat before he glanced down, as though surprised to see he held it. With none of the smooth grace Polly had noticed when he swung off his horse earlier, he awkwardly turned to hang the coat on the rack. It missed the peg on his first attempt, and he grabbed it from the floor and jammed it beside his hat. Facing Chrissy again, he held out his hand, as though getting ready to shake with another man. Immediately he must have realized how foolish that appeared.

Dropping his hand, he wiped it against his denim-clad leg and tossed Polly a helpless look as he shrugged.

Still peeved at him, Polly determined to hold her silence and let Sam muddle his own way through the start of his new relationship with his niece. However, Chrissy had never been one to tolerate a lengthy silence from the first moment she learned that sounds made words.

"Are you my Uncle Sam?" she asked. "I'm Chrissy. I was pretty sure someone would come, but I didn't know who."

Polly frowned in confusion over Chrissy's statement but quickly turned her attention back to Sam when he knelt down to Chrissy.

"Yeah, I'm Sam Butler," Sam agreed in a quiet, hesitant voice. "Your father was my brother, so I guess that does make me your Uncle Sam. I've never had a niece before, but I'm very glad to meet you, Chrissy."

Chrissy tilted her head and laid a tiny finger beside her mouth for a moment. Evidently making up her mind, she nodded before she crossed the floor, hugged Sam's neck, and then kissed his cheek. Sam's arms went around her and she remained within his grasp, though she stepped back far enough to study his face.

"You look sort of like the picture Aunt Polly gave me of my papa," she said after a second. "He's in Heaven, you know. With my mama."

"I know," Sam replied. "But I just found out a couple of days ago."

"I've always known," Chrissy said matter-of-factly. "Aunt Polly says it doesn't mean Mama and Papa didn't love me awfully much, just because they went on to Heaven without me. She says they're watching over me, even if I can't see them."

"Uh . . . I'm sure that's right, sweetheart." Sam tossed Polly another helpless glance, but she turned to move the stew to the side of the stove.

Let him bungle along on his own, she thought to herself. According to Christine one of Sam's worst faults was his attitude toward having a family. He'd told Christine that he would rather pamper and coddle his wife for a few years before children intruded on their life, but Christine had always had reservations about whether Sam ever meant to have children of his own.

For her part, Christine had picked up one of Polly's dolls as soon as she could walk. She'd had an entire family of dolls by the time she was Chrissy's age, and had spent hours building fantasy lives for them. She had never once hesitated when asked what she wanted to be when she grew up.

A mama. Christine's voice echoed in Polly's mind, and she smiled to herself. Glancing over at the clock, she reluctantly forced her thoughts back to her responsibilities.

"Chrissy," she said as she picked up a bowl and ladled it full of stew. "It's really past your bedtime. Sam will be here in the morning, and you can talk to him some more then."

She thought she heard Sam give a suppressed sigh but decided to give him the benefit of the doubt as she set the stew on the table and looked over at Chrissy.

"All right, Auntie," Chrissy said obediently.

Chrissy kissed Sam's cheek again and told him good night. Her ears might have wrongly interpreted Sam's emotions, but Polly had no problem reading his expression. The look on Sam's face clearly showed his relief as he stood and wiped his beaded brow.

"I'll be in to hear your prayers and tuck you in, Chrissy," she said.

"That's all right, Auntie. I'm big enough to do that all by myself now." Chrissy stopped in the doorway for a second and grinned at Polly. " 'Sides, I kinda gotta say something all on my own this time in my prayers."

She scampered out of the room before Polly could question her. Deciding that Chrissy must have some secret Christmas wish to recite, Polly let her go. Despite her reluctance to stay at the kitchen alone with Sam, manners bade she at least get his meal on the table. Besides, she always tucked Chrissy in at least twice before she went into her own room, and tonight, since she'd be sleeping in Chrissy's room, she could check on her as much as she wanted.

"Would you like some butter and jam with your bread?" she asked Sam.

"I was hoping that was for me," Sam admitted as he came over to the table.

"Well, of course it is," Polly said. "Chrissy and I ate over an hour ago. Oh, I'm sorry. I guess I didn't think to ask you if you were hungry. I just assumed you hadn't taken time to eat before you rode out here."

"Thanks," he said as he sat down. "And yes, I would like butter and jam, if it's not too much trouble. Or . . ." He shot her a grumpy look that reminded her of Chrissy when it got a little past her nap time. "Unless you think it might be too fattening for me."

Polly quickly caught her lower lip between her teeth to stifle her giggle and turned so he wouldn't see the merriment in her eyes. Giving herself a moment to control her mirth—though she didn't really know why she cared if he saw her laughing at him—she sliced off a couple more pieces of bread. Keeping her eyes downcast, she got everything else on the table, then poured him a cup of coffee and set it in front of him.

"Do you need anything else?" she asked.

"Yeah," he answered in a rather petulant voice. "Some company. I hate to eat alone."

Polly sighed and poured herself some coffee. Sitting down across the table from him, she clasped her hands around the cup.

"Then we might as well continue our discussion while I sit here," she said. "And we'll start with you explaining your comments about horse dung and sweat, although I'm pretty sure I've already figured out what you meant. If you've got any designs on making me sell this ranch, you'd better know right off that I'll fight you tooth and nail. This is Chrissy's heritage, and it was her father's dream, as well as my sister's. No one asked you to come here and get manure on your boots!"

Sam clanked his spoon into his stew bowl, then sat back in his chair. Face tight with anger, he glared at her, but Polly noticed he kept the piece of bread with butter and jam in his hand.

"Ranching's no life for a woman and a child alone," he growled. "Hell, I looked this place over a little when I arrived. You've got three cracked windows in the cabin, the barn door's about ready to fall off, and there's hardly any hay put up for your stock for the winter in the loft. Besides that, you haven't got enough wood stockpiled for even one blue norther. How the blazes do you think you're gonna manage all that on your own?"

Before she could stop herself Polly buried her face in her hands. He was only saying out loud everything she'd been thinking for the past two months, but he had no right to say it. No right at all. Where had he been while she struggled the last few years?

Getting a grip on her emotions, she dropped her hands to see Sam shoving the entire piece of bread and jam into his mouth. He chewed angrily, but the comic sight did not amuse Polly.

"We'll manage," she gritted. "Just as we have so far, without *your* help!"

"*I* didn't even know you were having to manage," Sam spat back. "You can't sit in judgment of my actions when I didn't even know Ron and Christine were dead!"

"And if you had known?" Polly demanded.

That set him back—or rather, he leaned forward and picked up his spoon. He moved a piece of beef around, shoved his spoon under it, then tipped it back into the bowl. He glanced quickly at her, grabbed his coffee cup, and took a swallow.

Finally he said, "I would've come to check on Christine. I wouldn't have left her out here on a godforsaken Texas ranch to starve."

"Even if you'd known she was going to have your brother's baby?"

"Of course," Sam replied after a brief hesitation. "Chrissy's my niece. She's family."

"And what would you have offered to do for Christine?" Polly asked in a deceptively mild voice. "Give her a job in your saloon after she had her baby?"

Sam shoved his chair back violently and stood, leaning toward her with his palms on the table. He opened his mouth, then shut it abruptly, though the rage continued to sparkle in his brown eyes.

"If my niece wasn't sleeping in the next room," he said in a quiet, anger-laced voice, "I'd give you the verbal thrashing you deserve for even suggesting I'd do something like that to Christine. For your damned information, my saloon's a gaming house. It's strictly a place for men to come to gamble and drink."

"It's a place for them to come and spend money on cards and whiskey, which should be spent on their families instead." Polly crossed her arms over her chest and glared right back at him. "And you're cursing again."

"Damn it, woman! You make a man curse! You've always treated me like I wasn't good enough to lick Christine's boots. I'll bet the happiest day of your life was when Christine gave me my walking papers and took up with Ron."

"My sister made her decision totally on her own. I had nothing to do with it. And since you brought it up, yes, I did think Ron was better for her. He treated her like an equal, not like some little puppy he wanted to parade around and show off."

Polly saw grief replace the anger in Sam's eyes and realized he was still dealing with his new knowledge of the deaths. Deriding him over how he had treated Christine so long ago had probably worsened his sorrow, and she was stabbed with guilt. Even though Polly had thought Sam and

Christine mismatched, she had been aware that Sam truly cared for her sister. Who could have helped loving Christine? She had been beautiful, loving and tender. It had cut Christine to the quick to have to hurt Sam and break their betrothal, but she had done the mature thing and faced her responsibility.

Polly remembered well the night she had listened as Christine poured out her heart—saying that she realized she was falling in love with Ron, her feelings for Sam paling in comparison to what she now knew was a true love. Christine had looked down the long years ahead of her and known in her heart she wanted to live them with Ron, not Sam.

She hadn't known those years would be cut short, but at least the brief time she had left had been with the man she loved.

"Sam, I'm sorry," Polly apologized. "It's just that you have to accept the fact that Christine made her decision because she knew it was the right one for her. She didn't make it lightly, either. She also felt you deserved a chance to find another woman who would love you in the way a man's wife should love him."

"I'm glad she was happy," Sam said in a lowered voice. He sat back down in his chair and picked up his spoon. "But sometimes marriages are made for other reasons than love. It's an accepted fact of life. Our marriage will have to be one of those."

"Our . . . what!" Polly's voice broke on a squeak of outrage.

Chapter Three

Sam waited until he'd chewed and swallowed his bite of stew before he answered. "Chrissy needs two parents, and our marriage will be the best way for us to take care of her. I still haven't decided what to do about this ranch, but I'd been thinking of selling the saloon for a while now. . . ."

"Of all the unmitigated gall!" Polly screeched before she remembered Chrissy in the next room. She surged from her chair and paced around the table, stopping with her hands on her hips and her face close enough to Sam's to make her point without shouting.

"What the hell makes you think I'd marry you? And who gave you any say in what to do with this ranch?"

"My, my," Sam said in a condescending tone. "The lady's cursing."

"Oh! You're enough to make an angel curse, Sam Butler! Answer me!"

Sam casually picked up another slice of bread and began spreading it with butter. "I think you're overlooking something here, Polly. As Chrissy's uncle, I have as much right as you to see that she has a reasonably stable, comfortable life. My brother would have expected me to make sure his daughter was taken care of."

"Well, my sister begged me on her deathbed to care for her baby, and that's what I intend to do. And you left out the fact that Chrissy also has the right to have love in her life while she grows up."

Sam threw the piece of bread down as though it had suddenly grown mold and stood. Facing Polly across the chair, he said, "I can give her love, too. I fell in love with her the minute I saw her."

"You still haven't answered my questions, Sam." Polly whirled away and walked over to the stove before she turned back to him. "I don't see one reason why we have to be married—or why you think you have the right to decide what happens to this ranch."

Sam rolled his eyes and got that patronizing look she had seen on too many men's faces when they spoke to women, but Polly held her tongue, silently demanding his reply. When it came she gulped back her growing feeling of entrapment.

"Under the law I have just as much right to custody of Chrissy as you do, Polly. If it came down to a battle, I'd think a judge would look at what either one of us could give Chrissy—what was in her best interests. You're a woman alone trying to run a ranch that's going quickly to seed. I'll bet you don't have more than a penny or two in the bank, or you'd have hired somebody to get your hay in and cut your winter wood."

"I've got José," Polly put in.

"José? Why haven't I seen him?"

"He's . . ." Polly's shoulders slumped. "He's getting old. Sometimes his arthritis makes it impossible for him to do much."

Sam nodded and continued. "Whether or not you approve of the type of business I operate, I have adequate funds in the bank to care for a child, and a wife, if necessary. The saloon's not my only investment. I've been careful with my money over the years."

Polly clenched her fists at her side, resolutely refusing to allow the gathering tears of rage to fall. "What you're telling me, then, is that if I don't marry you, you'll take Chrissy away from me. You'll sell the ranch and toss me out into the cold."

"Now, don't put it like that," Sam replied. "After all, you're family, too. I've got a responsibility here, for both you and Chrissy. I'm just deciding what's in Chrissy's best interests."

"Like a judge would."

"Like a judge would," Sam repeated.

"How . . . how long do I have to make up my mind?"

"I've got a competent manager running the saloon," Sam said with a shrug. "I can hang around for a while. But it's not going to do your reputation a lot of good to have me here for very long without us being married. And your reputation will reflect on Chrissy. So, let's say three days. That should give you plenty of time."

"And the ranch?"

"I'll use those three days to look it over—see

what needs to be done and if it's worth putting any more money into it." Any hopefulness Polly felt faded as he went on, "If I decide it isn't, what we get from selling it can go into a trust fund for Chrissy. And I'll expect your cooperation in being truthful with me about this place. I want access to the books you keep."

Three days kept echoing in Polly's mind while she tried to pay attention to Sam's words. Three days to make a decision that would affect the rest of her life.

"Ch . . . Christmas is coming up," she said without thinking. "I've already got a few things made for Chrissy. We always have a lovely time on Christmas Day. You can't turn Chrissy's world upside down right before Christmas."

"Christmas is too long to wait for your answer on whether you will marry me," Sam said dismissively. "It's over two weeks away, and your reputation would be ruined by then."

"Is it too long for you to wait to make your decision about the ranch?" Polly pleaded, despising herself for the beseeching tone in her voice. "We've already begun making plans. Moving right now, in the middle of everything, wouldn't give us much time to prepare all over again. And if it's Chrissy's last Christmas on the ranch, I'd like it to be extra special."

"Yeah, well, Christmas has always just been another day to me. But I can see where it would mean a lot to a child, and I guess I need to start remembering things like that. All right. We'll stay on the ranch after we're married until at least Christmas."

* * *

"Oh, that man!" Jo fumed. She crossed her arms, her wings fluttering in agitation. Beneath her robe, her foot tapped against the cloud floor upon which she and Matt stood.

"Darn it, Matt," she continued. "Chrissy's wish was for her Aunt Polly to be happy again. All Sam Butler's done since he arrived is upset Polly more!"

"Now, now, Jo," Matt soothed. "Sam's trying to decide what's best for Chrissy. He wants her to have a good life."

"There's more to life than the material possessions Sam has in mind There's love and caring. And Sam Butler has absolutely no idea what love is—or what the lack of it can do to a person's life. He's forcing Polly into a loveless marriage."

"Maybe they can learn to love each other. There are definitely some sparks there—and I truly don't believe all of it is anger. Let's just see what happens, all right?"

"Do we have any other choice?"

"No, we don't," Matt agreed.

Sam swung the ax and split another log into stove-size pieces. Grimacing, he lifted his hand to his mouth and sucked on a newly forming blister. He should have at least had sense enough to get his riding gloves from his saddlebag, but he supposed he wanted to prove to Polly that he wasn't afraid of calluses. Blisters, though—those were a different matter.

And why the heck did he care what Polly the Harridan thought of him? He had the upper hand here, and she ought to appreciate his shouldering his share of the responsibilities. He could have ridden away this morning and left her to her own devices.

Something had happened to him while he stood beside the twin crosses under the cottonwood tree, though. Beneath that dirt lay the only woman he'd ever loved, and his brother, both gone from his life forever. The barren years he'd spent with only his pride for companion had mocked him—rising in his memory now that he knew why Ron had never swallowed that damned Butler pride and contacted him.

Christine's letter had explained that his compassionate, caring younger brother had died in a way that characterized the man he had become. He could imagine the scene—the runaway team and a little boy standing crying and frozen in its path. Ron wouldn't have thought twice about the danger to himself, only the necessity of rescuing the child.

The little boy had been tossed to safety, but Ron's death under the iron-shod hooves of the horses had left his own forthcoming child fatherless. The only way Sam could make up for his self-righteous foolishness in cutting his brother out of his life after he and Christine had married was to make sure Ron's daughter never wanted for anything. Polly's dislike of him was a complication, but he'd be damned if he'd let her banish him back to a life he now realized had been lonely and hollow.

Chrissy, he reminded himself. *I'm doing this for Chrissy. She's the only person left on earth who's truly a part of me—who shares my blood.*

Why, then, didn't Chrissy's face keep him awake most of the night? Why did he keep seeing Polly's tear-misted eyes as she pleaded with him to at least have Christmas on the ranch? And why did he keep remembering how her slight figure felt when she held him—how comforting it had been for him to hold on to her in his grief? How silky that golden hair felt against his cheek? How her breasts, though small, had pressed firmly against his chest?

That sure as hell was a dangerous route for his thoughts to be taking. But it gave him an inkling that the physical part of their marriage might be somewhat enjoyable, if he could ever get close enough to Polly to show her that their bodies could please each other. *If* she agreed to marry him—but he didn't really see that she had much choice. He'd come to the conclusion that this would be the best way for them to share their mutual love for Chrissy. After all, Polly had never found a man to love herself, and he would never open his heart again. Together, they could have companionship and watch over Chrissy.

He glanced at the cabin. He sure as heck hoped she got up soon. He'd been out here at the woodpile since dawn first streaked the sky, and he hadn't even taken time to make a pot of coffee first, since he was reluctant to make any noise that would wake Polly. Well, a child like Chrissy needed her sleep, too.

Hearing a sound behind him, he turned to see the door of the small shack open. A weathered little man emerged, obviously fighting pain as he hobbled toward Sam. He held out a gnarled hand, and Sam carefully shook it.

"You must be José," Sam said. "I'm Sam Butler, Chrissy's uncle."

"Thank the Virgin you have come," José replied in a shaky voice. "Señorita Polly, she is almost wore out. I tell her I want to go back and be with my family—I have become one more burden for her since I cannot do much work. But she tells me she needs my company."

Sam studied José's dusky skin and white, curling mustache, the same shade as his hair. "Is your home in Mexico?" he asked.

"*Sí.* It is warm down there. I try not to let Señorita Polly know how much better my pain would be back there. I do not think she realizes it is this cold up here making me worse."

"Tell you what, José," Sam said. "I need to get a handle on how the ranch is doing, and I'm sure you probably know as much as—maybe more than—Polly. If you'll stick around till after Christmas, I'll see you're kept warm in your house and won't ask you to exert yourself. And I'll pay whatever wages you're owed, plus throw in your stage ticket back home and a little something extra to help your retirement."

"How did you know Señorita Polly owed me back wages?" José asked.

Instead of answering, Sam let his gaze run over the ranch yard, pausing now and then on the repairs needing to be done. When he looked back at José the man nodded in understanding.

"I do not want your charity, Señor Sam," José said. "I have some pesos put aside. I have been working in Texas most of my life."

"It won't be charity," Sam insisted. "It'll be payment for your services and knowledge. I know absolutely nothing about ranching—never had any desire to learn. But I promised Polly I'd check things out before I make a decision about whether to sell the ranch."

"Señorita Polly and the little Señorita Chrissy, they love the ranch," José mused. "I have seen them walking around at sunset, holding hands and smiling at each other. I have not seen that lately, though. Señorita Polly, she does not have much time to enjoy herself these days."

"Well, I'm here now," Sam said. "And the first thing to do is to get some more help around here. Do you know any boys looking for work?"

"Plenty, if you have the money to pay them, Señor Sam."

"Give me a quick rundown on how many you think we'll need. I want somebody with some carpenter skills to make the building repairs, as well as whatever hands will be necessary for the stock."

José smiled wryly. "Not too many for stock. Maybe two. They may be able to gather up twenty, twenty-five cows with the R Bar C brand, and the old range bull, if they can find him. Señorita Polly, she sold the steers at the fall roundup, but she only received half the money they brought. She had to pay her share of the roundup hands' wages. She didn't have her own hands to send to help out."

"Lord, what was she going to have ready to sell next fall?" Sam asked. "Even I know it takes steers a couple of years growing time before you get any money out of them. The spring calves next year won't be ready to sell in the fall. And with only twenty or so cows, it hardly seems worth the effort."

José went on to explain that the ranch had started out with around a thousand cattle. Over the years, though, instead of increasing, the herd had steadily decreased. Part of it was because there was never enough money to keep on sufficient hands.

Cattle were lost in the violent blue northers that bore down on Texas at times. One March a lot of calves didn't make it when the cold lingered well into spring. Even Polly had helped out that year, leaving Chrissy with a nearby neighbor while she rode with José and the one other hand they still had left then. They'd found the newborn calves hidden in the brush and carried them back to the barn to try to save them. Half of those had died, however.

One year drought took its toll. The following winter, hay was scarce, also due to the drought. The cattle had to make do with the dry, unnourishing forage on the range to supplement the lack of hay, and more died of starvation.

"The señorita, she did her best," José stoutly defended Polly.

"It must have been hell on her," Sam said. "Yet she still loves this place."

"It is her home now," José explained. "There have been good times, too. The neighbors, they gather, and in troubled times they help each other out. The ranching, it gets in your blood, señor. But perhaps only another rancher can understand that. I could have gone back home any time, but I wanted to stay. I would not go now if I were not so old."

Sam nodded, but without any real comprehension. He kept picturing Polly in his mind, bundled up in a coat and wool scarf, carrying a small calf across her saddle. Polly sweating in the hot Texas sun, staring at her cattle, which were dying of thirst. Polly grief-stricken over her sister's death, but pulling herself together for the baby's sake.

Polly and Christine had come from New Orleans originally. Theirs had been a blue-blooded heritage, but the family fortunes had long been squandered. Christine had told him once that they pretty much lived off a small trust fund her mother had somehow protected for them. He'd known all along there would be no large dowry for Christine, but it hadn't mattered to him.

Now he realized just who had held the family together. Polly had cared for their ailing father, who Sam guessed must have died shortly after Christine and Ron married. Otherwise, Polly wouldn't be out here in Texas. Polly had made sure Christine never lacked for anything. Christine didn't attend all the fancy balls but had a presentable gown at the ones she did attend. Funny. He never thought about Polly always missing out on the balls.

The object of his thoughts opened the back door and called, "Breakfast is ready! You, too, José. Come on in and eat with us since you're able to be up and around today."

"*Sí,* señorita," José called back.

Sam threw down his ax and José bent awkwardly to pick it up. With a wince of pain, he buried the blade in the cutting block.

"You must take care of the ax," José said. "There is no money for a new one."

"Make a list of the tools we need," Sam told him as they walked toward the cabin. "I'll go into town this morning—hire some help and bring back some supplies."

"If you plan to sell the ranch, why fix it up?" José asked.

"It'll bring more if it's in better shape."

"*Sí.* And I will tell you what we need, but you will write it down, señor. I do not do the reading and writing."

Sam nodded in agreement and pushed the cabin door open, motioning for José to precede him.

Chapter Four

Polly tightened her fingers on one of the last remaining glasses as it threatened to slip through her hand while she did the supper dishes. She'd broken four over the past three days, and with the new hands to feed at the noon meal, she only had a glass apiece left for each of them. She'd be darned if she'd ask Sam to buy some more, since that might mean explaining why she'd gotten so clumsy lately.

Sam had caused her clumsiness, she admitted to herself, swishing the rag around none too gently inside the glass. And he'd brought it on again just now, sitting there at the table with Chrissy, reading her a story and raising his voice in a growl when he imitated the bear in the book. His raised voice starkly reminded her of his presence and how soon Chrissy would be sent to bed, leaving her alone with him. Sam would demand her decision tonight.

Shoot, he could have demanded it the day after he told her she had to make it. She was just stubborn enough, though, to make him wait until the last minute. She would take no chances on losing Chrissy, even if it meant spending the rest of her life tied to Sam Butler.

What would Christine think? she wondered. She recalled Christine telling her, the night of their long talk, that Sam seemed better suited to Polly than her. Polly had laughed herself silly at that comment; at least it had lightened their somber mood. What could Christine have been thinking of to make a remark like that?

Sure, Sam was probably even more handsome than his brother, if you liked that sort of rugged good looks. His eyes were a deep, velvet brown rather than the cinnamon color of Ron's. His hair was thicker, and slightly more wavy. Sam's shoulders were broader, and though she thought she'd kept herself completely aloof from him the last three days, she realized she had noticed that his stomach was already firmer. Who could help noticing, she rationalized, with those form-fitting shirts he wore and the tight denims he'd brought back after his trip to town?

She stiffened when she heard Sam say, "It's bedtime now, sweetheart. Want me or your Aunt Polly to tuck you in?"

"You, please," Chrissy replied around a yawn. "Auntie did it last night. But . . ." After a brief hesitation Chrissy said, "Maybe you both could do it. That would be awful nice."

"Uh . . . sure, if that would make you happy," Sam said.

Polly heaved a sigh and picked up the dish towel to dry her hands. Sam had sure as heck gotten over his uneasiness with his niece. She admitted to a tiny bit of jealousy over that, but their closeness would make life easier for all of them. If Sam had to be the man in Chrissy's life, at least it would be nice for them to have a warm, loving relationship.

Pasting a bright smile on her face, Polly threw her dish towel on the counter and turned. "I'm ready, if you two are. I can let the pans soak a minute and do them when I come back."

Chrissy slid from Sam's lap and skipped out of the kitchen, with Sam close behind her. Polly followed more slowly, but it only took her a few steps to reach Chrissy's bedroom—too few steps. Sam stepped aside at the door and allowed her to enter. Then he leaned against the doorjamb, his gaze on Chrissy, who knelt beside the bed.

"I know I already said thank You a couple of times," Chrissy began. "But I really mean it—at least so far. I was just sorta wondering, though, if this is all of it—the help, I mean. There was that happy part, too, and I don't think that's happened yet."

Suddenly Chrissy glanced up at Polly and Sam, then bent her head a little more and whispered over her hands. Being a little closer to her, Polly caught a word now and then. Something about a dolly . . . or did she say Polly? And she made out the word crying at one point. After a moment Chrissy raised her voice so they could hear it again.

"And Preacher Jim says we have to ac . . . accept Your will, so I promise I'll do that. And please bless Auntie and Uncle Sam. And Mr. José. All our other friends, too. Tell my mama and papa I love them. Amen."

Chrissy leapt up and hurled herself into bed. After wriggling beneath the covers she held out her hands. Polly went to her and kissed her cheek, receiving a kiss in return. She turned to make room for Sam and found herself wedged against his chest. Since her back was to Chrissy, she gave him an icy gaze.

"I'll move out of your way, if I can," she muttered.

Sam snaked his arm around her waist and held her. He bent down and said his own good night to Chrissy, then turned to lead Polly from the room.

Back in the kitchen, Polly firmly removed Sam's hand and turned on him. "I have to finish the dishes."

"Leave them," Sam ordered. "I'll finish them in a while. You're exhausted. You've been dropping things all evening, and you've got big enough bags under your eyes to carry a week's worth of supplies in."

"Well, excuse me for being so clumsy and looking so ragged," Polly spat. "But have you thought it might not be all physical tiredness? I've had a heck of a lot to think about lately—not the least of which is the possibility of losing the child I love like she was my own!"

Sam reached for her again, his manner so gentle that she didn't fight him. He urged her into a chair by the table, then walked over to the stove and poured them each a cup of coffee. Returning, he set one cup in front of her before he reversed a chair on the other side of the table and straddled it.

"I've been doing a lot of thinking the past few days, too," he said quietly. "Whatever you decide, I want you to know that I'll never keep you out of Chrissy's life. You're the only mother she's ever known, and José's told me how much you both mean to each other."

"Then we don't have to marry?" Polly asked hopefully.

"I didn't say that. It's still the only option in my book. I want to be a part of Chrissy's life, too, and I want to make sure she's never in need. But I can also see that you might want to find your own husband—have kids of your own. . . . "

"Chrissy *is* my own!" Polly interrupted. "She's been mine since the day she was born! I would *never* give her up, even if it meant being forced to fight you with my last breath in front of every judge from here to Washington, D.C."

Sam nodded slowly and took a sip of his coffee. "Then that's the way it's going to be?"

Polly closed her eyes and took a deep breath. Her hands began to tremble violently, and she grabbed at her cup, clasping it in a tight grip. Her jerky movements sloshed coffee over the rim, and she opened her eyes and stared down at the red spot already forming on the back of one hand.

Sam hastily reached for the butter dish. Stretching across the table, he pried her hands from the cup and shoved it aside. Keeping her burned hand in a firm grasp when she tried to pull away, he dipped a finger into the butter and spread it across her hand.

"Better?" he asked. "I didn't think the coffee was that hot."

"My hands have been soaking in dish water," Polly murmured, resolutely refusing to acknowledge that his tender gesture had probably soothed the burn more than the butter. "The skin's still soft and more sensitive to the heat."

"Hum." Sam ran his fingertip up the inside of her wrist, and a cascade of what felt like goose bumps just under her skin ran up Polly's arm. "Yeah, it's soft, all right."

Polly wrenched her hand free. "We were discussing Chrissy's future," she reminded him.

Sam crossed one forearm on the chair back and propped his chin on it. "I guess we were. You were saying that we were going to have to go to court."

"No!" Polly cried, then softened her voice. "No. I . . . I won't put Chrissy through that. It would be horrible for her. Isn't there some other way?"

"Believe me, I've thought about little else the past few days myself," Sam admitted in a grudging voice. "And I just don't see any other alternative. We're both a necessary part of Chrissy's life. You might remember that this is affecting the rest of my life, too."

"That's one of the problems between us. You think of Chrissy as an *effect* on your life. To me, she's a joyful, wonderful part of it."

"No," Sam denied. "Chrissy's not the effect. You are."

"What's that supposed to mean?"

Sam straightened in his chair, and a slow grin spread over his face. He unhurriedly traced her face with his gaze, lingered a second on her lips and let his eyes wander down her dress bodice.

Polly's eyes widened when she felt a wave of sensation creep from between her legs up to her stomach. She clenched her thighs on the chair seat, but it only escalated the warmth, until her cheeks flushed with heat.

"Stop that!" she demanded.

"All right," Sam said with a shrug. "But I've waited long enough for you to answer me. You're tiptoeing all around the subject, and we need to get this matter settled."

Polly gulped and pulled her hands from the table, clenching them into fists on her lap. Her mouth went dry, and she licked her tongue around her lips, then bit the side of her cheek. Sam's gaze dropped to her mouth, and she saw the grin start again, but he quickly glanced up and met her eyes.

"I . . . we . . . we can be married," she forced out.

"Good." Sam stood and picked up both their coffee cups. "We'll go into town tomorrow afternoon and find a preacher. I had the man at the general store hold a ring I saw there, in case I needed it. We'll take José for one of our witnesses. Do you need a dress or anything?"

"You . . . you've already made all the plans, haven't you?" Polly said around an indignant gasp. "You knew all along I'd have to agree, didn't you?

"No, Polly," Sam contradicted her. "I merely believe in preparing for all the contingencies. It'll take us a long time to get to know each other well enough for me to be able to read your mind, but we'll have all the time we need for that through the years."

"What was your contingency plan if I'd said no?"

"We don't need to discuss that." Sam walked over to the sink and emptied the coffee cups before he turned around. "We'll start from now—start new, as though we'd just met. We can make a go of this, Polly."

"People don't usually marry each other when they first meet," Polly reminded him.

"Hum, not usually," Sam agreed.

He sauntered over to where she sat and grasped her shoulders, urging her to stand. Caught in the depths of his smoldering gaze, Polly helplessly obeyed him. He gently ran his index finger down her cheek and across her lips.

"People who get married usually kiss each other at least once or twice before the wedding," he murmured in a soft growl.

Cupping his hands on her face, he tilted her chin up and bent his head. He brushed her lips with a delicate kiss and Polly flinched. Instead of releasing her, Sam kissed her again, still gently and tenderly, but with a firmer pressure. The tension drained from her in one fell swoop and she lifted her hands to his waist. Sam broke the kiss only long enough to reach down and place her unresisting arms around his neck; then he gathered her close and captured her mouth in a kiss that tingled all the way from her mouth to her toes. It hardened her breast tips into nubbins and rekindled the warmth between her legs. A far-off corner of her mind told her, though, that maybe the hardness pressing against her stomach had something to do with this delicious new heat she had so recently discovered.

Sam raised his head and ran his hands down her back, grasping her hips and keeping her firmly pressed against him. Sparks flickered in his eyes as he spoke.

"Oh, yes, Polly, darling. We can make this work."

"That . . . that was three kisses," Polly murmured inanely.

"Four." He kissed her again, this time tracing his tongue around her lips before he lifted his head. "But who's counting?"

"I . . . you . . . we didn't talk about this being part of the agreement."

"Marriage, Polly," Sam growled. "It's not an agreement—it's a marriage. And, yes, it—*this*—will be part of it. Have no doubt in that pretty little head of yours about that. We're going to be spending a lot of years together, and there's no reason on earth for us to deny ourselves this pleasure."

"It's supposed to be for Chrissy," Polly insisted, somehow finding the will to push against his chest and step back. "We're getting married for Chrissy's sake."

"It's us now, too." Sam picked up a lock of her hair and rolled it between his fingers. "You and me, Polly."

She shook her head in a helpless gesture, pulling her hair free. Sam sighed and dropped his hand.

"Don't worry, Polly. We can take it slow—get to know each other better. I won't expect us to make love tomorrow night, or even the first week or so. But I will expect you to sleep in my bed—for us to have some time alone together. I want you to understand right now that this marriage will eventually be consummated—not only for legality's sake, but also because we'll be taking a vow of fidelity to each other. I intend to honor that vow, but I do not intend to spend the rest of my life abstaining from lovemaking."

Curling his fingers, he reached out and brushed them under her chin. "Go on to bed now, Polly. I want you to get some sleep, so your pretty green eyes won't have those dark circles beneath them tomorrow. I'll finish up in here."

Polly mutely turned away and walked out of the kitchen on unsteady legs. In Chrissy's room she quickly changed into her nightgown and sank down onto the cot. She knew her jumbled thoughts would never allow her to sleep. Mental pictures and sensations mixed together with snatches of words, keeping her from being able to form more than short, jerky images in her mind.

Sam's face. Her body's newly discovered reaction. Making love—Lord, she'd heard it hurt virgins. That part of him was big. He touched so gently—it felt so nice. Pleasure, he'd said. He called it making love. Love . . .

Chapter Five

Muted sounds from the kitchen woke Polly, and she uncharacteristically lay in the netherworld of half wakefulness for a few seconds longer. She felt so rested, so ready for the day. Keeping her eyes closed, she lifted her arms above her head and stretched luxuriously. The smile on her lips deepened as lingering traces of her dream loitered in her mind.

She'd been in the front parlor—the one other room in the cabin besides their bedrooms and the kitchen. Why didn't they use that room more often? Oh, yes. It took wood for the fireplace. But it had been decorated so nicely in her dream—a Christmas tree, with popcorn and berry strings, and tiny candles on the limbs. A cozy fire blazed in the fireplace, and garlands of holly decorated the mantel. A soft rug cushioned the floor.

They didn't have a soft rug in there, but she'd been lying on one. Not alone, either. And she'd felt so protected, so at peace. So sensual . . .

Her eyes flew open and she clasped a hand over her mouth. Sam. Sam had been lying there with her—kissing her—stroking her. It hadn't been the heat from the fire warming her body.

She flung back the covers and sat up on the side of the cot. Instinctively, her eyes went to Chrissy's bed and found it empty. Now she recognized Chrissy's muted giggles coming from the kitchen, interspersed with a gravelly voice that had recently murmured love words in her dream.

Oh, God. She was getting married today—to Sam. Suddenly a quick rise of excitement stirred in her, but she gritted her teeth and forced it back. Before she could contend with her garbled emotions, Chrissy stuck her head in the bedroom door.

"You're up, Aunt Polly!" Chrissy cried in an excited voice. Skipping into the room, she continued, "I thought you'd never wake up. We're getting married today, don't you 'member? Uncle Sam said you talked about it last night after I went to bed. Hurry, Auntie."

She flung her small arms around Polly's neck and hugged her tightly. Green eyes dancing with delight, she leaned back and pursed her lips into an impish pout.

"I helped with breakfast, so's you could sleep late. It's your wedding breakfast, and I told what your favorites were, and me and Uncle Sam fixed them."

"Uncle Sam and I," Polly corrected automatically.

"Huh-uh," Chrissy denied with a shake of her

head. "You didn't help, and he's my uncle, not yours. But that's all right, 'cause you always have to cook all the time." She stepped back and tugged on Polly's hands. "Hurry, Auntie. We got lots to do."

"I need to get dressed, Chrissy."

"Oh, we already got water heating for us all to take a bath after breakfast, so's you can just wear your robe. I'll go tell Uncle Sam to cook the eggs now. He didn't want them to get cold while we waited for you to wake up."

In a flash of energy, Chrissy ran from the room. Polly laughed softly under her breath as she shook her head. If she could only bottle that vigor, she could make a fortune selling it. Rising to her feet, she decided to take Chrissy's advice and just put on her robe; no sense getting dressed twice. After brushing her hair she pulled it back and tied it loosely, then walked out of the bedroom before she could change her mind and retreat to her bed again.

Sam cracked the last egg on the rim of the bowl and glanced over his shoulder. The egg slithered between his fingers instead of into the bowl, but he ignored the oozing mess.

He could definitely get used to seeing that sight every morning for the rest of his life. The dark circles were gone from beneath Polly's brilliant emerald eyes, and they sparkled with love and tolerance as she glanced at Chrissy, who was setting the table. Tendrils of golden silk curled around her forehead and sleep-flushed cheeks, and a soft smile curved her full lips—lips that had tasted like sweet honey to a starving man when he'd kissed her last night.

The loose fit of her robe only served to tantalize a man who knew exactly how some of those slender curves felt beneath his palms. A set of bare toes peeped out from beneath the hem as she adjusted the belt, and he'd bet his bottom dollar she didn't realize how her breasts were outlined when she shrugged her shoulders to adjust the fit of the robe.

Damn, he was the one with circles under his eyes this morning. He couldn't believe how relieved he'd been last night when Polly had finally agreed to marry him. During his tossing and turning search for sleep, he'd been forced to admit something to himself. This marriage meant more than just a way for him to take care of Chrissy. It meant he'd have Polly for his wife.

He knew she didn't love him—and he sure as hell couldn't be in love with her—but he'd seen another side of Polly through José's eyes, as well as Chrissy's. And he wanted just once to see some respect for himself on Polly's face.

He'd never before in his life thought a relationship with a woman would involve something like mutual respect. Part of his uneasiness with his thoughts last night had been because he was pretty damned mad at himself. He'd browbeaten Polly into agreeing to marry him, insisting it was the best thing for all of them. Polly was a strong woman who had faced and overcome a lot of obstacles in her life. It took a lot to bully her, and maybe another man would've felt a certain sneering satisfaction at subjugating her to his will. It left Sam feeling hollow—as if he'd destroyed a precious, irreplaceable treasure, the only one of its kind.

Toward morning, he had decided to let her out of their agreement. It surprised the hell out of him that he couldn't follow through on that decision. He wanted her—not because of Chrissy, whom he already loved enough to lay down his life for—but because he couldn't give Polly up. She was stronger than him after all.

"Oh, dear, Sam." Polly hurried across the kitchen and grabbed the dishrag. Moving his hand, she swiped the egg into the rag and shook it over the sink, then dunked the rag into the dishpan to rinse it. She tried to nudge Sam aside to finish cleaning up the goo on the counter, but he held his ground firmly.

"Was the *dear* for me, or were you only using it as an expression of aversion at the mess I made?" he growled in a soft whisper.

Her eyes swung immediately to his, and he was completely aware of exactly how many inches of her body pressed against his. His groin reacted instantly, and he could see the flicker of awareness that she felt it also. Her lips slowly parted, and a faint hint of hazy desire clouded her eyes, changing the color from new leaf to storm-tossed sea green.

She swallowed audibly and backed away a step. "The . . . uh . . . the egg. It's running down the front of the counter."

"That's not the only front of something being affected here," Sam whispered. "The front of my . . ."

Polly's elbow hit him in the stomach, and his breath whooshed out. She gave him a wide-eyed, innocent look and murmured insincerely, "Oh, *dear,* excuse me. I was trying to get to the egg to clean it up."

Sam caught his breath and threw back his head. Chrissy ran over from thc table and when he glanced down at her, a miniature of Polly giggled up into his face. A chuckle at his side drew his gaze, and he saw Polly's shoulders shaking and her head turned away from him. Forgetting about the egg on his hand, he reached out and pulled her face around.

"Yuck!" Polly said. She scrubbed at her face with the dishrag, then stared down in horror at the runny traces of raw egg still on it. Sam and Chrissy howled with renewed laughter. Polly's narrowing eyes and the devious look on her face should have warned Sam, but he was too caught up in his own hilarity.

Polly swept the dishrag across the counter and up at Sam's face. It landed in his mouth, and he spit and sputtered as she hastily backed away from him, a hand over her own mouth, which he knew damned well was open in a wide, pleased grin. Her glimmering eyes gave her away.

Sam picked up the bowl of eggs. He dunked the dishrag into it and held it aloft, allowing the mixture of whites and yellows to slide back into the bowl.

"Sam!" Polly cried. "You're ruining the eggs."

"You should have thought of that." Sam advanced on her, still holding the dishrag over the bowl. "We'll have to eat our johnnycakes and ham without eggs this morning."

She backed up another step, then another when he took a long stride. "What . . . what are you going to do?" she asked in a breathless voice.

"I've heard some ladies use eggs for a facial." He looked down at the dishrag for a second, and Polly whirled and ran, wildly giggling Chrissy following on her heels. They stumbled over each other as they tried to get through the bedroom door but finally slammed it shut. Sam could hear both of them giggling to beat the band on the other side of the door.

He thumped his boots on the floor as he crossed the room. Dropping the dishrag into the bowl, he twisted the doorknob. When the door swung open he said in a triumphant voice, "Ah ha! Now I've got both of you in my clutches. Who wants to be first?"

"She does!" Chrissy pointed at Polly and scrambled back onto a corner of her bed. In one swift movement Polly grabbed her and pulled her onto her lap.

"Oh, no, I don't! She does!" Polly cried, burying her face in the back of Chrissy's neck, her chortles of merriment matching those Chrissy couldn't hold back.

Chrissy managed to squirm around and grab Polly's robe, pulling it over her face. "No! No, I don't," she said gleefully. "Aunt Polly does!"

Sam waited for a long moment without saying anything else. Soon both of them fell silent, but each kept her face hidden. After another few seconds, though, they peeked at him apprehensively.

"Huh," Sam said. "If that doesn't take the cake."

"What, Uncle Sam?" Chrissy ventured.

"Well, golly," Sam mused, "I can't make up my mind which one of you to give the first egg facial to." With a shrug, he turned. "Guess I'll have to go eat instead."

Chapter Six

Sam slipped the wide gold band over Polly's trembling finger.

"By the power vested in me, I now pronounce you man and wife," the minister said solemnly. "You may kiss the new Mrs. Butler now, Mr. Butler."

Polly felt as though her eyes were glued to the face of the man all the children in church called Preacher Jim. Yet when Sam touched her chin she turned her face toward his in much the same way a flower seeks the sun. He covered her lips and kissed her tenderly, taking his time with it. Preacher Jim finally cleared his throat to get their attention, and Sam sighed and raised his head.

"Yippee!" Chrissy jumped from the front pew and ran over to them before Preacher Jim could speak, with José following more slowly. Sam swept her into his arms, and Chrissy reached out and pulled Polly closer. "Do I get a present, too, on our wedding day?" she demanded.

"A present?" Polly said with a smile. "Why, Chrissy, who told you we'd be giving each other presents today?"

"Everybody gave Mr. and Mrs. Pyle presents the day they got married," Chrissy contended. "I was only four, but that was just last year, and I 'member it. We give them that quilt I helped make."

"Gave them," Polly corrected.

"Gave them," Chrissy repeated agreeably. "And I don't want something like a quilt. It's . . ."

She ducked her head in sudden shyness, and Sam tilted her face back up. "What is it, sweetheart? If I can, I'll get it for you. This is your day, too, like we talked about this morning."

"Well . . ." Chrissy glanced at the minister. "You know lots about Heaven, Preacher Jim. I . . . I need to ask you somethin' first."

Sam allowed her to slide to the floor, and Chrissy took the minister's hand, leading him off to one side. They began whispering together, glancing now and then at Sam and Polly.

"I wish you both much happiness, Señor and Señora Butler."

Polly turned to José, at first wondering who he was speaking to before she realized her old friend was addressing her. José shook Sam's hand and reached for Polly's. He carried it to his mouth and kissed the back of it, patting the spot he'd kissed as he said, "I will go on back now. I will see you both at the ranch."

"Thanks for being my best man, José," Sam said with a smile.

"My pleasure, señor," José replied. "A great pleasure."

As José slowly limped down the church aisle, Sam and Polly looked over at Chrissy and the minister. When Sam focused on Polly again and lifted his eyebrows inquisitively, Polly shrugged her shoulders in disavowal.

"I have no idea what she wants," Polly said truthfully. "And you really shouldn't agree to give her whatever she asks for without knowing if it's something she needs first. You'll spoil her."

"I said I'd do it *if* I could," Sam responded. "And that goes for you, too. If you want something, all you need to do is ask."

Polly spoke before she could think. "All I want is for Chrissy to have a wonderful Christmas at the ranch she loves so much." She realized her mistake immediately when she caught the brief flash of anger in Sam's eyes.

He maintained a low-voiced control when he answered her. "I've already agreed to that. We're going shopping as soon as we leave here."

"Oh, I can't," Polly whispered, thinking of her embarrassment when she fingered all the things she would love to give Chrissy herself, knowing she had no money. "There's . . . we need to get back. There's supper . . . and evening chores . . ."

"I've already set up an account at the general store, and I expect you to use it, too," Sam said, making her realize he was all too aware of her lack of money. "I also told the hands to stay and do the other chores tonight, and one of their wives came over after we left. She'll leave supper waiting in the oven for us."

"You think of everything, don't you?" Polly said

in a resentful voice. "And you could have asked me before you did that. Maybe I didn't want some other woman messing around in *my* kitchen. But I guess it's easy to order things done when you've got money to pay for them."

"Listen to me, Polly." Polly glanced into his face and saw understanding there. "It's not your fault you need some help now. From what I know, you've done everything you could the past few years to stay on top of things. Let's not sully the rest of the day. It started out pretty nice."

The sincere tone of his voice melted a little of her annoyance, and when she remembered him chasing her and Chrissy with the gooey egg mixture a smile actually tilted her lips. "I'm sorry," she apologized. "I guess I do appreciate knowing I don't have to spend my evening cooking."

Sam hugged her and kept his hand on her waist as Chrissy skipped up to them. His touch reminded her immediately of what definitely did await her this evening—her wedding night. She would be sleeping with Sam in the double bed, which had always seemed so nice and large and comfortable—and lonely, when she had sobbed herself to sleep so many nights the last year or so.

She gnawed on her bottom lip. Sam was so large, he would probably take up most of that bed—Christine and Ron's former bed. A sudden stab of jealousy stormed through her. Would Sam be wishing it was her sister lying there with him instead?

Good grief, jealousy was supposed to be an emotion associated with envy—or love. She couldn't be falling in love with Sam Butler. He'd made it clear this was only a marriage for Chrissy's sake. He'd looked awfully cute that morning, though, with the egg white on his rugged face and that gonna-get-you look in his eyes. . . .

"Preacher Jim says it's fine," Chrissy said. "I can tell you what I want now."

Pulling Polly down with him, Sam knelt in front of his niece. "What is it, honey?"

"I was afraid my other mama and papa might get mad at me, but Preacher Jim says not," Chrissy explained in a serious voice. "I'd like yours and Aunt Polly's per . . . permis . . ." She glanced at the minister and he mouthed something to her. "Permission! That's it. Can I call you Papa and Mama now?"

Polly's eyes filled with tears, and she heard Sam's muffled sniff beside her.

"You've got my permission," Sam said gruffly. "And it would make me the happiest person around to have you do that."

Chrissy tilted her head inquiringly at Polly, and she reached out to pull the child into her arms. "You've always been my little girl, Chrissy," she said with a sob of joy. "I love you very much, and I'd be awfully proud to have you call me Mama."

"That's settled then," Chrissy said, astonishing Polly at the matter-of-fact way she sounded when held-back emotion clogged her own throat. "Can we go shopping now, Papa? You said this morning that we would."

That cocky grin Polly was coming to recognize slid over Sam's mouth, and he swept Chrissy with him as he stood. "Of course, sweetheart," he said, nestling her into the crook of his arm. "Let me speak with Preacher Jim, and then we'll go."

Polly watched him stride over to the minister

and hand him something. Money, she supposed, to pay for the ceremony. She smoothed her hands down the skirt of the dark mint-colored dress she had taken from her trunk that morning—one of only two dresses remaining from her days back in New Orleans. All the others had been refashioned into everyday dresses for her or Chrissy. But at least she hadn't had to accept Sam's offer to buy her a wedding dress. And this one had always been her favorite—its color almost matched her eyes and flattered her slender figure. The ruffles at the neckline added to her less than generous bosom.

Now, why on earth was she suddenly wishing for more on top? It had never bothered her before.

Sam shook hands with Preacher Jim, and a moment later they left the small church, climbed into the wagon, and made the short drive into town. Sam mentioned at one point their need for a buggy, and Chrissy bounced up and down with glee when he added that she might be thinking about what sort of pony she wanted, since she was old enough to begin riding. Polly managed to swallow her pique at being unable to provide such a pleasure for her niece and smiled into Chrissy's excited face.

As the afternoon wore on, her rancor grew. Sam made an even greater friend of Mac, the general store owner, within five minutes of them entering the establishment. Sam never asked a price—only gave the man a long list he evidently had already prepared, then led Chrissy up and down the aisles. The owner's wife tagged along, accepting the purchases and carrying them back to the counter.

Most of the things could be deemed necessities, Polly realized, although somehow they'd been able to get along without them recently. Chrissy picked out some mittens, a new winter coat with a matching hand muff and earmuffs, and some boots. She added some socks and underdrawers, as well as some frilly pantelets.

Polly glanced now and then at the store owner to see him carrying box after box of provisions taken from his shelves out to the wagon. He untied a huge ham hanging from the rafters, then a burlap bag that probably contained an entire side of bacon. He filled other burlap bags with flour, sugar, and coffee beans. She caught the smell of apples once, and saw him scooping dried ones from a barrel.

"Pssst."

Polly turned to see Sam motioning to her. "I sent Chrissy back to have some cookies with the owner's wife for a few minutes," he said as she approached. "We might not get back into town before Christmas Day, so I thought we'd better get that shopping done, too."

Taking her hand, he led her over to a shelf. "She seemed especially entranced with that one," he said, pointing to a beautiful doll with a porcelain face. "But for some reason she said she didn't need a dolly this year."

"It's beautiful," Polly admitted. "She would love it. All I have for her is a new nightgown I made her, and a robe. No toys."

Sam took the doll down from the shelf. "Have you seen anything you'd like to get her?" When she remained silent he frowned. "Please, Polly. We want to make this Christmas special for her. It's our first one as a family."

With a sigh, she turned and went to the front of

the store. At a glass case by the cash register she pointed to a music box, with tiny, woodland figures of bears, bunnies, and squirrels on it. The store owner immediately took it out and handed it to her.

Polly twisted the key on the bottom, and the top revolved as strains of Brahms's "Lullaby" tinkled through the room. When Sam failed to give her his opinion she turned to see him fingering a hand-tooled leather vest, the same chocolate color as his eyes. As though sensing her gaze, he dropped the vest and looked up, nodding at her.

"That's nicc. She'll like it. Now, why don't you go have a cup of coffee with Mac's wife and send Chrissy to me. We'll let you know when you can come out."

Polly started to protest, but Sam wagged a warning finger at her. "Ah, ah, ah. It's Christmas, a time for secrets, so don't you dare poke your head out until we give you permission to."

He had such a childishly delighted look in his eyes that Polly obeyed him. She even swallowed her pride long enough to send Mac's wife on a surreptitious trip into the store while she drank her coffee. When Sam helped her into the wagon a long half hour later she had her own packages in her arms.

Sam made a playful grab at one of them as soon as she sat down on the wagon seat, but she laughed and pulled them away from him. "Secrets," she reminded him, and laughed again when he pretended a petulant pout.

Tension replaced her gaiety, however, as they drove toward the ranch, and her thoughts kept veering toward the coming night. The two-hour trip seemed to take only a few minutes. She tried hard to join in Chrissy and Sam's chatter and thought she succeeded fairly well.

They arrived home at sundown, with Chrissy stretched out across both their laps, sound asleep. The hand who'd stayed behind to do the chores was just leaving, but he dismounted agreeably when Sam asked him to help unload the wagon.

She carried in both the sleeping child and her gifts, and managed to wake Chrissy long enough to change her into her nightgown and get her to eat a bowl of the soup she had found waiting on the stove. All too soon, Chrissy knelt and yawned a short prayer, climbed into bed, and immediately fell asleep again. Polly heard the sound of a horse's hooves as she walked back into the kitchen and knew the hand was on his way home. José would probably wait until morning to see them, since he went to bed along with the sun these days.

In the kitchen, she stood undecided as to whether to set the table or just get out the roast the hand's wife had left in the oven and set it on the counter, along with a plate for Sam. Her stomach was too knotted for her even to think of eating a bite, but Sam probably wanted something. She felt a stab of pain, and glanced down to see herself twisting the wide gold band around and around on her finger.

Moving closer to a wall sconce, she held up her hand. She hadn't really paid much attention to the ring at the ceremony. Now she saw delicate, intertwined vines encircling it. The gold gleamed with a dull but pleasant glow.

"Like it?"

Polly whirled at Sam's voice, a flush on her cheeks. "Uh . . . yes, it's beautiful."

"If you want, you can pick out your own ring for our first anniversary," he said in a quiet voice. "It's just that I saw that one and wanted Mac to hold it, so no one else would get it before me."

"This one's perfectly fine," Polly insisted, refusing to respond to his hint of the years to come. Darn, they'd only gotten married a few hours ago. "Uh . . . would you like me to fix you a plate?"

"Our plates are already fixed," Sam said with an enigmatic smile. "I did it while you put Chrissy to bed."

"Where?" Polly stared around the kitchen. "Oh, in the oven?"

"No. Come with me." Sam walked over and took her hand, which he'd been doing with frequency lately, and led her out of the kitchen and into the front hallway. He opened the door of the seldom-used parlor and pushed her inside.

Polly gasped and stared. The room had been dusted and cleaned, and a fire crackled cheerfully in the fireplace. Pine boughs lined the mantel, filling the room with a pleasant scent. One of the end tables had been drawn up in front of the settee, and a pair of candles burned on it, sending flickering light across the polished silverware and plates of food. The thick, cerise-colored rug on the floor drew her gaze.

"What . . . how . . . ?"

Sam chuckled under his breath. "I found the rug in town the other day when I went in, and hid it in the barn when I got back. The hand's wife got the parlor ready today. I hope it suits you. If not, we can put that rug in the bedroom maybe, and you can pick your own color for in here. . . ."

"Damn you!" Polly spun on him and pounded on his chest.

Chapter Seven

"Uh-oh." Matt flew back down the hallway into the kitchen, then stuck his head around the doorjamb, though he could have seen perfectly well through the kitchen wall. Jo remained sitting on the kitchen table, a worried expression on her face. She could gaze at the parlor door from her perch, and she watched Sam fall back from it, a startled look on his face.

Polly pushed past Sam and fled into the bedroom across the hallway—the one in which Sam had been sleeping. She slammed the door behind her, and Jo mentally dissolved the wall so she could see Polly fling herself onto the bed and beat her fists on the pillow, as though she wished she still had Sam's chest under those pounding thrusts. Tears flooded down her cheeks, and Jo's heart went out to her as Polly sobbed in both anger and agony.

"What the heck's wrong with her?" Matt asked in a confused tone. "She's got such a turmoil in her mind that I can't even read her thoughts."

Jo sighed in exasperation. "You always did understand the men in our assignments better than the women, and maybe it's time you tried to overcome that. Think about it for a minute."

Matt's face creased into a frown, and he glided over to stand beside her as Sam entered the kitchen. Shaking his head, Sam sat down at the table and buried his face in his hands, then ran his hands through his hair.

"I can't figure it out," Matt muttered. "But look at poor Sam. He's a lot more baffled than even we are. I feel sorry for him. Why, he had this all planned out, and he wanted it to be a special evening for him and Polly—sort of the start of his courtship of her."

"You feel sorry for *him?*" Jo said in an amazed voice. "What about poor Polly in there, crying her eyes out? We were supposed to make Polly happy, and what do you think Michael will say when he finds out we've failed on this assignment?"

"We've got until Christmas to fulfill Chrissy's wish," Matt insisted. "You can't say we've failed yet. We just need to get our thinking caps on here and figure this out."

Jo cocked an eyebrow at him, then pointed her finger. Matt swept his hand up, pulling the white nightcap from his head and tossing it at her.

"Funny," he said. "You think I'm so dense I need a cap to help me think!"

"You're the one who mentioned it," Jo said with a giggle. Then she tuned back into the sounds in

Polly's room, and her smile faded. "Matt, we'd better do something here. What if Michael picks this time to come check on us? He'll find Polly sobbing her eyes out and see Sam sitting there trying to tear his hair out."

"What can we do? We're not supposed to interfere. We have to let the relationship take its own course."

"Well, it sure ain't coursin' right now, pod'ner," Jo mocked in the voice Matt had used in his prospector guise. "Fact is, it's purty derned near as far off the path as it kin git."

"Well, it's Polly's fault," Matt grumbled. "She . . ."

"Polly's fault?" Jo jumped from the table and faced him, wings fluttering and palms on her hips. "She's been swallowing her pride all day long, while Sam spent money like it was water, making Polly remember all the things she hasn't been able to give Chrissy the last few years. She . . ."

Matt leaned forward and stuck his face up to hers. "She ought to appreciate it!" he interrupted. "Chrissy needed a new coat and mittens. And she only said she didn't want the dolly because she thought that was too much to ask for, along with her wish for Polly to be happy. She's a very unselfish little girl, Chrissy is!"

"Well, she won't stay that way long if Sam keeps buying her everything she sets her eye on. She'll get spoiled and be a whiner, just like Polly's afraid will happen."

"Shhhh," Matt said suddenly. "Look."

Jo turned to see Chrissy wandering out of her bedroom, rubbing at her eyes. The little girl stopped abruptly and stared at them, her eyes rounding in awe. They both knew in an instant that she'd seen them. That happened with children sometimes, especially a child as sweet, innocent, and loving as Chrissy. Jo recovered first and sent a thought to Chrissy, whispering to her not to let on to Sam that she and Matt were there. Chrissy smiled and nodded, and Jo waved her hand to make them invisible even to Chrissy. The little girl frowned in disappointment before she wandered over to the table.

"Papa," she said, tugging on Sam's sleeve.

Sam glanced down at her, then shifted around to pull her onto his lap. "You should be sleeping, sweetheart. What's wrong?"

"I heard them talk. . . . " Chrissy gazed around her for a second, then smiled secretively. "I mean, I woke up," she said. "Did the lady get the parlor all fixed up, like you whispered to me this morning she was gonna do?"

Sam rose reluctantly, with Chrissy in his arms. Jo could tell Sam didn't really want to go back into that parlor right now, but he carried Chrissy down the hallway, and Jo flew after them, waving a beckoning hand for Matt to follow. In the parlor Chrissy slid from Sam's arms at once and ran into the center of the room.

"Oh, it's so pretty," she exclaimed as she whirled around, trying to see everything at once. "Mama must love it! Where is she?"

"Uh . . . she went on to bed," Sam replied. "She was tired from all the shopping she did today, I guess."

Chrissy sat down in front of the fire. "Well, can I stay up for just a minute, Papa? I love to watch the fire."

"I suppose that won't hurt," Sam agreed. He walked over to the corner of the room and picked up the bottle of brandy he'd placed on the other end table earlier. Pouring himself a full glass, he joined Chrissy in front of the fire.

Chrissy wrinkled her nose. "What's that, Papa?"

"Brandy," Sam admitted. "Sometimes I have a drink of it before bed."

"It smells sorta nice."

"You can't have any brandy until you get older, honey. It's only for grown-ups."

"Sometimes I don't think I want to grow up," Chrissy said seriously.

Sam swallowed a quarter of the brandy in one gulp before he asked, "Why not? Everybody grows up, honey."

Chrissy considered her answer carefully, and Jo motioned to Matt to sit beside her on the settee. "Let's listen to Chrissy," she whispered. "I've got a feeling we're going to hear something important."

"Yeah," Matt agreed. "And maybe Sam will, too."

"Wellll," Chrissy finally drawled, twirling a golden curl around her finger. "You see, I'm so happy all the time . . . well, most of the time, except when Mama gets sad. But she hardly ever lets me know she's not happy, so I stay happy. Un'nerstand, Papa?"

"I think so," Sam replied. "But you're a child, Chrissy. It's part of our job to see that you grow up safe and happy."

"Uh-huh," Chrissy agreed. "And I like that part of it. Even when I am sad, though, it's real easy to get over it. I just make a wish with my prayers and I'm pretty sure things will be all right. Mama was happy today, wasn't she?"

I thought she was, until a few minutes ago, Jo read in Sam's mind. But he said, "Yes, honey. She seemed to be."

The fire crackled and a spark shot up the chimney. Sam rose to place another log in the grate, and secured the fireguard firmly before he sat back down. "You still haven't told me why you don't want to grow up, sweetheart," he reminded Chrissy.

She sighed delicately, her small shoulders hunched. "It's a lot of hard work," she said at last. "I don't mind work, really I don't. I gather the eggs for Mama, and I study my lessons. She's been teaching me to read, so I'll be ready for school next year, and I can already write my name. That's more like fun, though. I like the chickens, and in the summer they have babies for me to play with. And reading's loads of fun. I like books."

She glanced up at Sam as she continued. "But Mama's grown-up work is just work. She can't have any fun at it. Her hands get all red and cracked sometimes, and her back hurts. I know, 'cause I've seen her rubbin' it."

"Then we'll just have to see what we can do about that, won't we, honey?" Sam said, downing the rest of his brandy. "Right now, you'd better get back to bed. I don't want your mama getting mad at me for keeping you from your sleep."

Chrissy got to her feet agreeably but pushed Sam back when he started to rise. "You go ahead and sit here, Papa. You worked hard today, too, driving us into town and back. Mama says pulling the reins is hard on her arms when she drives us. I can go to bed myself."

"All right, sweetheart. Give me a kiss first."

Chrissy flung her arms around Sam's neck and kissed his cheek. A second later, she scrambled from the room. At the door she glanced at Sam, but he was staring into the fire. She waved at Jo and Matt, then ran down the hallway.

"Darn, we let the barrier slip while we listened to her and she saw us again," Jo said with a laugh. "But Chrissy won't say anything."

"What do you think Sam's going to do?" Matt asked in a worried voice. "Do you think it will be something to make Polly get over being angry with him?"

"His thoughts are a little clouded with the brandy and his confusion over the way Polly ran off crying, when he was only trying to please her," Jo mused. "He's not thinking straight himself right now."

"Guess we'll find out tomorrow," Matt said.

The next morning, after leaving a note on the table for Polly, Sam hitched up the wagon and left before daybreak. He drove into town and returned shortly after noon. Grabbing some things from the back of the wagon, he strode into the kitchen, where Polly was finishing up the noon dishes.

She turned to watch him set his burdens on the table. "Hello, Sam," she said when he looked at her. "Look, I'm sorry I acted like I did last night. I was . . ." She took a deep breath. "It was all new to me—being married, I guess."

Sam's heart softened and a hopeful look filled his face. "It's all right. We'll start over again today. Wait here. I've got some more things in the wagon."

"Things?" Polly said, her eyes narrowing.

But Sam ignored her and strode out the door, returning with his arms filled again. "There," he said after he emptied his arms. "Let's see what we've got here."

He untied some brown paper and set something out from among the rest. "Here's a new coffee bean grinder. That other one you have is getting real hard to turn. And this," he said, unwrapping more paper, "is a bigger coffeepot. You won't have to make two pots every morning, and we can each have all we want."

He glanced at Polly, surprised to see a scowl instead of a smile of delight on her face. But he shrugged and continued to show her what he'd purchased, unwrapping a new hand mixer, some more bread loaf pans, and a larger cookie sheet. A better knife sharpener and a new set of knives joined the other items, then a teakettle, twice as large as the old one.

"I got a popcorn popper, too," he said eagerly, tearing the paper off that. "We can use it in the parlor fireplace in the evenings. And out in the wagon there's a hand pump and some pipe. We'll pump water in here to the sink, so you don't have to carry it in."

"Take it back," Polly snarled. "Take every damned bit of it back!"

"What the hell?" Sam's head snapped up. "What the devil's it take to please you?"

Polly flung him an outraged look and raced from the kitchen. A second later he heard the bedroom door slam.

Chapter Eight

Polly kept finding the new *things* Sam had purchased mixed in with her other kitchen items over the next few days. She had to use the new coffee grinder, since the old one disappeared, as did the old coffeepot and teakettle. He had defied her demand to return anything. She found the new loaf pans and the cookie pan in among the rest of her cooking equipment, and the knives and hand mixer in a drawer. The first evening, she even smelled corn popping over the fire in the parlor when Sam and Chrissy went in there after supper. She, however, refused to enter that room.

After the first night, her wedding night, when she'd fallen asleep in the bed Sam had been using, she returned to sleeping on the cot in Chrissy's room. Chrissy didn't seem to find it strange. Polly guessed a five-year-old who had never had two parents didn't realize that married people usually slept together. She could feel Sam's eyes boring into her back each night when she carried Chrissy in to bed, but so far he hadn't pushed the matter.

They went to church as a family that first Sunday. Everyone in town already knew of the marriage, of course, since the minister had performed the ceremony and the general store owner had most assuredly bragged of the huge sale he'd made to Polly's new husband. Polly tried her best to respond graciously to the well wishes of the other parishioners, knowing they came honestly from the hearts of the friends she had made over the last few years. She even swallowed a stab of jealousy when she overheard a couple of the unmarried young women bemoaning the fact that Sam had married her so soon after his arrival, without giving any of the other women a chance to catch his eye.

Jealousy? Polly worked the handle on the pump harder and the water gushed into the new teakettle, overflowing the top. Sam had made it clear this marriage was for Chrissy's sake—so Chrissy would have two parents, and no taint of scandal would touch the relationship between herself and Sam. She wondered what those two biddies would say if they knew she slept on the cot, and that Sam had not touched her other than to help her in and out of the wagon last Sunday since their fight on their wedding night. Would they still send longing glances at Sam's rugged face, his broad shoulders and slim hips?

Dropping her hand from the pump handle, she stared out the window over the sink. The barn now had a fresh coat of paint and the door hung true on its hinges. Edgar Pyle had delivered three wagonloads of hay, and they were stored in the loft to feed the stock over the winter. Yesterday, Mac, the general store owner, had brought out panes of glass for the broken cabin windows himself, and stayed for the noon meal. Luckily, he had wanted coffee with his food, so she had enough glassware for everyone.

Her musings broke off abruptly as Sam came out of the barn, a plank over his shoulder and Chrissy trailing at his heels, as she had been almost ever since he arrived. Sam strode in his loose-hipped gait to the corral and easily swung the long plank into the place where he had removed a rotten one. Chrissy handed him a hammer, then one nail after another, until the new board was secured. When Sam stepped back to study his handiwork, flexing his broad shoulders and brushing his hands, Chrissy imitated him. Sam glanced down and saw her, laughed and swung her into his arms. Polly's mouth went dry and her cheeks heated up at the easy way he handled the child, the fitted shirt outlining bunched muscles and wide shoulders—his now-trim belly.

She tore her eyes away and grabbed the teakettle. Swinging around, she thumped it onto the stove, where water sloshed out and skittered across the hot surface in hissing droplets. She jammed the lid on the kettle before she stared around the kitchen, searching for some unfinished chore to keep her hands busy.

Nothing came to mind. With all the new help outside she'd had plenty of time to clean the past week. The floor was scrubbed, the cupboards arranged, and she'd even cleaned the pantry off the kitchen. Nothing waited in the other rooms, either, since Sam made his own bed and kept that bedroom picked up. She'd already made up her cot and Chrissy's bed.

With a grim set to her lips she walked down the hallway and checked the parlor. It could probably use a dusting, but why bother? Heart leaden in her chest, she sank down on the settee, allowing her eyes to scan the room.

It could have been such a wonderful family room. The huge stone fireplace took up most of one wall, and scent lingered from the pine branches on the mantel. The cerise rug matched the curtains well enough, its duller color a complement to the bright holly berries scattered across the mantel and the maroon settee and end chairs. She and Christine had made rainbow-colored throw pillows that first year, since both of them loved bright colors around them.

Yes, it could be a cheerful place to spend family evenings—but what family would enjoy it? Not the family she had now, which included Sam, Chrissy, and herself. Why was Sam doing this to her and Chrissy? It would have been hard enough to leave the ranch before, given its rundown condition and the backbreaking work it took to eke out a meager existence. With its new appearance and the life it was taking on, it would be heartbreaking.

Her gaze settled on the side window—the perfect place for a Christmas tree, if she could only stir herself to wash the windowpane Sam had replaced. It still had his and Chrissy's fingerprints scattered on it. They would have a tree, too. Sam had promised Chrissy they would find one on the way home from church tomorrow, and Polly had forced herself to join in Chrissy's enthusiastic chatter at dinner last night, even to the point of agreeing to show Chrissy how to string popcorn and berries for decorations.

That, of course, would mean spending an evening in this room while Sam popped the corn they would need. Steeling herself, she glanced at the rocking chair in the corner. Christine had sat there many evenings, stitching tiny garments for her coming baby. How many evenings had she sat there herself, rocking Chrissy to sleep and enjoying the warmth of the fire after a blue norther had blown in? She should never have allowed the room to fall into disuse, but firewood had come so dearly when she had to saw and chop it herself.

There was plenty now. Sam seemed to enjoy that chore, and she had a pile of wood on each side of the back door, handy for her to carry in if she ran low, though Sam and Chrissy usually kept the bin by the stove full. Sighing when she heard the teakettle sing out in the kitchen, she rose to her feet. Idle hands were the devil's work, and the room definitely needed cleaning.

Sam hesitantly entered the kitchen a half hour or so after the noon meal. Polly glanced at him, then finished wiping the plate in her hand and placed it in the cupboard. He smelled ginger and other spices in the air and saw a pan of gingerbread cooling on the table, beside a tray of sugar cookies. At the sink, Polly carefully wiped the new hand mixer before laying it in the drawer and picking up her mixing bowl. She stretched onto her tiptoes to reach the top cupboard shelf, and he muffled a groan of desire when her breasts strained against her bodice and her slender hips were outlined beneath her skirt.

Suddenly Polly gasped, and the bowl teetered on the edge of the shelf. He lunged forward and caught it, shoving it back to safety. He bumped Polly's body, and grabbed her when she staggered slightly and clutched at his shirt to steady herself.

Wide green eyes stared up at him when he glanced down, and her pink lips parted. The flush on her cheeks deepened and her fingers clenched in his shirt rather than pushing him away. For an instant he felt a stab of hope and gathered her closer, smoothing his hands over the curls tumbling down her back.

"All right now?" he asked.

"Uh . . . yes. Thank you for saving my bowl. The . . . uh . . . the shelf's a little high."

"I'll fix you up with a step stool," Sam murmured. Of its own volition, one hand came up to brush at a wisp of golden fringe on her forehead. At his touch she closed her eyes tightly and sucked in a breath. He started to bend his head—wanted desperately to touch those softly parted lips with his own—but her eyes flew open as soon as he moved. He faltered for a brief second, sure she would start struggling wildly in his embrace. Instead, she whimpered a soft sound and flung her arms around his neck.

Sam captured her lips softly at first, but quickly gave in to his surge of desire. Parting her lips with his tongue, he growled deep in his chest when she met his thrust with her own. Everything around him faded into nothingness, leaving his senses filled with this warm, willing woman in his arms.

He tangled his fingers in her hair and firmly clasped the back of her neck, holding her even closer to his greedy lips. Bending his knees slightly, he cupped her hip with his other hand and rubbed the ache between his legs against her, matching his thrusts with the rhythm of his tongue.

Polly sobbed against his mouth and her fingers clenched in his hair, the pain firing his raging lust even higher. He bent lower and grabbed her legs, pulling her up to straddle his waist. God, he had never wanted a woman more in his life, and his senses were just unclouded enough to realize that this deep, uncontrollable need came from Polly being the woman in his arms.

Suddenly Polly wrenched her mouth free and stared at him in dismay, then gasped and tightened her legs around him. Her head dropped to his shoulder, and he felt her shudder. A second later she frenziedly struggled from his arms and backed away, a hand clasped over her mouth, her eyes as dark as a storm-tossed sea.

"Polly, don't." Sam pulled her back, capturing her arms at her sides so she couldn't fight him. She strove to escape him anyway, but he held her until she gave up. Keeping one arm firmly around her waist, he tilted up her chin and waited patiently until she opened her eyes.

"Polly," he growled in a low voice. "Whatever the hell you're feeling, don't let shame be part of it. We're a healthy, normal man and woman who've been in close enough proximity to each other the last couple of weeks to keep our desire near the boiling point."

Polly shook her head and opened her mouth to

speak, but Sam kissed her into silence. "Yes, it's true," he said when he raised his head. "I've been aching for you, and you jump away like a scalded cat whenever I get close to you. I promised myself—and you—that I'd let these feelings between us develop naturally. But you have no damned idea how hard it's been for me to not kidnap you off that blasted cot every night after Chrissy goes to sleep and carry you back to my bed and show you just how beautiful things between us could be."

"It's . . . just lust," Polly managed to say.

"No, darling, it's not," Sam denied. "But you're not ready to accept that yet." Reluctantly, he released her, and she scampered around the table, placing it between them. A grating chuckle broke from his lips, and he smiled grimly at her.

"No, you're not ready yet," he repeated. "But I'm not about to give up."

"We . . . we got married for Chrissy's sake," Polly said. "You didn't tell me until I'd already agreed to marry you that . . . that . . . that *that* would be a part of it."

"Polly, sweetheart, you don't even have any idea what *that* is yet."

"I . . . do," Polly stuttered, and Sam could see the exasperation with her wayward tongue on her face. She'd stumbled over every sentence since he touched her. "J . . . just now . . ."

"Just now could have been only the beginning," Sam interrupted. "But try not to break any more glasses while you think that over for the next few days. We've barely got enough left as it is." He rumbled with renewed laughter when she flashed him a sparkling green look of indignation, then turned to take her cloak from the wall hook.

"Chrissy's going to stay with José for a while this afternoon," he said as he turned back to face her. "I thought maybe you'd like to go for a ride with me. Pyle told me about a couple of ponies he has when he delivered the hay, and I've been trying to find time to go over and take a look at them."

She stiffened and gripped the table edge with white fingers, shaking her head. "You can pick it out yourself. You'll be the one paying for it."

"Damn it, Polly," he snarled, his temper barely under control as he tried to ignore the still unsatisfied desire throbbing between his legs. "You haven't been out of this cabin since church last Sunday. José says he can feel in his bones that a cold front's coming in. This might be the last nice day we have for a while."

"There aren't any chores I need to take care of outside anymore," Polly said, tilting her chin in defiance. "You've got plenty of help now."

"That's no reason for you to stay inside and wither up like a dried rose. You can either get your ass willingly out to the wagon or I'll carry you. Which will it be? You're very easy for me to lift, remember? I did it a minute ago."

A violent blush crawled over Polly's cheeks, and she huffed out an incensed breath, her breasts rising and falling against her bodice. Sam took a step toward her, and she glared at him for another second. Then she rushed swiftly around the table and swiped her cloak from his hands. Jerking the door open, she disappeared outside. By the time Sam controlled his laughter and followed her, she was sitting on the wagon seat, her back as stiff as if she had a frozen icicle down her dress.

She didn't thaw an inch, either, on the ride over to Pyle's place, though he made it a point to take up more than his fair share of the wagon seat. Damn it, he'd had about enough of the impenetrable wall she kept around her emotions, even when he forced a physical closeness on her. He'd been working his ass off getting the ranch into shape. The hard labor had helped him sleep at night, after he managed to push Polly's face out of his mind. He couldn't seem to keep it out of his dreams, though.

More than once he'd caught himself during the day standing in the yard, admiring the newly painted barn. Many times he had pulled his horse up when riding back from checking on the cattle to stare at the snug cabin, where smoke from the chimney curled into the blue sky. He could imagine Polly inside, bustling around as she kept it tidy. The clear air out here filled his lungs a heck of a lot more pleasantly than the foggy, cigar-smelling air in the saloon. He'd never been one to eat regularly, but even with the three full meals he downed each day, his muscles continued to firm and his stomach was now trim and fit.

Not that it mattered a damn to Polly. She put on a good act for Chrissy, joining in their conversations at mealtimes when they discussed the happenings of the day. Yet she busied herself in the kitchen after supper, while he and Chrissy enjoyed a little while in the parlor, then feigned weariness and went to bed when Chrissy did. He knew damned well she did it to keep from being alone with him. How the heck could he court her when she avoided him? If that blasted bowl hadn't started to fall, he never would have gotten his hands on her a while ago.

As they drove into the Pylc ranch yard, Sam frowned to himself. He thought he'd put that bowl securely on the shelf himself—but then, his real attention had been on the outline of Polly's body beneath her dress.

Chapter Nine

Jo drifted down and settled on the pony's back, legs curled Indian-style in front of her. The animal turned its head briefly to glance at her, then continued trotting along behind the wagon, head bobbing in time to its movements.

"Oh, Matt," Jo breathed with a sigh. "Chrissy's going to love this pony." She leaned forward and ticked her fingers through the silky, white mane and ran a hand over the sleek chestnut withers. "He's a darling little pony, isn't he?"

"What happened to spoiling Chrissy?" Matt said as he floated above her. "We don't want her to get to be a whiner, do we?"

"A pony's different," Jo insisted. "A little girl needs to learn to ride as much as a little boy does. Horses and ponies are transportation. And even Polly fell in love with this one. She didn't argue with Sam about buying it."

"Polly's still trying to come to terms with her feelings for Sam, after what happened when you nudged that bowl off the shelf." Matt shook his head and chuckled. "Right now, Sam could probably buy out the entire general store for Chrissy, and Polly would only nod and say how nice it was for him to do that. Who would ever have thought a simple thing like a mixing bowl would finally get them in each other's arms again?"

Jo preened for just an instant, then glanced overhead and quickly changed her demeanor. Pride didn't belong in the inventory of angel emotions. She also might have been pushing the bounds of not interfering in Polly and Sam's relationship when she prodded the bowl from the shelf, but she had taken advantage of the situation without too much thought. Michael, though, could be around any time.

"I know I accused you of not understanding our female assignments, Matt," she said. "And we both thought this match a big mistake at first. But now we can see how right Sam and Polly are for each other. Why are humans so dense sometimes? Why can't Polly see that she's in love with Sam?"

"Aw, Jo," Matt replied, "you've got to remember that we've been around since Creation—and we continue to grow and learn all the time. Humans have such a short time to develop and understand their emotions. But I have to disagree with you here. I think what Polly's fighting *is* the knowledge that she loves Sam. And she wants his love in return, rather than only a relationship of convenience for Chrissy's sake."

"Sam does love her, Matt. It's Polly he wants to

make love with, not just any woman. He's still carrying remnants of the hurt of Christine jilting him, though. He's afraid to trust. After all, he's reminded of Christine every day. She's buried here, and he's in love with her sister—living with Polly. Everything here is a remembrance to him of Christine and his brother. He might enjoy working on the ranch for a while, but he's in no way ready to accept it as a home for the rest of his life."

The wagon pulled into the ranch yard, and Jo gave the pony a final pat, then drifted from its back.

"Wal, pod'ner," Matt drawled as Jo floated to his side, "we'll jist have ta see what shakes out here."

Jo nudged him in the side and laughed before they both looked down in response to Chrissy's shout of joy as she ran toward the wagon.

Polly shivered and tugged her cloak tighter as they headed home after church. José's aches had again proven to be a true forecast of the impending weather. Blue northers swept down quickly and severely this time of year, sometimes dropping temperatures as much as 30 or 40 degrees within an hour. This morning had dawned clear and barely cool enough for a wrap, but she had heeded José's warning and loaded a few blankets into the wagon.

Chrissy huddled in her new coat and continued to bounce along on her pony, which she had named Nicker within moments after its arrival. Polly asked her if she wanted to ride in the wagon and wrap up in a blanket, giving in at once to her pleading to ride Nicker. Chrissy hadn't needed more than a cursory riding lesson from Sam—instead, she moved naturally with the pony's rhythm from the beginning. She rode bareback now, but Sam had already hidden the almost-new saddle he'd also bought from Edgar Pyle in the barn until Christmas Day.

"There's a pretty one," Chrissy said for the tenth time as she pointed at a spruce tree and kneed Nicker away from the wagon.

Sam halted the wagon and jumped down. He held his arms up to Polly, and she allowed him to help her from her seat again. Shaking her head tolerantly, she smiled up at Sam.

"I wonder if this tree will suit Miss Perfection?" she asked. "According to Chrissy, the last one was too tall—the one before that had a missing branch where she thought the angel should be hung. One was too fat—one way too skinny."

"Well, I hope this one is it, because my feet are about frozen. There was a puddle of water I didn't notice back about three trees ago, and I stepped in it."

"Oh, Sam," Polly said in quick concern. "Maybe we should go on home."

"We're going to get a tree," Sam said in a determined voice. "I'll be fine."

He grabbed the ax from behind the wagon seat and strode toward Chrissy, who had dismounted and was walking around the prospective tree. She had her chin in her hand and her head cocked, studying it closely. Polly watched her and Sam for a moment longer.

With Christmas only three days away, it had been hard for her to maintain her irritation with Sam. He'd been like a little boy himself yesterday, his excitement almost as great as Chrissy's when he handed over the pony's reins to her. Last night in the parlor, the two of them had carefully paced off the area in front of the window, and Sam lifted Chrissy to his shoulders to measure the height of the room. As they strung popcorn and berries, the two of them had hinted at hidden gifts that would appear under their beautiful tree Christmas morning.

She heard the sound of the ax thunking into wood and breathed a sigh of relief. Chrissy had evidently found the perfect tree. Her thoughts continued as she waited for them to finish cutting it down.

She'd held herself aloof from the easy camaraderie between Sam and Chrissy up until yesterday evening but soon came to realize what she'd been missing. Granted, her remoteness had been directed toward Sam—an attempt to handle the intense pull she felt toward him, which had finally flared out of control the previous morning. Still, if this was to be her last Christmas at the ranch, she should make it as enjoyable for Chrissy as she could. After all, hadn't that been why she asked Sam to wait until after Christmas to make his decision about selling the ranch?

Chrissy screamed and Polly's heart leapt into her throat. Instinctively, she gathered her skirts and ran toward the tree, which now lay on the ground. Chrissy stood beside it, a hand over her mouth and her eyes wide with terror. She couldn't see Sam.

Oh, God. Where was he?

She found him behind the tree, his hands clasped around his blood-soaked leg. The ax lay next to him, its blade splotched in red.

"Oh, my God!" Polly ran to Sam and knelt by his side. Chrissy began sobbing behind her, but Polly couldn't handle both of them right now. She jerked her skirt up and began tearing off strips of her petticoat while she demanded that Sam tell her what had happened.

"Last whack, boot slipped on a frozen spot on the ground," he managed between lips set grim with pain. "Ax got me."

"How . . . how bad . . . ?"

"Mostly blood, honey," Sam muttered. "Tie it up 'til we get home."

Polly quickly wrapped several loops of petticoat around the wound. Blood continued to seep through, and she tore off another strip of material. She pulled this one tighter, her mind racing with images of what could happen. The wound needed cleaning immediately. A young man she had known in New Orleans had died of gangrene from a septic wound. And the blood—so much of it . . . Christine's blood had poured from her, taking the life and vivacity that was her sister with it. Polly choked on a sob and covered her quaking lips with her hands.

Sam touched her cheek and murmured soothingly to her, "Honey, take it easy. The bleeding's stopped now. I'll be all right until we get home."

"Oh, Sam!" She brushed a black curl from his forehead with shaking fingers. The cold sweat covering his skin told her how deeply he was suffering, despite his attempt to reassure her. She had to get him to the cabin. Chrissy ran over and flung her arms around Sam's neck, whimpering but stepping back hurriedly and sniffing for courage.

Pride surged through Polly when the little girl

said bravely, "We'll help you into the wagon, Papa. You can lean on us."

Sam struggled to his feet and wrapped an arm around Polly's shoulders. Though she insisted he let her take more of his weight, he hobbled to the wagon using his injured leg and letting Chrissy hold one hand as though she helped. With a grunt, he hoisted himself up to the seat and fell back. Polly's heart hammered in her chest at the shadowed depths of agony in his dark eyes and renewed cold sweat, now rolling down his tight face.

"Can the two of you manage that tree?" he asked in an attempted light voice.

"Forget the tree," Polly said. "We've got to . . ."

"Polly," he interrupted, with a glance at Chrissy's small, worried face, "I went to a lot of trouble to get that blasted tree. Try to get it in the wagon, won't you?"

She stared up at him, flabbergasted. Setting her mouth, she placed a foot on the wagon step.

"Please, darling?" Sam whispered.

Her shoulders slumped and she blew out an exasperated breath. Shaking her head in frustration, she turned and took Chrissy's hand to lead her back to the tree. They grabbed the trunk and dragged it back to the wagon. Her anxiety warred with vexation over Sam's stubbornness about the tree, lending her strength to almost fling the darn thing into the wagon bed.

"There," she said, dusting her hands together to dislodge the clinging pine needles as she tossed Sam a severe frown. "Now we're going home!"

Chrissy picked up Nicker's reins and Polly lifted her onto the pony's back. When Chrissy glanced at her with a tear-streaked face she took an extra second to kiss her cheek and pat her comfortingly on the back.

"Papa will be fine, sweetheart," she said. "Think you could ride ahead and have Mr. José get the medical kit ready? We'll be right behind you."

Chrissy nodded and nudged Nicker in the sides, galloping away as Polly ran around the wagon and clambered into the seat. Grabbing the reins and releasing the wagon brake, she flicked the straps over the horse's back and sent it surging after the pony. Sam muffled a groan when the wagon wheel lurched in a hole, and she forced herself to pull the galloping horse down to a trot. They were close to the ranch, though, and the wagon entered the ranch yard only a moment or so after Chrissy.

Chapter Ten

"You must do it, señora," José murmured. "My hands, they are too swollen today."

Polly clenched her fists and stared down at the wound on the calf of Sam's leg. They'd helped him into the house to his bed, and his denims lay in a blood-soaked heap in a corner. The sheet covered everything except the brawny leg, with towels beneath the wound to catch the blood again seeping out. It would take several stitches to close the gap—stitches that she must somehow force herself to make. She had learned at church that the only doctor in town was attending the birthing of the Pyles's baby, and they lived at the other end of the county.

"Chrissy, you better leave now," Polly said.

Instead, Chrissy crawled onto the bed beside Sam's head and took his hand. "I want to stay,

Mama. Please. It's gonna hurt, and I can hold Papa's hand and make it feel better. Like you do when I skin my knee."

Polly reluctantly nodded her head. It would probably be harder on Chrissy if she were delegated to listening outside the door, with no one to comfort her. She scanned Sam's face, and he gave her a brief nod of agreement.

"There's a bottle of brandy in the parlor," Polly said to José. "Would you fetch it?"

"*Sí,* señora."

While José was gone, Polly threaded the needle and steeled herself for the ordeal. Her hands trembled so badly, she missed the needle eye three times before she could thread it. When she finally managed the task she anxiously glanced at Sam, gnawing on her bottom lip.

Chrissy was curled up in Sam's arm, and he cupped her small chin, keeping her attention on his face. He caught Polly's gaze long enough to give her a reassuring look, which didn't quell the storm in her stomach even a tiny bit. But José came back in and handed the brandy bottle to Sam, and she watched him swallow a fairly large amount before he held the bottle out to her.

"I . . . don't want any," Polly said.

"It's for the leg," Sam said with a grin. "Though maybe you should take at least a sip. Wobbly stitches don't seem your style, but after all, it's my leg."

She choked out a sound, half laugh at his humorous attempt to relieve her anxiety and half misery over it indeed being Sam's leg she had to sew up. With a hesitant nod she accepted the brandy and took a delicate sip. Her eyes widened and teared, although a second later her hands did feel steadier. Tipping the bottle once again, she poured a measure over the wound, hearing Sam's indrawn hiss of breath and glancing at his face to see his jaw clenched and his lips a thin white line.

Her hands started shaking again, but she controlled them and poured a drop of brandy on the needle and thread, then handed the bottle to José and bent over the wound.

Polly clattered the pan onto the stove and poured some milk from a pitcher into it. Darn that man! He *knew* he should stay in bed, but he totally ignored her admonitions and limped around on that crutch José had dug up somewhere—probably from the time one of their hands had broken his leg when a still half-wild horse threw him. He hadn't even stayed in bed a full day. This morning he'd insisted on being at the table for breakfast and lunch; then he'd gone out onto the back porch and fashioned a stand for the tree—and talked her and Chrissy into helping him get it into the parlor. Now she could smell popcorn.

Well, they did need to get the tree decorated, since the next day was Christmas Eve. But they would just have to miss the afternoon service at church tomorrow; she'd be darned if she'd let Sam take a chance on reopening that wound by exerting himself to make that long drive. Her stomach vaulted a half circle as she recalled again the twelve stitches it had taken to close the awful gap on his leg. She'd counted every dad-blasted one of them—one for each day of Christmas, she realized inanely.

The milk steamed and she picked up a potholder, grasped the pan, and carried it over to the sink. While she shaved off some of the bar of chocolate Sam had brought in with one load of supplies, she glanced out the window.

Snow! It fell in soft, delicate flakes, wafting hither and yon on the barely perceptible breeze before settling on the ground, which already had a coat of whiteness covering it. Only once since Chrissy was born had they had a white Christmas, and she'd been too young to remember it.

"Chrissy!" Polly called in an excited voice. "Come see. Hurry."

Chrissy scrambled into the kitchen, and Sam followed right behind her, his crutch thumping on the floor and an alarmed look on his face.

"What's wrong?" Sam demanded.

"Nothing's wrong," Polly hastily assured him, hurrying over to place a steadying hand on his arms when his crutch threatened to slip on her newly shined floor. "Oh, do be careful. It's snowing outside. I wanted Chrissy to see it, since she's never seen snow before."

"Snow?" Chrissy said, her eyes wide in wonder. "Like in the pictures in our Christmas books, Mama? Can I play in it?"

"Yes, darling," Polly replied. "But we need to get our wraps on before we go out."

"Can I play in it, too, darling?" Sam whispered.

Polly stared pointedly at his crutch, her stomach fluttering at his endearment. How easily he could unnerve her with just one word.

"*You* can sit on the back porch in a chair," she said, attempting chastisement in her voice, which came out breathless instead. "I was making hot chocolate, but I'll put it on the side of the stove to stay warm, and we can have it when we come back in. Be sure you both bundle up well."

Chrissy whooped and ran to where their wraps hung on the pegs by the door, but when Polly started to move away from Sam, he wrapped his free arm around her waist. She tugged against him, but he bent his head and nuzzled her nose.

"If I get cold," he murmured, "will you warm me back up?"

"T . . . there's a fire in the parlor," Polly insisted, trying to still her trembling legs and maintain control over her arms. They seemed to have a mind of their own, though, creeping up his chest, her fingers playing briefly on his shoulders and then tangling in his hair.

"You're a better fire than that," Sam whispered. "You make me hot a lot faster. Have I told you what I want for Christmas yet?"

"N . . . no," Polly stuttered.

"You, darling," Sam growled in a low undertone. "You, my wife, only you."

"All right," Polly said before she even realized she had formed the words. She gasped and wrenched free, backing away until her rear hit the sink, and stared into Sam's gleaming eyes. "I . . ."

"It's Christmas," Sam cautioned, wagging a finger at her. "Little girls who tell lies get only coal in their stockings. We can't have that now, can we?"

"Aren't we going out to play in the snow?" Chrissy said in a persistent voice. "I'm all ready."

Sam chortled gleefully and held Polly's gaze for another long moment before he limped over to the door.

Polly whirled, grabbed the hot chocolate pan,

and carried it to the stove. After shoving it back into a corner she found herself looking down into the pan, comparing the lighter brownish shade to the deeper depths of Sam's eyes a moment ago. She lifted a hand and ran a finger across her nose, her breath catching in her throat as she recalled the feel of Sam's caressing nuzzle, the tempting nearness of his lips to her own as he moved his head back and forth.

The door opened and closed, allowing a draft of cold air into the kitchen. She turned to see Chrissy and Sam gone, but the chill on her back brought to mind Sam's words about her being able to warm him.

How could she have said that she would give herself to him for Christmas—aloud, at least, since more and more frequently lately she had caught herself wondering what it would be like to become Sam's real wife—reach complete womanhood in his arms.

But . . . besides her longing for the physical fulfillment her body had been demanding recently, she wanted something much more than that. She wanted the type of love she had seen between Christine and Ron—the love her baby sister had been mature enough to recognize. She wanted the tender touches, and someone to meet her eyes across a room and tell her with a smile that he shared her thoughts without a word being spoken. And she wanted the man sharing that love with her to be Sam.

She ached to be able to tell Sam how distressed she had been when she saw him lying behind that tree with blood flowing from his leg wound. The truth of her feelings toward him had been clamoring in her mind ever since, with her acknowledgment of what an inexorable part of her life Sam had become.

He was different now—or maybe she was seeing him through different eyes, which weren't comparing him to the proper mate for her younger sister. He was pushy still and very much a man who took sure charge, but his leanings were concentrated on Chrissy and her. His very presence eased each day along to a satisfying conclusion, with her pleasure in the day's accomplishments being due in part to what she could do in reciprocation for him.

If the wound had been worse, if the ax blade had cut an artery and she hadn't been able to staunch the flow of blood, he could have very easily bled to death and been gone forever from her life. His grave would have joined the other two beneath the cottonwood tree, and she knew in her heart that she could never have stayed on the ranch then. She could never have faced that third cross every day.

Giggling wildly, Chrissy threw herself backwards in the snow and waved her arms up and down.

"Wider," Sam called in encouragement from the porch. "Angels have real large wings."

"Make one with me, Mama," Chrissy called up to Polly, who stood over her with a tolerant smile on her face. "You're bigger. You can make an angel with great big wings."

Agreeably, Polly collapsed backward beside Chrissy and worked her arms up and down, her legs out to the side and back. Then, carefully, she stood and stepped over to Chrissy, helping her to her feet without blurring the outline she had made in the snow. Two snow angels were imprinted in the soft whiteness, one large and one tiny.

"Oh," Chrissy breathed in awe. "They do look like angels, don't they, Mama? Can we make some more?"

They made four more sets of angels, in a wide, curving swathe. It took them a while longer to roll the easily adhering snow into three varied-size balls, like in one of the picture books, and plant the snowman within the arc. While they worked, Sam hobbled back into the cabin and returned with Polly's old red shawl, a carrot, and a small burlap bag of dried prunes.

When Chrissy ran over to take the decorations from Sam he called to Polly, "We don't seem to have any coal. You'll have to use prunes for the buttons and face."

She blushed and hurriedly turned her attention to helping Chrissy decorate their snowman. As they stood back to admire their handiwork, she noticed Chrissy shivering and took her hand.

"We'd better go back in and get warm, honey."

"Our snowman won't melt while we do that, will he, Mama?"

"No," Polly assured her. "He'll be fine, as long as we have cold weather."

Once on the porch, Sam made them turn around and around while he whisked snow off Polly's cloak and Chrissy's coat with the broom. He teasingly wiggled the bristles against their ribs when they lifted their arms, and their giggles filled the area beneath the overhang. They really shouldn't have been able to feel the bristles through their thick wraps, but Sam's grinning face and wicked "gotchas" fired their delight. Chrissy wrapped her arms tightly across herself and laughed so hard she could barely stand.

After removing their wraps in the warm kitchen, Polly shooed Chrissy and Sam into the parlor, following a moment later with a tray of hot chocolate and cups. Now seemed as good a time as any to decorate the tree, and they went to work amid shared laughter and the singing of every Christmas carol they could remember. Once Sam's deep baritone blended with Chrissy's sweet young voice, and Polly stepped back to listen to them, brushing away a sentimental tear that trailed down her cheek.

She ended up making two more pots of hot chocolate before they were finally ready to place the small angel on the very top branch. Polly carefully unwrapped it and brushed out the white robe she had tatted for the angel that first Christmas on the ranch. She handed it to Chrissy, and Sam lifted her to his shoulders. Chrissy carefully secured the angel, then placed her palms on Sam's head and studied the result, her small lips tilting up in satisfaction.

Sam put Chrissy down, and she plopped on her stomach, propping her chin in her hands. "It's beautiful, isn't it, Mama? It's the most beautiful tree we've ever had. I can't wait to open our presents tomorrow night."

Polly felt Sam grasp her hand and pull her down beside him on the settee. "Uh . . . yes, it's very beautiful, Chrissy," she said, trying to keep her mind on the tree rather than the caressing hand on her shoulder.

"Beautiful," Sam agreed, but when she glanced at him he was looking at her instead of the tree. "You open your presents on Christmas Eve, not Christmas Day?" he asked with brows raised.

"Uh . . . well, yes," Polly admitted. Goose bumps tingled down her neck and across her breasts, and her eyes started drifting closed. She snapped them open. "I mean, no. Not really. Chrissy always seems to wake up just after St. Nick leaves, usually around midnight. It's become our tradition to open our presents then, but it's really Christmas Day, since we wait until after the clock strikes twelve. And last year we even stayed up until dawn to watch the sun come up."

"Hum," Sam mused in a voice too low to reach Chrissy's ears. "If we stay up all night, when will I get my present?"

Polly lost herself in his deep brown eyes and ran her tongue around her lips. Sam ever so slowly bent his head and imitated her motions by running the tip of his own tongue across the path hers had taken. He sipped a kiss, then kissed her more deeply, his mouth tasting of chocolate and sugar cookies.

"I had José take that damned cot out to the barn when you weren't looking today," he said when he released her mouth. "I won't demand my present early, but I want you in my bed tonight."

Her cheeks flushed and Polly dropped her eyes. "Chrissy will wonder. . . ."

"Chrissy talked to one of her friends after church Sunday," Sam interrupted. "Then she asked me why you and I didn't sleep in the same bed, like her friend said her mama and papa did."

"What did you tell her?"

"Luckily, a little boy ran up and tagged her 'it,' so she took off. But I had a lot of time to think yesterday, when you kept me locked up in that bedroom. We've got years and years ahead of us, Polly, sweetheart, and I'll be honest with you: I never knew how wonderful it would be to have a family of my own until the last couple of weeks. I want us to be a complete family—with you and me being a *real* husband and wife."

"*Real* husbands and wives discuss things and make their decisions together," Polly said grumpily. "You . . ."

"Mama?" Chrissy said, rolling onto her back. "How long does it take a baby to be born?"

Polly stifled her astonishment and shot Sam a warning look when he chuckled beside her. "You heard at church that the doctor was with Mrs. Pyle, I guess, Chrissy, helping her baby to be born. Is that it?"

"Uh-huh, I heard that, Mama, but that's not what I mean." She scrunched up her face. "You see, it seems like Mrs. Pyle has had her baby in her tummy—like you told me when I asked why she was getting so fat—for a long time. Now, I guess she'll have the baby for Christmas. I just wondered if we'll have enough time before next Christmas to have our own baby."

Polly's mouth fell open, but she closed it with a snap, struggling desperately to maintain her composure in the face of Chrissy's earnest gaze. She couldn't seem to stop herself from giving Sam a beseeching glance, but instead of the amusement she thought she would find on his face she saw a soft wonder in his brown eyes. And he answered Chrissy for her.

"Babies are a gift," he said, holding out a hand to Chrissy, who scrambled up and onto his lap. "We'll just have to ask for that next year and see how important our request is."

"Yeah," Chrissy agreed, resting her head on Sam's shoulder and seeming satisfied with his vague answer. "We gotta be careful what we wish for. Wishes should only be for the real important things. I think babies are *real* important, though."

Sam pulled Polly closer, and a peaceful sensation replaced the confusion in her mind for a moment as the three of them gazed at the tree, outlined by the fading light beyond the window. She could almost see a tiny baby lying in Chrissy's old crib, set beneath the tree. But immediately she realized she had no idea where they would set up their tree next year, and she swallowed a stab of already increasing homesickness for the small ranch and tiny cabin.

Chapter Eleven

Polly crept into her bedroom that night with trepidation so strong she could barely force herself to walk, but she saw Sam lying on his back and heard a soft snore issue from his throat. Relief filled her. He had suppressed yawns all through supper, and she realized he still had a ways to go to recover from his loss of blood. A tiny bit of pique, however, crept into a corner of her mind, which she immediately swept away when she realized she was actually resenting Sam's falling asleep, after he had so pointedly ordered her into his bed.

She undressed and slipped on her nightgown, then eased into the bed. Sam didn't waken, and for a few minutes Polly allowed herself to try to fathom these new sensations—someone in bed with her, the warmth instead of the chill she usually had to contend with until her own body heat counteracted it. Most amazing, she admitted to herself groggily, was the yearning to scoot across that empty space. . . .

She woke without the usual reluctance to face yet another morning in a long line of chore-filled days. Normally, she spent a few moments trying to will herself to toss back the covers and hasten into the kitchen to build up the fire. Now she felt so comfortable, so languid, yet so ready to face the waiting work. She had slept so well. She snuggled down against her pillow, which suddenly felt hard, rather than soft. Something tickled her nose, and she opened her eyes to see a nest of wiry curls—the culprit of the pesky aggravation.

Her mind ordered her to pull away—informing her at once that she was lying on Sam's chest—yet her body refused to respond. She took inventory of the other points where their bodies were in contact as she languidly lifted her hand and protected her nose by pressing her fingers into the curls before they made her sneeze.

Sam's left arm curled around her back, his hand resting on her hip. Her breasts pressed against his chest, feeling somewhat heavier than usual, and one of her legs curled over his thigh. Her stomach nestled against his side, and she heaved a small sigh. Probing her mind in silent inquiry, she found the answer to the question of what this wonderful feeling was.

Contentment.

"'Morning, sweetheart. Sleep well?" Sam's voice rumbled in his chest.

She pulled back to look into his face and answered him honestly. "Better than I have in a long while."

Her gaze locked with his for a long, precious moment, and she lifted a hand to caress his cheek. "Sam, there's something I want to tell you."

He quickly bent to kiss her, then placed a finger on her lips. "This evening. We'll talk this evening, all right? When we don't have to worry about Chrissy interrupting."

She saw a shadow of worry in his eyes, and her heart dropped. He probably wanted to tell her that he intended to put the ranch on the market the day after Christmas. She had to prepare herself for it, and for the responsibility of divulging to Chrissy that they would be moving. But she also firmed her resolve to tell Sam tonight that she would make her home with him wherever he wanted to live. She loved him. She had known it irrefutably ever since his accident with the ax, and come of it what may, she had to reveal her love to him.

"All right," she agreed. "Tonight."

The day flew by, with whispered conferences between Sam and Chrissy, black head bent to golden one in a corner of the room, and a new package appearing now and then under the tree. Polly joined in the excitement herself a couple of times, hiding a package behind her back and sidling up to the tree, then shaking a cautioning finger at Sam and Chrissy when they demanded to at least feel the packages and attempt a guess.

After the noon meal, when Sam handed a warm pair of gloves and an envelope to José and each of the other hands, he gave them the rest of the day off, ordering the hands to spend Christmas tomorrow with their own families. He'd pretty much discarded his crutch today, though he still walked with a limp, and he assured them that he could care for the animals himself.

A while later, he and Chrissy came into the kitchen as Polly finished the dishes. Each carried a wreath fashioned from pine boughs and red holly berries.

"We're going out to decorate my other mama and papa's graves," Chrissy told Polly solemnly. "Do you want to come with us?"

"Of course I do, sweetheart," Polly replied.

She hurriedly dried her hands and donned her cloak. José was walking toward the grave sites himself, and he waited for them to join him. They silently made their way to the cottonwood tree, and Chrissy and Sam placed a wreath over each cross, then stepped back and bowed their heads.

"Oh, Matt," Jo said with a sigh. "Isn't this wonderful? Can't you just feel the love here? It's so nice of everyone to remember Ron and Christine, too. This is going to be an absolutely splendid Christmas for this family."

When Matt didn't answer Jo looked over to see a frown on his face. "Now don't spoil things, Matt. Polly's going to tell Sam that she loves him this evening, and he's going to admit to her how he feels, too. They'll work everything out, once they declare their love for each other."

"I suppose," Matt finally said. "I'm tuned into Polly right now, though. She's just realizing that part of the reason Sam's uncomfortable on the ranch is because of his memories of Christine. But it's still breaking her heart to think about leaving here."

"Well, part of loving someone is wanting their happiness above and beyond your own," Jo insisted. "Maybe it will be better for them as a family to build their own memories in a new place."

"Maybe. I guess we can pop back here from time to time to see how things are going."

"We don't have to leave until right before midnight," Jo reminded him. "We can stay around until then, but we don't want to miss our own celebration."

Matt nodded, and they both watched the little party by the graves a while longer. Polly took Chrissy's hand, and José walked with them back toward the cabin. Sam remained behind, waving a dismissing hand when Polly stopped once to call back a reminder to him not to linger too long in the cold.

Suddenly a wide smile crossed Matt's face, and he glanced joyously over at Jo. She clapped her hands and sent a delighted look winging overhead.

Polly answered a faint knock on the kitchen door, and smiled into José's face when he shushed her greeting with a finger on his lips.

"It's all right," she said. "Chrissy's in bed. I guess you want us to come out and get the saddle."

"I have it here, señora," José replied. He pointed beside him, to where the tiny saddle lay against the wall.

"José! You shouldn't have carried that here. We would have come for it."

José ignored her admonishment and brought

something out from behind his back, holding it out to her. "My hands, they have not pained me so bad for a few days. I made this for the little señorita."

Polly accepted the tiny bridle, hastily cushioning it against her stomach when the little bells on it jingled merrily. Despite José's protests, she knew how hard it must have been for him to braid the leather for the bridle and tie the bells on with rawhide thongs. The wizened old man had made the bridle with great effort—love in every pained movement. She leaned over and kissed his weathered cheek.

"It's beautiful, José," she breathed. "She'll love it. Come on in and have some hot chocolate with us."

"No, señora, but I will come back after St. Nick leaves, as I have always done." He gave her a surreptitious wink. "I would not miss the joy of watching Señorita Chrissy open her gifts."

Sam appeared behind Polly as José walked away, and spied the saddle against the porch wall. He lifted it over an arm and carried it across the kitchen as Polly whispered to him that José would return around midnight.

In the parlor, Sam knelt and placed the saddle beneath the tree, then draped the bridle Polly handed him across the pommel. "That's everything, isn't it?" he asked, leaning back on his heels.

"I would surely hope so," Polly said with a smile. "The doll is beautiful, Sam. Chrissy will love it."

Suddenly she saw Sam's hand move nonchalantly toward one of the packages under the tree, and she instinctively dropped down beside him, grabbing his arm and jerking it back.

"No! I've been telling you all day you can't *feel* the packages. You're worse than Chrissy!"

With a chuckle, Sam pulled her into his arms and sat on the floor, snuggling her onto his lap. "Ah," he said, "but that wasn't a real attempt to feel a package. It was a trick. I knew you'd lunge down here and try to stop me, and I could get my hands on you, not the package."

Polly laughed and swatted him on the shoulder. Gazing up into his mischievously twinkling eyes, she felt a curl of the same contentment she had experienced that morning spread through her. "I don't recall giving you permission to feel *me,* either," she said. "But I don't appear to be denying you right now."

Sam cupped her chin and kissed her tenderly. "Merry Christmas, Mrs. Butler," he murmured when he reluctantly pulled back from her lips. "I want you to know, I'll remember this Christmas for the rest of my life. I didn't realize when I rode onto this ranch a little over two weeks ago that everything I needed to fill a great big hole in my life was waiting here for me. I love you, Polly. You're my very heart and soul."

Tears misted Polly's eyes, and she caressed his cheek, her fingers rasping on the new growth of shadowy beard. "I wanted to tell you first," she murmured.

"Tell me what?"

"That I love you. That ever since you came here the cabin has become a home again, instead of just a place to shelter Chrissy and me. My days have become exciting, rather than something to just get through. In fact, I've never been happier in my life than I have recently. I love you, Sam, and I'm very pleased to be your wife. Merry Christmas."

Sam captured her mouth again in a deep, thrilling kiss. He crushed her against his chest, but she gloried in the strength of his embrace. One of his hands tangled in her hair, the pins scattering across the floor as the heavy mass fell down her back, and Sam's muffled moan of desire fired a deep yearning in her.

She wanted to be his wife completely—shatter this one last barrier between them. The barrier of her virginity was secondary to what she somehow sensed would be the total completeness they would find together as lovers.

Sam groaned and raised his head to glance at the clock on the mantel, and Polly instinctively stretched back toward his lips. "There's lots of time left before midnight," she almost pleaded.

"Woman," Sam said with a low growl, "there's not enough time left in this world for me to love you as much as I want to. Once I get you in that bed, I might never let you out of it."

"Now, now, darling," Polly chastised in a teasing voice. "We have to let Chrissy and José open their Christmas presents, too."

Sam buried his face on her shoulder and nuzzled her neck. Her eyelids drifted downward, but an ember popped in the fireplace, and she glanced over to make sure the fireguard was securely in place. Her eyes caught on the rocking chair instead, and she tensed, some of the craving in her body diminishing. Sam appeared to realize immediately that something had intruded upon their closeness. He pushed her back a few inches and stared into her face.

"What is it, darling?" he asked. "You don't need to be afraid. I promise you, I'll open my gift slowly, cherishing every inch of it."

Polly threw her arm around his neck and shook her head. "Everything's fine. Please, kiss me again."

Sam tilted his chin and lifted his mouth beyond her reach. "No. Something's bothering you, and I want to know what it is. I don't want anything hanging between us this evening."

Polly bit her bottom lip for a second, then sighed. "I was just wondering if we could at least take the rocking chair with us. I don't care that much about the rest of the furniture. Well, except maybe this rug. But the rocking chair has a lot of memories attached to it, and they're all good ones."

"Take it where?" Sam asked in an innocent voice, though Polly thought she detected a shuttered slyness in his eyes when she glanced at him. "But I'm glad to know you like the rug. You never said."

"Of course I like the rug," Polly grumbled. "It's perfect in here. Maybe the next woman will want to decorate her own way, but if she wants this furniture, I don't mind. All except the rocking chair."

"Next woman?" Sam said in mock awe. "Are you telling me I can have two wives, Polly, love? But you're all I need."

Polly shoved at his chest and scrambled to her feet. Setting her hands on her hips, she glared down at him.

"If you ever so much as sneak a sideways peek at another woman, Sam Butler, I'll crack you upside the head with my rolling pin so hard, you won't have any interest in even me for at least a week. And you know exactly what I'm talking about."

She swung around and looked at the tree. The few candles they had fastened to the limbs remained to be lit, but not until gift-opening time. Then they could keep a close eye on them, what with the danger of the drying pine needles catching fire. But the flickering flame in the wall sconce outlined the tiny angel on top, and Polly frowned in confusion when she imagined that the angel winked at her. She stomped over to the settee and grabbed one of the decorative cushions, pillowing it against her stomach as she sat down and glared again at Sam. He had a damnable grin on his face.

"Sam, my home is with you now," she said. Her voice came out rather huffy, instead of soft and loving, as she had anticipated this conversation with Sam would be, when she told him that he meant more to her than the ranch. The grin stayed on Sam's face, and she tightened her grip on the cushion, fighting the urge to throw it at him. " 'Wither thou goest,' " she quoted. "When you sell the ranch, though, the new owner's wife will probably want things her way."

"Sell the ranch?" Sam rose to his feet. "Sell this ranch, after I've worked my fingers to the bone trying to make it a decent home for my wife and child? When we've got all this good, clean air to breathe and open spaces for Chrissy and our future children to grow and thrive in? Why, just look at me." Sam patted his flat stomach. "See? I'm in better shape than I've ever been before in my life. Ranch work seems to agree with me."

Polly clasped a hand to her neck, blinking her

eyes furiously to try to hold back her tears of joy. "I thought . . . you said . . . when did you decide?"

Sam crossed to the settee and knelt before her, taking both her hands in his. "Only today," he admitted. "But I think the decision has been in my subconscious for a long while. I've promised myself to be honest with you, Polly, as part of our marriage. You know I thought myself in love with Christine."

When Polly cocked her head in question he continued, "Yes, *thought.* Your sister was a lovely person, but I only found out what real love was when I realized I was in love with you. Today I thanked Christine for knowing what was best not only for herself but also for me. Any memories I have now of Christine on this ranch will be grateful ones, since because of her I found you. I found my own soulmate—my own true love."

Polly threw her arms around his neck, almost tumbling them both to the floor. Somehow Sam managed to steady himself, and he rose, sweeping her up and swinging her around once, then again. The room circled, with flashes of fireplace, rocking chair and Christmas tree passing her by, but she barely noticed them from the corners of her eyes. She couldn't tear her gaze from Sam's face.

"I love you, Sam," she said as soon as he came to a halt. "With all my heart."

"I love you, Polly, sweetheart," he replied. "With my heart, too, but . . ." He glanced once more at the clock. "I do believe there's plenty of time left before midnight to show you how much my body can love yours, also."

"Oh, but what if we don't want to leave the bed once we get into it?" Polly asked in mock horror.

"Chrissy will be so disappointed if she sleeps past our traditional gift-opening time."

"Well," Sam mused, dropping a kiss on her nose, "I've come to another decision. The best Christmas gifts are the ones you can savor all year long. I'll force myself out of bed at least five minutes before midnight, knowing that *my* Christmas present will be something that lasts forever."

"Forever," Polly agreed on a sigh. She snuggled her head against his shoulder as Sam carried her out of the parlor, *forever* whispering in her mind.

The angel atop the Christmas tree glowed with a light too bright to be reflected from the wall sconce, drawing Jo and Matt's satisfied gazes to it. The light drifted upwards, leaving the angel in place on the branch.

"Michael!" Jo said in a delighted voice. "Michael, did you see? This has been a wonderful assignment."

"I saw," came the voice from the light. "I had faith the two of you could do it, despite your own doubts. Let's drop in on Chrissy before we leave."

The three of them drifted through the wall and hovered over Chrissy's bed. Matt reached down and brushed a lock of hair from Chrissy's forehead, and she opened her eyes slightly.

"Thank you," she whispered. "Thank you for making my wish come true."

Her eyes closed again, and Jo said softly, "Merry Christmas, Chrissy."

"Merry Christmas," Chrissy breathed in response.

The angels floated through the ceiling, and Jo paused a hundred yards or so above the small cabin to scan the ranch. Reflected starlight sparkled on the snow, dotting it with brilliance. Smoke curled lazily into the blue-black night from the chimneys on the cabin and José's smaller shack. The scene was so peaceful and serene, a wondrous joy filled Jo's heart, and she looked over at Matt and Michael. They both gave her a nod of agreement and wide, delightful smiles.

Suddenly a shaft of light cut through the sky, bathing the ranch yard in new radiance. The three of them turned as one toward the star glowing in the eastern sky.

"Oh," Jo said. "Let's go. Our own celebration will begin pretty soon."

Merging and separating in joyous abandon, the three angels flew toward the Christmas Star.

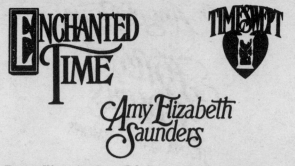